Rave Reviews for
Devon Monk's Age of Steam Series

TIN SWIFT

"Action and romance combine with a deft precision that will keep readers turning pages—and anxiously awaiting the next volume."

—*Publishers Weekly*

"Monk flawlessly blends fantasy, steampunk, and Western in this fantastic series." —SciFiChick.com

"An exhilarating adventure thriller that grips the audience. . . . Fans will want to soar with the crew of the *Swift* as they struggle to survive the pact made by two evil essences." —Genre Go Round Reviews

DEAD IRON

"Featuring a cursed hero, fabulous secondary characters, a world torn between machines and magic, and a plot that hooks your interest from the very first chapter, *Dead Iron* is a must read."

—*New York Times* bestselling author Keri Arthur

"A relentless Western and a gritty steampunk, bound together by wicked magic. The action is superb, the stakes are sky-high, and the passion runs wild. Who knew cowboys and gears could be this much fun? Devon Monk rocks—her unique setting and powerful characters aren't to be missed!"

—*New York Times* bestselling author Ilona Andrews

"A novel and interesting take on the steampunk tropes, with generous nods to other genres, and plenty of odd but human characters and Mad Science."

—*New York Times* bestselling author S. M. Stirling

continued . . .

BOOKS BY DEVON MONK

COLD COPPER

The Age of Steam

DEVON MONK

A ROC BOOK

ROC
Published by the Penguin Group
Penguin Group (USA) Inc., 375 Hudson Street,
New York, New York 10014, USA

USA | Canada | UK | Ireland | Australia | New Zealand | India | South Africa | China

Penguin Books Ltd., Registered Offices: 80 Strand, London WC2R 0RL, England
For more information about the Penguin Group visit penguin.com.

First published by Roc, an imprint of New American Library,
a division of Penguin Group (USA) Inc.

First Printing, July 2013
3   5   7   9   10   8   6   4

RoC REGISTERED TRADEMARK—MARCA REGISTRADA

LIBRARY OF CONGRESS CATALOGING-IN-PUBLICATION DATA:

Monk, Devon.
Cold copper: the age of steam/Devon Monk.
p. cm
ISBN 978-0-451-41860-9 (pbk.)
1. Bounty hunters—Fiction.   2. Werewolves—Fiction.   3. Steampunk fiction.   I. Title.
PS3613.O5293C65 2013
813'.6—dc23   2013001054

Set in Electra   •   Designed by Elke Sigal

Printed in the United States of America

PUBLISHER'S NOTE
This is a work of fiction. Names, characters, places, and incidents either are the product of
the author's imagination or are used fictitiously, and any resemblance to actual persons,
living or dead, business establishments, events, or locales is entirely coincidental.
    The publisher does not have any control over and does not assume any responsibility for
author or third-party Web sites or their content.

For my family

ACKNOWLEDGMENTS

Here we are at the third book in the Age of Steam series, and I have a lot of thanking to do. Thank you to my terrific agent, Miriam Kriss, for your wise and understanding counsel. Thank you to my extraordinary editor, Anne Sowards, for helping me make this book the best it could be. My gratitude goes out to the fantastic artist Cliff Nielsen, whose stunning work has flawlessly captured my world. To the many awesome people within Penguin who have gone above and beyond to make this book beautiful and strong, I thank you from the bottom of my heart.

I want to give a huge thank-you to my brilliant first reader Dean Woods for all your input, questions, and insight. You're amazing. To my first reader Dejsha Knight, thank you so much for all your support, last-minute late-night reads, and helpful conversations.

Also, a big thank-you to my wonderful family and friends for all your encouragement and help along the way. I couldn't do this without you. To my husband, Russ, and sons, Kameron and Konner, thank you for being the best part of my life. I love you.

Last, but not nearly least, I want to thank you, dear readers, for giving me the chance to share this world and these people with you once again.

COLD COPPER

CHAPTER ONE

There were plenty of good ways to die. Cedar Hunt wiped ice off his face and pushed through the knee-deep snow, leaning against the wind. Some people said drowning wasn't bad; others said hanging was a peaceful way to go. But he had decided real quick that dying in the teeth of a blizzard wasn't any way to lay a soul to rest.

Cold just made him angry and anger fueled his determination to keep right on living.

"Mr. Hunt," Miss Dupuis called over the howl of the wind. "A river, I believe."

He looked back at the people following him as he broke trail through the drifts. Miss Sophie Dupuis was an acquaintance of the Madder brothers.

She looked like a French diplomat but was part of a secretive group of people who, as far as he could reckon, spent most their time taking the law into their own hands to try to rid the land of the Strange, those unholy creatures from myth and legend intent on killing good folk.

But now there was an even greater threat than the Strange. The Holder—a strange-worked weapon made of seven ancient metals—was scattered across this land.

Cedar had seen the destruction even just one piece of it had caused.

It wiped out a town of people, left their bodies as playthings for the Strange, and nearly killed his friend Rose Small.

The remaining pieces of the device would do the same or worse. And if they fell into the wrong hands, they could bring the United States, and all within it, to its knees.

His instinct for the Holder's whereabouts had sent them north out of Kansas, heading up to Des Moines. But this snowstorm had fouled his senses.

"Which way?" he called out to Miss Dupuis.

She adjusted the compass in her hand and pointed west. They'd been hoping to catch a direction toward civilization for hours now, and following a river was their best hope of doing so.

Behind her loomed the Madder brothers' wagon, pulled by a team of mules. Alun Madder sat the driver's seat. A miner and deviser by trade, he was a bear of a man: heavy coat, wide-brimmed hat, messy curls of hair, and beard adding to the wild look of him. Even in the pounding snow, he kept his pipe hot, pulling cherry red coals from the bowl.

His two brothers, Bryn and Cadoc, were behind the wagon, pushing when the mules weren't enough to pull the sleds they had rigged up beneath the wheels. In the back of the wagon, out of sight, was the woman Cedar loved, the witch Mae Lindson. His brother Wil, who carried the same Pawnee curse as Cedar and currently wore a wolf's shape because of it, was also in the wagon.

The wind thrashed harder, picking up snow and ice. Cedar shivered under the onslaught.

If Mae Lindson hadn't cast a spell of warmth on his hands and feet every few hours, he knew he'd have lost his fingers and toes yesterday.

It had taken Mae several attempts to find a way to bind warmth to skin without scorching flesh. He figured he'd carry the scars on the back of his wrists for years to come, but didn't regret a moment of the pain.

Because of her, they might make it to shelter. If shelter could be found.

One thing was certain: there was no turning around now. It was well past midday, and the path behind was blocked by fallen trees and piles of snow. The mules and horses struggled with every passing hour.

They were running out of daylight and running out of time.

Cedar tipped his head so he could see up from beneath the brim of his hat to where Miss Dupuis pointed. Nothing but snow and hills ahead, though he thought he could make out a downward slope.

"Are you sure?" he called back over the wind's howl.

"Yes. If the maps are correct, there should be a river there." Miss Dupuis's voice quavered. She was shaking even though she wore a long wool coat over her several layers of skirts, kidskin gloves, a rabbit-skin muff, and a rabbit-skin shawl across her shoulders. Her hair was tucked up beneath a woolen cap covered in a heavy layer of white that would not melt.

The compass in her hand burned a bloody red and let off enough heat to stay the snow from its surface. She'd shown him the contraption the Madders had devised—a combination of sextant and compass housed in an enameled case filled with sand that could be heated to keep the user's hands warm.

Now she tucked her palms into the furred hand warmer to keep her gloved fingers from freezing.

Miss Dupuis had refused the warming spell from Mae, knowing that every time Mae cast the spell, it drained Mae's strength.

"You should return to the wagon," Cedar said.

"Not yet. I'll watch for lights, town, rail. If we come on the river and follow the banks, we should see a town."

Cedar didn't waste breath arguing. Truth was, he could use a second set of eyes in all this white. "Shout if you see the river. I'd rather not find it by falling through the ice."

He adjusted his course west, every step sinking into snow up to his knees, despite the snowshoes he'd strung together out of strips of leather and willow. He'd fashioned the shoes a week ago, when he and Wil had first felt the weather taking a shift toward the worse.

Neither of them had expected this storm.

"Where you think you're going now, Mr. Hunt?" Alun Madder hollered from the seat of the wagon.

"Des Moines!" Cedar had been telling him that the city should be the nearest shelter for two days, but the Madders refused to believe him. Refused almost to admit Des Moines was a city that existed in the world at all.

He didn't know what nonsense they had in those stubborn heads of theirs, but ignoring a town didn't mean it wasn't there.

Alun let out a hard whistle and pulled the mules up short. Even Miss Dupuis's horse jerked at the sound and stopped, head drooping, grateful for the rest.

Alun lifted a lantern to better see through the snow, and sunset light slapped across his round, weathered face, revealing a beard white from snow, a bulbous nose stuck in the center of his close-set features, and glass-sharp eyes looking out from beneath bushy brows.

Quick tempered and quirky natured, Alun Madder was the eldest of the brothers. The blowing snow turned him into a ghoulish figure, as if the face of death itself was peering out at Cedar through a casing of ice.

"We will not stop in Des Moines," Alun said flatly.

Cedar was pretty sure that was the first time the miner had actually spoken the name of the town. But he didn't care to point it out. He didn't care in the least if the Madders acknowledged that the town existed.

"We will, or we won't last the night." Cedar spaced his words like hammer strikes. "The mules are near dead. The horse too. We won't last long enough to dig our own graves. We stop in Des Moines."

"I say otherwise," Alun yelled. "And so do my brothers."

As if called to battle, the other two Madder brothers strode through the snow alongside the stopped wagon, both carrying geared-up shotguns against palms and shoulders.

Near freezing to death did a lot of odd things to a man's sense of reason. It was said some went raving mad, tore their clothes off, and ran through the snow naked while their blood turned to ice.

Maybe the cold had frozen up the Madder brothers' brains.

Maybe Cedar didn't give a damn about that.

"Do not stand against me, Alun Madder, and think you will win," Cedar said. "And do not think I will stand here and waste time fighting you instead of finding our path to salvation. If you have some device or matic you've bolted together that can change the weather or give us speed, I'll wait for you to bring it out here; otherwise I am going to find that city."

"A city of devils," Alun said.

"Good. I expect they'll keep the fires warm."

Alun scowled and returned to puffing smoke out of his pipe.

That was answer enough.

Cedar turned his back on the brothers and their guns and pushed through the snow down the next slope.

They could shoot him in the back for all he cared. He wasn't going to stand still in the middle of a blizzard and argue his heartbeats away.

After what seemed a long time, the mules let out hoarse brays, and the crunching hiss of the wagon's sled runners scraped through the snow behind him again.

Good. They were still following him.

The spell of warmth around him gradually wore away and the cold sank through skin down to bone. Hands, face, and feet went numb, but he pushed on.

It seemed all the world was ice and death. There was nothing but putting each foot down, one after another, breaking through to solid ground for the horse behind him, who left a path for the mules and wagon.

Cedar lost all sense of time to that rhythm, and soon the Pawnee curse showed him other things riding that storm. The Strange were thick in that wind. Ghostly fingers and teeth clawed at him, catching at his coat, his feet, his hat.

Angry. But not solid enough to draw blood.

He could kill the Strange, even in this ghostly form they took. It would make the world a much better place without them and eventually, if he killed them all, he might again regain a normal man's life. The curse he carried forced him to hunt and kill the Strange. All the Strange in the world. He suspected he'd breathe out his last days before that was done, and still not be free of the curse.

But he was too exhausted to fight them today. He ignored these Strange that plucked and wailed and bit. Life was all that mattered now. And life, for all of them, meant moving west.

Wil, beside him, growled. Cedar looked down, surprised to see his brother out of the wagon.

Wil's ears were flattened against his wide, gray-and-black skull, his copper eyes the only flecks of color in the snow. Wil saw the Strange too, likely smelled the moldy green of them as Cedar smelled them, likely saw the flash of eyes and heard the trebled laughter warbling through the air.

The Strange couldn't do serious harm unless they took on a shape, a form, a body. As Cedar had learned firsthand, dead people were the clothing preferred by the Strange, though there were times they could inhabit other bits and matics.

He wasn't going to give them any corpses to waltz about.

"Don't," Cedar said to Wil. "There is no time to chase them. They'll lead you to your death."

Wil growled but stayed close, snapping at the swarm of Strange and holding them off as daylight drained away and the shadows deepened.

"Mr. Hunt," Miss Dupuis called out. "Please, Mr. Hunt. You must stop!"

The heat in her tone finally soaked through the cold that gripped his thoughts. Cedar stopped. Wil's teeth were dug in the cuff of his coat, and he was pulling backward, whining.

For good reason. They had reached the bank of the river. If Cedar had walked even three steps more, he'd have slid down the steep embankment and landed in the water.

The Madders behind him were talking—no, they were arguing, loudly—about ice and rivers and speed and something else Cedar couldn't hear except for the smattering of curses and the phrase "that devil," followed by words that must have been their mother language of Welsh.

"We've found the river," Miss Dupuis said.

Cedar lifted his free hand and rubbed his stinging eyes. His vision was blurred by the snow, his hand lifeless in the heavy gloves.

The river was not flowing. It was a frozen ribbon that wound off to the northwest, black and dusty as an old chalkboard.

"Good," he croaked, his mouth and throat on fire. He needed water, he needed rest; but there was no time for either with night fast approaching. "Town won't be far."

"We're going to step back, Mr. Hunt," Mae Lindson said, "so the Madders can come through."

Cedar jerked at her voice. When had she climbed out of the wagon?

"Cedar," Mae said again, her tone stern, as if trying to pitch her voice over a fever snuffing out his senses. He supposed she wasn't much wrong to do so.

Along with the cold confusing his head, his ears were filled with the eerie voices of the Strange, calling him. Pleading for him to follow.

"Just take a few steps to the side," Mae said. "The Madders are bringing the wagon down now." She pulled on him and he followed her guidance, stopping with her near a leafless tree while Wil paced a tight circle around both of them.

"You've been walking for hours," Mae said. "And you are nearly frozen." Her hand was firmly in his, holding tight to him, even through her thick mittens and his gloves.

The magic she had placed on his skin seemed to warm again at her nearness. Or it could just be his natural response to her. His want for her.

"You need food, you need water, and you need sleep," she went on, as if he were not really listening.

"We're all tired, Mae," he said, gazing down at her.

She looked up at the sound of his voice, a smile playing across her pale lips.

Her yellow hair was tucked up beneath a wide-brimmed blue wool hat. She wore a thick red scarf buttoned up under her leather coat, and red mittens she had knit to match the scarf. Her face was heart-shaped, her cheeks rosy and softly arced.

Life had left the echo of hardship across her features, a tightening at the corners of her eyes, a furrowed line across her forehead when she frowned, but here, bundled against the cold, with the wind plucking pink from her cheeks, and her wide brown eyes for him alone, she was a beauty who caught at his heart like no other.

"Yes, we are all tired," she said, "but only one of us just tried to walk off a cliff."

He gave her back the smile and felt his lip crack and flash hot with blood.

"Here, now." She reached into her pocket and produced a handkerchief. She dabbed it to his lip, though the blood there had already frozen.

"You need water, Mr. Hunt, rest, and food," she repeated. "Maybe we could build a fire—"

Her words were smothered by the earsplitting racket of limbs cracking and brush breaking.

Alun and Cadoc Madder stood at either side of the mules that were still hitched to the wagon. They were leading the two reluctant animals down toward a more gentle incline than the one Cedar had been about to step off of.

Seemed the Madder brothers couldn't go a day without doing something to "improve" the wagon. Cedar secretly, and not so secretly, suspected it was just the deviser madness in them needing something to meddle with.

This time they had pulled two lengths of canvas out of the wagon, tied them to long wooden poles, and lashed them down the wagon sides. Ropes ran slack from various points on the canvas poles, and then were gathered up into the hands of Bryn Madder, the middle brother, who sat in the driver's seat instead of his eldest brother, Alun.

Cedar noted that Bryn had donned a pair of dark goggles and a woolly hat that flapped down over his ears and tied beneath his beard. He looked ridiculous and was grinning like a fool.

"They're going into the river?" Cedar asked.

"Onto, if what they say holds true," Mae said. "They said we'll make better time on the ice."

Cedar ground back a frustrated growl. "They can't be sure the ice is thick enough. They can't be sure they aren't all going to fall in."

"I asked about that," Mae said. "They have a device that can tell them if the ice is solid. Brother Cadoc was already down on the river testing it. He says the ice is at least a hand deep. It will hold."

"I do not share their confidence, and don't like them risking our supplies." Cedar started off toward the wagon, and caught himself just before his knees gave out.

He was tired. More than that, he was exhausted. Mae was right. He couldn't go on much longer.

It wasn't just the walking. It wasn't just the cold. The moon was coming up soon, and it would be full. But if the beast took him over in this state, and ran through the night chasing and killing Strange, Cedar would wake in the morning, naked, more than exhausted, and lost in the blizzard.

Wil, standing in front of Cedar, glanced back at him. The intelligence and concern in his brother's eyes were clear.

"Fine," Cedar said. "I'm fine. I'll be better if the Madders don't fall through that damn ice with everything we have."

Cedar took another step. Satisfied he wouldn't fall, he kept moving.

Mae walked beside him. He didn't say anything, didn't pull away when she slipped her hand into his. They walked, together, hand in hand, through the blizzard toward the wagon.

The wagon and mules, urged forward by Cadoc and Alun Madder, tipped onto the slope and made a rather quick journey down the bank.

Mae gasped, but the whole lot of them—man, beast, and contraption—came to a full and surprisingly easy stop several feet away from the bank of the river itself.

Miss Dupuis, who stood beside her horse at the top of the bank, just shook her head at Bryn Madder's whoop of excitement. "They enjoy this," she said. "I believe they truly enjoy this."

"Come on down!" Bryn Madder yelled. "The water's fit as a fiddle!"

Miss Dupuis hesitated. "Do you trust their judgment?" she asked Cedar.

"Doesn't matter if I trust them," Cedar said, already making his way down the hill, and helping Mae to make hers. "Right now, we have to rely on them. In my experience, they've never been the sort of men overly interested in reaching their graves early."

After another, probably sensible, moment or two of doubt, Miss Dupuis left the horse, who was too tired to wander off, and started down the slope too. Cedar saw to it Mae had her footing on the ice. She made her way over to the wagon, where Alun Madder was waiting, his hand extended for her.

Cedar turned and met Miss Dupuis halfway up the hill and helped her down.

A Strange reached out of the snow and slapped at her. It tugged a lock of her dark hair out from under her hat, pulling enough to hurt.

"Ouch," she said.

Cedar took a swat at the thing and it disappeared, as insubstantial as air.

"They are thick here, aren't they?" She lifted her skirts to step over a twisted root.

"The Strange?" Even though he and Miss Dupuis had been traveling together for some time now, and had even fought the Strange together, he often forgot that she too could see the creatures.

She couldn't kill them, although some of the weapons the Madders and other devisers had made could hold, slow, and harm the Strange. As far as Cedar knew, only he and his brother Wil, both tied to the Pawnee curse, could kill the Strange.

Two men against an entire country full of ghouls and bogeys. Two men cursed to kill them all.

It was madness. A task they could never fulfill. The Strange were growing in this country, more and more each day.

"I can see them," she said. "Do you see them now, Mr. Hunt? You and Wil?"

"Yes," Cedar said. "The storm is lousy with them. I've never seen so many in such a small area."

"Poor weather doesn't usually bring them out," she said. "Most Strange prefer rain and lightning storms, if they're to be in bad weather. Not blizzards."

"Oh?" Cedar asked, extending his hand to help steady her.

"We've studied them, Mr. Hunt. We of the Guard. We know some few things about their ways."

"Was there a chance you might want to fill me in on your knowledge of the Strange? Knowledge of the Guard for that matter. The Madders talk in riddles whenever I ask questions."

"I had hoped there would be time to speak of such matters on this trip, but . . ." She shrugged. "Everything has been difficult."

"Perhaps when we reach Des Moines," he said, "you and I could spend more time together."

Miss Dupuis glanced up at him through her thick snow-heavy lashes. The expression on her face was part surprise and something more. Something like pleasure. "I would like that very much, Mr. Hunt. To spend time with you."

Then she took the last few steps with him to the edge of the ice.

Mae, who was helping the Madders lead the mules onto a platform they'd lowered from the back of wagon, glanced over at him. Miss Dupuis released his hand like she'd been caught cheating at parlor games. She tipped her chin up just a fraction and waited for Mae's reaction.

Mae frowned, then went back to work.

"Bring the horse, will you, Mr. Hunt?" Alun called from the rear of the wagon. "We've got room for him too. And a long way to go."

"Shouldn't be long to reach Des Moines," Cedar said.

"We'll go where the winds take us," Alun said. "Find a smaller town to wait out the storm. Trust me, it will be for the better."

He'd just told Miss Dupuis trust didn't matter. But there was something about the three Madders' avoidance of Des Moines that wasn't adding up. Still, they'd saved his life more than once, even though they'd made sure he was owing to them for their favor.

"Find us shelter and you'll have no argument out of me," Cedar said. Then he turned and, with Wil beside him, climbed back up the bank to fetch the horse.

CHAPTER TWO

ose Small tucked her head against the spit of rain brushing down the roofs of Hays City, and avoided a steam cart full of barley rattling down the street. A little bad weather couldn't keep the people of this Kansas town from their work, chores, and errands.

Nor would a little bad weather keep her from running down that low-life, cheating son of a grease licker Captain Lee Hink.

It was eight in the morning, and the corner baker had already sold out of the day's bread. A storm was on the horizon and creeping close with the promise of rain. Folk were hurrying with their necessities, business, and trade, all that hustle giving the town the feel of a kicked beehive.

The sweet faraway clang from off north a ways, where the blacksmith was bending horseshoes and rims for the steam carts, called her heart like a church bell ringing for service. The noises of the city just proved the whole town was open for business.

And so was Sweet Annie's Saloon.

Three nights this week. Three nights Hink had gone off to "see to a few matters" or "pick up some parts for the *Swift*" or "check on the crew in town."

She had stayed behind at the farm owned by a coven of witches who had taken them all in when they'd nearly crashed the *Swift* trying to bring Mae Lindson back to the sisters. The coven had been happy to see Mae, Cedar Hunt, Wil, the Madder brothers, and Miss Dupuis leave the property in search of the Holder, but she, Captain Hink, and his crew had stayed behind to repair the *Swift*.

Hink had grown more and more restless and made up lies and excuses to go to town, while she nodded and smiled and believed him, just like the backwoods bumpkin he knew she was.

He'd even had the nerve to bring her back a wallpaper flower, cleverly folded and perfumed like a red velvet rose. He'd said it had come in on the rail all the way from France. He said he'd bought it up when he saw it because it reminded him of her.

She'd loved it. It had been the first time in her life a man had bought a pretty thing just for her. She'd been wearing it on her bonnet and scarves for weeks.

She'd even been so delighted by his gift that she had kissed him for it.

Kissed him. More than once.

And she'd made him something in return: a little compass on a chain that would always point toward a matching little compass she wore on a chain. It had taken some doing to make the two devices point only and ever toward each other, but she'd traded work at the watchmaker in town for access to his instruments after hours.

The compasses were the finest things she'd ever devised. And they'd cost her almost every cent she'd earned in the last two months.

But now she knew the truth.

He could try to wrap his lies up in pretty paper roses all he wanted, but she wasn't falling for them again. Sweet Annie's was more than a saloon; it was also a bordello.

Two nights ago, he'd gone into town for some boiler tubing for the *Swift*'s new guns, and hadn't come home.

One of the younger sisters in the coven mentioned she'd seen him step into Sweet Annie's while she was at the post office picking up the coven's letters. Said he'd been clutching a half-empty whiskey bottle and was half out of his shirt, his arm around some plump raven-haired girl of the line.

It wasn't like they'd taken vows. It wasn't like he'd ever said she was his only one, or that he'd told her she was special. Still, she thought they had a beginning that was headed somewhere. She thought that somewhere might be love.

He'd told her she was beautiful.

He'd told her he didn't want to live without her.

He'd given her a *rose*.

Which she'd been sure to stuff in the pocket of her overalls this morning so she could throw it in his cheating face.

Rose paused and stomped the snow and mud off her work boots, tipped back the flat cap she kept her hair tucked up into, then shoved open the painted red door to Sweet Annie's.

She stepped in and got a face full of stink—alcohol, lavender, kerosene, wood fire, leather, and linseed overpowered by tobacco, sweat, and perfume. She clenched her teeth against the smell, straining it through her teeth as she inhaled.

This was what betrayal smelled like.

A man at the piano against one wall played out the strains of "Long, Long Ago," sweet and sad.

The decor was done up nicer than she'd expected: wood ceiling polished to a dark shine, walls covered in paper with cream and gold designs. Tables set out to one side were in good repair, crowded with fellows playing cards and dice and women looking on.

The bar itself was honey-colored oak, and so high-shined you could see the reflection of the men who stood around it, boots propped on the brass foot rail with matching spittoons at their heels. Someone had gone and hung up a red, white, and blue star banner in loops across the back of the bar, and the gaslight chandeliers gave off a cheery halo of light, while the Franklin stove at the far end of the room on the wall between two closed doors kept the whole place warm.

There were three sorts of people in the room: workingmen who had already dealt with livestock for the day, there to drink away the weather until they could tend fields or see to their evening work; travelers with shiny shoes cooling their heels, stuck until they could strike out west for more temperate lands; and the employees of the place—a bartender and six saloon girls. Out of sight in the back rooms would be the other ladies who worked there, the sort who took a man's money in exchange for a certain kind of attention.

The saloon girls were dressed in the prettiest finery Rose had ever seen.

Feathers adorned their hats, and their bright silk corsets and skirts were covered in tassels and sequins. All of the dresses—if you could call them that—were worn cut in such a way a man didn't have to imagine what kind of woman was under the layers. The hem of their skirts were so high, you couldn't help but see their stockings, all the way up to the knee.

They were rouged, coal-eyed, and . . . and *pretty*, with hair done up in curls and shiny pins and flowers.

Rose was suddenly very aware of her grease-stained overalls, her heavy, square man's coat and boyish flat cap with her hair tucked up. She didn't look a thing like these women. Wasn't even in their league when it came to pretty.

And right there, sitting at a table near the corner of the room with a woman on his lap, was Captain Lee Hink. Hat off, sun-pale hair mussed up, he hadn't shaved for a day at least. He was a strong man and a tall man, and had just the sort of rakish swagger to him that made women swoon.

He saw her stopped just inside the door. He didn't smile, didn't move a muscle. His eyebrows, however, lifted up into his uncombed hair, shifting the black patch over one eye.

While she had been busy studying the saloon, every single person in that place had turned to look at her, as shocked as if a three-headed mule had come strolling in.

Women weren't allowed in the saloon. Not a woman in boy's clothing. Not even a proper woman.

But Rose wasn't a proper woman. She was an angry woman.

And she was angry at that man.

"You can't be in here, miss," the bartender called out from behind the bar. "No women allowed."

Rose ignored him and stomped across the room, gunning straight for Hink.

The corner of his mouth cupped a smile, and just as quickly poured it out into a frown, though that damn eye of his twinkled with mirth.

"Mr. Hink, I need to have words with you." Rose stopped in such a way that most of the table was between her and that painted vixen on his lap.

"Don't think this is the sort of place for you, darlin'," he said. "Why don't you run on home now like a good girl?"

The vixen giggled and leaned her head down a little closer to Hink's ear, all the while giving Rose the kind of look that was usually reserved for buying cattle at auction.

"Run on home?" she asked. "I don't know what's gotten into you, Lee Hink," Rose said with as steady a voice as she could muster. "But if you think for one minute I'm going to do anything you ask me to do, ever again, you are sore mistaken."

"Now, Rose . . ."

Rose reached into her pocket, and couldn't help but be pleased when Hink twitched.

He was darn right to twitch. She carried all sorts of trinkets and more than a few weapons in the pockets of the knee-length wool coat.

But today, right now, all she pulled out of her pocket was the paper rose he had given her.

"I won't accept false gifts from sweet-talking men like you."

She tossed the fragile velvet and paper rose at his feet.

"Rose," he said almost softly, as if the air had come out of him.

She shook her head. No honey words would change her mind. He'd been carousing while she was rebuilding his ship, refitting the boiler and setting the new guns. He didn't care a whit for her feelings. He only wanted her devising skills.

She turned and walked across the saloon floor and straight on out the door. The door hadn't even clicked shut before the piano man started playing again, and one of the women laughed.

She kept right on walking. It was cold out, Rose knew that. But she didn't feel the wind, didn't hear the clatter and racket of people making their way along the wide dirt streets with horse, wagon, carriage, and the grumbling steamer carts.

All she could hear was the echo of Hink's voice saying her name. Saying it like he was trying to catch up a fleeting thing.

Too late. It was too late. He wanted a life of drinking to soothe the anger of losing his eye and crashing his airship. If he wanted a life with a woman full of ruffles on his lap, then he could have it. She had other things planned. Greater things.

And she was the kind of woman most likely to be wearing goggles or men's trousers rather than ruffles and perfume.

Maybe they weren't made for each other after all.

It was time to be moving on. She'd sold just enough devices through the watch shop; she'd have money for a train ticket east. Straight through to Chicago, then on to New York City. She wanted that, wanted to shake this town and the coven soil from her boots and get on with seeing the wonder this wide world could bring.

But she hadn't planned on seeing it alone. Her best friend, Mae Lindson, was gone with Cedar Hunt, the Madders, and Miss Dupuis, looking for the next bit of the Holder.

She knew what they were doing was important work—the ache in her shoulder and terrible scar where the tin scrap of the last piece of the Holder lodged in her flesh reminded her daily of what that dangerous device could do. She was glad they were hunting for it before it brought plague, madness, and destruction to all it touched.

And now she wished she'd gone along with them instead of staying here with the witches at the coven and, most especially, with that no good, cheating air pirate Captain Lee Hink.

"Out of the way!" A set of hands—no, a whole body: hands, arms, and the rest—slammed into her all in one motion and sent her spinning down to the ground.

She braced for the fall, throwing hands out in front of her, but instead two hands quickly moved around her waist and stopped her fall.

Suddenly finding herself suspended an inch or two off the road, Rose watched as her cap took a tumble in the wind and rolled down to the corner of the sidewalk.

"Please excuse my manners," a man's soft tenor said. "I am terribly sorry for our collision. I'm going to hoist you up on your feet now, if you'll pardon my handling of your overcoat."

Rose nodded, wondering if she was about to be pickpocketed by the most polite thief she'd ever met.

The man shifted his grip so that he stood close against her, then lifted. In a moment, she was standing, and for a tick or two longer than that, the man held her with his fingers resting lightly on the top of her hips and all the rest of his body pressed against her back.

Rose had spent most her life in Hallelujah avoiding the sort of men who manhandled women. She knew how to break free of a man's embrace, knew how to hurt a man, in both polite and less-genteel ways.

But she found herself wishing he might just turn into some kind of fairy-tale prince, come to save her from that airship pirate, come to put the happy back into her ever after.

"Are you recovered, miss?" he asked.

"Yes," Rose said. "Yes, I am." She finally stepped away and turned so she could properly thank him.

That nice voice of his went with a smooth shaved face, sharp jaw, and an elegant sort of arc to his cheekbones and nose. He wore spectacles, gold-wire circles that couldn't contain his wide and startling green eyes. The man also had on a bowler hat that didn't quite cover the brown bangs swept across his forehead.

He wasn't much taller than her, and had a trim, thin build.

"Excellent," he said with a smile. "I must apologize. Wearing that . . . fashion, I mistakenly took you to be a . . . well, one look at your face and I would have known. I certainly don't want to make a reputation of running down lovely ladies."

Flattery, mostly. Rose knew what it was, knew how men used it. But his smile didn't have that kind of hook behind it. He looked nice, sincere, a little flustered by nearly running her over.

It would be the perfect cover for a thief, but she knew by the weight in her pockets that he wasn't that either.

"Apology accepted," she said. "It was my fault as much as yours. I wasn't watching where I was going." Rose glanced up at the street to see exactly where her wandering feet had taken her.

Hardware store, tinsmith, tailor, but not the shops familiar to her.

She'd walked most this town, coming in to pick up necessaries for the witches of the coven, and more often than that, to linger at the blacksmith's or talk to the elder Mr. Travis, who spent most his time repairing watches while his sons and grandsons minded the shop and customers.

But she wasn't on the side of town she knew best.

"I'm not sure I know quite where I am, to tell you the truth," she said.

"Oh?" He looked up and down the street, and at the rambling townsfolk, horses, and buggies, as if trying to get his bearings himself. "We are just east of Bucker's Run, I believe."

The man had a deep blue canvas-covered book in his hand, which he used to point at the shingled cottage and hitching post behind them a bit. "That's Old Miss Bucker's place, if you're of the curiosity."

Rose scowled. "There'd never be enough curiosity in me to want to know about Miss Bucker's place or any other place of such negotiable affections, thank you very much," she said archly.

The man frowned, his eyebrows dunking down to the tops of his glasses. "I'm not sure I understand why you wouldn't want—oh," he said. Then, a little louder, "Oh! No, I assure you, ma'am, Miss Bucker isn't a . . . isn't one of those . . . Why, it's not . . . It is a lending library."

He held up the book as if to prove the use of the place, and she noticed that his cheeks had gone a high color. "I would never, I assure you upon my honor, I would never suggest a woman with your obvious"—he swallowed hard and stepped back just a bit so he could gesture toward her—"qualities would be interested in a place of ill repute."

The poor man was tying his cinch in knots, trying to secure her favorable perception of him while defending her honor. It was . . . sweet.

"Please, Mr. . . . ?" she said.

"Wicks," he supplied. "Thomas Wicks, at your service." He gave her a small bow.

Rose smiled again. Such manners on this man, she wondered where he'd been raised. "I am surely sorry for my hasty and poor estimation of you, Mr. Thomas Wicks," she said. "I'm afraid you haven't caught me at my best."

"That collision of ours may have jumbled us both a bit," he said. "Miss . . . ?"

"Small," she said. "Rose Small."

"Pleased to make your acquaintance," he said. "Might I accompany you back to roads more familiar?"

Rose looked around again. A steamer cart chugged down the half-frozen street, high walls painted with DIRKSON'S CELLAR ICE across the side.

The weather was taking a turn for the worse, and that stone-colored sky was about to dump more than rain over the town. She wasn't the only person who knew it. All the folk on the street were rushing to get business done, and get back to warmth and walls before the storm hit.

Everyone was in a hurry except one figure—a man. He stood on the corner of the street, his broad shoulders leaned against the wood telegraph pole there, his hands in the pockets of his long leather duster, and his head tipped down so his eye patch was shadowed by the brim of his hat.

But from out of that shadow, his remaining eye, blue as a heart-break, shone.

She would recognize that man anywhere, in any town, for the rest of her living days: Captain Lee Hink.

He knew she saw him, and still he stood there, watching her as she talked with a very handsome, educated man.

He had followed her. She didn't know why. Maybe just to tell her she was wrong. Maybe to tell her more hurtful things, like he never wanted to see her again.

She'd had enough hurt for one day. She just couldn't talk to him right now.

"Miss Small?" Mr. Wicks said. "Is something the matter?"

"No," she said, turning to give him her best smile. "Nothing at all. If you wouldn't mind terribly, I'd love to see the library."

His face lit up. "It would be my pleasure." He held out his arm for her and she took it.

Just as they reached the door, Rose glanced over her shoulder. Captain Hink strode away into the storm, a paper rose falling from his fingers into the muddy street behind him.

CHAPTER THREE

Cedar Hunt never once doubted that the Madders were crazy. He had no need for them to prove it to him so thoroughly again.

The miner brothers laughed and hollered at one another as the mule-drawn wagon-turned-ship set sail to catch the punishing wind of the blizzard and barrel down the frozen river.

To turn a wagon into an ice-fairing vessel was a genius bit of thinking. But to sail the whole thing faster than a horse at full gallop upon a frozen river in a blizzard they could barely see through was the kind of madness reserved for those who live very short, albeit colorful, lives.

Cedar sat in the driver's seat of the wagon, holding tension in the ropes to the port sail, his goggles keeping the stinging snow out of his eyes, but not doing much else to help him see through the blinding white. Alun Madder sat on the far side of the seat, minding the starboard sail. Cadoc Madder sat between them, holding the reins not for mules but for the steering contraption they'd made. All of them were taking orders from the middle brother, Bryn, who sat atop the wagon with a compass in one hand and lantern in the other, yelling out commands.

Mae Lindson and Miss Dupuis were in the back of the wagon. Mae had cast a binding of calm over the two mules and one horse that stood on the wooden platform being dragged behind the back of the wagon. Just to be sure the animals didn't panic and harm themselves, they'd also blindfolded them. The combination of witchcraft, blindfolds, and exhaustion of the last week of travel insured the beasts remained docile.

"Bend in the river, west five degrees," Bryn yelled out.

"West five degrees!" Alun Madder said.

Cedar and Alun both leaned hard on the sails, muscling them into trim to slow the wagon. Cadoc pulled hard on the rudder near his foot, sending their mad craft skidding to the west.

They made the corner without tipping, let the sails loose, angled to catch the wind, and picked up at top speed smoothly.

"Spent some time sailing, Mr. Hunt?" Alun Madder yelled as they successfully completed the maneuver.

"Enough," Cedar yelled back.

"Thin ice, starboard!" Bryn bellowed. Cedar didn't know how they'd made a device that could predict the depth of the ice. Bryn Madder's rushed explanation, while they'd been attaching the rods with springs at the ends so they stretched in different directions beneath the wagon, about how different sounds of ice thickness were akin to thumping a ripe gourd to check for hollowness didn't do much to clear things up either.

Cedar hated trusting his life to other men's wild-hair ideas. But they'd been shooting across the ice for near an hour now, and had stayed on a solid path.

Cadoc pulled on the rudder again, adjusted course to guide the wagon to the thickest ice in the center of the river.

The river took a soft push to the right, then left again, snaking a path between the trees. The rise and fall of hills became visible and were gone as they flashed past them.

The wind shifted, slowed. The wagon slowed too as they came round the bend, all the rattling and clattering of the vessel quieting some as the trees on either side of the river bent in closer.

"Go on now," Alun muttered. "Go on."

Cadoc, next to Cedar, leaned forward as if urging the wagon to pick up speed.

COLD COPPER • 25
COLD COPPER • 25

Cedar glanced up at Bryn. Every fold of his coat and hat was covered in snow, the goggles over his eyes reflecting bloodred in the yellow glow of the lantern in his hand.

Tense. These men sensed a danger ahead of them Cedar did not feel. They wanted the wind, wanted speed to escape whatever was ahead.

He inhaled, exhaled, scenting for the Strange. Yes, the Strange were close, but not as close as they had been before Cedar had set sail on this ice trundler. The Strange were not the danger the Madders were trying to outrun.

His ears were good under normal circumstances, and now, with the full moon just a day off, they were even sharper. He didn't hear anything other than the push of wind in trees farther off, the shifting of the ice beneath the sleds and the crack and muffled *thump* of branches breaking beneath the weight of snow in the distance.

"What is it?" Cedar asked.

"Nothing," Alun snapped. "Can't you find us a breeze on that compass of yours, brother Bryn?"

"Might have to fashion ourselves our own gale," Bryn said.

"No wind will take us far enough away," Cadoc said in a soft tone most often reserved for storytellers. "The wind is gone and has left a song made of strings, knotted notes that tie and bind. We gave our word. Our word drags like an anchor."

"There are more important things than an old promise," Alun said loud enough to be heard a half mile away. "The Holder comes before anything, or anyone else."

"We gave our word, and with it our right to choose," Cadoc said even more quietly.

"Our word can be upheld another day," Alun said. "The world is in danger. The Holder, even now, is poisoning rivers, fields, cities. The longer the Holder is unfound, the more of this land it will destroy. We will not set one foot in that town. Not before the Holder's found."

Cadoc turned enough in his seat so he could look at Alun. He raised one finger, as if pointing to the heavens.

A sweet song rose on the chill stillness of the night, a flute-pipe of notes that seemed so near Cedar glanced in all directions to be sure the player wasn't hiding in the muted darkness and falling white around them.

Wil was back in the wagon with Mae and Miss Dupuis. He whined softly at the sorrowful song.

The tune tumbled to its end, repeating the last five notes slowly. All three Madders turned, as if pulled by the same string, to face west.

Then Cadoc spoke. "I have given my word, and I will keep it."

"No," Alun said.

"A Madder's vow cannot be broken," Bryn said from above them.

"We move on," Alun growled.

"I will stay," Cadoc said.

"I will stay," Bryn said.

Cedar had heard the brothers argue before, usually loudly with fists and threats and insults. But this was serious, the tension between them hard-edged. Something very important, or very dangerous, rode on this decision. A decision Alun Madder appeared to be on the losing side of.

"Our promise is not easily given," Cadoc said. "It is nearly impossible to earn the Madders' oath, the Madders' favor. But once given, it cannot be broken. Especially not by us, Brother Alun."

Alun swore one hard, burning word. Then he rubbed his mittened hand over his beard, scraping away snow and ice. His gaze searched the shadows around them as if he had lost something valuable.

"We knew this day would come," Bryn said.

"Aye." Alun sighed. "We did. This will be the last of it. No man there will have another promise from me. But on this old vow, they will collect. And it will be the last time I set foot in this devil's town."

"It will be the last time any of us set foot in this devil's town," Cadoc said. "He, I am sure, will see to it."

"He?" Cedar asked. "Who?"

"The devil," Cadoc said.

The wind picked up again and snow sifted down like flour through a sieve. The wagon scuttled onward, crawled along as fast as a man could walk.

Ahead a glimmer of gold sparked and burned brightly, perhaps a lantern on the west edge of the bank.

"Just a ways now," Bryn said. "Catch the wind's march, boys. We'll be to land soon."

Cedar adjusted the sail, and so did Alun. Just as Bryn had said, the wind drew them smoothly, slowly, as if dreading the journey, while Cadoc steered them toward the ever-brightening light.

Soon Cedar could make out its source.

A man in a full cloak with a wide, heavy hood sat on a horse on a rise over the bank. He held an oversized lantern, mirrored to enhance its flame. The light threw shadows against his face so thick, Cedar couldn't make out a single angle of his features.

"Trim the sails," Bryn said. "This is our stop."

"Do you know that man?" Cedar asked as the wagon came to a creaking stop, sleds skiffing over the ragged ice at the river's edge and riding up to settle in the snow on the bank.

"No," Alun said. "We knew his family, I expect."

"Ho, stranger," Bryn called out. "What town lies beyond this bank?"

"Des Moines," the man answered, his accent pressing hard on the spaces between the words. "Where do you fare from?"

"Long away and better days." Alun jumped down out of the driver's seat and lashed the ropes of the sail tight so the wagon didn't go wandering off onto the ice again.

"Was it your song playing?" Cadoc Madder stepped onto the snowy ground too and saw to resetting the hitch so the mules could pull the wagon on land again.

"It was the song of my father, and his before him," the man said.

"Father's, eh?" Alun asked. "I suppose it has been some years since we were last through. We'll need shelter for the night and a place for the animals out of the storm."

"Yes," the stranger said. "Follow me."

It didn't take long to get the animals situated to pull the wagon. Mae released the calming spell, and the mules and horse all seemed a little spooked to find themselves in the middle of a snowstorm.

With some pushing, pulling, coaxing, and cussing, they managed to get the wagon up the bank and onto a road.

It was well and dark now and the only light came from the lantern the man carried, the lanterns on the wagons, and the occasional flickering behind the thick glass of the houses they passed.

The streets of Des Moines rambled between haphazard structures built with the hurried signs of sudden growth now that the railroad joining the Mississippi and Missouri Rivers had come through town. That, along with the mines of coal, lead, and a rare vein of copper, had put the city's star on the map.

The town was quiet beneath the snow. Houses gave way to warehouses, shops, and brick buildings. Now and again a shout broke the night, a gunshot cracked, or the rattle of laughter and piano reminded Cedar of this city's restless state.

Des Moines had grown dense with the people who had settled here for years. Now more were coming through, building businesses, clearing land for farms, working the mines, and seeing to the shipping of grains, cattle, devices, and other goods between the east and west.

The railroad and telegraphs that connected this great land had been a boon to the town and had given it enough spunk to build tall buildings, airship fields, and foundries.

It was a city now. Called itself the capital of Iowa.

Cedar thought it might be the sort of town Rose Small was hoping to see one day: full of busy and bustle, fed by all the new ideas coming on rails from the east. He wished, for a moment, that she might be here with them. Then the wind scraped across his exposed skin and he was glad she was safe and warm back in the Kansas coven.

They turned down a street lined by unlit lamps, then left that street for another, and finally came to a winding lane.

Cedar rolled his shoulders. The press of people sleeping just behind the tall walls was a palpable weight on his nerves. Dawn would come too soon. By moonrise tomorrow, he'd be full under the hold of the Pawnee curse and in the body of a beast.

Hungry for Strange blood.

The Madders hadn't said a single word as they traveled the streets; neither had their host, who led them down the lane.

In short time, a structure rose at the end of the path.

A single candle in a high arched window flickered in the framework building. Above that rose a blocky bell tower with a simple cross atop it. A church. From the look of it, a very old but well-kept house of worship.

The rider took them past the building to a barn that was larger than the church by half. He dismounted and motioned them forward into the shelter.

The barn wasn't large enough for the wagon, but there was a generous lean-to, beneath which the wagon would be shielded from the worst of the weather.

Their host led his horse into the barn and they followed.

"There are stalls for your animals here." The man pushed the wide hood of his cloak away, revealing black hair smoothed back from his wide forehead and tied in a single braid that fell at least halfway down his back. He had the tanned skin and carved angles to his face that spoke clearly of native descent. And yet, he wore a modern man's clothing. At his neck hung a simple silver cross.

An Indian preacher? Cedar didn't think he'd ever heard of such a thing.

"Mr. Hunt," Alun said. "Please see to the mules and our host's horse. We have business to conduct with Father Kyne here. I assume there's room in the church?"

The native man nodded. "Find your welcome. I will follow in a moment."

Alun strode out of the barn, impatience clipping his step. "Brothers," he said. "Let's get this done with."

Bryn and Cadoc turned heel and followed him.

Wil was waiting in the shadows. As soon as the Madders had passed by, he slipped into the barn.

Mae and Miss Dupuis led the mules and horse toward stalls, all of the animals too tired to care about the unfamiliar surroundings.

"They're in a hurry," Mae said. "Do you know why?"

Cedar took the horse's reins from her. "I'm given to understand they owe a favor to someone here in town."

"Perhaps that is why they wanted to avoid it?" Miss Dupuis said.

Cedar watched Father Kyne, who stood in the stall, removing the light saddle from his horse. He was watching them all but, most especially, him and Wil.

"I don't know the Madders' business," Cedar said. "And they seem content to leave it that way. I do want to thank you, Father Kyne, for guiding us to town. It's been a long, hard ride."

"My pleasure," he said quietly. "You and the wolf. He belongs to you?"

Cedar nodded. "My name is Cedar Hunt. The wolf is named Wil. This is Mae Lindson and Sophie Dupuis."

Father Kyne nodded to them each, and draped the saddle over the stall door, followed by the bridle. "You are all welcome to my home, for as long as you have need."

"We don't want to be a burden, Father Kyne," Miss Dupuis said. "Perhaps there is a hotel with room for us this evening?"

"Not so late in the night," he said, stepping out of the stall. "In the morning, I would be happy to take you to better accommodations. But tonight, no one should be out on the streets. There are . . . strange happenings in our town. I do not think it would be safe."

He pulled the hood of his cloak back up and then left the barn, disappearing into the snow.

Cedar finished with the saddle, blanket, and bridle from the horse, then closed the stall door behind him.

"Well," Miss Dupuis said, "I, for one, am looking forward to some time out of this weather. Perhaps a cup of tea, or a hot meal."

She adjusted her scarves and hat, tucked her hands into her woolen muff. "Do you need any help with the animals?" she asked.

"No," Cedar said. "We'll be right behind you. Wil, please go with her."

She walked out of the barn and so did Wil.

Mae lingered in the stall with the last mule.

"Mae," Cedar said. "Are you all right?"

She patted the mule on the nose before ducking under its neck and stepping out of the stall. "Better now that we are out of the storm. How are your hands? The burns?"

"Fine," he said. "I don't feel them. The burns," he clarified. "I wanted to thank you. For the spells, the warmth against the cold. I wouldn't have survived that without your witchcraft."

"I think you are overstating that a bit," she said gently. "Nothing could have stopped you from finding our way through that storm."

He gave her a slight smile.

"Tomorrow will be the full moon," she said. "Do you want me to try to cast something to ease the beast?"

They'd tried that, more than once. Spells didn't seem to have an effect on the curse he carried. The best way to be sure he didn't roam the night killing Strange—or accidentally any people who got in his way—was to chain him up and wait until dawn gave him back his mind and body.

Mae strolled up next to him. He could see the fatigue in her step, but she held her shoulders back and her eyes were clear. "Or do you want me to chain you?"

She paused, her gaze searching his face. It was suddenly no longer the beast that he was thinking about. It was Mae and only Mae.

Mate, the beast whispered in his head.

Cedar very gently brushed a stray lock of her hair away from the curve of her cheek, his fingers hot and stinging. "I want," he said softly, "you."

They had had too little time alone together since they started this journey. Only enough for a caught hand, a stolen kiss. He hadn't even had a chance to tell her how much he loved her. To ask her if she would be his wife.

Mae looked down and smiled, but shook her head slightly, taking this moment away too. "We need rest, you need rest. I want . . ." She looked away, swallowed, then looked back to him, her expression calm, clear. "I want you to eat something, and drink."

He took in a breath, knowing he should say more, explain to her that he wanted her in his life, forever.

But before he could say a word, she slipped her finger gently to his lip, and then very carefully kissed him. She pulled away, and he could see a small drop of his blood on her bottom lip. She took out her kerchief and dabbed at her lip, then at his.

"You are injured, Cedar," she said softly. "You might not feel it now, but you will. You need rest."

The beast inside him pushed, wanting out, wanting her, and if not her, then wanting the hunt.

But she was right. He needed rest, warmth, and a man's mind for as long as he could have those things. He took a deep breath and ignored the beast's demands. He offered her his arm. "Mrs. Lindson," he said.

"Rowen," she corrected. "My maiden name is Rowen. I think I will use it again."

Cedar's heart leaped at that and he smiled. "It's a good name."

"Yes, it is," she said.

It was a short enough walk to the church, and the glow from the windows made of small colored panes lay a patchwork quilt across the snow.

Mae stepped into that light, and for a moment he imagined her at the altar with him, exchanging vows. Then she stomped snow off her boots and stepped through the door.

He shook his head. This was something new to him. When he'd been a much younger man and asked his wife to marry him, it had been a whirlwind of plans, and preparations, and a wedding before spring was over.

But Mae . . . Mae was worth waiting a thousand springs for.

He climbed the church steps and paused.

An eerie call, like the weeping of the dead, echoed through the night.

He snapped around, hands to the side, feet spread, bracing for an attack.

Nothing moved in the snow. Nothing he could see. The call rolled out from the city, a sobbing wail.

The Strange were crying. He'd never heard a Strange weep, but he knew with every inch of his being that it was the Strange behind that sound.

The crackle of lightning licked copper against the sky. Once, twice, three times. Then thunder rumbled in its wake. He thought he heard a gun fire far off, then all was quiet again, smothered by the falling snow.

There should not have been lightning in the middle of this snowstorm. Copper lightning. There should not have been thunder.

And the slight scent of blood in the air told him there was something else here that didn't belong: the Holder.

CHAPTER FOUR

Rose had never been in a library before. The small town of Halle-lujah, where she'd been raised, had a few books in the schoolhouse and a few more in the church, but there wasn't a proper library within a hundred miles.

But here the entire house was filled with shelves that reached up two stories high. Off where one might expect bedrooms were chairs and tables and lamps set easy for the eyes. The whole place smelled of summer—that peculiar dust-and-dry scent of well-tended books, oily ink, leather, and wood that was shared with the season.

"I could live here," Rose sighed, drawing her fingers along the mounded spines of the gold-lettered volumes.

Thomas Wicks chuckled. "Do you read much, Miss Small?"

"I've always endeavored to do so. Mostly the periodicals coming through my parents' shop. Sometimes a novel or poems, but those were usually ordered by people in town who were quick to pick them up."

"Come now. You never once snuck a book off in a corner and took a peek?"

She looked up and across the room. Thomas was half-turned from the shelf there, in shirtsleeves and vest, having draped his coat and jacket across the back of a chair. He'd taken off his hat too, revealing his dark, wavy hair. She thought he looked rather at home here, as if he did indeed have a cot stashed away in some corner of the place and would at any moment kick off his shoes and settle in by the fire.

He smiled, waiting for her answer.

"Maybe once or twice," she admitted with a laugh. "Old Mrs. Pruce loved her romantic fiction, and Mr. Donaldson asked every week if a new bit from his favorite, Longfellow, had come through."

"Did you have a favorite too?" He turned back to the shelves and tipped his head just slightly to one side to better read the titles on the spine. "Poetry, intellect, suspense?"

"Oh, I like it all, especially the popular fictions. But really, anything at all to set my mind dreaming." Rose noticed a stout brown volume and tugged it out gently by its top. *The Handbook of Household Sciences.* She tucked it under her arm with her other finds, *The Lady's Oracle* and *The Lamplighter.*

"And you, Mr. Wicks? Do you have a preferred sort of reading?"

"I am particular to the philosophies."

"Really?" She glanced back over at him.

He nodded, even though he was still facing the shelves. "I have a horrifying fascination about such things. Seeing the world through other people's eyes and minds. Imagining the implications of varying arguments and scenarios. About the world. About the heavens. About the human heart. So . . . fascinating."

The way he said it all, it sounded like poetry. Rose folded the books against her chest and studied her companion. "Do you live here in town, Mr. Wicks?"

"Presently." He tucked his hands behind his back and bent nearly in half, browsing the books on the lower shelves.

"What is your occupation?"

"Currently? A purveyor of fine literature. Previously? A railroad and express agent. And before that, other, less interesting things."

"You've worked for the railroads?"

"Just so."

"How exciting," she said. "Have you been to all the great cities, then? Boston? Philadelphia? New York?"

His shoulders tightened just a bit at the mention of the cities. He pulled himself up to his height again, then, casually: "If one may consider them great. Yes. Those places and many more."

The way he said it, she suddenly wondered why he had left them for this rather out-of-the-way spur in Kansas.

The wind battered at the shingles and sieved through the cracks around the door, reminding her that outside this cocoon of ink and page, winter was on a wail. Time had slipped away. It was dark out, and here she was lingering with a perfect stranger after hours.

Best she be moving on.

"Well, then," she said, giving her words a lift. "Thank you for showing me around the place, Mr. Wicks. I'll just be signing out and on my way."

"Yes," he said. "Of course." He seemed to choose a book at random off the shelf, then picked up his jacket and coat. "I do hope you'll allow me to see you to your front step?"

Rose narrowed her eyes. What did she really know about this man? Nothing other than the rather idle chitchat over the last few hours. He seemed a kind, polite, and guileless sort. But it had been her experience that sly-hearted people often hid behind kind smiles.

"Oh, I wouldn't want to be bothering you," she said. "I know my way about. Why, I suppose Mr. Davis might be headed out to the farm, and I'll just hop his wagon."

He frowned while donning his outercoat. "It has never been my experience that Mr. Davis is reliable. It must be—"

A train whistle hooted, two short, one long howl. When it softened a bit, Rose was sure she could hear the call of the conductor, urging passengers aboard.

"—five o'clock exactly." He tucked his watch into his pocket. "Mr. Davis should be halfway to the creek by now."

"Do you pay such close attention to all of Hays City's residents?" Rose wandered up to the librarian's desk and placed the books down.

"Well, no. But you have to admit he is difficult to overlook. I think he quite prefers it that way."

That was true. Mr. Davis had a bit of a drinking habit, and by evening each night as he rambled out of town with his tinker wagon, he was usually singing at the top of his lungs.

"Is that everything now?" Miss Bucker wore round glasses much like Mr. Wicks, only hers had glass in them as thick as a thumb. That glass didn't appear to be strong enough to take the squint out of her eyes as she flipped each book over and took note of the title and author in the ledger at her side.

She picked up the fountain pen and quirked her head to one side, pen raised, looking down her nose at the same time as looking up at Rose. "Name, my dear?"

"Miss Rose Small. I'm currently at Miss Adaline's farm."

"Is that so? I heard an airship came crashing into the orchard just a few months ago. Were you there to see it?"

Rose had indeed been there. She'd been injured, very sick, and aboard Captain Hink's airship, the *Swift*. They nearly hadn't made it to the farm that was owned by the coven of witches where Mae had been raised. The *Swift* hadn't so much crashed as barely limped the winds to come down less than easily in the orchards.

"I didn't see a ship crash at all," Rose said quite truthfully.

"Well, I expect such things to become common now," Miss Bucker said. "Such comings and goings with the rail line and ships and strange travel devices. This town used to be a quiet place. A nice place." She planted her pen back in the ink pot and shook her head. "Look at it now. New faces every day, bandits and roughs just adding to the mess of it. I wouldn't be surprised if we burst our boundaries by next spring."

"Hays City is busy," Mr. Wicks said. "That is the price for the advance of civilization, I'm afraid. But it's not growing as quickly as some other towns. The rail connections in Council Bluff and Des Moines have more than tripled the size of those cities in under a year."

"Civilization can advance all it wants," she said with a huff. "In those cities."

He grinned at Rose when Miss Bucker wasn't looking, then slid his book onto her desk.

"Oh, you can take it, Thomas," she said more kindly. "I know you'll have it back by the morning."

"Thank you, Miss Bucker."

Rose tucked the books inside the inner pocket she'd sewn into her heavy coat; then, knowing the books were safe from the elements, she tugged the door open and stepped out into the night.

Wet, dark, and cold. It wasn't snow coming down; it was waves of freezing sleet that the wind snapped out like sheets on a line.

Rose swore under her breath. She hadn't ridden into town. She'd stormed her way on foot, five miles or so, without once thinking how she'd get back in the dark.

Well, she knew the way, and there wasn't anything wrong with her feet. She'd be cold and wet by the end of it, but neither of those things would be her death.

Time to get walking.

She'd made it down to the end of the block when Mr. Wicks called out.

"Miss Small." He all-too-quickly caught up to her strong stride before she'd even reached the hardware store. "You aren't going to travel the night alone are you?"

"Yes, I am, Mr. Wicks. Don't bother yourself over my welfare. I can take care of myself."

"It isn't a bother—"

A horse loped down the street toward them. Rose paused on the wooden sidewalk, squinting against the sleet catching like sparks of gold in the wedge of shop light.

She knew that rider. Captain Hink.

"You're coming home," he said, pulling the horse up short and glaring down at her.

"Not with you, I'm not," she said.

"Excuse me," Thomas said. "Are you a relation to Miss Small?"

"No," Rose said. "He most certainly is not. My relations aren't lying, cheating dogs."

"How would you know?" Hink asked. "You run across one of your real relations lately?"

"If I had, I wouldn't tell you."

"Rose Small, I do not know what has gotten into you." Hink pushed his hat back off his eyes a bit.

"Give me your horse." She held her hand out.

"What? No."

"You won't need it, will you?"

He leaned forward a bit to drape one arm on the saddle horn and the sleeting rain shattered down like diamonds from the brim of his hat. "If I wanted to be standing in the street with my boots in a puddle, that's where I'd be. What has gotten into you, woman?"

"Clarity," she said. "You don't need the horse. You have a warm bed waiting for you right down Whore Street."

Hink opened his mouth, but instead of yelling, he laughed.

He *laughed*.

Rose took a deep breath and clenched her hands into fists. Hot white fury filled her, and the taste of melted metal filled her mouth. How dare he make fun of her. How dare he try to laugh his way out of his betrayal.

Did she mean so little to him?

"Is that what this is all about?" he asked. "My . . . other interests? I suppose you've made up your mind without once hearing my explanation."

"Mr. Hink," she said through her teeth. "Do not *slight* me so. I am not a fool."

He had the sense to straighten up and lean back.

"The only thing you have that I would even consider accepting," she continued, "is that horse. All the rest of you is abhorrent to my eyes."

Hink hitched one shoulder back as if taking a punch.

"Rose, you're just not seeing it straight," Hink said.

"Excuse me, Mr. Hink, is it?" Thomas said. "The lady is obviously unwilling to entertain your company. In this weather, at this hour, a gentleman's duty is to give up his mount so that the lady may find shelter."

Hink turned his single blue eye down on the slender man next to her.

"Who the hell are you?"

Rose had seen that look on his face before. It was the sort of look he gave men who stood between him and the *Swift*. Possessive, angry, and harder than iron, Captain Hink didn't hesitate to kill men who threatened the one thing he loved—his ship.

And it was the look he was giving Thomas.

But not because he was threatening his ship. The *Swift* was safely tucked away in a shop on coven land, being rebuilt by Mr. Seldom, Hink's second-in-command; Rose; and Hink himself, when he wasn't drinking and carousing.

So why the look? Because Thomas was threatening to take his horse away? Hink won that horse in a card game. As far as she knew, he didn't care that much for the rambling old beast.

Then what had put the calculating, killing look into the man?

Could it be his feelings for her?

No, he'd made it clear just exactly where, and who, he wanted to spend his time with.

"Wicks," Thomas said. "Thomas Wicks."

"Are you speaking for her now, Mr. Wicks?" Hink rumbled.

"No," Rose said. "Of course not. It's—no man speaks for me. But at least he knows how to be courteous to a woman."

Hink nodded slowly, still looking at Thomas, who stood beside Rose, his shoulders back, stock straight. He stared Hink right back, unafraid, or unaware of just how dangerous that man could be.

Rose was secretly surprised. Thomas had seemed a little distracted, and maybe a sweetly bumbling man, when they'd run into each other. But now he looked like someone who knew how to take care of himself and any situation that came his way.

She suddenly wondered if he had a gun on him.

Oh, for glim's sake. She didn't want either of them shot over this.

"Never mind," Rose said. "The both of you. I'll walk. Keep your horse, Mr. Hink. I'll find my way home on my own."

"I wouldn't have it," Thomas said. "I'll see you home safely, Miss Small."

He turned half away from Hink and touched her arm.

"I don't need—," Rose started.

"Step off, now, boy," Hink warned. "Woman said you don't speak for her. I'd be more than happy to see that's a permanent sort of condition for you." He dismounted and took the three steps or so to close the distance between them.

Now they were all huddled beneath the overhang of the hardware shop, wet and shining in yellow lamplight.

Rose was close enough to Thomas that even in the low light she could see his eyebrow arc and a hard, cool sort of look cross his face. She decided he most certainly had a gun on him.

"Please," Rose said softly to him. "Let it be."

He glanced at her, his wide eyes shifting just over the frames of his glasses to take in the all of her face. Then he nodded and leaned in a little closer, whispering, "As you please. I do hope I'll see you again, Miss Small."

Hink chucked his chin up and stared at Rose from behind Thomas. She heard the creak of leather in the seams of his gloves straining as he clenched his hand.

"Thank you, Mr. Wicks." She stepped back so as to lessen the chance of Hink walloping the man.

Thomas moved out of the way and Hink pushed past him to hand Rose the horse's reins. "I'll see you out at the farm," he said.

"Don't bother yourself, Captain." She clomped past him, half expecting he would reach out for her, try to stop her, try to tell her that he was sorry.

But he just folded his arms across his chest and leaned back on one foot, glowering in the darkness as she swung up into the saddle—glowering at her as she turned the horse and started away.

The stirrups were too long, set for his legs not hers, but she pretended that it didn't matter, just as she pretended he didn't matter.

She had loved him, given him her heart, even if she hadn't said so much in words. He had broken that trust and spent weeks in the arms of other women.

She didn't want that, didn't want a man who gave his affections to any pretty painted bird. But she had wanted him—so much so it had made her ache to think of leaving. But she knew she must.

She urged the horse into a quick trot as the cold sleet scrubbed away her tears.

By the time Rose got back to the farm, she was all cried out and numb, both inside and out. But the numbness brought with it a certainty she hadn't possessed before: she was going to catch the next train out of town, head up to Kansas City, or maybe St. Louis, then off to Chicago, New York, Boston.

She had horizons to see, and she wasn't going to let any man take them away from her.

She walked Hink's horse into the barn, dismounted, lit the lantern with shaking, cold hands, then put the horse in a stall and gave it a quick wipe down with a cloth before tossing some hay in for the poor thing and setting the saddle and bridle in the tack room.

Her room was in the main house, a sort of large lodge building that housed all the people who worked the farm in the spring and summer, and fell empty during the wintering months. The witches all shared in the labor and the harvest of the land, but most lived in town or on their own smaller lots of land.

The gathering room of the main house was empty and quiet, fists of coal from the wood fire that had burned down to ash whispering softly. The rocking chair Mae Lindson had sat in while she was recovering her mind and sanity when they'd first arrived stood empty.

The quiet of the place just made Rose more lonely. And determined. She might have made the wrong choice agreeing to take the boilerman job on Captain Hink's ship, but she didn't have to sit around moping about it.

Not wanting to disturb the coven members who might be sleeping in the guest rooms, she made her way on tiptoe across the hall.

Halfway across the room she heard hushed voices, and almost called out softly to the sisters to ask why they were awake so late after sunset.

Probably spells. All of the sisters had been busy lately, mixing herbs and other blessings, making trips into town for supplies come by the mail or train, and then shipping them off again. She hadn't seen any of the things they'd made their magic with, and since they'd told her it was of both a private and business nature, she hadn't thought it right to ask.

Better just to pass by quietly.

"But he's asking for more," Margaret said. "We've already fulfilled our side of the agreement. I don't know why Sister Adaline doesn't tell him we're done with this business. It's worrisome. Do you ever think what that family of his might be doing with those things?"

"We have to think of what's best for the coven," Sarah replied. "Times are changing, Margaret. Witches can't just stand by while the rest of the world falls apart. We must choose a side. Do you remember what happened the last time witches were on the losing side?"

"I don't see any good coming of this. Since when do witches choose sides in wars? Our calling isn't for these kinds of . . . devices and curses. He can do his own dirty spells. Or buy them from someone else."

"Shush, Margaret. Don't speak of him so. He'll hear you." She paused, then, quieter: "Sister Adaline wouldn't lead us wrong."

"Something bad will come of our good work," Margaret said. "Nothing good can come of those things."

"Shh!"

Rose knew they had heard her walking, breathing.

Then Sarah said much more loudly, "Good night, Margaret. I'll see you in the morning."

The shuffle of bare feet crossed the hall floor, and two doors closed firmly.

They had known she was there. They must have known.

She felt a little guilty for eavesdropping, but didn't know what they were talking about. The world was falling apart? As far as she could tell, the witches had a good communal farm, were respected citizens in a town willing to turn a blind eye to their practices, and even managed to keep their witchery mostly quiet. Outsiders would never suspect an entire coven sat right outside Hays City. And since that's how the sisters liked it, Rose had thought things were going very well for them.

She wondered who that man they were doing business with was, and why it made Margaret so uncomfortable. Devices and curses. That certainly sounded worrisome.

Rose walked down to her room, shucked out of all of her clothes, and pulled a blanket around her shoulders. The finder compass hung against her chest, its burnished metal warm from contact with her skin. She tipped it up and saw the fine needle pointing northeast toward the other finder compass she had made, Hink's compass.

There was a time she thought she'd never want that man to be lost to her. That had changed now.

Rose hung her wet clothes over the back of the chair and on the wall hook to dry. She dragged her carpetbag from the corner of the room and packed her clothes, her metalworking tools, and the twine, wax, oil, and bits and pieces of metal and gears she had slowly gathered up over the last few months. Finally, she draped her practical trousers and a dry pair of socks over the back of the chair for the morning.

She considered the clothing. No. She was starting a new life. She'd meet it looking her best. She packed away her spare trousers and pulled out her best dress and underskirts. That was the way to meet her horizon: like a lady.

The train left early. She'd be dressed and ready to meet it.

She settled into bed, pulling the rough wool covers up over her nose. Just before she slipped into sleep, she realized with a pang of regret that she hadn't had a chance to read the books she'd borrowed from the library. There was no changing her mind now. Those books were just one more thing she loved that she'd have to leave behind.

CHAPTER FIVE

The Madder brothers sat at the table in the church kitchen, hats off, hair and beards still dripping wet, hands wrapped around mugs filled with tea.

They looked as uncomfortable as schoolyard bullies under a teacher's disapproving glare.

The teacher, in this case, was Father John Kyne, who seemed quite at home putting the kettle on the back of the stove now that he had seen to the filling of everyone's cup. It was proper manners, almost English manners, and not what Cedar was used to seeing from a man native to these lands.

But then, he'd never known a native man who had taken the Almighty as his personal savior.

"Let's get this over with," Alun said. "What favor do you want from us, Kyne?"

Father Kyne paused with his teacup resting on his bottom lip. He regarded Alun Madder from over its rim. "You are not the men I expected to answer my call," he said mildly.

All three Madders swiveled their heads to peer at him.

"What sort of men did you expect?" Bryn rubbed at his bad eye while staring at Kyne from the good one. "Did you think we'd be taller? People always think we'd be taller."

Alun snorted and Cadoc turned his head to the side a bit more, like a bird trying to sight a worm.

"I heard stories. Stories of the noble Madder brothers. Brave, ingenious, and wise." Kyne sipped his tea, then sat at the head of the long wooden table.

"Stories are just that," Alun Madder said. "No matter what your father told you."

"My father told me you owe my family a favor."

"We promised a German man named Kyne a favor. Not a man born of this soil," Alun said.

"Lars Kyne took me in when my family was killed. He raised me as his own and had no other."

"But you are not, in fact, of Kyne blood," Alun pressed.

Father Kyne leaned back and placed his fingers together, tip to tip, his hand curved loosely on the table. "I am not of his blood," he agreed. "Did you give your promise to the blood or to the man?"

"We promised Holland Kyne three favors," Cadoc said. "One favor for each of our lives saved."

"He saved your lives?" Miss Dupuis asked, surprised.

"It was long ago," Cadoc said.

"It was that," Alun agreed. "And a promise made to a dead man. We've done Holland his favor and the favor to his son, Lars. That's two favors. Now that Lars is gone, the last favor dies with him."

"Brother," Cadoc said with soft reproach, "he saved our lives."

Alun turned and glared at Cadoc. "We've repaid enough."

Cadoc only shook his head slowly, the dark of his hair curled out to the side into points, his close-set, rounded features visible between beard and hair and scrubbed red from wind and snow.

"Perhaps your life was repaid," Cadoc said. "Perhaps Bryn's life. But not mine. Not all of ours. Three promises given must be kept. Madders do not break their vows."

Alun grunted and pointed a finger at John Kyne. "This better be good. We are doing important work, Mr. Kyne. Work that might just save this land and a fair more people than who sit in this room. Now we have to halt that important work to tend to your favor that couldn't wait. So tell me, what is it you want? And if you say more favors, I promise you it will be the first time I've shot a man in a house of God."

"Mr. Madder," Mae cut in. "Please, show some gratitude for our host. He brought us in, gave our animals food and shelter, and is offering the same to us. Without him we would be lost in a blizzard."

"We weren't lost."

"Yes," she said, "we were. And now that we are found, we will show our appreciation."

There was a clear threat in her tone. A threat Cedar knew she could follow through on. Mae's magic ran toward curses and bindings. She could make a very formidable foe, though he'd never seen her raise magic in anger.

"Widow Lindson, I do believe you are threatening me," Alun said with just a bit of a glint in his eyes.

"Believe what you will, Mr. Madder." Mae took a sip of her tea.

Father Kyne watched the exchange without much change of manner. He seemed to be a man with little expression beyond a serious, almost sad stare. Still, Cedar could tell there was something weighing on him. He certainly hadn't brought the brothers here on a whim.

"What is your trouble, Father?" Cedar asked. "And how can we help?"

Kyne nodded. "Thank you, Mr. Hunt. The trouble is not mine alone. Although many of the town do not choose to worship in the church my grandfather built, our congregation was once very devout. Common people, miners, farmers, millers, and a few merchants, all gathered here.

"Many families too. Some young and of distant homelands, pushing west, looking for a beginning. Children worshiped here until three months ago when the children began to disappear. Called into the night, and gone, never to return home."

"Children?" Alun asked, a little startled at the story. "How many?"

"Dozens. Perhaps hundreds. Ever since the star fell out of the sky."

"Is this your favor?" Cadoc asked.

"Yes."

"Then give it words that bind and speak it true," Alun said. "Tell us exactly what you want us to do for you. And we will do that exact thing."

"Find the children. All the missing children and return them to their families. Do not leave this city until you have done so."

All the Madder brothers sat back, their chairs creaking. "That's your favor?" Alun asked.

"Yes."

"You had to say it that way, didn't you?" Alun muttered. "You want us to find children who have been lost for months. Not just one, not just the living, but *all* the children. Did you see the blizzard beyond the doors? We promised a favor, not a miracle."

"We will do it," Cadoc said, throwing a stern look at his brother. "Just as you have said. We will find all the missing children and return them to their families. We will not leave this city until we have done so."

Alun threw up both hands and exhaled. Then he crossed his arms over his chest and scowled at Father Kyne.

"Is there more you can tell us about their disappearances?" Bryn asked, ignoring Alun. "Has the local law been involved?"

"Yes. Sheriff Burchell has searched the city. He has found nothing. No trace of the missing children. But the mayor has done nothing."

"Over a hundred children?" Alun grumped. "This could take years."

"Was my father wrong, then?" Kyne asked Alun.

"Probably."

"When he spoke of the Madder brothers, he said they were men above all others. Men who cared about the misery of their fellow man. Men who would never shirk to help the innocent."

Alun scowled, his dark brows pushing wrinkles across his broad face. "Your father had a way with words."

"What is the mayor's name?" Miss Dupuis asked. "Perhaps I could speak with him."

"Vosbrough," Father Kyne said. "Killian Vosbrough."

All three brothers looked at one another. They knew that name. They knew that man. But none of them spoke a word. Even Miss Dupuis seemed a bit startled.

"I see," she said.

"But it is late," Father Kyne said. "Perhaps morning will bring us all more rested to this endeavor." He stood and gestured toward the doorway to the right. "There is a room, a fire, and blankets for sleeping. I am sorry I don't have beds to offer."

"No, that is fine," Mae said. "We are grateful, truly, for everything you've given us."

"Yes, thank you, Father Kyne," Miss Dupuis agreed. "The tea was lovely, and your kindness most welcome."

Cedar pushed up away from the table. He was bone tired. "I'll do what I can to help find the children also."

"Mr. Hunt," Alun said. "You aren't forgetting your promise to us, are you?"

"How could I? You remind me of it constantly." He nodded at Father Kyne, then walked from the room with the women.

Wil lifted his head from where he had been drowsing near the stove. He got to his feet, then stretched and yawned hugely before padding off after Cedar.

Cedar wondered if he should stay and see what the Madders and Father Kyne discussed. Wondered if he should do what he could to warn the priest that making deals with the brothers could land a person in more trouble than bargained for.

But this time the shoe was on the other foot. Father Kyne was owed a favor by the brothers, not the other way around. It was no wonder Alun was so angry. Cedar didn't know if the brothers had ever owed any man or any country anything ever before.

He smiled. It was about time the table was turned.

The narrow hall ended in a room that must have once served as a bedroom, but now looked more like a storage space. There was a chest of drawers and several shelves built into the wall. The shelves held some canned goods, three books, boxes of candles, and several bottles of kerosene and medicine.

Wool and cotton blankets sat folded on top of the chest, enough to make up fifty beds. A small stove in the corner put out enough heat to make Cedar wish he were dry and curled up beneath every last one of those blankets.

Mae and Miss Dupuis spread quilts on the other side of the room, then untied boots and took off their wet outercoats. Mae drew the combs out of her hair, and used them to brush through her long honey locks.

He found himself yearning to touch her, to draw his fingers through her hair, to hold the heat of her body against his.

"Do you suppose they'll be coming to bed too?" Miss Dupuis asked as she rolled up a quilt to use as a pillow.

Cedar blinked and wondered how long he'd been staring, transfixed by Mae.

"I would assume so, eventually." He walked over to the chest and pulled out five heavy blankets, then turned his back so the women could strip down to their undergarments. "I think Father Kyne was weary and ready to turn in."

"And so am I," Miss Dupuis said with a sigh. "I could sleep for a year, right here on this hard floor with nothing more than my dreams for a pillow."

"Do you think they'll start in the morning, looking for the children?" Mae asked.

Cedar shook out two blankets near the door, for Wil and himself, careful to keep his back turned so the women had some privacy. Enough time on the road together had afforded them a certain sort of ease around situations more civilized people might shy away from.

Time on the road had also set them into much worse sleeping arrangements than this.

"You heard them as well as I," Cedar said. "Cadoc seems set and ready to see this promise through to fulfilling it, and so does Bryn."

"And you?" she asked. "Are you going to search for the children? If they're lost . . . like little Elbert Gregor . . . ?"

"Yes." Cedar resisted the urge to look over his shoulder at her. "Even if they aren't lost like little Elbert Gregor."

"Good," Mae said over the shush of crawling beneath blankets. "I had hoped you would."

Elbert Gregor had been kidnapped for a man named Shard LeFel by the Strange creature known as Mr. Shunt. Cedar had killed Mr. Shunt, had felt him fall apart into bits and pieces of bone and bolt and spring. There was no chance that monster was still alive.

But there were other Strange, other monsters. The wind was thick with them. Likely, the town was thick with them. And Strange were known to steal children, though he'd never heard of a hundred missing at once.

As long as there were no bodies available for the Strange to wear, whether the freshly dead or the rare Strange-worked creatures built of cog and sinew, like Mr. Shunt, the Strange couldn't directly harm anyone. They were spirits—bogeys and ghouls—reduced to haunting the living world and desperately looking for ways to become a part of it.

No, it made the most sense that the children of Des Moines had been taken for more common evils by more common men—to work mills and factories in faraway cities, or to do some other labor in this quickly growing land.

With the railway connecting coast to coast and all lines pointing to Des Moines, it would be fairly simple to send a large group of children off to the far corners of the country. But a child-smuggling business that large had to have a reason to pull so many from one place alone.

Cedar lay down and dragged a thick, well-patched quilt that smelled of pine up to his chin. He'd left his boots on and laid his hat on the floor next to him. Wil settled down too, groaning as he stretched out.

Cedar dropped one arm out to the side, and dug his fingers into Wil's fur. They'd track the children tomorrow. He'd have most of the day to do so. He'd look for the Holder too.

And when the moon rose full, Cedar would ask Mae to make sure he was locked up, in the wagon or in a cellar.

The Pawnee curse turned him into a beast like his brother, but he had far less control over the animal instincts. When he changed, all he wanted, with every pump of his heart, was to kill the Strange. This tired, in this unknown city, he would be too likely to kill at random, kill people in his rage to destroy the Strange. He didn't want to lose control near a city this size with Strange so near. He didn't want innocent deaths on his hands.

He'd spilled enough innocent blood. With that grim thought, sleep finally claimed him.

Cedar startled awake as the Madder brothers tromped into the room. They each took a blanket and made beds, rolling up without removing coat or gloves, and snoring nearly as soon as they hit the floor. From the rhythm of breathing in the room, he knew Mae and Miss Dupuis slept through their arrival.

Wil twitched his ears. Other than opening his eyes into slits for a moment, he didn't move.

Cedar closed his eyes again, but sleep shifted further from his reach. He rolled over, which didn't do anything but make his back hurt, so he turned the rest of the way, facing the stove, the women, and the window, with Wil and the door behind him.

He was exhausted, mostly dry and warm. Why couldn't he sleep?

The skitter and odd scratch of tiny footsteps brought him awake, all of his senses open.

Something was in the room with them. Something was moving with uneven clawed feet toward the women. Toward Mae.

Cedar reached to the floor for his gun. He tugged it from the holster, then sat, aiming at the noise.

The noise stopped. It took a moment, no more than that, for Cedar's eyes to adjust to the darkness.

Then he saw it.

A creature with too much head for its spindly body, fully the size of a grown man, hunched over Mae, who lay sleeping. Its big head turned toward Cedar.

It was made of bits of straw, spun in a tight twist as if from a spindle, with dirt and leaves and long, wet pine needles caught within it all. The arms were too long, overwide hands dragging along the floor next to buckled legs that ended in tiny hooves.

The head was round, but the face was sharp, with no nose and a wide, slotted mouth full of pointed teeth. Two very human eyes glittered with damp light.

Strange. It had to be. But the beast inside Cedar was not stirring to kill it; Wil was not stirring to kill it.

He'd felt no warning that it was in the room, no warning it had crossed window or threshold. Yet it was so close to Mae it could strike her.

It opened its mouth and made a sound like a hissing moan, almost like crying.

If Mae held still, he could shoot it. He would miss the curve of her hip by inches. But if she or the creature moved, he'd surely hit her.

"Mae," he said softly, raising the gun slowly to show the Strange that he was about to blow it to bits.

"Mae."

And then the creature rushed him. It screeched and howled as it ran on all fours across the room and leaped for him, mouth wide, teeth glistening like knives.

He raised the gun again, this time pointing it toward the creature as it whispered, "Hunt-er. Run." It opened its huge mouth and sank teeth into his neck.

COLD COPPER • 55

Cedar yelled and turned the gun.

"No! Cedar, don't!"

Mae Lindson grabbed for his gun hand, pulling it away.

The creature was gone.

Cedar blinked hard, instinctively pulling his finger away from the trigger, since the gun was held by both him and Mae, and remaining very still until he gained his wits.

"You were dreaming," Mae said. "A nightmare. A nightmare."

Cedar took in the room. No more than a few hours must have passed since they bedded down. The Madders were still snoring. Miss Dupuis was awake, sitting wrapped in her blankets, staring through the dark at him. Wil stood in front of him, head lowered, eyes glowing.

Mae crouched in front of him too, wearing nothing more than her chemise, with one white strap having fallen off to reveal the creamy curves of her shoulder, collarbones, and breast.

"You were dreaming," she said again, pulling the gun gently the rest of the way out of his hand. "We are safe here."

"There was a creature. A Strange."

Wil's ears flicked up, and he started around the room, scenting for the intruder.

Mae took a deep breath and let it out slowly. "Here? Now? Can you see it?"

He peered at the corners, looking for any shift, any odd shadow.

"No. It wore straw and leaves. It was bent over you."

"I'm fine. Nothing touched me. Do you want me to light a candle to see if you're hurt?"

Cedar glanced at Wil, who had finished a full search of the room. Wil's ears flicked and he gave Cedar a steady stare.

There were no Strange in the room. Maybe there never had been. Wil would have woken up if there were, wouldn't he?

He wiped his hand over his face, rubbing away sweat, and realized Mae must have woken to see him holding his gun to his own head.

"Mae," he said. "I'm sorry. I . . . It must have been a nightmare."

"It was," she said firmly. She slid his gun back into the holster. "Can I get you anything?" she asked. "Help you in some way?"

She sat on her knees, beautiful and soft in the darkness. But she was also worried, and from the goose pimples on her skin, he knew she was chilled in the cold room.

"No, I'm fine," he said. "Just fine. Go on back to bed. Morning's coming soon enough."

She paused, then leaned forward and gently pressed the palm of her hand against his cheek.

He wanted to hold her, draw her in to him, bring her beneath his blanket and warm her. But then she leaned away, walked back to her bedding, and folded down beneath her covers.

Miss Dupuis, still across the room, released the hammer on her gun like the slow crack of knuckles.

Cedar nodded slightly. She'd had a gun beneath the blankets aimed at him. Practical. But unsettling, nonetheless.

She shifted and stretched out under her blankets, but lay facing him.

Cedar rubbed at his hair and tried to settle his mind. His neck ached from where the dream creature had bit him. He pressed his fingers there and didn't feel blood, though it was too dark to see.

He was no stranger to nightmares or the Strange. And he knew that creature had been watching them. It had known what he was and had called him "hunter."

Maybe he wouldn't let Mae chain him at the full moon. Maybe it was time for the hunter to hunt.

CHAPTER SIX

Rose left the house at a run. She'd overslept and dawn was already starting to shine up the sky. There was no time for walking now. If she was going to catch the train out to Kansas City, she was going to have to steal Hink's horse.

But before she left, and even though it might mean she'd have to gallop a mile or two, she wanted to take one last look at the *Swift*. She was the first airship Rose had ever been aboard, and the first she'd ever had the chance to help repair. She couldn't leave without saying good-bye.

The door to the big wooden shed was propped open by an overturned bucket. The voices of two men drifted out.

". . . get word back to you soon, so watch the wire," Hink said.

"Chicago, you think?" said another voice, that of Mr. Seldom, Hink's second-in-command.

"It's where I'll start looking. If you hear anything, send me a dove. There has to be another connection between the east and west trade and I want to know what it is, and who's behind it. And watch Miss Adeline. I've a feeling the witches are in this deeper than they'll admit."

"What about Miss Small?"

Rose skidded to a stop and ducked just behind the open door.

"She's . . ." Hink sighed. "Look after her for me. Keep her on the boilers. She's got a hell of a knack for steam and I have no doubt will be the best boilerman the *Swift* has ever had if she gets over her stubborn foolishness."

Rose made a small sound but clapped her hand over her mouth.

There was a pause, wherein she wondered if he'd heard her. Then he said, "Do me a favor, Seldom. There's a man named Thomas Wicks who's sweet on her. Kill him."

"No!" Rose gasped. She stormed around from behind the door.

And ran straight into Hink's massive chest.

"You were spying on me." Hink reached out and caught her elbows to keep her from falling.

Rose adjusted her wide-brimmed hat and pushed away from his embrace.

"I was not. You were talking too loud."

"I was having a private conversation. I can talk as loudly as I please."

"You. You." Rose felt the heat creep across her face. Too many thoughts were colliding in her brain, and too many emotions in her chest. He'd said she was good at her job, a better boilerman than even his last crew member, Molly Gregor. He'd told Mr. Seldom to look after her for him.

Because he cared about her, or cared about getting the *Swift*'s boiler repaired?

"You will not have Thomas killed," Rose blurted.

"Thomas?" Hink tipped his head down just a bit so that his eye was covered in shadow. "Are you on a first name basis with a man you've just met?" he asked softly. Too softly. "You *did* just meet him last night, didn't you?"

Rose closed her mouth and glared at him. "I was on first name basis with you quickly enough. Why not also with an educated gentleman?"

"I had to beg you to use my first name."

"You never told me your first name! I had to bribe it out of Mr. Seldom."

"Aha!" Hink turned to his first mate and stabbed a finger toward the man. "I knew you told her."

Mr. Seldom was a thin man with close-cut red hair and a face most often set in a droll expression. He wore coveralls, leather gloves, goggles, a flat cap, and a tool belt with an alarming range of things attached to it, each of which he could handily use as a weapon. He gave Hink a bored look.

Behind Seldom, filling every spare pocket of the shed was the *Swift*.

It didn't take much imagination to see that she was an airship, even though bits of her were scattered out across the floor, stacked up against the shed walls, and hanging by chains from the rafters.

Her huge tin envelope was almost whole now that they'd had a couple months to rivet, bend, and weld. And all of her internal framework, also made of tin, was strong again.

The ship had been nearly blown out of the sky, and been so filled with holes, Rose didn't know how she'd limped all the way to Kansas.

It had been good to work on her, to know her quirks. Even now, Rose's fingers itched to pick up a wrench or a hammer, and start in on making her whole again, strong and fast.

But that was done now. Breaking up with the man meant breaking up with his ship. She was sure she'd miss the ship more.

"I'll have your word," Rose said, looking away from the beautiful airship. "Mr. Seldom, I'll have your word that you'll not harm Mr. Wicks while I'm gone."

"While you're gone?" Hink asked. "Where are *you* going? And in a dress, I might add."

"I'm leaving Hays City. By train. Like a lady."

"Are you now?"

"Yes. And I'm already late. Mr. Seldom, please do nothing to harm Mr. Wicks. He seems a decent, upstanding man, whom I spoke with only once. Also"—she stabbed Hink in the chest—"you have no right ordering innocent people to their deaths."

"Need I remind you I am a U.S. Marshal? I could hang the man before you could say Nelly."

"Nelly."

Seldom snorted.

Hink gave him a deadly glare.

Seldom went back to stitching up the net he had hung over a rafter, pulling the rope through it to rebuild one of the *Swift*'s glim-harvest trawling arms.

Rose walked over to Mr. Seldom. She stood with her back to Hink, hoping he hadn't seen what she carried in her hand. "I trust you, Mr. Seldom. Please don't bother Mr. Wicks." She handed him the finder compass, which he took with a frown. "I think this should stay with the ship," she said quietly. "A ship should always know where her captain is."

She turned before he asked her any questions. He knew what the object was, had been mighty interested in her making a version for the ship, but now she wouldn't need to. Seldom would be able to find Hink anywhere he was in this country. At least some good had come of all this.

"Good-bye, Mr. Seldom. Marshal Hink." Rose turned and strode toward the door.

"Cage," Hink corrected her. "It's Marshal Cage or Captain Hink."

"I'll leave you to the sorting of your special names," Rose said. "I have a future to find."

Hink was quick and caught her arm.

"Without me?" He stepped up close, so she had to tip her head up to see the all of him.

Her heart about beat its way out of her chest. He'd left her. He'd gone sleeping with other women. Was he asking to be in her life, her future?

"Well . . . I have a train to catch," she said softly.

"Isn't that something?" he said with a smile. "So do I."

She narrowed her eyes. "No, you don't."

"Oh?"

"I don't know why you are so set upon bothering me!" she said. "I am leaving you behind."

"This has nothing to do with bothering you. I'm set to leave on that train." He stepped back and hooked his thumbs into the pockets of his long, heavy coat, then shrugged. "Bothering you is just a happy accident."

"Happy for whom?" Rose demanded.

"Me," Seldom said. "Because then both of you will be out of earshot. Winds are turning, Captain."

Hink looked up and over Rose's shoulder, his eye widening at the brightness of day. "Hell, woman. I have a train to catch. Why'd you have to go and make me late?"

"I'm so sorry to get in your way!" Rose shouted. "Oh, and by the way, I'm taking your horse."

Seldom snorted again.

"We both take the horse," Hink said.

"I don't think the horse can carry me and all the people you claim to be."

"Ho there, airship people!" a cheery voice called out over the rattling of a cart.

Rose glanced over her shoulder. It was Margaret, one of the witches she'd heard in the hall last night. Margaret's wild brown hair curled across her forehead just beneath the brim of her bonnet, pulled back to reveal her rounded features, which were covered with a liberal sprinkling of freckles. She was just a few years older than Rose, and smiled brightly, bundled up in the driver's seat of a horse-drawn wagon. Half of the wagon was filled with supplies of some sort, covered over with a canvas tarp.

"I'm going in to pick up mail," Margaret said. "Do you need a ride?"

"Yes," Rose said, spinning on her boot heel and quickly securing the seat next to her. "Thank you so much. Quickly, I need to catch a train. We're running out of time."

Captain Hink said one last thing to Seldom and handed him a thick fold of bills. That would be enough money to finish the repairs on the ship and some.

"What about Captain Hink?" Margaret asked.

"He has other plans. Go. Go."

Margaret flicked the reins and the horse started off at a brisk walk.

Unfortunately, Captain Hink had long legs. He jogged after the cart and jumped up into the back of it before they'd gone more than a short distance from the shed.

"Captain Hink," Margaret said. "I thought you had other plans."

"Not at all," he said. "I'm bound for the rails. Seems there's a future out there needs finding."

Rose rolled her eyes and settled in for a long ride of ignoring him. Hands always restless for something to do, she reached into her pocket and pulled out a small lock that she'd found broken on the ground in town the other day.

She ran her fingers across the tools and bits of metal, twine, and cloth she kept in her pocket. The feel of all those little oddments was as soothing as a hot bath and she felt her shoulders relax and her mood lighten. There were so many things she could do with the castaway bits in her pocket. Right away, she had half a dozen ideas of how it could all join together to make half a dozen different little whimsies.

The last thing she'd made and tucked in her pocket was a little hollow wood ball, spring loaded and filled with sharpened nails that shot out when the trigger was hit. It was just a model to see if that kind of nonexplosive grenade might do some damage in a fight aboard an airship. She had planned on showing it to Hink.

Not now.

Still, she loved putting things together, seeing her ideas take form between her fingers, exploring the world through screw and bolt and curiosity. But today, on this ride, she worked on the little lock. She felt the need to fix, to repair, to make something work, since nothing else seemed to be going right in her life.

All through the ride, Captain Hink talked up the witch, making her laugh with that damnable charm of his. Rose wished she could block out the sound of his voice, but there was nothing else to listen to.

In the past, she could hear the sound of growing things, trees and bushes and the like, though mostly their comments were about sun, or shade, or water, or wind. But she hadn't heard a single thought of any green since she'd been injured by the tin piece of the Holder.

The witches didn't know what to say about it when she'd discussed her ability with them. Some of them had that same natural hearing of greenery. But none of them had just up and lost their abilities. And plus, she wasn't a witch.

It was winter now and everything was sleeping, guarding roots, waiting out death, silent.

Maybe spring would bring her world back into full song again.

Margaret laughed and Rose hunched a little deeper into her coat, holding tight to the broken lock as they rattled over the rough trail.

Nothing about her world seemed worth a song right now.

The rail station was bustling with activity and noise. Rose looked up and away from the lock that she'd nearly gotten fixed. All the insides of it had frozen up, and she'd had to pry the pieces apart to get to the trouble. Once she had it opened, she'd been so distracted a cannon could have gone off and she wouldn't have noticed.

She needed to put just a little grease inside to make sure the mechanism moved smoothly, but there wasn't time for that now. Reluctantly, she dropped the lock into her pocket and took in the excitement around her.

The train station was a long, narrow wooden building, two stories tall, with a steeple right up the middle of it. The platform around it was built nearly six feet off the ground to make loading and unloading onto the train from wagons and carts all that much easier.

Dozens of steam-powered wagons and at least that many horse carts and carriages surrounded the place on three sides, while the huge, hulking black train sat huffing on the track along the remaining side of the station. Beyond the train was a row of warehouses and silos.

There had to be at least fifty people hugging, handshaking, and saying their good-byes. The squall of babies and barking dogs made up all the middle-ground noise, punctuated by the yell of workers loading crates and boxes and bags onto the back cars of the train, while laughter and shouts from the soon-to-be passengers muddled up all the calm of the day.

It was exhilarating. Rose found herself wondering what each of the people might be getting on the train for, where they were going, and why they were leaving friends and family behind.

"I'll pull up here so as not to get us run over," Margaret said. She guided the cart to the far side of the muddy road, just avoiding a family of four—a father, mother, boy, and girl—who dashed out in front of the wagon as they headed for the platform stairs, clutching one bag each, hands on their hats to keep them in place.

"Thank you," Rose said, "for all the kindness you've shown me. I wish you and the sisters all the best."

"Travel safe," Margaret said, giving her a quick hug.

"Oh," Rose said, "One other thing. I left some books in my room. Could you return them to Miss Bucker's library?"

"I'd be happy to."

Hink jumped down out of the back of the cart and was around to the front before Rose could swing her boots over the edge.

He held his hand up to her. Didn't say anything. Just raised his eyebrow.

She took his hand and stepped down off the cart into the straw-filled mud.

"Might be difficult keeping that dress clean while adventuring," he said.

"I'm a woman, Mr. Hink. I can keep my dress clean, and my shoes bright no matter what adventure may bring."

"I thought you liked mucking about in trousers. Said they don't get in the way like petticoats and whatnot."

"Well, since I am no longer employed repairing your ship, I feel much more comfortable in proper dress and belted coat."

He grunted. They made their way through the hiss and puff and heat and noise of the place. "You have enough for your ticket?"

"Yes."

"And for food?"

"Mr. Hink." She navigated around a cart with six men unloading crates of apples, potatoes, and bags of grain. "I am perfectly capable of taking care of myself."

"Couldn't hurt to have some company. It's a long way to Kansas City. Might be dangerous."

"On a train? I don't think so." She kept walking and he dropped his pace to hers.

"Rose," he finally said as they strode up the wide wooden steps onto the platform. The station house was ahead and to their right, the train running the full length on their left. "I didn't sleep with them."

"I can't hear you, Captain Hink. You'll have to lie a little louder." The day was noisy, but she could hear him just fine. And she didn't believe him for one hot second.

Hink swore and stopped pacing her. Fine. She had tried to get rid of him all morning. She was glad he had finally taken the hint that she didn't need him for where she was going.

Rose strode into the station and stood in the short line of people purchasing tickets from the agent in the ticket booth. She had been here once before, just out of curiosity, but this would be the first time she'd ever ridden a train. Here she was, Rose Small, with nothing to her name but a change of clothes and her wits, ready to take her first steps out on the adventure of her lifetime.

She couldn't wait to see the big cities. Couldn't wait to build her place among them. Someday she would own her own airship. Faster than the *Swift*. Stronger too. She'd fly halfway around the world for tea every morning, if she so cared.

The line moved forward and Rose's stomach fluttered with a mix of excitement and a dose of doubt. She knew heading off into the unknown could bring joy, but it was also filled with danger. And heartache.

She swallowed hard and glanced out the window, wondering if Hink was still following her. He was a tall man. With his hat on, he stood a good hand or two above most other men. But there was not a hint of him out there.

She was surprised at how sad that made her.

Maybe she wasn't being honest about her own feelings. Maybe she was angry with him but still sweet on him, though she didn't know how the two emotions could take up space in the same heart.

"Miss, may I help you?"

Rose blinked and looked back to the ticket agent. All the people in front of her were gone, leaving a wide empty space between her and the man. She'd been dreaming in her boots again.

She pulled her shoulders straight and put on a smile as she walked up to the agent.

"I'd like a ticket to Kansas City," she said.

"First class?" he asked, though from the tone of his voice he already knew what her answer would be.

"No, second class, please." She put her money on the counter. She'd done the math. At two cents a mile, she'd make it to Kansas City and would have a few cents left for food when she got there.

She didn't like the idea of arriving in a new town nearly penniless, but didn't fear it either.

The agent took her money and handed her a stamped ticket. "Just give this to the conductor when he comes by. Best be hurrying. Train's about to pull out."

"Thank you." Rose glanced at the ticket, then held tight to it as she walked out on the blustery platform. She hurried down the line of cars, steam fogging the air with the thick smell of ash, until she reached the second-class passenger car.

Down toward the end of the train, a crowd of workers quickly loaded long crates that looked like coffins and several dozen smaller square crates into the last car. Dark green letters, V and B, were inked onto the crates. The workers looked over their shoulders a bit too often and hurried a bit too much. They were nervous handling that freight, trying not to be noticed as they transferred the VB cargo onto the train.

It must be very valuable indeed.

To Rose's surprise, she caught a glimpse of Margaret handing them one last crate with VB on its side. She'd thought the witch was going for the mail, not to deliver crates for shipping.

A terrible curiosity caught her up. What were the witches shipping? She had never heard of them sending produce or grain anywhere but to the markets in Hays City. And those crates were handled like something fragile or valuable were inside. Rose called out Margaret's name, but the noise of the engines covered her voice.

Margaret strode away and never looked back.

What could the witches be shipping?

The conductor yelled out a hearty "All aboard!" The train blew two hard whistles, signaling it was time to get moving.

Rose ran up the steps into the train itself and then entered the car. It wasn't much warmer in here than out in the weather, but with all the windows closed, it smelled of wet clothes, mud, and sweat. She'd been so late to get on, every seat in every aisle was full. But she wasn't the last on the train. A boisterous group of young men dressed so fine their shoes shined crowded on behind her, talking loud enough to beat the band.

She made her way down the narrow aisle, looking for an open spot, but every bench seemed filled with more people than it could hold.

Then she spotted Captain Hink. He took up one full bench on his own, his arms draped across the whole back of it as he slouched there, looking like he didn't have a care in the world.

He watched her come down the aisle. She searched for any other place, even for a spot on the floor, but there wasn't any seating available.

As she neared, Hink stood up into the aisle, leaving the seat he had just been in open.

She took a deep breath and let it out. She'd managed his company before. Enjoyed it too, more often than not. And if she didn't take the seat, that group of men behind her surely would.

"Thank you," she said stiffly.

"Ma'am." He tipped his hat.

Rose sat, moving over close to the window so that he could take the spot next to her.

He folded down with a grunt and stretched his long legs out as far as he could.

The group of men glanced over, probably hoping for spare space, but Hink glowered at them and they moved on.

Before Rose had settled herself with her luggage at her feet, the whistle blew out again. She sat a little straighter, excited for the sensation of being on the rails.

With a hard lurch, the train started off. It was a strange sort of motion, like being atop a horse with a limp, but it was much smoother than she imagined it would be.

She pulled the window curtain back enough to see the landscape go by. Rose couldn't help it: she smiled. While she might prefer her travel high above the earth, rail travel was now her second favorite way to go.

If only she'd had better company, this trip might have been thoroughly enjoyable.

"Rose Small? Is that you?"

She turned at the same moment Hink did.

Hink swore.

She grinned. "Hello!"

Standing in the aisle, with a smile on his face and a book held open in one hand, was none other than Mr. Thomas Wicks.

CHAPTER SEVEN

Cedar rose before the sun was up. He hadn't slept, his mind too restless to keep. He paced the church quietly.

Father Kyne wasn't in any of the rooms Cedar walked through. The worship room was a small square the size of a schoolhouse at the front of the building, which was made with meticulous care. Old and worn, the walls were rubbed to a hickory shine, and dark pews kneeled in pious lines beneath the morning hush.

A light coat of dust covered the corners and windowsills, either ash from the now-cool stove in the corner or a sign that people did not pass this way often.

He didn't sense the Strange here in the old echoes of the faithful.

Cedar walked the aisle to the front door and stepped out into the fresh air.

The sky was still lead heavy and dark as night. The wind had teeth, but at least it wasn't snowing.

He buttoned his coat up to his chin, turned his collar against the wind, and took a deep breath. There were Strange in the air. Not here, not near the church. Still, they were close enough he could taste the scent of them like blood on the tip of his tongue.

Too intent on the scent and trail of Strange, Cedar did not hear the footsteps behind him until it was too late.

Pain cracked the back of his skull, and the world slipped away as he fell.

He woke, too hot and too groggy, pain roaring in his head, tied to a chair. The room was dimly lit with lanterns and smelled of hot metal and other sharp chemicals. Glass jars and vials lined a shelf to his right, and at his left he glimpsed the edge of a table with sharp medical instruments across it.

He tried to move, but his head, arms, wrists, chest, thighs, and ankles were all strapped tight. He was gagged, coatless, arms bare to the elbow.

"I could kill you," a man's friendly voice said from behind him. "It would be the simplest of things. But instead I am going to change your fate. This, Mr. Cedar Hunt, is a gift. We have been looking for you. For the man who kills the Strange. We thought perhaps you'd been killed by the blizzard. But here you are. And you've made it so much easier for us, coming here. Thank you. Now, I will give you your gift."

Cedar's heart was pounding. He might not be able to see the man, but he could smell the soap he bathed with and the oil he used in his hair. They were not uncommon scents, but mixed with the man's sweat and the slightest tinge of hickory and cherry that clung to him, they became unique. A signature he could hunt.

If he survived.

"You see the Strange, you track them, kill them. Because of that curse you wear. We have the solution for you."

The man stepped closer. From the corner of his eye, Cedar saw a gloved hand pluck up a needle and vial from the table.

"We are a curious people, Americans. We like to experiment. Sometimes when we discover something, we like to keep it quiet. My family has discovered some of the most interesting things that can be done. With man. With metal. And with the Strange."

The clink of glass and metal made Cedar twitch. Sweat ran a bead down his neck, stinging the nightmare bite there.

"You won't remember this, Mr. Hunt. Which is how I prefer it. This solution will make it so you will no longer see the Strange. A cure for your curse. Temporary, I'm afraid, but it should last long enough for my needs."

A needle stabbed into his arm and Cedar grunted from the pain.

The man took care to stand just out of his line of vision so that all Cedar could see were his gloves and the sleeve of his overcoat. He pushed down the needle's plunger.

Whatever had been in that vial washed hot up his arm and burned across his chest, then his body. He felt as if he'd been dipped in flame. The scent of copper and taste of blood filled his mouth and burned his eyes. He yelled, but the gag muffled his cries.

Then the man stepped behind the chair again and returned with another needle and vial.

"And now. This solution will make sure you forget this meeting of ours. If I give you too much, it will kill you quickly. However, if I give you the correct dose"—he stabbed the needle into Cedar's arm and ice-cold pain shattered across his nerves—"it will still kill you. Only slowly.

"There is some chance you might find the antidote in time, but since you won't even remember being poisoned, I doubt very much that you will survive a month."

He tugged the needle out of Cedar's arm. "Just one last thing before I return you to your companions, Mr. Hunt: I am an old-fashioned man. And while I find new advancements in the scientific world fascinating, I find it best to rely on tried-and-true methods. I do hope you'll humor me."

Cedar could barely think past the pain storming through his body. Too late, he realized the man was casting a spell.

And then the world went dark.

• • •

The wind clattered against the frozen treetops, sifting snow down through the branches like sand through fingers.

Cedar sat on the church porch stairs, his head resting against the rail. He glanced up at the sky. It had been dark just a moment ago. But the sky was bright with dawn. Had he been walking in his sleep? Dreaming? He remembered being restless and pacing through the church, then finally stepping outside.

He rubbed at his face and at the tender pain at the side of his neck from his nightmare. His arm hurt, but then, he hurt everywhere from nicks and bruises gotten on the trail.

The cold could do strange things to a man's mind. Hallucinations. Madness. And he had been far too cold for far too long in that snowstorm.

It must have rattled his mind more than he realized.

"Good morning, Mr. Hunt," Father Kyne said quietly as he walked up from the barn, a bucket of water in his hand. In the muffle of snow, even his soft voice carried.

"Good morning," Cedar said. "Need any help with the animals?"

"There is no need. I gave them hay and water. They'll be fine until tonight. Is there something else that brought you out so early?"

He remembered he'd come out to look for the Strange. To find the one who had found a way into the room and bit him. To discover whether it had been real or a dream.

Most people didn't believe in the Strange. Thought them to be ghosts and stories and things to frighten children into doing their chores.

"There's a restless wind in this town," Cedar said. "Restless souls ride it."

Father Kyne nodded as he walked up the back steps to the church. "It has been so for many years. Some people say it is the rail that brings unrest. Some say it is the people rushing to build this city into a road for civilization. Others . . ." He paused and opened the back door to the kitchen. "Others say it is the earth shivering beneath the tread of strange devils."

Cedar followed him into the house. "Strange devils?"

Father Kyne set the bucket of water in the sink and caught Cedar with his sober gaze. "There are ghosts who walk this town. They come in at night and flood the streets. So many, the mayor must send men to walk the streets with copper guns. Guns that sweep the ghosts away."

"Have you seen this?"

"Yes."

"So you believe in ghosts? In spirits?"

Father Kyne smiled briefly and Cedar realized he was not as old a man as his serious eyes made him out to be.

"Why would I ignore that which is in front of my eyes? Do you think the ghosts are to blame for the children disappearing?"

"I don't know. But I plan to find out."

"You have my gratitude. The Madders do not seem as deeply concerned for the children's welfare. Why do you travel with the Madder brothers, Mr. Hunt?" He turned and began gathering eggs and small potatoes for breakfast, and set them beside the stove.

"They did me a great good. Helped me find my brother," he said.

"Your brother?"

"The wolf. He is beneath a curse. A curse we both bear."

Kyne was silent for a bit. "Do you know why I am a minister, Mr. Hunt?" He scooped water from the bucket to the pot on top of the woodstove, then reached for the jar of oats on the shelf and dropped handfuls of the grain into the water.

"Followed in your father's footsteps?" Cedar said.

"He wanted it so. I was taken in young enough the people, the tribe, refuse me as their own. I am a man between worlds. But God accepts all His children. I had always thought the people of this church had accepted me. But when my father died . . ." He shrugged. "I was mistaken."

"Do you have a congregation?"

"A few remained, for a while. Now they no longer come. I believe we must all find God at our own pace. Do you pray, Mr. Hunt?"

"I used to."

"And now?"

Cedar didn't say anything.

Kyne waited, then quietly said, "The curse?"

"Prayed to any god who would hear me for months," Cedar said. "Not even the devil lent me his ear."

"Have you tried breaking the curse? Gone back to the one who put it upon you?"

"I don't remember much after the curse. By the time I had . . . reasoning back, he was gone."

"Was he a man?"

"He didn't seem to think so. Seemed to think he was a native god. Pawnee."

"I do not know those people. Have you looked for him?"

Cedar heard the approach of hooves in snow. He walked over to the window near the door and peered out. "Not sure I know how to track a god, Father Kyne."

Riders were approaching: four men on horses in front of a towering black and green three-wheeled steam carriage. The carriage itself was suspended between two wheels taller than a man, with a driver sitting right atop a single front wheel. Gray plumes of smoke poured out of the single chimney pipe sticking up at the back of the coach.

The first horseman wore a bright silver star on the breast of his sheepskin coat. He had a long, mulelike face, narrow at the chin, with a forehead full of wrinkles beneath a flat-topped hat. He was clean shaven except for thick sideburns; his eyes brown and cold as grave dirt.

The sheriff.

The riders stopped in front of the church stairs. The carriage rolled to a stop farthest from the church, turning enough to show the footman who stood on the backboard. Painted in gold on the doors were two gilded letters: V and B.

Father Kyne moved the oatmeal to a cooler burner, but kept stirring. "How many men?" he asked.

"Four riders, two with the carriage. Lawmen on horses. Probably the sheriff."

Kyne nodded. "Is the coach green and gold?"

"Yes."

"You may want to make sure your companions are awake. That's the mayor's coach."

"Why send the law? We barely hit town ten hours ago. Is there something I should know, Father Kyne?"

"The mayor is much beloved by many in this town. By most," he added. "I do not trust him. He has lied to my family far too often. Lied to the people of my church. Hidden things."

The lawmen tied their mounts to the snow-covered hitching post, then stomped up the stairs to the short porch. The sheriff knocked on the door.

"Go," Father Kyne said. "I will invite them in."

Cedar left the kitchen and met Wil in the hallway.

He heard the kitchen door open, and Kyne's greeting. He couldn't catch any of their words before he was in the bedroom.

Everyone was already awake. Mae and Miss Dupuis were dressed, coifed, and folding blankets into neat squares atop the chest of drawers. The Madders were awake too, caught up in some kind of dice game where the stakes appeared to be who would go outside in the cold to take inventory of the supplies in the wagon.

"We have company," Cedar said.

They all looked up sharply, and Cedar was reminded how quietly he often walked. "The sheriff, his men, and a carriage are here. Kyne says they do the mayor's bidding. He thinks they want to see us."

"Mayor?" Alun said. "Isn't that an interesting turn? He's getting slow. Thought he'd be by last night."

"Wonder what that devil wants." Bryn pocketed the dice and pushed up from a crouch.

"We don't have to wonder," Cadoc said. "Killian Vosbrough wants what he has always wanted."

"So you do know him?" Mae asked.

"There's a reason we should have avoided this city." Alun settled his coat around his shoulders with a dramatic flair. "It wasn't just because of our promise owed to the Kyne family. But you wouldn't stand for it, would you, Mr. Hunt? Insisted we stop at this town. And now, see where you've landed us? Summons. From that snake of a man."

"Why are you worried," Cedar asked. "Do you owe him a favor too?"

"No," Alun said. "Quite the opposite. We've been asking him for a favor for years." Alun ambled out of the room.

"What favor?" Cedar asked the other two brothers.

"To lay down and die," Bryn said. "He seems reluctant to grant our request, but I am looking forward to the day we collect on that."

"As am I," Cadoc said with a sharp grin.

Cadoc and Bryn sauntered out of the room after their brother.

Mae raised her eyebrows and Cedar shook his head. He had no idea what their issue with the mayor might be. The Madders were given to moments of drama and foolery, and moments of sobering truth. He didn't know which of those this was.

"Do you know anything about the mayor?" Cedar asked Miss Dupuis.

She finished placing the last blanket on the dresser and smoothed it while she considered her answer. "I know the Madders have made a great many friends in their efforts to keep this land safe. I know they have made a great many more enemies. Vosbrough is an old family, rooted in the beginnings of the country, in the money and influence that holds it together."

"Are they famous?" Mae asked.

"Powerful, which buys them fame if they so wish. Some even say it will buy them the country."

"The New York Vosbrough?" Cedar knew he'd heard that name before.

He'd guess there almost wasn't a man in these United States who hadn't heard of them. They were millionaires, thriving on glim trade between the states and into England, France, and Spain. The elder patriarch Vosbrough had died more than thirty years ago, leaving the running of his thriving glim empire to his three children.

"Are there any others?" Miss Dupuis asked with a faint smile. She adjusted the pearl hatpin in her hat, then walked across the room, smoothing her skirt. She had chosen to put on her coat and kidskin gloves, ready to face the storm.

"I'll see what, exactly, the sheriff wants," she said.

Cedar turned to Mae. "You could stay here."

Mae shrugged into her coat and shook her head. "I have nothing to fear from a rich man, mayor or not. It is possible he wants to have words with the Madder brothers and we will be left behind. Or perhaps Mayor Vosbrough doesn't want to speak to any of us. Perhaps he wants to talk to Father Kyne."

"And so he sends the sheriff to fetch him?" Cedar asked. "And four other men?"

She gave him a quick smile. "Well, whatever the case, I can't imagine it would be a bad idea to have a witch at hand, do you?"

"No," Cedar said, catching her hand and walking with her, "I don't."

The kitchen was empty. Father Kyne leaned in the open door looking outside, and glanced back at them. "The mayor has asked for your company," he said. "Breakfast at the manor."

"Aren't you coming?" Mae asked.

"He asked for the company of the Madders and their traveling companions. He did not ask for me."

Cedar looked out past the minister.

Alun, Bryn, and Cadoc were standing in the snow near the tall carriage that hissed and steamed up the air. Their hands were in their pockets and they stared at the sky like they were expecting an airship to cross it any minute now. From the buzz in the distance, Cedar could tell there were airships out today, though he had always thought snow made for bad flying.

Miss Dupuis was at the back of the carriage, stepping up a ladder to the back door of the coach.

"Coming, Mr. Hunt?" Alun shouted.

Instinct said, *trap*. If it were, then Miss Dupuis and the Madder brothers, who were all within easy range of the mounted men's firearms, were already in danger.

"I'll look after your brother," Father Kyne said as he moved aside so Cedar and Mae could step past him. "Be careful."

Cedar walked onto the porch.

"Are you Mr. Hunt?" the sheriff asked from atop his horse.

"I am."

"Pleased to make your meet. I am Sheriff Burchell, and this is my deputy, Greeley." He nodded toward a clean-cut man, built stocky with slicked-back black hair and an old scar running from the edge of his mouth to his temple.

Greeley tipped his fingers to the brim of his hat.

"You and your lady friend are invited to breakfast with the mayor," Sheriff Burchell said. "He sent you a carriage. We'll see you returned here or to other more suitable lodgings after your meal."

"Seems an awful lot of guns for a stroll to the mayor's place," Cedar said as the Madders all clambered up into the tall carriage.

"Father Kyne there doesn't care to have the telegraph lines hooked up to his church, so there was no faster way to send an invite," the sheriff said. "Besides, there are plenty of people passing through town out to make trouble. We get our share of tramps and rowdies. Wouldn't stand for you to be delayed."

"Delayed?" Cedar said as he walked down the porch with Mae. "I'm surprised the mayor knew we had arrived."

The sheriff's mouth curved up for the briefest of moments, but no humor took hold in those dark eyes. "We hear all sorts of things from both sides of the Mississippi here in this town. Every corner has a wire, and every house a telegraph key. Isn't a thing that happens in this town the mayor doesn't know about."

"That's *thorough* of him." Cedar and Mae walked to the tall coach.

"He's a very caring man," the sheriff agreed. "Always has the good of this city on his mind."

"Hurry up, now, Mr. Hunt," Alun called. "We wouldn't want to keep the mayor waiting."

Cedar had followed Alun Madder and his brothers into danger before. He didn't enjoy making a habit of it. But Mae was right. If there was trouble, it would be good to have a witch at the table. And it might not be bad to have a bounty hunter either.

They climbed the ladder and Cedar ducked his head through the coach door and settled onto the plush green velvet of the seats arranged on either side of the carriage.

The coach was roomy, luxurious. The three Madder brothers sat on the bench opposite him, Mae, and Miss Dupuis.

The footman shut tight the door, and then the driver let loose the brake. The carriage pulled forward rather smoothly through the snow and chugged along at a smart pace.

"Do you know what this is about?" Cedar asked over the creak and jostle of the carriage.

"It's about old debts and new wars, Mr. Hunt," Alun said. "Mayor Vosbrough has never quite sided with the people who have the best interests of this country in mind. We've wondered why he settled in Des Moines. Now that the railroad hub is here in the town connecting rivers and lands and coasts, well, seems to make some sense as why he's here."

"He's powerful and wants more power," Bryn said.

"Power," Cadoc mused. "Perhaps that is all the town is made for."

"And what does this have to do with you?" Cedar asked. "He wouldn't be the first man to use money or other means to bend the law and the progress of civilization to his favor."

"He's not a man," Cadoc said so softly only Cedar's sharpened hearing allowed him to make out his words. "He's a devil."

"Oh, it's worse than that, brother Cadoc," Alun said. "He's a devil with plans. The worst sort of devil to have. Mr. Hunt, promise me this: you will look for the Holder. No matter what happens."

"I've never gone back on my word, Mr. Madder," Cedar said. "I caught the scent of the Holder. I think it's nearby."

"Is that so?" Alun said. The brothers exchanged a look.

"Lucky for us," Bryn said.

"Lucky for someone," Cadoc said.

"Luck or otherwise, I expect you to be looking for it," Alun said. "If, of course, we survive meeting the mayor."

"That sounds rather final," Mae said. "Do you think this is dangerous?"

Alun raised one bushy eyebrow and dug in his pocket for his pipe. "Don't think it, I know it. Life is danger, my dear woman. Today we happen to know just exactly where the danger's coming from."

"What did you do to him?" Cedar pressed.

Alun paused and gave Cedar a hard look. Then he patted his pockets and Bryn offered him a welding striker, from which Alun lit the tobacco in the bowl.

"The Madders and Vosbroughs have history, Mr. Hunt. It is a long history. That's all you need to know."

Alun puffed away on his pipe and folded his arms over his chest, staring out at the passing city. It was clear he would say no more.

Drama or foolery. Cedar didn't have time for either.

"A man deserves to know what foe he might be facing," Cedar said.

But none of the brothers said a word.

Cedar settled back. Fine. He'd gone blind into war before. He didn't think breakfast would be the worst battlefield he'd ever navigated.

The frozen landscape of the city shifted from trees and two-story wood-frame houses to wide lanes cleared of deep snow, drifts piled up on either side of the roads teetering against tall brick buildings and wrought iron gates.

Down those roads rattled every manner of steamer cart: brass and wood, and one that seemed made of silk handkerchiefs and fine embroidery. Horses added to the muddle, and heavy muler wagons belched out smoke and hot ash that flashed red before dying gray in the wet snow.

Plenty of people were in the street, in tailored coats and high hats, bonnets with lace that matched the hem, boots in bright blues and yellows tied up in black. All those people crowded together wearing browns and gray and sensible black, with scarves or mittens adding a coy flip of color, like birds flocking beneath the shadow and bleak light of the day. Mixing and milling, they ducked under bright red awnings that were stretched out from towering buildings.

All the shops had glass windows, goods stacked for display, and door latches polished bright.

But the thing that caught Cedar's eye was copper wires that spooled from roof edge to roof edge. Crossed and tangled, caught up with glass globes, looping down poles, and spun along windows, the copper wires looked like a great metal spider had gone mad and stitched the entire city together with thread.

Telegraphs in every house. The sheriff hadn't been boasting.

Des Moines might have once been a sleepy town, but no more. Rail, river, and sky had packed its streets with people eager to work, businessmen in smart suits and jackets, bowler hats and canes, and women in silk tuck-edged umbrella skirts and parasols.

Mixed among the upper class were cowboys, farmers, and miners, all in sturdy workaday clothes, overalls, and heavy boots, walking with the sort of determination found in men who sweat for their pay.

Newspaper boys called out the morning headlines at street corners, and the airships rattled fans overhead as they hummed toward the sky-scraping tether towers just outside the city, dragging bulbous shadows over the streets and buildings.

This was a working town, a shipping town, a building town.

This was a city.

The old yearning of days long past, when he had sought a scholarly life, settled around him again. It wouldn't be so hard to imagine himself out in those streets, hurrying for a meeting, for a class, for the day's business. It wouldn't be so hard to imagine the nice suit, the companionship of learned men, the steady dignity of education, reading, and other comforts.

Mae shifted a bit, her hand upon the tatting shuttle she wore beneath her coat. She was worried, uncomfortable. He didn't know if she'd ever been to a city this large. Most of her days had been spent in the coven and then on the farm she and her husband owned. He touched her hand where it rested on the seat between them, meaning to lend her comfort.

She turned her gaze away from the window to him.

All the thoughts of his previous life faded away.

She was his life now, his future. Maybe they'd settle in a city once he found all the pieces of the Holder for the Madders. Maybe they'd settle on some faraway hill and take up farming.

Whatever they chose, he knew wherever this woman was, his heart would find home.

She searched his face, and he wondered what she saw there. His long sorrows? His fleeting joys? He wondered if his growing love for her was plain in his eyes, wondered if it was clear without words how he felt about her.

She frowned. "Are you all right? Did you sleep at all?"

"No. Not a wink. But I'm fine enough."

She gave him a fleeting smile, then looked back out the window. She didn't remove her hand from under his, and they rode the rest of the way through the loud, busy city to a grand manor house.

The carriage rolled up right in front of the marble stairs that made a half circle in front of a four-story brick building with spires and creased copperplated roofs. The building was a fine specimen of architecture, sporting crisp white balconies and scrolling trim that framed every window.

"Remember your promise, Mr. Hunt," Alun said. "The Holder is all that matters. The longer it remains out of our reach, the more damage it does. Wars, disease, and madness. And if it falls in the wrong hands, our civilized world will be gone in a snap."

Alun shoved the door, nearly nicking the footman who jumped down out of the way.

Bryn lifted his woolen hat, smoothed down his tousled hair, and adjusted the monocle over his bad eye. "We'll know if you aren't looking for it," Bryn said. "We'll know if you falter. Do not disappoint us in this, Mr. Hunt." He ambled out the door behind his brother.

Cadoc reached out for the doorframe but paused.

"This is long coming, this encounter between the Vosbroughs and Madders," he said. "Remember your promise to us and all those living. Finding the Holder is all that will save us in these dark days. This is a grim time, and it is a grim game we play with the world in the balance. The winning or losing hinges on you, Mr. Hunt—on you finding the Holder."

And then he was out the door too.

"They have always been so theatrical," Miss Dupuis said, tugging her gloves tighter to her hands. "Once they gave farewell speeches fit for a king when all they did was walk from one room to another to get a beer."

"So you don't think this is serious?" Mae asked. "You don't think they are serious?"

Miss Dupuis frowned just slightly, setting a thin line between her brows. She had seemed pale and often frail since her man, Otto, died. But not now. Now she considered the facts as presented with the mind of a scholar.

"From what little I know about the Vosbrough family, I think it is very serious," she said sadly. "And the Madders are not wrong about the Holder. Each piece is enough to tear down this great country, to hold all lives hostage. Those who want to possess it and use it as a weapon will go to great lengths to do so. Killing. Torture. The Holder is a poison that will spread quickly. I wish it had never been made."

Something about her words was familiar, and tugged at his gut. But the faint feeling was gone as soon as it came.

She stepped down out of the carriage, and after a brief moment Mae followed and Cedar did the same.

The cool morning air seemed colder now. The Madder brothers swaggered up the wide steps, passing between the smooth marble columns like soldiers come to declare victory. These three short, bull-built men in the plain clothes, worn from long miles of travel, carried about them an air of something more dignified, something strong and righteous.

If Cedar didn't know them, he'd think they were royalty come to inspect an outpost of their rule. Or conquerers come to take the spoils of war.

Cedar made note of the manor's doors and windows that could be used for escape, and kept count of how many guns and other weapons the men who accompanied them into the house carried.

Sheriff Burchell walked in front of the group, and scar-faced Deputy Greeley and one other man followed behind Cedar.

The manor was warm inside and well lit with high chandeliers of cut crystal and electric lights strung on copper wire. Green and gold wallpaper padded the walls, and the marble floor was covered by an expensive carpet, resplendent with flowers and vines.

The high arched ceiling was stamped with copper that reflected light like a low fire. Opulence.

Standing at the far end of the massive entry hall was a man.

He was dressed in a respectable, but not overly expensive, three-piece gray suit, tailored well to his solid, lean frame, and he was shorter than Cedar, but likely just under six feet. He had yellow hair brushed back that curled just below his ears. He was clean shaven, his eyes a bright blue. His nose might have once been straight, but someone had flattened the bridge of it so that it crooked to one side.

When he smiled, a dimple shadowed his cheek.

"Welcome, my friends!" he said in a friendly voice, arms wide. "Welcome to my home. I hope you're hungry. Breakfast is hot and delicious and served. Please come on in this way."

He gestured toward the wide double doors to his right, and Cedar caught a strong scent of cologne with hickory and cherry overtones.

The scent triggered pain that rolled down his spine. His palms slicked with sweat. There was something very dangerous about this man. Cedar wanted to take Mae's hand, turn, and leave the manor. Run, if they had to. But it was an unreasonable fear that seemed to spring from his nightmares.

And he was not the kind of man who gave in to nightmares. He forced himself to stroll into the room.

The mayor walked into the dining room, still talking.

"It has been years since I've had the great honor to dine with the infamous Madder brothers. As soon as I'd heard you'd come to town, I couldn't wait to invite you and your . . ." Here he tossed a look back at the rest of them, his quick gaze weighing and balancing Miss Dupuis, then Mae, before resting on Cedar.

He showed no reaction on meeting Cedar's steady stare. Cedar knew most people didn't like holding eye contact when the beast hovered just beneath his surface. But Mayor Vosbrough only smiled.

". . . most interesting traveling companions to join me in a meal," he finished. "I always trust the Madders to find the most fascinating people, and I am not disappointed today. Please, be seated."

Cedar had seen dance halls smaller than this room. A long wide table took up the meat of the space, with equally impressive cushioned and carved chairs set along it.

It was a beautiful place. A plush place.

Just the kind of place where Cedar would expect the devil to sit down for a meal.

CHAPTER EIGHT

"Mr. Wicks," Rose said. "How wonderful to see you here. I didn't know you'd be traveling on the train. I thought you were staying in Hays City for some time."

"That had been my plan. But an unexpected opportunity arose that requires my attendance in Des Moines."

The train jostled over a rough spot in the tracks and Wicks grabbed the luggage rack to steady himself.

"Please," Rose said, "sit with us."

"Well, I . . ." He looked up and down the aisle as if just noticing where he had gotten to. "If it wouldn't be too much bother, yes. Thank you."

Captain Hink hadn't moved an inch. "Nope."

"Move over," Rose said.

"There isn't enough room on this seat for three." He glanced up at Mr. Wicks again. "You'll need to be moving on."

"Captain Hink," Rose said. "Please move aside."

"I said there isn't room for him."

"There doesn't have to be." Rose stood. "Please let me by."

"Where are you going?"

"For a stroll."

"Why? Where?"

"Because I want to. And anywhere"—she leaned in a little closer—"anywhere away from your terrible manners, Captain."

Hink shook his head slowly, then took a hard breath and pushed up onto his feet. He stood out into the aisle, face-to-face with Mr. Wicks. Rose hadn't realized how tall and wide Captain Hink was when compared to the willowy Mr. Wicks.

But Thomas did not back down from the impressive man hulking over him.

"It's good to see you again, Captain Hink," Mr. Wicks said calmly. "Are you enjoying your travel?"

"This isn't my first time on a train, Wicks."

"It is mine," Rose said, stepping away from the seats and trying to stand near Thomas, but unable to get around the looming Captain.

Mr. Wicks's eyebrows shot up into the curls beneath his bowler hat. "Your first time on a train? Would you like to see a Pullman car?"

"I only bought second class," Rose said. "I don't think they'll allow me into that kind of luxury."

"Oh, I daresay they would. Please"—he offered his arm—"you will be my guest."

"You have first class accommodations?" Rose asked. She was impressed and didn't try to hide it.

"Of course." He smiled. "Shall we?"

Hink was still in her way. She waited. Wicks waited.

Finally, Rose stepped on Hink's foot. Hard.

He tipped his glare down at her. "You're not really going with this bluestocking, are you?"

Calling a man a bookish old woman was fighting words from where Rose came from. She glanced quickly at Mr. Wicks, gauging if she'd have to try and stop a fistfight in the middle of a moving train.

But Mr. Wicks laughed. His arm was still extended for Rose. "Black, actually, if you so care to know. My stockings," he said. "Now, let's go see what we can see."

Rose took Thomas's arm. "Excuse me, Captain. But I will be going now."

Hink leaned back, just the fraction of an inch, so Rose could step between them.

"Good day, Captain Hink," Mr. Wicks said.

Hink turned to the side and they moved past him and down the length of the car, managing the swaying of the rail rather well. Once at the door at the end, Mr. Wicks turned to her. "It's a bit blustery between cars, and the shaking—"

As if in answer, the entire car swung hard to one side and back again. Rose almost lost her balance, but grabbed a brass rail above her to keep her feet.

"I've flown on an airship, Mr. Wicks," she said. "I know how to keep my boots down and my head up."

"Excellent. Here we are." He pulled open the door. A great rush of wind and smoke and dust curled up into the train. There was a walkway between the cars and enough railings to hold for balance. They made quick work of crossing the short space, Rose going first and Mr. Wicks making sure to shut the door firmly behind them.

The next car was much like the one they had left. A single aisle down the center, a stove in one corner, and seats crowded with people down both sides. They strode through it and three others like it. One of the cars contained the mail and telegraph station, something she would have liked to have seen, but that car only had a narrow hallway to pass through, with two locked doors on each side where the mail and telegraph men worked.

"Next stop," Mr. Wicks said as they paused on the crossway. "First class." He opened the door and they stepped across the threshold.

She was surrounded by luxury.

The ceiling, walls, and floor glowed with the warmth of deep, rich cherrywood, and the large, plush seats were all red velvet with gold trim. All the brass shone to a mirror finish, and chandeliers dripping in cut crystal glittered merrily across the arched ceiling, making the pastoral scenes painted there dance.

There was even a neat little piano to one side in the middle of the car that stood silent, waiting for someone to strike a tune.

While the other cars had been crowded and jolly, with plenty of people and plenty of talking and wailing babies, the Pullman was much more sedate.

Men in sharp suits and the shiniest shoes she'd ever seen sat reading papers, smoking cigars, and drinking from cut crystal glasses. Women in jewel-colored dresses that Rose only dreamed of were reading books or tending to needlework, fine china cups on the tables beside them. She noted the young men with shiny shoes at a table, smoking and playing cards.

Wide windows set close together strung down both sides of the car. For a moment, she felt a little dizzy as trees whipped by quickly to each side of them.

"This way," Mr. Wicks said, with a gentle pressure on her elbow.

She walked down the aisle, feeling more out of place than a duckling in a desert, but then even that passed. She forgot to worry about her dusty boots and disheveled hair; instead she wondered how the bunks hinged down and stowed away, how the heat here remained so steady and pleasant—likely from hot water piped through from the engine itself—and other such minute details of the construction of the place.

Mr. Wicks led her over to the empty chairs and waved his hand toward one by the window.

Rose settled her skirts and took the lush seat while he took the chair opposite her.

"What do you think?" he asked.

"It's . . . it's wonderful, Mr. Wicks."

"Please. Thomas. And it is rather, isn't it? They have a library too. Just a small stash of books, but some worthy reads to pass the time."

She looked about the car and he pointed to a shelf not far from the piano. "Are they for any passenger to use?"

"Any in first class. Or his friend, of course."

Rose smiled and Thomas settled back, looking pleased as could be. He removed his bowler hat and placed it on his knee. His hair was wavy but combed back, so the worst of the curls seemed to fall in a semblance of order.

"Your destination is Des Moines?" Rose said. "I've never been."

He shrugged. "It's not nearly as exciting as the big cities, but it's grown quite a bit with the rail. There's a man I need to see about a business he's starting. Exciting prospect that I hope to have a hand in."

"What sort of business?"

Wicks glanced out the window and his eyes narrowed just a bit. "Shipping, I believe. Although it will require my knowledge of the telegraph system and, if I may say without it sounding too much like a boast, my skills as an operator."

There was something about his manner that made Rose think he was being very careful with what he told her. Perhaps there was something about this business that wasn't on the level.

"That sounds very exciting," she said. "So many opportunities for someone with your skills."

"This is the land of opportunity," he said, brightening. "Not a road any of us can't follow. I plan to follow a lot of them. And you, Miss Small, what is it you do to occupy your time?"

"Please, Rose. Just Rose."

"Very well then. Rose."

"I have a few handy skills. Know how to mind a store, keep a ledger. And I enjoy working with metal and steam. Thought I'd work a boiler on an airship for a while there. But now I am following new horizons."

"I see. And what distant shore are you and your companion, Captain Hink, traveling toward?"

He leaned forward just a bit and seemed a little too keenly interested in Hink.

"Oh, I'm not traveling with him. He's not my companion. Well, he was—we traveled together, with a few other people before landing in Kansas. But now . . . now he's just . . . well, we just happened to be leaving on the same train, is all."

"You've known him for some time then?"

"No. Not really for long at all."

"But you must have a destination," he pressed.

"Must I?" She glanced out the window. Snow was falling, tiny flakes like seeds of white planting the fields with winter. The train could take this kind of weather without a pause. It wasn't like airship travel, where too much snow and ice would bring a dirigible down to the earth like a rock in a river.

"I thought I'd step off at Kansas City. Find a job, see what the town has to see, then save up for a ticket east."

"How far east?"

"As far as I can go. Big cities. Universities, sciences, industry. I want to see this great new world we're building. I want to see it all."

"Alone?" he asked.

"I don't know," she said. "I guess if I must."

"Sometimes it is better to go it alone," he said.

She looked over at him. He was staring out the window too, though he watched the countryside as it pulled away from them, seated as he was with his back to the engine, whereas the world all seemed to be rushing toward Rose.

"I was . . . grateful to run into you, truth be known," he said without looking over at her. "I know we've only briefly met, but I rarely run into anyone who is so . . . curious."

"Curious?" she asked.

He looked away from the window. "Oh. Not in an odd sort of way."

He folded his hands over the book in his lap and looked up at the ceiling as if reading words there. "Inquisitive. Yes, far better choice of phrase. You have a wonderfully inquisitive way about you, Rose." He lowered his face and smiled.

The reflection of bluish light from the window frosted the lenses of his glasses, hiding his eyes in the pale glow. "From the moment you nearly ran over me"—Rose rolled her eyes—"I thought," he continued, "'This person is lovely and self-assured.' And now that I know you've traveled with an airship captain, I simply must know everything about you."

"Mr. Wicks—Thomas," she corrected when he lifted one long finger. "I am certainly flattered you think me interesting. But really, we've only just met. Other than a taste for books, and a remarkable ability with telegraphing, I don't know a thing about you either."

He sat quietly for a bit, then leaned forward to look at her from over the top of his wire glasses.

"I'm not a very interesting story, I'm afraid."

Rose very much doubted that, but kept her smile in place.

"But there are other things we could do to pass the time," he said. "Would you like to explore the train with me? The freight is in a locked car." He reached into his vest pocket and pulled out a key on a fob. "I managed to get my hands on a key."

"How? You didn't steal it, did you?"

"What?" He gave a fair go at looking surprised. "No. Someone just left it where I could find it and I thought it'd be good for a lark." He waited to see if she would challenge that.

"I'm not sure that taking that key is legal, Mr. Wicks."

"I don't intend to do any harm. Just look about a bit. It's a long way between here and Kansas City. So, would you like to see the rest of the train?"

"I don't think it's my business, seeing other people's goods. I worked my parents' store for years. I know what a crate full of straw looks like."

"Of course," he said, settling back. "I understand. Still . . . while everyone else was boarding the train, I was watching the workers load freight. There seemed to be some unusual items placed aboard."

"How unusual?"

"Very."

He sat there, not saying a word, and not looking away from her. Rose knew she shouldn't. Her curiosity had gotten her into trouble all of her life. But she'd never seen a freight car full of packages, since the railroad hadn't made it to Hallelujah yet.

And she still wondered what was in the crate that Margaret had handed those men who looked nervous they would be caught loading it.

It could be nothing. It could be dangerous. It could be the only time she had a chance to see such a thing, just like this probably had been her only chance to see the inside of a Pullman car.

"Let's go," she said.

"Really?" he asked, startled.

Rose stood. "I'm a woman seeking adventure, Mr. Wicks. As such, I can't just turn timid when the first romp presents itself. Let's see what this train can offer."

He stood, placed the book on the seat of his chair, and settled his hat back on top of his head, giving the brim an extra tug to make sure it was secure.

They exited through the doors and cars they'd already passed through, and Rose felt the tingle of excitement in her bones. It was probably nothing; there were probably no secret items on the train. Probably nothing more in the hold than magazines, potbelly stoves, and cooking pans.

She supposed there might be something worth snooping over, even if it was all ordinary things. Books would be fun to see, perhaps a clever use of gear or spring for the house or field. There might even be parts of airships or glim-harvesting gear on board. She wouldn't mind setting her eyes on that.

It wasn't unreasonable to think there might even be glim on board. It would be locked in a safe so no one could see it, but since the rail ran from coast to coast, glim from the Rocky Mountains or the Cascades might easily be shipped along the main route, which cut a horizontal line through Iowa and then connected with Chicago, New York, and went all the way to California.

There certainly seemed to be people in the Pullman car who looked rich enough to have a dram of glim. Although she suspected a person would keep it near if they actually owned any of the rare substance.

They rushed through the car where she had been sitting with Mr. Hink. She glanced over at the seat he should be slouching in, and was surprised not to see him in their seat, though her luggage was still stowed under the bench.

She didn't have much time to wonder where he'd gotten off to; Thomas was already out the door. She hurried behind and stepped into the crowded immigrant car, filled near to busting with men, women, and children, coats hung to dry on every available hook or line, the bare wood floor and benches covered by families or strangers crowded together.

The car smelled of cabbage and pork. Someone was breathing the harmonica through a sweet tune she'd never heard before and a baby was fussing. It was messy in a homey sort of way, crowded, and no one looked up as they passed.

Passing through the back door, they entered the first freight car. Rose stepped in close behind Thomas, and he reached back and shut the door behind her.

The car was dark and cold. There were no windows and the only light tongued in through the cracks in the walls.

"There should be . . . ah, yes, here." Thomas took a few steps to the side and pulled a lantern off a hook on the wall. He ran his thumb over a flint and steel built into the bottom of the lantern, and the whole thing came to life with a warm yellow glow.

He held it up and Rose couldn't help but whistle. "This is all mail?"

"Well, those bags"—he pointed to a lumpy pile of canvas—"and these boxes and crates." He nodded at the stack of crates piled up and secured with rope and buckles all the way up to the ceiling. "And well, all the rest?" He spun a circle with the lantern held out, like an actor on a stage revealing a great wonderland. "Yes."

"How many freight cars are on this train?" she asked.

"Not many out of Hays City. Just five. This is first-class freight. Two cars of livestock at the end, and two cars of produce and such goods in between."

"How do you know?"

"I told you, I've worked for the railroad, and I'm a very observant man. So, let's see what sort of shipments we have here." He walked over to the huge pile of crates and rocked back a bit on his heels so he could stare all the way up, the lantern held high.

"Sewing machines, bolts of cloth, musical instruments, baby buggies . . . firearms. Hmm. This!" He wandered over to the far corner and Rose followed along, her eyes fully adjusted to the light now.

"Odd shape, don't you agree?" Thomas said.

"It looks like a coffin."

"Yes, it does, doesn't it?"

"That's not odd. Not really," she said.

"I agree, but I noticed there were gold letters on the side." He bent down. "Yes, here. VB. Initials on a coffin?"

"The maker?" Rose suggested.

"Unusual, don't you think?"

"I suppose. You don't think there's, um, a person in it?"

"No, no. They ship corpses on ice. No ice car on this train, though it's cold enough without it, isn't it?" He turned from where he was kneeling by the coffin and smiled up at her, his words catching cold curls of smoke in the light of the lantern.

The light bounced off a smaller crate to one side and Rose noticed the green VB painted on the side. "I wonder what's in that," she said. "I saw a crate very like it being loaded and unloaded today."

"Is that so? Let's open it."

"We shouldn't."

"We shouldn't even be in this car," Thomas said airily, "but here we are. Tell me you aren't curious, hmm? What's in the crate and what's in the coffin? Both sharing the same initials."

Rose shook her head but her curiosity was getting the best of her. "I figured you for a law-abiding man, Mr. Wicks."

"Oh, I am," he assured her. "But there is no law against a quick look if we put everything back the same as we found it, now is there?"

"Yes, I believe there is, actually."

"Well, then, you can hold the lantern, and I will do the dirty work." He handed the light to her.

Thomas did a quick search, found a pry bar, and set the forked end of it beneath the lid of the first crate. With the skill of a career burglar, he pulled the nails free and carefully lifted the lid off the top of the crate.

"Now, let us see what sorts of things are shipped beneath the VB letters." He pushed the lid to one side, balancing it across the top of the crate.

"Well?" Rose asked.

"I . . . don't know. Lighting? Lanterns? Care you to apply your curious mind to it?"

She stepped up to the edge of the crate and glanced inside.

A chorus of not-quite voices and not-quite strings and not-quite woodwinds burst through her mind. It was as if the device—whatever it was—was eager to speak, to reveal its secrets, to tell how it was made and why it was made and what it could become.

Growing things used to fill her mind like this, used to speak to her like this: the device, the thing made of metal, sang.

Copper—so much copper—gave off the hardiest sound, twisted as it was in coils around a central glass orb the size of a large apple. Four solid plates of cold-pounded copper spread out from the center orb and coils. Holes allowed the copper coils to thread through those plates into long, thin, almost delicate strands that looked like spider legs.

The possibilities of what it could be, what it was intended for, rushed over her like a hard wind, and she gasped trying to catch her breath and wits. Her mind swam with the wonder and the complex concepts of this odd creation.

She knew this was not a creature, not a lantern. It was more. It was built to hold something. Carry something.

And it was built to power something. But the possibilities of what, specifically, it could power flashed hot behind her eyes, then, just as quickly, burned to ashes.

"It's . . . amazing," she exhaled.

"Don't move!" a voice called out.

Rose blinked hard, trying to pull her racing thoughts away from the device and back to the dark train car.

"Put your hands up and step away from that crate."

Who was speaking? Thomas? No, not Thomas.

Three rough-looking men were headed their way, guns drawn.

"You." One of the men jerked his gun toward her. "Put that back in the crate."

"Put what?" She looked down at her hands. She was holding the device in one hand, the metal casing and glass globe cradled in her palm, spidery wire legs draped through her fingers like threads.

When had she picked that up? Why hadn't Thomas stopped her from accidentally stealing?

She glanced up at Thomas, who stood just a bit in front of her, one hand up, the other still clutching the pry bar.

"I'm sorry," Thomas said. "I don't believe we've met. Who are you gentlemen?"

"You don't need our names," the lead man said. "You only need to know we have an interest in keeping thieves out of our goods."

"Your goods? These crates have no shipping labels. Unless you give me your name, I can only assume you came back here to burgle the place." Thomas tipped his head just a bit.

"We aren't the robbers here."

"Nor are you the law," Thomas said with a bit more steel in his tone. "As long as it is on this train, all goods are under the protection of the United States Postal Service and the Kansas Pacific Railway."

"This gun says otherwise."

"Yes, well. I see that it does," he said. "Before we begin shooting each other, let's let the lady go, shall we? This wasn't her lark."

"It is now." The three men closed the distance and Rose saw Thomas tense.

"Rose," he said, tightening his grip on the pry bar. "Run."

CHAPTER NINE

The devil certainly knew how to lay a fine table. Cedar hadn't eaten his fill for weeks now, getting by on hardtack, grits, and whatever game they could bring down while on the road.

But here, at Mayor Vosbrough's manor, breakfast was served hot and heaping on fine white china with gold trim around the edges. Thick planks of seared beef, chunks of fried potatoes, eggs over easy, and thick, fluffy biscuits were enough to make his mouth water before he even picked up his fork. Accompanying the meal were tall glasses of heavy cream milk and coffee so dark and rich, it went down like aged Scotch.

Besides Mayor Vosbrough and Cedar's traveling companions, two other people sat at the table. Mr. Charles Evans Lowry was a ruddy-faced man with black hair oiled back smooth, his mustache trimmed to meet his sideburns. He dressed finer than the mayor and had been introduced as a prominent real estate developer.

Their other breakfast companion was Miss Lydia Daffin, a round-faced young woman with clever eyes and a quick tongue who wore her hair curled at the temples and drawn up off of her neck. She was, Cedar was given to understand, the heiress of Daffin Coal Company.

"Please excuse the plain spread," Mayor Vosbrough said as he waved a knife of fresh butter over the top of a split biscuit. "If I'd known you were coming to our little town, Mr. Madder," he said to Alun, who had refused to sit at the mayor's right and instead had dropped down in the seat at the foot of the table, "I would have planned a proper meal. Maybe set up a whole parade to welcome you all in." He buttered the biscuit and took a huge bite.

Miss Daffin laughed lightly. "A parade? Are you and your brothers such a sight to see?" she asked. "Perhaps you have valiant histories, honors in battle to share with the people of Des Moines?"

Alun shook out his napkin, but instead of using it, he brushed his fingertips over the front of his shirt. "I'm afraid we're plain men, Miss Daffin. Mayor Vosbrough here has a queer sense of humor."

She considered Alun, then Vosbrough, and finally glanced at Cedar. He gave her an even stare. A small knot of confusion knit her brow.

"Well, certainly it is delightful to have new people here in town. Important people." She left that hanging in the silence, fishing for more information.

"Not sure that I've heard of you gentlemen," Mr. Lowry said, picking up the conversation. "But, Miss Dupuis, I believe I was in Virginia when you gave that speech before the statesmen there. Made a convincing case for further educational reform, if I recall correctly."

"Thank you, Mr. Lowry," she said. "It was a stirring debate."

"Stirring? Why, you had every man in that building eating out of your hand." He took a drink of coffee, lifting his cup just a bit in toast before he did so. "Wouldn't mind seeing that sort of pepper out of my people in Washington."

"You are too kind," Miss Dupuis murmured. "I understand you've been very influential in rail construction lately."

"Well," he took a bite of steak and chewed, then wiped his mouth on the linen napkin. "Let's just say it has been my greatest pleasure to work with Mayor Vosbrough. There isn't a sharper mind in this great country."

Vosbrough chuckled. "Flattery always so agrees with my digestion, Mr. Lowry. Please do go on."

Alun and his brothers ate their way methodically through the meal. On the surface they didn't seem particularly worried, but Cedar had traveled with them long enough to know their body language.

The brothers were tense. Waiting for an ambush. Waiting for a chance to fight.

He'd never seen them quite like this before, and he'd seen them face down terrible devices, creatures, and men.

The mayor, apparently, was worse than any of those things.

Maybe Cedar's instincts hadn't been that far off.

"I'd rather be flattering that sister of yours," Mr. Lowry said. "I don't suppose she'll do us the honor of a visit again soon?"

"Yes," Alun said. "How is your sister, Killian?"

The mayor's eyes narrowed for a moment. Then he sat forward and took a drink of coffee. "Fully recovered, thank you. And so is my brother."

"I didn't realize they were ill," Miss Daffin said.

"They weren't," the mayor said. "Some time ago they suffered a bit of a . . . setback in their business dealings. Water under the bridge. The family business and fortune, as you well know, is thriving and growing. Just like this town."

"No surprise there," Bryn Madder muttered. "Bought off half the government. Funded both sides of the war. Can't see a downside in profits from that."

Vosbrough took another drink of coffee. "Now, now, Mr. Madder," he said with a smile. "Accusations do not always equal the truth. Besides, all men have interests. Mine and my family's happen to fall toward the good of people. Such as the good of this little town. Made sure Des Moines wasn't left behind by the railroad. Made sure we are all part of the iron hub and spokes between the great Mississippi and Missouri rivers. Which in turn allows us all to do our part to bring this country into the position of greatest wealth and power in the world. Feeding the gears of progress feeds the good for all."

"Yes, Killian," Alun said. "The Vosbroughs are humanitarians to the marrow. Nothing but the heart and country on your docket."

"Just so," he agreed, stabbing a chunk of beef and chewing away.

Miss Daffin glanced at each one of them in turn. "Well, I sense there may be a disagreement between these two gentlemen. How exciting. I wish you'd have invited a reporter or two for breakfast, Mayor Vosbrough. Think of the gossip."

"Won't have to," Mr. Lowry said. "If I know you, Miss Daffin, there'll be a letter to the editor in time for the evening edition."

She patted her mouth with her napkin and gave him a coy look. "I have no idea what you are talking about, Mr. Lowry. However," she said, turning her full attention to Alun Madder, "I am very interested in what started this feud."

"Guns and glim and gold," Cadoc said, "a price he puts on every man's soul."

Vosbrough pointed his potato-filled fork toward Cadoc. "I've always liked your poetry, Mr. Madder."

"It isn't poetry," Cadoc said, his hands on either side of his plate as if waiting to be excused. "It is the truth of you."

"Well, you got the truth of me wrong, then. Here we mine coal." He nodded toward Miss Daffin. "Good rich veins to power trains, airships, water-going vessels and, of course, warm the family home. Here we lay lines for every house to have the latest in luxury. Even the most poor has a telegraph on the corner. Why we've strung cables through the rivers themselves and will soon connect every corner of this country into our system.

"When the East makes a decision, the West will know it instantly. We are fuel, we are communication, we are roads and sky. That is a properly modern way to run a country. Des Moines will be the hub that holds these states united. And no false accusations on your part will change what we've built by the sweat of our brow and spark of our genius."

"I never accuse," Cadoc said, unimpressed with Vosbrough's speech. "I see the what of things. And the why. It is the truth of me."

"Delightful," the mayor said. "Incorrect, but still, a whimsical addition to the meal. What did I tell you, Mr. Lowry—aren't they a treat?"

Alun had finished with his breakfast and was picking at his teeth with his pinky. "What do you want, Vosbrough?"

"Pardon me?"

"What do you want? You drag us in here, feed us like pigs to the slaughter, and baste us in compliments. What do you want?"

Vosbrough laughed. "Where are your manners, Mr. Madder? After all these years. All these *long*"—he practically snarled the word before affixing his smile back into place and pleasantly continuing—"years, you need me to remind you of what I want?"

Cedar didn't move, but from the corners of his eyes he saw shadows crossing the light coming in beneath closed doors, and heard the creak of many quiet footsteps.

They were surrounded. And he didn't think it was the serving staff.

"Let me refresh your memory of what I want, then, Mr. Alun Madder," Vosbrough said. "I want peace in the world, I want America to become a civilized shining example of progress, and I want you and your brothers dead."

Miss Daffin gasped.

Vosbrough snapped his fingers and dozens of gunmen flooded through the four doors of the room.

"Alun, Bryn, and Cadoc Madder," Vosbrough said in the steady voice of a judge. "For crimes upon my family, for crimes upon this country, you are hereby sentenced to the gallows, where you will be hung by the neck until dead."

Alun laughed. "Hanging? That seems so beneath you, Vosbrough, so *common*."

"I've acquired a taste for a much simpler life. Sometimes it is best to rely on tried-and-true methods."

Cedar's mouth went dry. He had heard those words before. Heard that tone before. His heart picked up a hard beat and every instinct told him to run.

Or kill.

"They are due a trial," Miss Dupuis said.

"Excuse me?" Vosbrough said.

"A trial. As citizens of this United States, and beneath the employ of the government, they are due a trial."

Vosbrough's eyebrows went up when he heard that. "Government? Is that what you're playing at now?"

"That's only fair and square, Mayor Vosbrough," Mr. Lowry said. "A trial for their crimes. Justice. That's what this civilization is built upon. And, as you say, Des Moines is a civilized city."

"It is so exciting," Miss Daffin added. "A notorious case here in Des Moines. Stop the presses and tap the wires. This will turn more than a few eyes toward our town."

"Well." Vosbrough looked between Miss Dupuis to Mr. Lowry and Miss Daffin. "Well, well. I suppose this might attract some attention."

"Wouldn't hurt for folks to know just how safe it is around these parts," Mr. Lowry said.

"But they'll need representation," Miss Daffin said. "You don't happen to have a lawyer you could call for, do you?" she asked Alun.

"Yes." Miss Dupuis stood. "He does. Miss Sophie Dupuis, Esquire. I will be defending the Madder brothers."

"You'll let a woman speak for you?" Mr. Lowry asked.

"Why wouldn't I?" Alun replied calmly. As a matter of fact, all of the Madders were taking this turn of events with something almost akin to boredom.

Vosbrough lifted the fine cotton napkin from his lap and wiped at the edges of his mouth. "Esquire," he repeated. "Government servants and the law. Isn't this a pleasant divergence. Well, for me, anyway."

"As always," Alun said, "you talk like a man and act like a fool. Killian, you have always been such a chore." He sighed heavily while Vosbrough's color rose.

"The papers will pick up our trial and all the eyes will be on the wire," Alun said. "Miss Dupuis will make sure the whole country knows you put innocent men on trial over trumped-up charges. Mighty big risk. Might lose your standing, lose your power with those you court, and those you are indebted to."

Alun sucked on his teeth, trying to dislodge a bit of breakfast. "What will your brother say? How do you think that sister of yours will survive your disgrace? Your family business and name aren't without fault. I suppose there's a reason your brother and sister sent you all this way west to get you out of their sight, out of their hair."

Cedar didn't think shaming a man would turn him away from the chance at revenge, especially when he had all the cards on his side.

He also knew they were outgunned ten to one. He glanced at Mae.

She was looking at the Madders. Maybe waiting for a signal, though he didn't know what spell she could cast to keep them safe from bullets. Her magic was mostly bindings, curses, and vows.

Vosbrough turned a shade darker red, staring at Alun Madder like a bull ready to kill.

"What do you have to lose?" Cadoc said into the stagnant silence of the room. "Time," he answered just as quietly, then, "What do you have to gain? Our abject humiliation."

Vosbrough swiveled his head as if his neck had been oiled, turning his gaze from Alun to Cadoc.

Cadoc was still staring down at his food, hands still on either side of the plate. He lifted his head and met Vosbrough's gaze.

"Abject humiliation," Vosbrough repeated. "Poetry, Mr. Madder." He pushed back from the table and stood, then slid his chair into place at the head of the table. "Poetry to my ears. Men, arrest them. Throw them in the jail. I will hold court for their judgment tomorrow."

The mayor's men moved forward and pointed guns straight at the Madders' heads.

Miss Daffin clapped happily, as if enthralled by a dinner play.

Cadoc had just talked the mayor into a trial. Why?

"No," Cedar said, standing.

"Mr. Hunt," Alun warned. "This is old history. You have other, more important things to do with your time."

"Do you want to go to jail?" Cedar asked.

"Old history," Alun repeated. "Not important. Not important to you."

"On what charges do you intend to jail them?" Miss Dupuis asked.

Vosbrough seemed to notice she was in the room again. "Excuse me?"

"What are the charges you are leveling against the Madder brothers?"

"Treason to the country to begin with," Vosbrough said. "Thievery, murder." He clapped his hands together and rubbed them. "Why, a whole list of things. Plenty for a hanging."

"And a rousing trial," Miss Daffin said.

"Yes." Vosbrough gave her a bit of a bow. "And for a rousing trial."

"I will expect to see a full list of their crimes by the end of the day," Miss Dupuis said.

"Of course, of course." Vosbrough smiled, showing his straight white teeth. "I'm rather looking forward to this lawful proceeding. I'll have my secretary write everything up and bring it straightaway to where you're staying. Where, exactly, is that?"

"The church on the edge of town. With Father John Kyne."

At the sound of the man's name, Vosbrough's face shifted to flat contempt. "When you find *suitable* accommodations," he said, "I will send my secretary over."

"The church," Miss Dupuis repeated firmly. "Send the papers there. Before the night is upon us, Mr. Vosbrough."

The Madder brothers were on their feet now too, and being hustled out of the room, without making so much as a fuss.

Cedar would never understand the brothers and their ways. Walking off to jail as if they were being escorted to a fine hotel made no sense. Unless they had a plan.

Which was likely. He'd never seen them without one.

"So nice of you all to stop by," Mayor Vosbrough continued. "Stimulating conversation. I hope you enjoy our city and all it has to offer. Oh, here." He strolled over to a table in the corner of the room and retrieved a sheet of paper. "New hotel opening up on Seventh Street. Looking for renters. Might be more to your comfort." He held it out for Miss Dupuis, but she didn't take it.

Mae stood and walked over to the mayor. "It's been an interesting morning." She took the paper. "Good day, Mr. Vosbrough."

The remaining men in the room moved aside as Mae walked out. Miss Dupuis followed. Cedar walked up to the mayor to follow. Vosbrough took hold of his arm to stop him from passing by.

"Mr. Hunt, was it?" he asked in a friendly tone.

Every muscle in Cedar's body froze. That was the voice of death.

"I don't know how you fell in with those men, with the Madders, but I am doing you a favor. Stay away from them. Stay out of their business, whatever they have told you it is. And stay out of my way."

Cedar looked down at the mayor's hand on his arm, then back up at his face. "The last man who threatened me is dead, Mr. Vosbrough."

"Is he, Mr. Hunt?"

Vosbrough removed his hand and tugged on a smile. "I see I've misjudged you. My advice, however, remains. They are not what they seem to be."

"And neither am I, Mayor Vosbrough." Then Cedar turned and walked away.

CHAPTER TEN

Rose clutched the copper device tighter. The three men in the train car stood across from Thomas, who was just ahead of her. Thin streams of light swung in the darkness, pinstriping every crate, bag, and person with the jostle of the train.

"Don't you move an inch," the lead gunman said to Thomas. "You." He lifted the gun toward Rose. "Put the battery down."

Battery? she thought.

"Yes. Of course. I'm going to put it down now, just as you said." She knelt, as if to place it on the floor, then tucked her other hand into her pocket. She wrapped her palm over the wooden ball filled with nails. Looked like she was going to have a real life test for the little grenade after all. She threw the device straight at his knees.

Hit him too. Nails flew out like shattered glass in a yard radius, striking all three men.

They yelled and stumbled backward, firing wild shots as they ducked for shelter behind the crates.

"Run!" Thomas shouted.

Rose was not running. She took aim and threw the battery at the men.

Thomas swore, grabbed her by the arm, and dragged her to the door. "I said run!"

"You can't just order me around!"

"Then consider it a suggestion," he said with a grin.

Thomas yanked the door open and all but shoved her out of it. She threw her arms out to the side to catch her balance, then ran across the narrow walk to the next car. She expected Thomas to be behind her.

She turned. He was inside the freight car, hands in the air as a gunman slammed the door behind him. Her gun was back in her luggage by her seat two cars away. She didn't know if she could reach it in time.

She pulled the door open.

"Miss, there you are." A middle-aged man with a brimmed flat-topped cap and the uniform of a porter reached through the door to help her into the car.

"Let's get you inside now." He reached past her to close the door and shuffled her into the train car.

"I was told you've been running between the cars. That is not allowed. Not allowed at all. I believe your seat is in second class?"

"There's a man in trouble," Rose said. "Back there. In the freight car. We need to help him."

"I'll see to it he returns to his seat after I escort you to yours. Please," he said, pressing a small gun to her ribs. "The sooner you return to where you belong, the sooner I can look in on your friend." He leveled his other hand at the crowded aisle indicating she should get walking.

Was he in on this too? Was he a part of the men keeping Thomas trapped in the freight car?

Several faces turned her way, but hardly anyone could hear the conversation over the rattle of the train. She was sure no one would notice the gun before he had a chance to shoot her.

She could try to rouse the passengers to help her, but as she met each person's gaze, they quickly looked away. Helping a friend was one thing; getting into trouble with the porter for a stranger—and getting thrown off, family and all, because of it—was an entirely different sort of risk.

Rose made up her mind. She needed her gun, and needed it fast.

The porter opened the next door and helped her across the narrow space between the cars before repeating the process all over again until she was back in the car where she and Hink had sat.

"I believe this is your car," he said.

"It is," Rose said. "You don't need to worry about me now."

"I'll just show you to your seat."

Rose bit back her frustration and quickly walked down the aisle and to the open bench.

Captain Hink was not there.

"This is it," she said. "My luggage is right where I left it. This is my seat. Thank you. I'm sorry to have been a bother."

"Just see that you don't go out again, miss. It's dangerous out there. Very dangerous." He leaned down over her, smiling as if he were her best uncle, but his tone was hard and clipped. "As a matter of fact, if I were you, I'd make a point to stay right here the rest of the trip. Stay out of the cargo, forget your 'friend' back there, and stay out of things that aren't your business. When you get off at the next stop, don't look back."

Then he straightened, his hand still on the gun in his pocket. "Do you understand me, miss?"

Rose nodded. "I promise to stay completely out of your business, if you'll just let my friend go."

"That isn't going to happen."

"Isn't it?"

"No," he said. "It is not."

He walked down the aisle and stopped in front of the door that would lead her down to the freight car, turning his back to the door so he could look down the aisle at her.

Thomas might not be dead yet. He was a smooth talker and seemed to keep his wits sharp. He might have talked his way out of the fight. Which could have left him wounded or tied up.

Or he might have talked enough that the men in the freight car shot him dead.

She couldn't just sit here if there was a chance she could save him. But how?

"Get tired of the tenderfoot and come back here for a real man's company?"

A man's shadow fell across the bench. Captain Hink stood blocking the light and the aisle, one hand up on the brass rail above the seat, the other tucked in his belt loop.

He still wore his hat, and, Rose thought, he smelled a bit of tobacco and whiskey.

"Where have you been?" she asked.

He raised one eyebrow, but did not smile. "On the train," he drawled.

"I walked through the car. I walked through several cars. You weren't here." She pointed at the seat.

"Maybe I was. Maybe I was sending a wire to Seldom telling him where to meet me with my ship. Maybe your eyes were filled with that toff, Wicks."

"He's in trouble," Rose said. "Three gunmen have him."

"Three?"

"I don't think he's armed. You must help me save him."

"Must? Don't recall ever signing a waiver as that dandy's protector. He get himself in a row? Fine by me. Might look better with a few less straight front teeth."

"Paisley Cadwaller Hink Cage, I cannot believe you can be so heartless."

"Heartless? I never threw my lovers in *your* face."

"Lovers? So you did fraternize with those women!"

"No," he said leaning down so that there was nothing to be seen but his tightly controlled anger. "I did not sleep with those women. Don't," he warned when she opened her mouth, "start talking. Listen. Just listen."

He tipped his head slightly, waiting for her agreement.

"He could be dying right now. Or dead," she said.

"If you sit there and listen to me, I promise to go look for the dandy. Agreed?"

"We go look for him."

He considered for a moment, then nodded and sat down next to her.

For the first time, she realized how much he had been making it a point not to touch her. When he sat, he made sure his leg didn't brush her skirts and deftly turned so his wide shoulders fit the space available.

"I haven't been completely true to you about my . . . activities," he began. "You're right that I haven't told you everything. Honestly, it's such a habit to keep certain things . . . private. Things I don't even share with my crew."

Rose clenched both her hands together and resisted the urge to stare out the window to see if Thomas was bouncing down the track.

"You know how I was raised, what sort of business my mother was engaged in."

"Yes," she said. He had been raised in a brothel. He'd told her that was one of the reasons he had so many names. His mother believed in giving him one from each well-off man who had visited her bed, hoping to secure a father for him.

"As a younger man, I found myself feeling quite at home in such places," he continued. "You may not believe this, but I made friends with some of the women over the years."

"Years? Is this supposed to be making me feel more kindly toward you, Captain?"

"This is meant to tell you the truth." He inhaled, held his breath a moment, then exhaled. "I've visited hundreds of brothels, dance halls, and parlors. Maybe thousands. And while I do not pretend to be a saint, the truth of it is, I visit such places for information."

"Is that so?" Rose said with a smile clenched between her teeth. "So this is purely altruistic of you. Of course. You are only exchanging *information* with thousands of beautiful, available women of ill repute."

A smile tugged at one corner of his mouth and she glared at him. The man was maddening. The angrier she got, the more he seemed to enjoy the challenge of testing her temper. If only he wasn't so frustrating, she might be able to ignore him.

But he made her blood heat up. In more than one way.

There was a roguish charm and power about him. Even with the eye patch, he still looked every inch the U.S. Marshal and airship pirate. And when he was this close to her, it didn't take much for her mind to wander to the kisses they'd shared and . . . gentler moments.

"They are that, just what you say," he said calmly, his voice a warm burr beneath her skin. "I'd expect a woman who plans to live her life adventuring to be more open-minded about women who are also trying to make their way in the world with their *particular* talents."

"So you are just helping these women make their way. Lovely."

"I am helping them, and they are helping me."

"I am certain they are!"

He gave her that grin again, enjoying her reaction. "By spying," he said. "They spy for me. Well, not just for me."

Rose opened her mouth, then shut it fast.

"They spy," he repeated, "for the American government. No better place to harvest a man's secrets than between the sheets." At her look, he added, "Not my secrets. Well, not always mine. There was this one woman . . ." He pulled back just a bit at her glare.

"Guess that's a story for another time," he said. "These women gather other men's secrets. Important men, unimportant men. Rumors, brags, lies, pillow-talk truths. All gathered up by the doves, and given to me. For a reasonable payment. For money.

"Telegraphs can be intercepted, but a message by dove always comes through."

"Spies? Do you expect me to believe the president of the United States would use women, *those* kinds of women, as spies?"

"Women like my mother?"

Rose closed her eyes. The man made her want to shout. "I didn't mean it like that."

"Yes, you did."

"All right," she said. "I did. I just can't believe a word coming out of your mouth, Captain Hink. Weeks. You spent weeks at that bordello. No secret takes weeks to hear."

Hink looked down at his hands folded on top of his leg. "There are things happening, Rose, things I cannot tell you for fear of you falling in harm's way. Those things take more than a week to piece together."

"And you want me to believe that you alone, naked and sweaty on your back, are somehow saving the world?"

"Don't have to be on my back, necessarily."

"Is that all?" Rose asked archly.

He nodded and tipped a glance her way. "It is all I can say now. And it is the truth. Is it enough?"

"For what?"

"Forgiveness."

Rose thought it over. She could lie to him, and tell him yes. But he'd know. For all he was a charmer and a man of lose morals, he had a keen eye when it came to reading people—her especially.

"No. But it's enough that I'll think it over. What you said. About what you have and have not been doing. Now will you help me find Thomas?"

At the mention of his name, Hink visibly tightened. "I don't understand what you see in that cheap suit."

"Discussing him wasn't part of our bargain," Rose said.

Hink just shook his head slowly. "All right. So where did he get himself caught up?"

"We were in the freight car—"

"What in the blazes were you doing there?"

"He'd seen some odd packages getting loaded. I was curious."

"The man lured you into a dark private train car so he could show you his package?" Hink said it real evenlike, but something about the way he asked it made Rose hesitate.

"I was curious," she repeated.

"I bet you were."

"About the freight," she continued. "Margaret had a box that was loaded aboard. She looked like she was trying to hide it. The initials VB were stamped on the side, and when Thomas said he'd seen something unusual . . . what? What is it?"

Captain Hink had gone a shade whiter than just a moment before. "Be very clear with me, Rose," he said in a voice befitting a U.S. Marshal. "Margaret Wood from the coven had a crate with the initials VB on the side?"

"Yes."

"Were there more of those boxes in that freight car?"

"Yes. Is that bad?"

"Yes. And you say Thomas is trapped there? By men?"

"Three men with guns. Looked like ranchers, but they told us to get away from the goods, and put them down."

"Down? You didn't take one of the crates, did you?"

"We . . . he . . . opened one."

"Oh, for the love of glim, Rose. What were you thinking?"

"I wasn't thinking, I was curious."

"Well, your curiosity might have just killed a man." He stood, and took a step toward the end of the car.

"We can't go that way," Rose said. "The porter threatened me with a gun. I think he's with the other gunmen."

Hink tipped his chin up so as to better sight the man standing at the door. "He pulled a gun on you?"

"Yes, a small pistol."

"Stay here."

Hink strode down the aisle, imposing as a blackened summer sky, storming to kill. Rose hurried behind him. Her gun was still packed away in her luggage, the ammunition in a separate pouch.

She'd just assumed taking a civilized sort of transportation meant she wouldn't have to get into a shoot-out before they'd even made the first station.

Hink had a long set of legs on him and was already in front of the porter. Rose paused, ready to duck or run or find something to throw, but neither man drew a gun.

Hink just grabbed ahold of the man by his lapels, picked him up off his feet, and walked with him through the door.

She rushed after him just in time to see him throw the man off the speeding train.

"Wait! No!" Rose yelled. "What are you doing?"

"Throwing a man off a train, what does it look like I'm doing?"

"But he's . . . he's the porter."

"I don't care if he's the king of England," Hink said. "He was in my way."

Hink walked the short distance to the next car, then turned to look at her. She nearly ran into him and had to grab the railing not to tumble the way of the porter.

"You, stay here," he said.

"We do this together."

"We?" he said, maybe angrily. But then he smiled, and it was a wicked smile. "You are a crazy soul, Rose Small." He pulled a gun out of one of the many pockets of his heavy coat. "This shows how much I trust you. Can't think of another woman as angry as you are that I'd go and give a gun to and then turn my back on."

"Don't worry," she said. "If I'm angry enough to shoot you, you'll see me coming."

"Promises, promises," he said with a soft smile that made Rose wish that maybe she weren't quite so angry with the man.

He reached out to clasp her hand, which she took, and then they were moving together, walking across the span, then in through the next door, and once again all the way down through the cars until they stood at the end of the third-class car.

Rose was beginning to think rail travel wasn't all that wonderful, and was tired of keeping her balance while getting half blown off and half frozen between cars, since it was now raining icy pebbles.

But when they came to that last door, and Captain Hink squeezed her hand once before letting go, she was tingling and alive. This was adventure. This was the world. Her world. And even if it was wet, cold, and full of danger, she was going to face it, gun drawn.

"Don't crowd me," Hink said. "Don't get in the way of fire. And don't go heroic, woman. Understand?"

"Clearly. Same goes for you, Captain."

"Ain't never been a hero a single day of my life," he said.

"Yes," Rose said, gathering up the material of her skirt, twisting it, and then tucking it into her belt so it stayed out of her way. "You have. You've been my hero."

When she looked up at him, he had such an expression on his face: maybe a bit of surprise, maybe a bit of hope.

"Ready?" she asked, her hip braced on the railing.

"Since I took my first breath," he said. Then Captain Paisley Hink drew his gun and kicked in the door.

CHAPTER ELEVEN

The Madders were quickly pushed into the back of an enclosed steam wagon, which puffed its way down the lane toward the heart of the city.

Cedar paused on the stairs outside Vosbrough's manor. From the height of this hill, he could see the towering buildings, brick and wood, and the brass tether towers spiring up above even the tallest structures. There were no airships at rest there now, probably because of the snow that fell in bitter, ragged squalls.

He'd heard at least one ship pass over when they'd been coming this way, so likely there was a landing field and air sheds outside the city.

Black smoke curled out of chimneys, wings of coal smudged the sky.

But there was more than just smoke in the air. There was the sound of the Strange, a low, slow weeping he'd never heard before. And with the sound of the Strange came the faintest scent of the Holder.

The Holder was here. Somewhere.

"Mr. Hunt?" Mae said from a short distance ahead.

He glanced one last time over the buildings. He didn't see the Strange, though if they were close enough he could hear them; he should be able to glimpse them. They weren't invisible. Not to his eyes anyway.

He tipped his hat down over his eyes and walked down the stairs.

"Are we going to let them take the Madders to jail?" Mae asked.

"For now." He walked with her toward Vosbrough's carriage and helped her navigate the slick steps up into it.

Just before he entered the carriage something bright on the snowy ground by his boot caught his eye.

He bent, picked it up. It was a piece of copper, flat and shaped like a triangle, bright as a sunrise. The edges were smooth and even, and in the center of the triangle was a punched hole, just as smooth and even as the edges. Tied through that hole was a small length of kite string.

But it wasn't the copper or shape of the piece that surprised him. The moment his fingers touched it, he heard again the Strange. Crying.

He pocketed the copper and string and stepped up into the carriage.

The driver started off toward the church.

"Can you defend them?" Mae asked Miss Dupuis.

"I can if I know what they've been accused of."

"Won't the mayor stand as judge?" Mae asked.

"No. There is a full and active courthouse here. There is an appointed judge."

"Appointed by the mayor?" Mae asked. "It won't matter to a man like him whether or not justice is being served; he has already declared them guilty. He intends to hang them no matter how the trial plays out."

"We'll have them out before the trial ends," Cedar said.

"I agree," Miss Dupuis said.

"How?"

Cedar just shook his head, and Mae's eyes widened a bit. She understood. If they had to, they'd break the Madders out.

"What about the missing children?" she asked quietly, even though the driver and footman wouldn't be able to hear her over the noise of the coach.

Cedar frowned and stared out the window. "I'll do what I can to find them while the Madders are in jail. But in this weather . . ."

He didn't have to finish. They'd all known it was a lost promise. Children gone wandering in snow, in blizzards, were rarely found alive.

And if they hadn't gone wandering, if instead they'd been stolen away by boat or airship or rail, there would be no trace of them now.

"I will look for the children," Mae said.

That brought Cedar straight out of his wandering thoughts. "Mae."

"You need to find the Holder, and you must. Do you think it is anywhere near here?"

Cedar nodded. "Close enough I've caught wind of it. But not enough that I know which direction to turn."

"Then it's settled," she said. "You will find it. And if it is near—"

"And if it is not?" he asked.

"We were following its trail before the blizzard hit. It must be near. I do understand," she added quickly, "that Miss Dupuis will be busy preparing her argument to save the Madders. I'm not going to just stand on the porch worrying while she defends the Madders and you hunt for the Holder. So I will look for the children. I may even have some spells that could help locate them."

Cedar pressed his lips together to keep his objections behind his teeth. He didn't like the idea of her searching alone. "You'll take Wil with you."

She shook her head. "Wil should go with you. To find the Holder. Especially since you'll be . . ." She didn't say it, didn't have to. They all knew the full moon was coming tonight. Then he'd be a wolf with barely a man's mind. Lost in a killing lust for the Strange, and caring nothing for hunting the Holder.

"I won't leave you alone," Cedar said.

Mae gave him the sort of smile that reminded him she'd traveled a good lot of this country at great risk to herself when she'd left the coven to start a new married life years ago. And that had been when she was sworn and bound to not use her magic.

"I will be careful," she said. "As I hope you will be."

He nodded, having no words to give her. If he lost her, if her search for the children brought her harm, the vestiges of his humanity would fall from him like an unbuttoned shirt.

And then it wouldn't be just the Strange that he killed.

The city was fully awake and even more crowded than when they had driven through on the way to the mayor's. The clash of voices, ringing of bells, and the constant ruckus of wheels over snow, harnesses, and the rattle and chug of steamers stirred the pulse of the living city.

And beneath it all, Cedar could hear the Strange. Wailing, crying. Their voices snatched away by the wind as quickly as he heard them.

Why were they caught in sorrow? What could make an inhuman thing grieve? He searched the street, peered in windows of buildings, and stared at shadows. Although he heard the Strange, he didn't see them.

Odd.

The carriage took a side street and detoured through a poorer part of town. Here the windows were covered with boards and newspapers, laundry hung in lines and over copper wires between buildings, even though the day was freezing.

People were just as busy here, but most wore much plainer clothes. It was here, more than in any other part of town, that the obvious lack of children on the street struck him.

Women with infants bundled close against their chests walked the slick streets with sacks of goods from the market. A lame boy, perhaps ten or twelve, leaned on a corner post, trying to keep the newspapers tucked beneath one arm dry from the snow. He saw no other children. The missing sight and sound of children among the noise of the place was like a piano lacking every other key.

It was this street that reminded him Des Moines was a hardworking shipping and coal-mining town that had built itself up on the shoulders of those who bent their backs to hard labor.

Mayor Vosbrough, Mr. Lowry, and Miss Daffin might be enjoying the luxuries of life, but the rest of the citizens were not as fortunate.

"What do you know about Des Moines, Miss Dupuis?" Cedar asked.

She shook her head. "Not much, I'm afraid. Several years ago we heard that one of the Vosbrough family had set himself in a powerful position and lobbied, bribed, and blackmailed to have the railroads meet here."

"The rail doesn't cross in Des Moines itself," he said. "There are spurs, but the main line is north, isn't it?"

"Yes. But this is the capital city of the state and, as Vosbrough is prone to remind us, seated between both major rivers, which run north and south.

"Between the rail and rivers, the town can be reached from all corners of the land, and with the airship fields, all corners of the sky." She paused. "Des Moines is quite well-set between mountain ranges and all the goods they offer."

"Access to glim harvested above the western mountains," Cedar said. "And access to store it, use it, or sell it anywhere in the country they want."

"Yes. That is one of our concerns," Miss Dupuis said. "It is too much of a coincidence that one of the richest families in the country is so conveniently seated in the hub of all modes of transportation and shipping."

"And communication," Mae pointed out. "All these wires."

Cedar ducked a little to better see the poles and lines stringing the city. She was right. Telegraph wires connected like a weave over the top of each roof, knotting together and marching across every rooftop, carried on the arms of overhead poles.

"Communication to whom?" Cedar asked.

"As Mr. Alun Madder said, the Vosbroughs are in contact with those in the government," Miss Dupuis said. "Congressmen, speakers, officials. And with those others who are connected to the Vosbrough family and are building their fortune in line with them."

"Like Mr. Lowry," Mae said. "If Alun Madder is correct, the Vosbroughs traded weapons and supplies on both sides of the war. Isn't that also what General Alabaster Saint was accused of?"

"We have long suspected Alabaster was on their payroll, before, during, and after the war," Miss Dupuis said. "The Vosbroughs have paid and blackmailed commanders to lose battles, have opened glim trade with pirates and brigands to stockpile the rare substance and control the price on the market, and have bought land from impoverished farmers, securing river passages, minerals, and supply points."

"Do you have proof of these things?" Cedar asked.

Miss Dupuis shook her head. "Not enough. Even the president himself, with all his men, hasn't managed to force the Vosbroughs to take the stand. The Madders were right in wanting to avoid this town."

Cedar had never heard of these charges against the Vosbrough family. Which meant they not only could sin, and did so, but they could also keep their sins hidden.

That made Mayor Vosbrough a very, very dangerous man. Cedar's stomach knotted with an uncertain fear. There was something about that man that bothered him to his core.

A steamer wagon bumbled out in front of their carriage and slowed to a stop, the driver cussing up a storm at the boiler breaking down.

Miss Dupuis glanced at the broken vehicle. "This might take some time."

From this vantage, Cedar noticed tall scaffolding piercing the steam and smoke of the city. Behind the buildings around them was a factory of some sort. Great billowing clouds of black smoke poured out from it, and a distinctive smell of scorched metal filled the air with the stink of hot blood.

Copper. It was a foundry or a mine refinery. Cedar frowned. The scent of the Holder tinged the air, then was gone.

"Copper mining," Cedar said as several people in the street pushed the faulty steam wagon out of the way. "Do you know much about it, Miss Dupuis?"

She shook her head. "Why do you ask?"

Cedar wrapped his fingers around the copper in his pocket again. "I can taste it on the air. Copper. All these cables and wires powered by electricity. There appears to be a foundry or refinery beyond the town."

"Lead is mined near here," Miss Dupuis said. "And, of course, coal. But copper?" She shook her head.

"Rivers, rails, the sky . . . and resources." Cedar rubbed at the back of his neck, unable to dislodge a restlessness growing in his bones. Fear peppered his lips with sweat. There was something he wasn't seeing here. Some dangerous thing.

The driver found a way around the broken-down cart and got their carriage going again.

Yes, the Strange were near. But it was more than that.

"How long before you think the mayor will just hang the Madders?" he asked.

Miss Dupuis looked back out the window as the city rolled past. "Most trials don't last longer than a day."

There wasn't much time, then. He'd promised the Madders he'd look for the Holder, and Mae insisted he do so. For the day, and if his reasonable mind remained for the night, he would hunt the Holder. And then he would get them all out of this town before Mayor Vosbrough decided to hang not just the Madders, but all of their companions as well.

The carriage finally came to a stop outside the church and Cedar stepped down first, offering his hand to Mae and then Miss Dupuis. The driver and footman didn't even say so much as a word to them as the carriage turned around and left them standing in the spitting snow.

As the women walked to the church, Cedar lingered behind. Pain stabbed his neck, like teeth biting deep. He pressed his fingertips there, blinking hard to try to clear his vision.

Where the coach had been moments before stood a Strange.

It was made of bits of snow and ice swirling in one place, pulled together to form a manlike shape, easily Cedar's height, the head overlarge, with no mouth and two huge holes where its eyes should be, showing the forest behind it. It lifted one hand, snowy palm upward beseechingly.

The beast within him coiled to spring, to tear at the creature with empty eyes.

Cedar snarled, reached for his gun.

"Please . . ." the Strange said in a voice made of the brittle ice cracking. "Help . . ."

"Cedar, what is it?" Mae's voice.

He blinked.

The Strange was gone.

Snow still fell, without eyes, without voice, without shape, onto the ground, then was whisked by the wind up to the treetops.

"Cedar?" she asked again.

He glanced down the road after the carriage, then at the bushes and the building. Nothing. There was not even the smell of the Strange in the air.

"Strange," he said.

She looked in the direction he was staring. "Is it still there?"

"No."

"But you did see one?"

"Yes. The same one from last night. It had the same empty eyes."

Mae scanned the trees again, then turned and walked with him toward the stairs. "Would a bullet have killed it?" she asked quietly. She knew the answer as well as he did.

"No."

They entered the kitchen, and were wrapped in the warm smell of woodsmoke and pine.

He pulled his hat off and dragged his hand through his hair. "It spoke."

"The Strange?" Mae said. "We've heard them speak before. Mr. Shunt did more than just speak. He walked this world in a body and passed among us like a man. The evils he did . . ." Her voice trailed off and Cedar knew the horrors of her memories. He'd been there too. He'd watched Mr. Shunt butcher and kill.

He'd almost died tearing Mr. Shunt apart with his bare hands.

"Yes," Cedar said. "Shunt spoke. But he was the only Strange I'd known to do so. This one outside just said two words: 'Please help.'"

Mae picked up mugs from the sink and filled them with hot water and a few mint leaves. "The Strange are wicked. They delight in playing on our sympathies."

Cedar nodded, taking the cup she offered and sitting at the table. Mae had fallen for a Strange that made itself look like a little lost child. So yes, she was correct in thinking the Strange enjoyed that kind of game. But this Strange had seemed sad. Hopeless.

Strange weren't human. They didn't have feelings, not human feelings.

Cedar rubbed at his neck again, at the pain there. He still ached from the trail, muscles already tired though the day had barely begun.

On top of that, the beast within him turned, pushing for control. It wanted to hunt and kill the Strange. But Cedar suddenly, for the first time in all his years killing Strange, felt a pang of empathy.

Father Kyne walked into the kitchen. "Are you not well, Mr. Hunt?"

"Well enough," Cedar said. "Do you know what this is?" Cedar placed the copper piece with the broken kite string on the table.

Kyne took a step back, his hands slightly out to the side as if Cedar had just deposited a snake on his kitchen table.

"Copper," he breathed. "Cold copper."

"Cold?"

"It is cursed metal. All who touch it go mad. Then they die."

Cedar picked it back up.

"Don't," Mae said.

"I'm already cursed." Cedar balanced the triangle in the center of his palm. "And my mind appears to be whole. This looks like kite string or a line a child would use to fish. It fell from the mayor's coach."

"People drop things in cities," Mae said. "Children drop things."

"It could just be a bit of trash, but when I picked it up, I could tell the Strange had touched it. Tell me about cold copper, Father."

The minister hesitated, then nodded. He sat at the table, placing his hands loosely in his lap. "There is a mine north of town. Not a coal mine, not a lead mine. It is the place we do not speak of. Not even the men and children who work there speak of it. From that pit into hell, they bring up cold copper."

"And it's cursed?" Cedar asked again.

"Damned."

"How?"

He shook his head. "It steals souls. It is the devil's work."

"What is cold copper used for? Trinkets for curses?"

"No. Cold copper is used for the devil's devices. There is something alive beneath this city. That is what is whispered. Something that feeds on cold copper. But no one knows. Some say there are mines beneath the city. Mines where the devil makes matics that drink down men's lives and steal the children away."

"Have you seen them? The mines? The devices?"

He shook his head again. "But I have heard them screaming in the night."

"The devices?"

"Yes. On the full moon, all doors are locked, all windows shut. No one is on the street except the mayor's men, who patrol. All through the night, the sounds of screaming pour through the cracks in the ground."

Cedar was silent. It seemed far-fetched that a demon or devil lived beneath the city. Still, he wouldn't rule it out. He'd certainly run across enough people in his time who didn't believe in the Strange, didn't believe in witchcraft, didn't believe in the Pawnee curse he carried. And each of those things was as real as the cold, cold copper in his hand.

"When did the children disappear?" he asked. "Was it during the full moon?"

"No. Not just then. But in the nights, other nights, the children who were tied to their beds were gone. Ropes unknotted, coats and boots left behind."

"People tie their children to their beds?" Mae asked.

"For months now, though it has done no good. Ever since the star fell."

"What star?"

"In the autumn night sky a star caught fire. It came from the west and fell to the earth."

"And that was when the children started disappearing?"

"Yes."

Cedar closed his hand over the copper bit. He could already feel the rising power of the beast within him. Soon, the moon would offer him its whiskey escape from this body, from this lingering ache, from his reasoning mind. Then all his world would be blood.

"Mr. Hunt?"

Cedar had squeezed his hand so tightly, the copper sliced his palm in three places.

"Is it the curse that drives you?" Father Kyne asked.

"My curse is no concern. Not until nightfall. Mrs. Lindson will make sure I am secured. Until then I will help look for the children."

Mae raised her eyebrows.

"Or the Holder."

Father Kyne frowned. "The Holder? Is that what you seek? Is that the task the Madders have bound you to?"

"You know of it?" Cedar asked.

He shook his head. "I'm afraid that I don't."

"Better for you that way," Cedar said.

"In what manner does the curse take you?" Kyne asked.

"Like my brother, I gain the beast's senses and body. Unlike my brother, I lose the man's mind."

"I believe I can help."

"No, that's fine," Mae said. "I think it's best we take care of this. We have done well enough so far."

"Not help in . . . restraining him." He nodded toward Cedar. "Not help in chaining the beast within him. But in breaking the curse. I believe I can break his curse."

CHAPTER TWELVE

"Gentlemen, if you're gonna shoot, better do it now," Captain Hink bellowed as he strode into the freight car. "You ain't gonna get a second chance."

Rose couldn't make out anything in the dark. But Hink, the fool, walked right down the narrow path between stacks of crates as if there weren't three armed men in the shadows.

"Stop right there," one of the gunmen said. "And get the hell off our train."

"Your train?" Hink bulled across the distance like a man storming the deck of a ship, making enough noise for three. "Unless you can show me where you branded its haunches, I don't think I'm inclined to believe you own this train."

Hink drew something out of his pocket with his left hand, scraped his thumb over a section of it, and threw it off to one side.

The entire freight car lit up with a blinding orange flash that just as quickly snuffed out. It was one of the flares airship crews used, and in this dark, enclosed place, it was devastating on vision.

Two voices yelled out. Then, gunfire.

Rose ran into the darkness, her flash-ruined eyes no good to her. She found the crates by feel and ducked behind them.

She didn't have a gun to draw, didn't have a flare, and now, she didn't even have clear vision. She wasn't sure Hink was helping rescue Thomas or just getting into a fight for the sake of fighting.

The loud scuffling was followed by that particularly meaty sound of fists hitting bone; then everything went quiet.

Except for the sound of one man's breathing.

She knew better than to call out. One against three? What were the chances it was Hink who still stood?

"You're lucky I don't throw you and that silly hat of yours behind bars," Hink said.

He was standing? He'd won?

"For what, Mr. Hink?" Thomas said with a grunt, as if he were getting up on his feet. "Last I knew it wasn't against the law to be roughed up by men of poor reputation."

"Thomas?" Rose said. "Are you all right?"

She moved out from behind the boxes, her vision still muddy but clearing up quickly.

"Rose? I am fine, just fine. I would have been out of here in a moment or two. I was just waiting for my opportunity."

Hink snorted. "You weren't waiting for an opportunity; you were waiting for rescue. And I'm the one who did the rescuing."

"I understand how you could see it that way," Thomas said distractedly. "But I was just holding them here until you came and arrested them."

"Arrest them?" Hink asked. "I would have pinned a medal on them for keeping you out of my way if they hadn't shot at me. Seemed a favor keeping you out of my sight."

"But you are a man of law, aren't you? Captain Hink? Or is it Marshal Hink?"

"What I am, Mr. Wicks, is all out of patience. Get walking."

Thomas stepped out from the corner of the car and tugged his jacket better into place. Then he dusted his hat and ran his fingers over the brim before placing it on his head.

"Miss Small," he said with no small amount of delight. "So wonderful of you to return."

"I couldn't leave you here with those roughs," she said.

He gave her a smile and a nod. "I am in debt to your kindness."

Hink had stayed behind. He grabbed hold of one of the unconscious men and dragged him across the car. "Step aside," he said as he passed Rose and Thomas. Hink opened the door, walked out with the man, then, a moment later, walked back in empty-handed.

"What did you just do with that man?" Wicks asked.

"Same thing I'm going to do with the next one." Hink stormed down the car again, and did indeed drag another man with him to the door, then out the door.

"You're throwing them off the train!" Mr. Wicks said. "They're unconscious. Bleeding."

"Don't worry," Hink said. "I left them their guns." Then he strode over to the remaining gunman and slapped him conscious.

"I've just tossed both your friends off this train, and I plan to do the same to you. Unless you tell me who you're working for."

The man spit in Hink's face.

"Wrong answer." Hink grabbed him up by the coat and dragged him to the door.

"Wait," Wicks said. "I'd like to know why they nearly killed me."

Hink opened the door. The man in his grip whimpered. "Last chance. Tell me who you're working for."

"I'd rather be tossed in the dirt."

"Happy to oblige." Hink stepped outside, the door slamming behind him.

"They were trying to kill you over those crates," Rose said.

"True," Thomas said. "Unpleasant business, wasn't it? I think it's best we find a more comfortable place to finish our ride." He offered her his arm.

Just then, Hink strode back into the place. He paused long enough to give Thomas's extended arm a look, then, shaking his head, walked farther into the car, obviously looking for something.

Rose wondered what it was.

"Rose," Thomas said again. "I'm sure there is a cup of tea and book waiting for us back in the Pullman car."

Rose stepped away from Thomas. "You go on ahead, Mr. Wicks. I'll be right there in a tick."

"I wouldn't think of it," he said. "A gentleman always escorts a lady."

"I don't need a gentleman," she said, surprising herself with that sudden truth. Then, a little kinder, "It's thoughtful of you, but I need a word yet with Mr. Hink. In private."

Thomas frowned and, for the barest moment, anger swiped across his face.

Rose held very still, startled by his reaction.

He swallowed and drew his bottom lip beneath his teeth once, as if folding words back into his throat. "Of course," he said with careful casualness. "I'll wait for you there."

He walked out the door and closed it behind him.

"Why?" Hink asked from halfway across the car. "Man was offering you tea and comfort."

"Because you need to see this. And I'm not so sure I'm interested in Wicks's company." Rose found the crate with the loose lid, and pulled the lid off. The men must have repacked the crate, setting the copper and broken glass carefully in the straw. She held her breath as a song poured out, copper notes cold across her thoughts speaking of pain, of sorrow, and of power.

Hink strolled up next to her and peered into the box.

"What the hell is that thing?" he asked.

Rose shook her head. "I . . . I don't know. The glass is broken now. They called it a battery?"

"For what?"

Neither of them was touching it. Rose knew if she did, she'd lose what was left of her wits to its song.

"I don't know. This is like the crate Margaret was carrying. With the initials of VB," Rose said. "That coffin over there has the same initials."

"Bring a lantern." Hink walked off into the dark, and Rose checked for a lantern.

There was one on the floor, the one she'd held before, tipped over and leaking. She hoped it had enough oil to hold a flame. She picked it up, and dug in her pocket for a striker.

Careful to lift the glass, Rose struck flint to steel and sparked the oil-drenched wick, catching a yellow flame there.

She and Hink stood next to the coffin. "See there?" Rose said, pointing at the side of it. "VB."

Hink brandished the pry bar. "I see it. Now let's see what's inside."

He set the bar in between the lid and case and pulled. The coffin lid rocked up, locks breaking. Hink pushed the lid full open.

"Hellfire," he swore. "Rose, don't look."

But it was too late. Rose had already seen the contents.

A body. Not whole like a person, but pieces and bits. One leg, an arm, and a torso. There wasn't even a head.

"Oh, God," Rose breathed. "Why?"

Hink turned so the bulk of him blocked her view, but it didn't do much good. She couldn't unsee what she'd seen.

"Lot of strange folk in the world," he said. "Or maybe this was all that was left of him to bury and his family wanted it home."

"There's no smell," Rose said, her mind suddenly working on the puzzle of how to fit what she'd just seen into the here and now of the world. "Death has a stink. Death always has a stink." She tipped her head up, searching Hink's face.

He nodded. "There are some solutions that can take care of that," he said. "And those bits aren't all hooked up, so a more thorough cleaning might have been done. Still . . ."

He turned back around, but was still positioned so she couldn't see past his width. He reached into the coffin.

"Huh," he said.

"What?"

"This isn't living."

"You just noticed?" Rose asked.

"I mean it wasn't ever. Living." He shifted so she could step up to the coffin again.

He lifted the arm up a bit. "Bring the light closer."

Rose held the lamp inches away from the severed limb.

"Wrist and elbow move like they're on a hinge." Hink once again shifted the arm and it gave a slow, dead wave. "And this skin? It's animal. Fine tanning, but not human. Not soft enough for meat to be underneath it either. Wood, I think. Maybe metal."

"It's pieces of a . . . a puppet?" Rose asked. The twist in her stomach screwed down to dread. It was very lifelike for a puppet and fully the size of a grown man, or pieces of a man, in any case.

Hink frowned. "Heavy for a puppet."

Rose looked from the arm in his hand, which was topped off with a fully articulating hand on one end and strands of thin, veinlike wires coming out the stump where the shoulder might be.

Those wires reminded her of something. They reminded her of the copper and glass device. "Is there a, um . . . hole in the chest or back?" she asked.

Hink set the arm back in the coffin and tugged on the shoulder, leaning the torso forward. No blood, no meat in the severed neck, but if Hink hadn't told her it was leather and metal or wood, Rose would have sworn it was the upper half of a man sawed in two.

"This is the back," Hink said, nodding toward the part facing them. "Whoever packed it put it in chest down."

Rose slid right beside Hink, so close she could feel the slight heat radiating from beneath his coat, could once again smell the tobacco on his breath as he exhaled steam into the cold railcar, and could sense the tension in him.

He had some idea of what this thing was meant for.

And then she saw it. Where the heart should be was a hole. Cut clean on every edge and fitted with a copper band along the inner walls about four inches wide.

"Something's meant to be set in there," Rose whispered. Then: "Oh. Oh! I think it's the copper piece. The copper piece was built to hold something in the glass, like water or a solution. To contain, and to . . . generate power of some kind to run like a matic?"

"You're saying you think this puppet runs on steam power?"

"I don't know. I don't know why it would," she said. "Do you?"

He held his breath for a moment. "I do. I think I do. Hold this." He moved just enough that Rose could grab the shoulder and keep the torso propped up.

He headed back to the crate and lifted the broken copper and glass device out of it.

"Cold," he noted as he carried it over to her. "Even through my gloves."

"You're not going to put it in there, are you?" Rose asked.

"Just to see if it fits. Can you prop it up a bit more?"

Rose leaned back and pulled the torso up so that it was balanced on the hips. "Why aren't all the pieces here?"

Hink shrugged. "Lots of crates. Might be the rest is packed away. Might be this is just a test sort of thing." He took a moment to glance between the hole in the torso and the device in his hand and then turned the device so that what was left of the shattered glass globe was facing outward.

"Like this, I'd say." Hink placed the copper and glass device into the torso, then twisted. It fit into place with a *snick*.

Nothing else happened. No lights, no movement, nothing but a disembodied torso with a contraption of copper filling the hole in the chest.

"That's disappointing," Hink said.

"What did you think it'd do?" Rose asked.

"It should have . . ." He glanced at her, then shut his mouth. "I don't know."

"Yes," Rose said. "I think you do."

"All right, yes. I think I do too. There have been rumors about a new kind of matic being built. A thing that can labor in factories or in the fields. There's also been rumors of a weapon coming out of Chicago. Could be this is part of it. Or none of it."

"Do these rumors give it a name?"

"Homunculus."

Hink twisted the copper piece and it fell out into his hand. "Set that back down," he said. He slid the copper piece into the inside pocket of his coat, then helped Rose get all the body parts arranged and the lid fit back into place.

"But you think it is part of . . . part of something dangerous?" she asked. "The copper device? The, um, homunculus? The coffin?"

"Not a good place to talk it over. Best we button this up and get moving."

Rose helped put the crates in order, then extinguished the lantern. By the time Hink opened the door to the passage between the train cars, Rose's stomach was in a knot. She didn't like the idea of Hink keeping that copper device. They didn't know what it could do, even if it was broken.

They crossed between the railcars in silence, since talking would mean shouting over the wind and rain. By the time they finally reached second class, Rose was soaked, cold, and tired.

Hink paused by their seat and gave a couple of the young boys lounging there a hard stare. They scuttled away, back to their families down the car a bit.

Hink removed his hat, brushed his fingers through his hair to get it in place, and then stood aside so Rose could take the seat.

Rose thought about the Pullman car and Thomas waiting for her with tea and a book. It would mean getting wet again, more than once, to reach first class. And it would mean sussing out that sudden anger he had showed.

Maybe she would just sit here for a bit and dry out.

She ducked under Hink's arm and settled onto the bench.

Hink dropped down next to her. "Thought you were headed up to luxury seating."

"I look like a drowned rat: my skirts are dripping, my shoes are covered in straw. They'd turn me away."

"They'd be fools," Hink said, pulling his hat back on and down over his eyes and stretching his long legs out as far as he could. "You're a beautiful woman, wet or dry."

Rose felt the heat of a blush brush her cheeks. Man could charm when he wanted to.

"Are you going to sleep?" she asked.

"Might as well. Next stop's still an hour or more off."

"What happens at the next stop?"

He didn't reply, so Rose poked him in the shoulder with her finger.

"Ow," he grunted. He pushed his hat out of the way and looked over at her.

"Well?" she asked.

"Next stop is where I get off and see to some business."

"What about me?"

"What about you, Rose Small?" he asked with that soft drawl that made her want to kiss him. "Aren't you going on to whatever destination that horizon of yours has painted for you? For you and your greenhorn?"

"Yes," she said. "Of course. But what if I don't?"

"You're sweet on him. Why wouldn't you go with him?"

"I'm not . . ."

He raised an eyebrow, waiting.

"No matter what you think, Captain, I've just met Mr. Wicks. I'm not looking to . . . to fall in with someone. My horizon is my own."

He grunted. "You are a changeable thing lately."

"I'm not changeable," she said. "I'm just full of surprises."

That got a smile out of him. "Aren't you just?" Then, quieter: "Wouldn't want you to be any other way." He settled back, tipping his hat down again. "Get some rest, Rose Small. Your horizon's coming up quick."

Rose shifted until she found a fairly comfortable position cradling her head against the wall. She didn't mean to sleep, just to rest and think for a while.

The train swayed hard to one side and she jerked awake.

Hink was awake too, looked like he had been for some time, sitting forward and keeping an eye on the other passengers and the door at the end of the car.

"Are we there?"

"Kansas City?" he said quietly. "No."

"What's wrong?"

"We're not moving."

That must have been what woke Rose up.

"See that man up there?" He nodded just slightly.

Rose leaned to the side so she could see around the woman seated in front of her.

At the head of the train car stood a man. He wore black from hat to boot, including the heavy duster that hung open to reveal the black of his shirt, tie, and suit beneath, with only the shine of his silver gun at his hip and the other gun in his hand to draw any light.

He wore a black kerchief over the lower half of his face.

"A bandit?" Rose asked, her heart pounding.

"Appears so."

"Appears?" His shoes most caught her eyes. Shiny and familiar. He was one of the men from first class.

"Ladies and gents," the bandit said in a voice that would carry to the North Pole even without the windows open. "You are being robbed. Do not get any ideas about drawing on me. My friend there at the end of the car is a crack shot."

Rose twisted to see another man, also in all black and with covered face, aiming a triple-barreled gun rigged for bullets and also emanating that ear-pinching whine of an electric coil shot. He had shiny shoes too.

If he was any good with that gun, he could pick off a dozen people before anyone could get a shot off.

"We will spill your blood unless you cooperate. If you want to stay alive all the way to Kansas City, then put your money and jewelry into this bag and pass it on to your neighbor to do the same." He held up a canvas bag and threw it at the man in the seat nearest him. "Now."

The man dropped a pocket watch and a few coins into the bag and handed it to the man next to him.

"Aren't you going to do something?" Rose whispered over the frightened muttering of the fifty or so people in the car.

Hink hadn't moved, his eye still on the bandit ahead. "They're not the problem," he said.

Two metal-on-metal impacts rang out through the car twice, as if something had just hit the train. The car jerked.

"That," Hink said, "is the problem."

"Did they uncouple the train?" Rose asked.

Hink shook his head. "Not this car. But one of the cars."

"Why?"

He nodded again, this time toward the window. "For that."

Rose looked out the window. She didn't see anything but a snow-covered field.

"What?"

"Listen."

That's when she heard the low buzz of an airship drawing near. Not the *Swift*; this ship had a much deeper roar. At least a four-stack. Maybe six. It must be massive.

"Do you know it?" she asked.

Hink and his crew were good at identifying other vessels by the sound of their fans alone.

He shook his head. "When I tell you, duck."

Rose pushed at her luggage with her foot, then bent a bit to pick it up and sling the strap over her shoulder. Her heart was hammering, but she couldn't help but feel a little happy thrill. She'd seen Hink get out of all kinds of life-threatening situations. If he had a plan, it might not be safe, but it might work.

"That's right," the bandit bellowed. "All of your valuables. I want to see coins, jewelry, and paper money. If you've got a deed in your pocket, it better be in that sack."

Hink leaned back, pulling something out of his right inside coat pocket as he did so.

The bag was passed, hand to hand, seat to seat, the clink of coins and rattle of contents revealing its passage.

Rose was practically holding her breath.

The airship boilers chugged on, fans growling louder and louder, like a beast snarling down at its prey.

The man in front of Hink twisted around and handed over the sack. Hink took the bag and dropped something inside it. "Duck," he said quietly.

He stood and hurled the bag at the bandit at the front of the car.

A rapid cacophony of gunshot rattled out; everyone screamed and ducked while blinding flashes of orange light splattered through the air.

The car fell into chaos.

People rushed to run or hide, yelling and pushing, though there was no space to do either.

Hink stayed calm during it all, twisted to face the back of the train car, pulled his gun, and shot the bandit there straight through the head. A second later, he turned back and shot the other bandit right through the heart.

Both men crumpled to the floor.

Then Hink faced Rose and offered his hand.

She took it, and with one smooth, waltzlike step, he exchanged places with her so that he was near the window and she was nearer the aisle.

People were rushing to the doors, crowding and pushing and trying to get out.

"What?" she asked as he held her tight against him with his left arm. With his right, he fired three shots to clear the glass from the window.

He looked down at her. "Stay with the train, Rose," he said. "Keep your gun ready, and when the train starts moving again, go on up to Wicks in first class. Kansas City ain't far."

"Where are you going?"

"To stop the real robbery."

The airship fans added to the chaos, their sound so thunderous and so close above the car that the glass lampshades rattled in their casings.

Hink tugged Rose close for a brief moment. Then he bent and kissed her.

Rose knew there was no time for this sort of thing. But at the touch of his lips, all time seemed to slip, and then the world was filled with him, her senses overwhelmed by him, and she found herself wondering how she could possibly go on without this man in her life.

Right then he pulled away. The sharp whip of winter wind poured in through the window, cold enough to hurt, as he let her go.

Hink bent, shouldered through the window, then dropped down outside.

A handful of heartbeats ticked off the seconds. And then the whole of the world came back.

Rose glanced up and down the car. Passengers pushed and shoved, some yelling for people to calm down, some just yelling. Several men surrounded both bandits. Someone had hold of the robber's sack and was beginning the process of convincing the crowd that this could all be sorted out amicably.

She could stay here. It would be wise. Hink said they weren't far off from Kansas City, and once there she could put this kind of nonsense behind her and keep her hands busy building a brighter horizon.

Or she could jump out that window, find out what he meant about "the real robbery," and get her eyes on that massive airship.

That would be foolish.

And a chance she'd never get again.

Rose stood on the bench and hoisted herself up into the window, kicking the wet, heavy ruffle of her skirts out of the way and pulling her satchel close to her.

The wind was brutal, slashing from above and all around. She sat in the window and squinted skyward.

Only there was no sky. Swallowing the heaven, from end to end, was a monstrous airship as black as coal. Smoke shrouded and parted in random, ragged patterns as at least a dozen fans roared along its side like the oars of a great vessel, each fan set so it could swivel independently.

Genius, she thought.

The roar of the ship made her want to cover her ears, but she needed both hands to slip her feet up under her and then drop down onto the narrow edge of the train car. She might be able to hold on to the outside of the windows and make her way along the train car, but not for long. She looked around for Hink.

And saw him on the ground running full-out down the line.

What was he running from?

Jumping down off the train would mean no going back. But then, there was a robbery in progress on the train, likely in every car, so going back might just get her killed.

But if she let go of the train, she'd be stranded out here, in the middle of nowhere, chasing a man she wasn't sure she loved.

Only she did know. She'd known all along.

It was why him leaving her for those other women had hurt so much. It was why she was so angry. Not because she disliked him. Quite the opposite. Because she had never stopped loving the man.

"Blast it all," she said through gritted teeth. "You're bound to be the death of me, Lee Hink."

Rose let go of the window edge and jumped down. It was a longer fall than she expected, but she knew how to manage it without hurting herself and didn't do more than kick up some snow as she hit ground.

Hink was still running alongside the tracks. He wouldn't hear her if she shouted.

The airship's boilers belched out smoke and the fans shifted, delicately adjusting the big blower's position above the train.

And then she saw why.

A massive rope, large enough to tow a frigate, extended down from the airship to one of the train cars.

The rope had a huge hook on the end that attached to the top of the freight car.

The same freight car where she and Hink had saved Thomas. The same freight car filled with coffins full of body parts and boxes full of strange copper devices.

What could that huge ship do to the train car? Tip it over? Pull the top of it off like a knife prying at a can of beans?

She couldn't tell from here. So Rose ran. Toward Hink. Toward the freight car.

It was almost impossible to see anything through the coal smoke. She caught a glimpse of Hink as he reached for the ladder rungs on the outside of the freight car and climbed up.

Rose ran the remaining yards between them, then stopped.

The airship boilers changed tempo again. This time a low, rolling growl boomed out in repeating echoes and all the fans shifted position at once.

Then the airship began lifting the entire freight car off the tracks.

Rose didn't wait. She didn't think. She leaped at the freight car, grabbed hold of the ladder rungs, and held on for dear life as the earth dropped out below.

CHAPTER THIRTEEN

Cedar had given up trying to track the herbal combinations, strengths, and conversation of prayer and spells Mae and Father Kyne had been poring over at the kitchen table for the last hour.

It was quickly apparent that Father Kyne had spent some time learning about the herbs and spells witches used. He had told Mae that his father's stories about the mysterious Madder brothers had fueled his curiosity as a child. A curiosity that had led him to study the ways of witches, Strange, and even glim. He was convinced each of these things was a part of God's will and world, and therefore it was his responsibility, in some small way, to understand them.

A native-born man taking up the Word of God didn't surprise Cedar much. But a man of God willingly combining his knowledge of those things beyond a man's understanding with a witch's spells was something he'd never thought to imagine.

But then, this land was changing quickly, from frontier to civilization. A man unwilling to adapt could soon be left behind.

"Will this do more for me than the Madders' chain?" Cedar asked Mae while Father Kyne was retrieving another book from the other room.

"I think so, yes. The chain helps you keep some of your logic and human thoughts. This should keep you from taking beast form at all.

You will remain yourself, just yourself, during the full moon. With no compulsion to hunt the Strange."

Father Kyne came back into the room. "This volume speaks of the herb I think might help us."

Mae gave him a quick smile, then went back to studying the text.

Cedar pushed up away from the table and paced the pain out of his legs. While they puzzled over whether or not they could really hold off his and Wil's curse enough to give them both a man's mind and body during the full moon, he puzzled over why the Madders hadn't put up even a small fight back at breakfast. It wasn't like them to just stroll off in shackles to jail because some old enemy said so.

No, they were more the blowing-up and breaking-out kind of men.

If they were in jail it must be because they wanted to be.

But why?

So he'd stay and hunt the Holder? He'd given his promise to do just that. They knew he was a man of his word.

Staying in jail certainly wouldn't fulfill their promise to Father Kyne to track down the children. Cadoc and Bryn Madder had been adamant about holding to the vows they'd made, even if Alun was not.

There was something the Madders weren't telling him. Something they felt they could gain by going along with the mayor's wishes.

The crunch of hooves in the snow brought him to the window. The rider wore a heavy coat, gloves, and black Stetson against the softly falling afternoon snow. The only color on him was his scarf, thickly woven in deep green and gold stripes. One of Vosbrough's people.

Built light and short, he was not one of the men who had escorted them to the manor this morning. He hitched the horse and retrieved a leather satchel from one of the saddlebags.

"Who is it?" Father Kyne asked.

"Vosbrough's man. With papers, I'd guess," Cedar said.

Mae was already headed out of the room. "I'll get Miss Dupuis," she said.

Father Kyne closed the books he and Mae had been consulting, then opened the door.

"Welcome here, Mr. Peters," he said.

The man took the stairs and drew his hat off upon entering the building, but other than a brief nod toward the priest, he treated him as if he wasn't standing in the room.

Fear. Cedar could smell fear on the man, could see it tied up in the stiff angle of his shoulders and set of his jaw. The man wasn't afraid of Cedar.

No, he was afraid of Father Kyne.

Cedar took a moment to look at the priest, trying to see the threat in him this man obviously felt. He sensed nothing threatening about the priest, nothing that made him uneasy. Only a calm sort of certainty emanated from the man. As if he unflinchingly knew who he was, and just as unflinchingly knew his place in the world.

"How is your wife?" the priest asked quietly.

"Fine," he said without looking at Kyne.

"No sign of Florence?"

He shook his head, mouth pressed tight.

"The baby is doing well enough?"

"Wife keeps him tied to her at all times, night and day. Even sleeps with us now."

Father Kyne looked past the man to meet Cedar's gaze.

"Florence is six," he said. "A sweet child with a wide imagination and several playmates that only she could see. Disappeared just last week. We've been saying our prayers for her."

"Prayers haven't brought my girl back," Mr. Peters said stiffly. "You won't speak of her again. God's given me his answer."

"Yes," Father Kyne said, holding Cedar's gaze. "I believe He has." And in his eyes was the faith that Cedar, or perhaps the Madders, was the answer to all their prayers. The answer to finding the children.

Cedar didn't much like being the servant of things beyond this world. But it wouldn't be the first time he'd been called to help those in need.

"Hello," Miss Dupuis said, sweeping into the room with a rustle of taffeta and wool. "Have you brought the charges leveled at the brothers Madder?"

"Are you Miss Dupuis?" he asked.

"I am."

"Then yes, these are from the mayor. Trial begins at dawn tomorrow. Good day, ma'am." He turned and was out the door like his heels were on fire.

Cedar watched him mount and ride off. He didn't even throw a single backward look.

"His wife and I were children together," Father Kyne said. "Her parents were faithful to the church when my father guided the congregation. Once my father died, she did not return. Then, three days after her daughter went missing, she came to me. Asking for my help. Pleading for me to find Florence. To do anything in my power."

"So you called the Madders."

"I searched for her daughter, before the snow set deep. Found nothing. Nothing but sorrow in these winds. And then I remembered the promise, our family promise. Yes, I called the Madders."

"Who have been thrown in jail," Miss Dupuis said as she untied the leather strips and opened the satchel.

"They promised to find the children," Father Kyne said. "I think they meant for you to do so for them now, Mr. Hunt. That you would find the missing sons and daughters. That you would find Florence Peters."

"I said I'd look for them," Cedar said. "But I think the Madders want my favor for the Holder repaid first."

"You said you were once a God-fearing man," Father Kyne said. "Can you be a God-trusting man if it will mean the burden of your curse is lifted?"

"Trust isn't something I shrug into and out of, Father Kyne. If you want me to kneel before God so that the children can be found, I'll do so. But if you expect me to become faithful to Him, it would be a lie."

Father Kyne nodded, dark eyes weighing Cedar's soul. "There is a reason you are on this earth. There is a reason you bear this burden. God knows the heart of every man, and sees the good in each of us. He will guide us down this path, you and I."

"Will breaking the curse take long?" Cedar asked.

Mae shook her head. "I'll need to go into town for some herbs, but if what Father Kyne and I have discussed is possible, it will only take a few minutes to put the spell together for you and Wil, and, hopefully, not much longer for it to come to full strength."

"Why are we waiting?"

Mae glanced at Father Kyne, then back at Cedar. "We both agree it won't last for more than a few hours. We'll want to begin it after sunset if it's to last most of the night."

"So it's temporary?"

Mae smiled, and for the first time in a while looked excited and pleased with something that had to do with magic.

"It should be," she said. "A very gentle sort of way to stave off the curse for a short time. If it works well, we should be able to do it again tomorrow night and the next. Perhaps even . . . even as often as you like. A respite when you want it. A way to control the beast. But first I'll need those herbs."

"I would be happy to take you into town," Father Kyne said.

"Thank you," Mae said. "Miss Dupuis, is there anything we can pick up for you while we're there?"

Miss Dupuis was leaning over the table already reading through the documents she had pulled out of the satchel. "No, I don't believe so. I'll just put some water on for tea. I have reading to do, then an argument to reason out. They've been charged with theft, claim jumping, and suspicious activity toward the United States." She turned the page. "Oh."

"What?" Cedar asked.

"Murder." She looked up, her brown eyes wide with surprise. "They've been charged with murder."

Cedar stepped over so he could read the paper in front of her. In tight, clean script it clearly said that all three brothers had been involved with the disappearance and murder of a man named Roy Atkinson.

"Who's Roy Atkinson?" Miss Dupuis asked quietly. She glanced up at Father Kyne. "Have you heard of him?"

"He was mayor of this town. Before Mr. Vosbrough stepped in. A good man, interested in connecting Des Moines to the rail, interested in the city growing and thriving. But he was unwilling to do the sorts of . . . immoral things Vosbrough has done."

"Do you have any proof of those immoral things?" Miss Dupuis asked.

"No. No one does. A Vosbrough buys favor as easily as most people buy wax."

"I wasn't expecting murder charges," Miss Dupuis muttered, more to herself than anyone else in the room. "Perhaps I will go into town with you and Mae, Father. The city hall should have records, business records, land records, things that might help me understand what Roy Atkinson was involved in and why someone may have wanted to kill him."

"You don't think the Madders actually . . ." Mae said. "Actually may have killed him?"

Miss Dupuis picked up all the documents, tapped them endwise on the tabletop, then placed them back in the satchel. "The Madders don't shy from force, when necessary. They have a moral code that isn't always discernable. But they don't kill in cold blood. It is against the vows of the office they hold."

"What office?" Cedar asked.

She closed her mouth and shook her head slightly. "That is for another time, Mr. Hunt. For now, I need information if I am to make a coherent argument toward their innocence."

"We'll all go to town then," Mae said. "Let me get my coat."

"I'll follow behind a bit," Cedar said.

Mae stopped and waited for his explanation.

He closed his hand around the cold copper in his pocket. "There are a few things I want to check on. I'll meet you either at the herb shop or city hall."

"We will try the shop on Ferry Street first," Father Kyne said. "If they don't have what we need, we'll try the shop a few streets over."

It didn't take any of them long to dress for the weather and saddle the horses. Cedar saddled up too, but waited until they were well down the lane toward the city before leading his horse out of the barn.

Wil, who had been sleeping off the day, waited for him in the shadows of the trees outside the barn.

Cedar drew the copper from his pocket and held it out so his brother could catch the scent of it. "Found this under the mayor's carriage. Kyne says it's cursed. Cold copper. He says it's the devil's metal."

Wil sniffed at it and his ears flattened. He showed fang.

"It smells of the Strange," Cedar said. "And glim. But it looks like a child's toy."

Wil took a step back and then lifted his head, scenting for both on the wind.

He trotted down the lane, and Cedar mounted and followed. At the end of the lane, another, wider road wandered along the bare-branched forest. Wil slunk into the trees, keeping to the shadows, the gray, black, and white of his fur rendering him nearly invisible.

Cedar followed the road, and Wil, north. He could smell the copper in the wind, could smell the strange mossy sweetness of the Strange. But even though his senses were heightened, Wil's were a hundred times stronger than his.

There were no signs of missing children. No fabric caught on stone or branch. No scuff of shoe or drop of blood. There were plenty of animal tracks, and the evidence of horses and wagons traveling the road.

Some clues of what those wagons had carried—coal, wheat, corn, potatoes—were scattered alongside the trail.

If the children had strayed off this way, the trail was long destroyed by the bustle of the city's trade.

The road forked, the right branch crooking back to the north part of town. Cedar heard water to the left, and caught a scent of the Strange. He turned his horse that way.

Wil was already waiting for him in the brush by the bank of the river. There was no bridge, no sign of a ferry, but this is where the well-traveled road stopped. There must be a reason for that.

The river bent tight, the width of it upstream squeezing through a slot in stone that forced the river to nearly half its size. Even though it was narrow, it would be a difficult water to cross in good weather, much less bad, stretching as it was at least a hundred feet across.

Cedar dismounted, exhaling a grunt when his boots touched the ground. Pain shot across his chest, and it took him a few minutes of breathing before it eased. He pulled his coat closer around his body and pushed his hands in his pockets for warmth. He didn't know why he hadn't recovered from the trail yet. Usually the curse helped him heal quickly.

He tossed the reins over a low branch and the horse nibbled at the few leaves still clinging to the brush.

The wind shifted, drawing like a slow finger across the water. The scent of copper and the Strange filled his lungs.

Cedar made his way carefully down to the frozen bank. There were footprints here, several dozen frozen in the mud and snow. All small enough to belong to the children. But they disappeared just before the edge of the water. None of the footprints were pointed back toward the road.

It was as if they had walked into the water and disappeared. Or perhaps fallen in.

He glanced at the river, frozen at each bank nearly out to the center, where water ran a thin ebony ribbon around stones and ice down its middle. Ice that could be easily broken, though he saw no signs of that now.

On the other side of the river, the bank was much the same as this one: ice, snow, dried brush, and beyond that, trees. No footprints that he could see, and the ice was far too dangerous to cross.

The smell of the Strange was strong.

Strange had been known to lure children away for the wicked sport of seeing them lost and suffering. But he'd never heard of them taking more than a child or two. Father Kyne had said it was dozens missing. Nearly all the children of the town.

Were there that many Strange who delighted in the suffering of children, or was it something else? Revenge against their parents? Could the Strange have a use for the young, like Mr. Shunt, who used little Elbert Gregor's blood to power the spells of his devices?

Or were the Strange innocent of the children's disappearance? Men could have stolen the children.

It didn't make sense. He'd spent years hunting Strange, killing them whether they wore a physical body or none. But he'd never run across even a single Strange who had gathered up children like a shepherd herds sheep.

Wil tracked up and down the bank and returned without indicating he had found any evidence of the children there.

It was a dead end, then. Cedar turned toward the road and heard the soft sorrow of Strange grieving on the wind.

Wil heard it too, and growled, a low rumble rising in his chest.

Nothing about the children's disappearance, or the weeping Strange, made sense.

And there was no trace of the cursed cold copper here. Maybe if he found the mines where the demons were rumored to dwell, he would find answers. Cedar swung back up into the saddle, and started toward town.

"Afternoon," a man called out from down the road a bit.

The man himself wasn't all that remarkable. Square face under a low derby hat, and clothing warm enough for the chill. It was the rifle he carried that caught Cedar's eye. Made of equal parts walnut and steel, copper tubes wrapped around it from the overwide muzzle to the stock. Those tubes fed into a square box about the size of a large tobacco tin, hooked to the saddlebag behind the man's leg.

Possibilities of the gun's use rolled through his mind, but Cedar could not suss what might be contained in that box, or what ammunition the gun fired. Not for the first time, he wished Rose Small was with them on these travels. Her quick eye and devising mind would have easily worked out what that gun could do. She probably would have come up with several improvements and modifications for it too.

"Afternoon," Cedar said.

"Name's George Hensling," the man said. "Lost, are you?"

"Not much."

George brought his horse alongside Cedar's and paced him toward town.

"Most people new to town don't realize the bridge washed out years ago. Some maps still show it, but there's no way to cross that river except for south a ways."

"Looks traveled for a trail no one uses."

Mr. Hensling pushed his hat back just a bit. "Like I said, people get lost."

"I heard there's been a lot of children gone missing this winter."

"Maybe. We have our share of runaways. Parents don't like to admit to such a thing."

"Dozens of runaways?" Cedar asked. "Sure there isn't something, or someone, stealing them in the night?"

The man laughed, but it was humorless. "Someone's been telling you ghost stories, I'm afraid. Where exactly are you staying in town?"

"The Kyne church."

If Cedar had been expecting the man to be angry at that, which he did since that seemed to be the reaction of anyone who heard the mention of Kyne's name, he was fully disappointed.

"Well, that explains it. Father Kyne hasn't been the same since Kyne Senior passed away. Started up with such nonsense tales about ghosts and blood drinkers and strange things wandering this land out for revenge. Any person of a reasonable mind soon realized he's gone quite mad.

"Sad state, but then, he is a savage; what can you expect? They're not made for a civilized world, don't have the constitution for it. And don't you believe that act of him being a preacher. There isn't a single person who attends his church. Not a single soul in this city who thinks he stands on the side of God Almighty."

"You think he's insane?" Cedar said.

"I'd say there ain't no wheels turning in that head of his. He's made up the story of missing children. For months now. Ever since some kind of star fell out of the sky." They had reached a crossroads. Off to Cedar's left he could see a flat field where two large structures and metal towers stood. Beyond that were barns and silos, airship sheds, probably storage sheds too, and half a dozen tether towers.

The road that led to the structures was cut down the middle with a single, wide metal rail that had a slit down the length of it. The single rail continued to Cedar's right, into town.

"Is that an air-rail cable line?" he asked.

Mr. Hensling nodded. "The only one this side of the Mississippi. Better than the ones in New York, Boston, Philadelphia, or Chicago. Ever seen one?"

The man started into town and Cedar followed.

"Not while it was in use," Cedar said. "Saw one being built once, lines laying down. Is this air rail for passengers or freight?"

"Bit of both," he said. "Ever since the coal mines went into full production and the Transcontinental hammered the spike in Ogden,

Des Moines has gone from a farming town to a genuine high-class city."
He nodded toward the rise of brick buildings ahead of them. "Had to be
replatted a dozen times already to take on the growth. Hear even Smith
& Wesson are thinking of putting in a production warehouse. Building
a new theater too, since the three we have are busting at the seams."

"You must think highly of Mayor Vosbrough then," Cedar said.

"I get paid on time every week. Got a paper every evening, telegraph's cheap, and there's enough jail space for those who like to cause
trouble. That's enough for me," he said.

"What about the mayor before him? Atkinson, was it? Did he treat
the town well?"

The man went quiet for a bit, and the brush and trees were replaced
by buildings, sheds, a farrier shop, a blacksmith for matic work, and
shops turning wood, casting clay, melting glass.

"Don't remember much about how Atkinson ran the town. Had just
come out of the battles down south when I started paying attention to
such things."

"Was his death suspicious?"

"His murder?" He shrugged. "I suppose any man in power is setting
himself up to stand in another man's sights."

"You know who did it? Who killed the mayor?"

"They say it was a gang of brothers, riding rough. Broke into his
manor demanding gold, glim, and anything else of value. Atkinson didn't
have servants other than the cooking and cleaning staff. He started off as
a farmer and didn't take much to people waiting on him. There were no
guns that night to defend him.

"Found him dead the next day flat on the floor by his safe, all his
riches gone."

"Who found him dead?"

He thought a minute. The road had brought them solidly into town
now, and every cross street grew busier and busier. There were still a lot
of horses in the street, carrying riders or pulling wagons and coaches,

but the closer they came to the center of the city, the more devices and steam matics crowded the roads.

People on foot rushed between the steamers and animals, narrowly avoiding getting run over.

Cedar couldn't help but smile. He'd missed this: the hurried pace of city life. While the wilds spoke to his blood, this was the life of his memories. Of his happiest days as a husband and father, back when he was a teacher in the universities, with a wife and daughter. Back before they had died and he and Wil had struck out west, escaping Cedar's grief.

There was a small break in cross traffic and both Cedar and the man urged their mounts out into it.

"I think it was the mayor," the man said.

"What?" Cedar had lost track of the conversation to the memories unfolding in his mind.

"The mayor, Vosbrough, found Roy Atkinson dead. Declared a manhunt for the killers and put a price on their heads. They were never found as far as I recall. Vosbrough took up where Atkinson left off."

"What about the copper mine?" Cedar asked.

The man shrugged. "Not much of a vein, but enough not to waste. That's just north of town back along the crossroad where you saw the air-rail line. But since there's more money in coal, and more coal to be found here, that's what we mine. They pull lead up around Dubuque and gypsum out Fort Dodge way, ship it all by rail east and west, river north and south, and anywhere else by sky. Hold up, now."

He heeled his horse to sidle over to Cedar's mount. Cedar noted everyone else was making a clear path down the left side of the street too, leaving the center of the street empty.

For good reason. That single rail cut a straight line down the bricks of the street.

The distinct plucked-bow hiss of a heavy wire moving through the air was immediately drowned out by the rumble of overhead fans.

He glanced up and over his shoulder.

A dirigible floated toward town, the stacks puffing slow, low smoke as it navigated the sky above the buildings.

A long cable hung from the airship, latched down inside the rail, rolling on metal wheels and guiding the dirigible through the town as easily as a needle pulling thread. Too many ships had crashed into buildings buffeted by winds between tall structures. But ever since some wild deviser had invented an air trolley system, people and goods could be delivered by airship more quickly and safely than by carts on the ground.

No wear and tear on the roads; no adding to the already traffic-heavy street. It opened up an entire sky full of shipping lanes.

Good for precious goods or particularly heavy freight too.

The fat shadow of the ship bobbed down the street, then was ladled up the sides of hotels, restaurants, and shops. The cable sped down the road, fast as a horse at full gallop, smooth and mindless as the wind.

As soon as the cable passed by, the townspeople went back to business, barely pausing for it to be out of the way before moving on.

There had been some arguments over the safety of installing air trolleys. Fears that the racing cable would cut horses and carts in half. But the accidents and deaths caused by collision with the cable had been fewer than expected. People quickly learned to stay out of the way of the device, and animals already had the good sense in their heads to do the same.

"This is the end of my ride," the man said. "It was nice meeting you, Mr. . . . ? I don't believe I got your name."

"Cedar Hunt."

"Well then, Mr. Hunt. Enjoy your stay in Des Moines." He kicked his horse into a quick walk, taking one of the side streets along which signs advertised lodging, laundry, and cheap hot lunches.

Cedar had kept an eye on Wil and knew he hadn't entered the crowded city. Too easy to be seen. Too easy to end up a trophy on the wall.

But he didn't need Wil to lead him to the place that would give him the most answers. The copper mine was just north of town. Cedar clicked his tongue against his teeth and set off at a trot.

There'd be answers at the mine. Answers to the copper in his pocket. Answers to the demons beneath the city. Because even though that man thought Kyne was insane, Cedar knew the priest was right about one thing: the children were missing, and the people of this town were wrong to think that nothing Strange was involved.

CHAPTER FOURTEEN

Rose clung to the side of the railcar, her head tucked down to keep the worst of the smoke, ice, and snow out of her face.

She wanted to climb to the top to see if Hink was still up there or if he had fallen to the ground, now a long distance below, but she couldn't seem to force her arms to unlock from their death grip around the ladder rungs.

She usually loved flying. Wasn't a bit frightened of heights. But she preferred to be safely inside the ship rather than hanging below it like a bobber on a fishing line.

"Hand!" a voice yelled, barely breaking through the noise of the overhead fans.

She looked up.

Captain Hink lay flat at the top of the train car, one hand held out for her. The first thought through her mind was relief that he was alive. The second was disbelief that he thought she would unlatch her hold on this crate even if she could.

She shook her head.

"Damn it!" he yelled.

Then he backed away from the edge and in a moment a rope lowered down, the end of it knotted in a loop big enough to fit down over her shoulders and latch up tight around her ribs.

She'd have to let go to get the rope in place. A terrifying thought.

"Rose!" he yelled.

She didn't want to let go of this slight safety, but had no idea how far the frigate was transporting the train car. And once they landed, they might not take into account the fact that there was a person on the side of the car, especially if they were taking it somewhere like a forest or a dock with other freight stacked upon it.

Just her luck, she'd get scraped right off the side.

The top of the car didn't seem much safer. But there might be a way down into the inside. She liked that idea. Liked it very much. And even if Hink hadn't gotten around to finding a way in, she'd be more than happy to do so.

Rose braced her left arm tight and uncoiled her right. She reached up for the rope and guided it one-handed over her head, then under her arm. She relocked her right arm over the rung, then positioned the rope under her left arm. The rope fit nicely around her ribs, and even though it was only a slight improvement in her situation, it lent a strong feeling of security.

The rope tugged, and Rose reluctantly let go of one rung, reached up for the next, and convinced her feet to do the same. She did not look down. And she tried very hard not to think about just what, exactly, she was doing.

Then she was over the top. Hink walked backward with the rope over his shoulder, then expertly tied a knot in it around the huge loop where the main cable attached between the freight car and the airship. He walked back over to her and bent, his hand extended.

He wasn't tied down to anything, not a safety line in place, and yet he strode around up there like he was stomping across a barn floor.

His days as a glim pirate were paying off. He was as steady on his feet as any seagoing captain.

Rose reached up for him, and with his help, was soon standing on the roof of the freight car, a rope still tight around her, and Captain Hink glaring down at her.

"What in the blazes are you doing here?" he yelled.

"Let's get inside," she yelled back.

He looked up and around, obviously completely unconcerned that any hard gust of wind would send them toppling, or worse, that the weather would drop and the whole of the thing would be covered in ice.

"This is not a game," he yelled.

Rose held up one finger to silence him. Then she pointed at her feet. "Inside."

His lips moved through an impressive array of cusswords, which Rose ignored. Then he took her by the arm and stomped along the top of the crate to a hatch.

So there was a way inside. Good.

Her heart leaped at the thought of having four strong walls safe around her.

Hink kicked the hatch open with the toe of his boot and held her arm as she crouched at the edge of it. She held her breath and dropped down inside.

A soft landing was out of the question with the entire car swaying in the wind. Her ankle shot with pain, and she barked her knees, but she was on the floor, the rocking floor, more whole than less.

In a moment, Hink dropped down over the edge, a much shorter fall for him since the tall of him took up a good chunk of distance between the top of the car and the floor.

"What in *hell* are you doing here?" he repeated almost before his boots hit the floor.

"Where did you expect me to be? Back on that train while it was getting robbed?"

"I told you that wasn't a real robbery."

"There are two dead men back there who might think otherwise."

"Yes. Two men *I* shot," Hink said. She pulled her shoulders back and stood up to him, craning her neck so she could stare into his stormy blue eye. "They were robbing the train, and you left me there. With them."

"They weren't breathing much when I was done with them. You'd have been safer there."

"I saw you jump on this . . . on this blamed train car and then the ship yanked it off the track. I thought you were going to die."

He closed his mouth around whatever he'd been about to say.

"Rose." He said that much softer than before. "You know I have a dangerous job. You throwing yourself into danger after me doesn't make it any easier. Or safer."

"I don't care," she said. "I know what I want, Lee. And it's you."

She reached up on tiptoe and kissed him.

He stood there for a second or two, caught by the surprise of her bold move. Then his arms wrapped around her possessively and for that world-erasing moment, she was once again right where she most wanted to be.

"Ain't that sweet?" a man's voice said from the corner of the car.

Hink broke the kiss and swung himself between Rose and the man, the whole of him wide enough to set Rose completely in the dark.

"Get both your hands out where I can see them and drop your gun on the floor," the man said. "Slow and easy."

Rose made to step out from behind Hink, but he had snuck his hand around his back. In it was a flare with a flint-and-steel starter.

"We have no quarrels with you, friend," Hink said, as he adjusted his hold on the flare up to his fingertips, offering it to Rose.

Rose took it and stuck it up her sleeve.

"I ain't no friend of yours," he growled. "Now show me your palms. Both of them. And, miss, I know you're behind him. Won't do you any good to hide. Step on out."

Rose couldn't get to her gun at the bottom of her bag without an awful lot of maneuvering, but she unlatched the top of her satchel so if there was a chance, she'd be on it faster.

"Don't get her involved in this," Hink said. "She tumbled out the window and caught on hold of this box by accident."

"That so?" the man said. "Don't believe a word of it. I've seen just as many women in this war as there are men. Step out."

War?

Rose stepped out from behind Hink, her hands clenched together, and tried to look frightened and helpless. The frightened part wasn't all that hard to manage, but the helpless had never come very easily to her.

"Please, don't shoot," she said.

The man was in dark clothing from hat to boot, just like the robbers. Only he didn't wear a kerchief over his mouth. Rose made a point to memorize the wide angles of his face, narrow-set eyes, and large nose.

"We don't mean you any trouble," Hink said.

The man jerked his gun. "Put that peashooter of yours on the floor, and kick it to me," he said.

Hink reached for the gun under his coat.

"Slowly."

Hink reached slower for the gun under his coat.

He pulled it out, holding it by one finger, then dropped it on the floor.

"Good. Now kick it."

Hink put the sole of his boot on the gun. He didn't say anything, but there was tenseness in him, like a coil wound too tight.

Rose knew that was her signal. It was time to throw the flare.

She slid her hand up her sleeve and struck the flare, then hurled it at the man. The crate filled with blinding orange light.

Rose ducked and dug in her satchel for her gun, but Hink was already rushing the man, then was on him, fists slamming into his face and stomach.

The man got off a shot or two, then both of them fell to the floor, just as the entire crate tipped alarmingly to the side, forcing everything not tied down to slide from one end of the car to the other.

Rose slid too, but held tight to her gun as she thunked against the crates and coffins. The flare went out and darkness thumped down so thick it felt like a blanket fell over her eyes.

The freight car leveled somewhat, and she stood with the help of the ropes tied around the freight.

She couldn't see anything. But she heard someone breathing heavily. Then a groan.

"Rose?" It was Hink.

"I'm all right," she said. "The gunman?"

"Out cold. Find a light, will you?"

He groaned again, then moved off to her left, probably toward the man. Maybe to tie him up.

Rose felt her way along to a wall, and then felt for the lantern that should be hanging there. Found it. It only took a moment to bring the wick to a cheery yellow fire.

Hink sat back on his heels, looking down at the man, who was not moving. She didn't think he was alive.

"Is he dead?" Rose asked.

"Hope to hell he is," Hink said. "Don't feel like breaking my knuckles on his face again."

Hink stood, and lifted his hands out to the side for a second, gaining his balance. But the car was level and smooth at the moment.

That's when Rose noticed the blood on his shirt.

"You've been hurt," she said.

"Not my blood," he said.

Rose got around in front of him and pulled his coat open. Steam from the heat of his blood wafted up from his shirt, which was soaked. "Yes, it is," she said. "Sit down and let me try to stanch it."

"Stanch what? I said I'm not wounded. I feel fine. We need to knock out one of these boards so we can see where this crate is flying."

Rose pressed her fingers against his ribs and he hissed in a hard breath.

"Good God, woman. Why you have to be jabbing at me like that?"

"Let me take care of the bullet hole in your hide."

He shook his head.

"Paisley Cadwaller Hink Cage," she said sternly. "Sit down before I kick out your kneecaps."

He blinked hard, then gave her half a smile. "You would, wouldn't you?"

"Faster than you could say Nelly."

"Don't know what I did to deserve the likes of you," he muttered as he made his way over to a stack of crates and carefully—very carefully—lowered himself to sit in the dust.

"Well, it wasn't all those years of you being an altar boy," she said, kneeling beside him.

He chuckled and pressed his hand over his side. "Never quite got the hang of spiritual purity. Or any other kind of purity for that matter. Too many interesting things that needed being done."

"Move your hand." Rose set the lantern down and dug in her satchel. She didn't have much in the ways of medicine, but had kept the black salve Mae used on her shoulder wound when she'd been hit with that piece from the Holder, and she had her sewing kit.

"Hold this." She placed the jar of salve in his palm and then unbuttoned his shirt.

"Had dreams about this sort of thing," he said in a soft drawl. "Me, you. A dark train car. You ripping off my shirt . . ."

"You're delirious," she said.

"I'm clear as a bell."

"Well, then your bell is cracked," she said. "A fact I'm willing to ignore since you are also bleeding. Oh." She lifted the lantern to better see the wound. A wet, stone-red gash in his side was pouring blood rather freely.

"I think it went straight through," she said.

"Told you it was just a graze."

"You said no such thing."

"Huh. Did I mention me dreaming about you pulling off my clothes?"

"Yes."

"Good. Wouldn't want to die without you knowing that. The things I think about you."

"You are not going to die." She twisted the lid off the jar and dipped her fingers into the mixture. "And I know exactly what you think about me."

"I really don't suppose you do."

She spread the salve on as gently as she could, and he held his breath through it. Even though there was no bullet buried in his gut, that gash had to hurt. She pulled out her sewing kit, grateful she'd left the needle threaded.

"You think I'm young, untested in the world, and innocent," she said as she pushed the needle through the skin as quickly as she could.

Hink winced, but remained silent, watching her.

"You think I don't know what a man can have on his mind when he looks at a woman. Or visits them in their parlors for weeks at a time."

She tied a knot and then cut the thread with her sewing scissors. The stitches should help slow the bleeding. But this was not a minor wound. She reached over for another fingerful of the salve.

He caught her wrist gently. "Rose Small. There aren't many people who bring the truth out of me, but you are one of them. I did not sleep with those women. There's only one woman who has the key to my heart. Only you."

This close, she knew he was not lying. Knew he meant every word he said.

But she wondered if she could give as fully her heart to him. She'd just barely begun to see this great and wild world. Tying her star to this man would mean not meeting any others. It would mean settling for the sort of life he intended to lead, just as much as it would mean him settling for the things she intended to do.

Of course, given the chance, they'd both jumped on a train car being stolen off the rail by a massive and unidentified airship, without so much as a pause. Maybe their intentions were compatible.

"At least you're smiling," he said, letting go of her wrist so she could spread the salve. "I prefer my doctors to be in a forgiving sort of mind-set when they're jabbing fingers in my innards."

"Hush," she said as she reached into her satchel for a clean handkerchief. She pressed that against the salve-covered wound. "Do you think you can hold this here while I try to make a window we can look out of?"

"I'll help."

"You'll help by staying right here and concentrating on not bleeding."

He took a deep breath to argue, but must have thought better of it since he stopped with a wince, halfway through. "Might be something in the crates you can use," he said.

"My thought exactly." Rose swung the strap of her satchel off over her head and left it there next to Hink. She took the lantern and first walked over to check on the gunman. She placed her hand over his mouth, felt no breath, then placed her fingers on the side of his neck, searching for a heartbeat there.

Nothing. Rose tried not to let his death bother her. He'd been more than prepared to kill her and Hink. And she didn't think he'd have any regrets if he'd done just that. She lifted the lantern, spotted a sheet of canvas, and pulled it over the man's prone body.

Then, with more delight than she should probably be feeling, she started digging into the boxes and crates to see what sort of useful thing she could build.

CHAPTER FIFTEEN

The road to the copper mine didn't appear to be much used. As soon as it wound out beyond the edge of town, it became a narrow path that snaked off to a small hill a short distance away. In that hill was an iron door that stood slightly ajar, revealing a narrow mine entrance.

He didn't see any workers coming or going, though there were carts and a rail spur on which small steam matics about the size of a pony rested, coal black and covered in snow.

Wil paused next to his stirrup, ears peaked high. He whined, took a step, then glanced up at Cedar.

"Don't like the look of the place," Cedar said. "It almost looks abandoned. I thought it'd be a larger operation. Some kind of working site."

Wil turned his wide head toward the mine and waited. This was Cedar's call. To decide if instinct was leading him the right way by checking out the copper mine, or if instead he should head back into town to find Mae and Father Kyne so they could break his curse.

He glanced up at the sun, already on its slow decent to the horizon. The moon would rise in a few hours. Night would be on them. And so would his curse.

A movement near the door of the mine caught his eye. A boy in cap and short pants stood there, looking at Cedar.

And then, as Cedar watched, the boy faded from sight.

The wind snagged across low bushes, pushing against his back, then scattering down the hill. In the wind was the sound of crying. Only it wasn't the weeping of the Strange, it was the weeping of children.

Could be a Strange trick to lure him into the mine. Could be a ghost.

But then the faces of children, many more, appeared in the slim wedge of darkness beyond the mine's entrance.

These didn't fade away.

"Seems like we have ourselves an invitation," Cedar said. "Let's see what it brings us."

He urged his horse on, Wil pacing him. It didn't make sense that the children would be stolen and locked up to work the copper mine. The mine wasn't far enough outside town for people not to look here, for people not to search for their children here.

Surely, this mine had been searched.

Cedar rode across the flat field toward the mine and came upon it at a trot. As he neared, he saw bits of brush and rocks and snow, tangled up like whirlwinds. Wil growled, as if he saw Strange in those gusts of debris. Cedar studied the whirlwinds and saw nothing but sticks and snow.

"It's fine," he said to Wil. "No Strange there."

Wil growled softly in disagreement.

Cedar dismounted with care so as not to trigger any more aches and pains that seemed only to be getting worse.

He led his horse the remaining distance to the mine and tied the reins on a hitching post.

Wil was still snarling at the wind. Cedar looked around again, but saw nothing.

"There is nothing in the air, Wil," he said. "Calm yourself." He pulled a lantern off the saddle, and lit it with a striker from his pocket.

The side of his neck stung, and Cedar pressed his fingers there.

Wil growled louder.

And Cedar finally knew why. A ghostly Strange stood at the mine entrance with eyes made of cold copper. "Please . . . ," it breathed, in a voice made of bits of wind scratching though leaves and stone and ice. "Help . . ."

He had seen this Strange before. In the bedroom, on the road outside the church. He was sure it was the same creature that had bit him.

And then it disappeared, torn apart by the wind that scattered him with a hailstorm of snow, branches, and dirt.

Wil snarled and paced the area, scenting for the Strange, but came quickly back to Cedar, ears up, and no indication that he had found a trail.

Why would the Strange ask him for help? Twice now. Cedar pulled his gun and walked up to the mine's entrance. A dozen or so small stones had been positioned in a straight line across the entrance to the mine, but there was nothing else impeding his progress.

There were no children in the doorway. Wil slipped past Cedar, head low, and entered the mine. Cedar followed behind.

The mine was braced by iron girders that jutted up from the walls and crossed over the ceiling like scaffolding constructed around a tower. The ground beneath him slanted downward and was fitted with a rail. To either side were metal staircases, bolted into the stone walls.

He made his way down into the mine, looking for any sign of the children who had been in the doorway.

Usually stealth was his best option, but if the children were here, hiding, then he'd need to convince them to show themselves.

"Hello," he said just loud enough to be heard. The stone and metal seemed to swallow his words, and the deeper he descended into the mine, the more it felt like his ears were stuffed with wool.

"Is there anyone here? I've come to help you. If you're lost, I can take you home. There's no need to be afraid."

Nothing moved. There was no wind in this hole, just the damp smell of stone and wet metal and the dusty arc of dirt all around him.

"I can help you," Cedar said.

The hush of something scraping over stones scratched in the shadows ahead. Something was moving down here. Cedar lifted the lantern higher and held his gun at the ready. He strode toward the sound.

The mine shaft took a hard right toward town. The tunnel narrowed, and metal bracers, which now also supported thick copper wires, closed in around his head and shoulders. Wil padded softly in front of Cedar, silent as darkness.

Another scratch, almost a buzzing, rattled through the tunnel.

Cedar's heart was pounding. It was harder to breathe here, though Wil didn't seem to be having any trouble.

The tunnel was tight and near-impossible to fight in. If someone ahead had a gun and saw him coming before he saw them, he'd be dead. He considered dampening the lantern, but hated the idea of wandering these tunnels blind.

There was a side tunnel to his left. He lifted the lantern, but could see nothing but a stone tunnel supported by wood bracers marching downward. The sound had come from ahead, not to the left.

Wil paused at the edge of the lantern light, head up, nose scenting the air.

Cedar walked up behind him. The tunnel split left and right, a rail line set smoothly down both paths. The scratching was coming from the right.

Cedar and Wil turned that way. Here the stone was no longer just brown and charcoal black. Spidery thin lines of blue and white spread down the wall and arced across the ceiling like lightning caught in stone.

Copper. A much richer vein of it than he'd expected.

At the end of the tunnel was a steel door. It stood ajar and the slight scratching came from beyond it.

Someone or something wanted him to go in there. Someone or something had been leading him this whole way.

It could be a trap. But who would go through this much trouble to try to lure him out here?

Cedar pressed his fingertips on the edge of the door. He gasped as the song of the Strange filled him, and with the song, their sorrow.

Cedar let go of the door and lifted the lantern.

The room beyond the door was massive. Easily two stories tall, it was a wide, smooth chamber that looked like it had been carved out with water and then polished down to a smooth sheen.

Lantern light caught a surreal turquoise glow from the walls and ceiling and floor. The entire room was the center of a massive copper vein. Cedar felt like he'd just stepped into the heart of an ocean-colored jewel.

But it was not just the stunningly rich deposit of copper that made him catch his breath in wonder; it was the huge iron and copper devices that filled the center of the room.

Five tanks stood at one side, wires connected to the top of each and spreading outward. Those wires also connected to a boiler and an alternator that were both taller than Cedar. And in the center of all those wires and connecting pipes was a transformer made of metal and wood and thick blown glass.

The room was noticeably damp and warm, which meant the boiler was still hot, and the device had recently been in use. The scratching sound could have come from the boiler cooling.

Cedar walked around the contraptions. They were built to power something, maybe to send an electric pulse of some kind down the copper wires hammered over the walls and ceiling like a net thrown across a blue wave.

The scratching hiss crackled down one of the wires, perhaps latent energy bleeding away into the walls.

Cedar walked over to one wall and touched the copper wire with his palm.

No heat, it was just the opposite. The metal was so cold, it drank the heat out of his skin. He pulled his hand away and could make out red lines left behind from the wire. Cold copper. What kind of energy could it carry, a metal that heated so slowly? What kind of power could it drink down?

Wil had made his own search of the room and came to stand next to Cedar.

There were no children here. There were no Strange. Whatever they had seen at the mine's entrance, whether it be an illusion cast there by Strange, ghosts, or his own tired imagination, they were not here.

But the one thing that Cedar had discovered in the room was the smell of hickory and cherry cologne, the scent he'd noticed on Mayor Vosbrough when they'd met. His stomach knotted, and he paced his breath to calm the sudden fear that rolled through him.

The mayor had been here. Recently. But Cedar had no explanation for his fear.

"What a pleasant surprise."

Cedar turned. The mayor walked through the door and froze as soon as he saw Wil.

"A wolf—," he started.

"Belongs to me," Cedar said. His heart was still pumping. This man, the mayor, set Cedar's instincts clamoring. He was danger. He was pain.

The mayor smiled, but did not move. "You certainly are an interesting man, Cedar Hunt. Would you like to tell me why I've found you in our generator room? And do make it a good reason; otherwise I'll be obliged to escort you to jail."

"I was told there are children missing in your town. Thought I saw them out at the mine entrance when I was riding by. Thought they might have wandered down these tunnels and gotten lost."

"How altruistic of you," he said, then, in a more friendly tone, "And how thoughtful. Most men would have notified the authorities instead of trespassing on private property."

"I saw no signs posted."

"That's because this is Vosbrough land and a private Vosbrough mine. I don't have to post signs. The town understands that if I find anyone near these tunnels without invite, I'll shoot them dead."

Cedar's fear crystallized into anger. "Is that what you're planning to do?" he asked very calmly.

The mayor glanced at Wil, then back at Cedar. He smiled. "Of course not, Mr. Hunt. I'll chalk this up to an honest mistake on your part. But I insist on escorting you off of my land."

He took one step, eyes on Wil. Wil growled.

There was nothing that would make Cedar agree to let this man walk behind him up these narrow tunnels.

"How about we follow you out," Cedar said.

Vosbrough's eyes tightened. He didn't like the idea of Cedar at his back either.

"The wolf can go first," Cedar offered.

"Yes, I suppose that will do." Vosbrough took three steps to clear the doorway for Wil to pass.

Wil walked through it, and paused, waiting for Vosbrough to follow.

"After you, Mayor," Cedar said.

Vosbrough ducked out into the tunnel, Cedar behind him.

"What is the generator for?" he asked.

"Nothing, yet," the mayor said. "But I have plans to bring this town into the modern world. To make it a wonder of communication and transportation. This generator is only part of that plan. An advance I expect you to keep quiet, Mr. Hunt."

Some of what the mayor was saying might be true, but one thing wasn't. The generator was being used. It was still hot, electricity still crackling down the wires.

"Have you tested it?" he asked.

"I don't see any reason to continue on this subject, Mr. Hunt. How exactly did you come across a tame wolf?"

"He's not tame."

"Then you'd best keep him out of my city. We shoot dangerous animals."

"I'll keep a close eye on him," Cedar said. It was both a promise and a warning.

They stepped out into the cold air.

"I know you travel with the Madder brothers, Mr. Hunt. And I hate to judge a man by his companions. But if you cross me"—Vosbrough smiled and swung up onto his horse—"I will make your remaining days very unpleasant."

Vosbrough urged his horse down the hill, away from the mine.

Cedar doused his lantern and tied it to the saddle. Remaining days? It had not been an idle threat. Cedar searched his memories. A moment, a memory of Vosbrough, his voice, his threats, slipped through his mind, blurry and incoherent.

Something. There was something important about Vosbrough that Cedar should know, but escaped him.

He rubbed at his arm, and the bruises there. He usually healed more quickly than most men. But these aches from the blizzard were slow to mend.

He took some time walking around the place, looking for signs of Strange, of children, or of anything else.

Nothing. He mounted up and headed back to town.

Nightfall was only a few hours off. He'd need to be under Mae's spell, or under chains, before moonrise. If not, he'd be hunting Strange and, in his current frame of mind, killing people too, beginning with the mayor.

The wind, pushing cold down his spine, was thick with the scent of Strange.

Why had the Strange asked for his help? That was something he'd never seen before.

It made him wonder, for the first time, what sort of thing the Strange would fear.

CHAPTER SIXTEEN

ose hadn't even gone through half the freight before she found a cutting torch and rigged it so she could catch a fire to the tip. She'd tried opening the doors, of course, but when the airship had lifted the car, it had done something to lock the doors from the outside.

She braced herself as best she could with all the swaying and then burned out a square hole in each of the doors at the ends of the train car.

The cold air that howled in through those holes was lung robbing, but if she squinted against it, she could see that they were being carried over hills and plains. Now and then she saw a river snake by.

She was going to share her observation with Hink, but he'd fallen asleep, likely trying to outrun the pain of his wound.

As day filtered into evening, Rose settled down too, putting a blanket she had found in a crate over Hink and wrapping up in one herself. But instead of sleeping, she set out bits and pieces of the puppets to see if she could fathom what they could do.

The puppet pieces fit together well enough, screwing in and hinging. She could make a roughly man-sized thing with feet, legs that included hinged knees, arms with all the bendy parts, a torso, and a neck. It had one hand with fully articulated fingers. She didn't know where the head was, and couldn't tell if it was intended to have one.

Also, there was that hole in the middle of the chest that didn't make a whole lot of sense, with its copper band binding the cavity's edge. Yes, one of those copper devices fit the hole, but how exactly did it power the thing? She'd assumed steam or maybe oil, but there was no evidence of either.

Plus, she hadn't found another of those glass-and-copper devices, just the broken one that Hink had in his pocket.

It would have to do.

Rose got up and took the few steps over to Hink.

She gently lifted the edge of his blanket and pushed his coat to the side. First, she checked to see if there was more blood from his wound than there should be. No, the handkerchief was soaked through but there was no blood on the floor beside him and he didn't seem to be leaking from anywhere else.

A wash of relief overtook her, and for a moment she just sat there, looking at his sleeping face. He didn't seem so worried and sullen when he slept, although pain pulled tight at the edge of his good eye and even at the corner of his eye patch.

"If you're waiting for a good time to kiss me, I'd say now should work," he said without opening his eyes.

"I thought you were asleep," Rose said.

"I was. Then you pulled near everything off me." Hink opened his eye and gave her half a smile. "You weren't going to pickpocket me, now, were you?"

"No!" she said too quickly. "Of course not."

"Rose Small." He shook his head, that grin growing wider. "You *were* going to pat my pockets. What are you after?"

"Nothing. I only came over here to check on your injury."

"For a girl so clever with her hands, you don't lie well. Go on now. Tell me. What were you after?"

"The copper device."

"Why?"

"After I cut a hole in the doors I got bored and started piecing things together."

"You cut holes in the doors?"

She nodded. "Can't tell where we're going though. Just snow-covered trees, fields, and a river or two."

He straightened a bit and grunted at the movement. Then he pulled a compass out of his pocket. "Let's find out before we're all out of daylight."

"I'd like to bind that wound."

"Do you have anything to bind it with?"

She pulled the strips of cotton she'd made out of a table linen she'd found in the crate.

"All right, let me get out of this coat."

She helped him take off his heavy outercoat; then with unspoken agreement, he stripped down to his undershirt too.

He shivered while Rose replaced the bloody handkerchief with a clean square of cloth, then wrapped his ribs, knotting the whole thing tightly enough to keep the wound closed. Or so she hoped.

"How's that feel?"

"Tight," he said. Then, "Fine. It should hold, and that's good. Now let's see where we are."

He got up to his feet with only a whispered swearword, then took a step. Finding himself steady, he shrugged back into his overshirt. When he was done, Rose handed him his coat and he pulled that on too, though she noticed he was breathing a little heavily by that point.

"Maybe you should rest," she said.

"No, I'm fine. Let's see what we can see." He walked over to the hole in the door, stepping around the puppet she'd pieced together. "That's what you've been fiddling with?"

"It's got my curiosity in a twist," she said. "So? See anything familiar?"

"I'd say . . ." He paused, looked away from the hole to the compass in his hand, then back out the hole again. "We're headed northwest by the lay of the sun. Still toward Iowa, by my estimation. We'll know soon enough."

"Why?"

"Can you hear it?" He paused. "The fans changed speed. We'll be on the ground before sunset, which"—he looked back out the door again—"will be in about two hours. Should be long enough."

"For what?"

"To see what that device on the floor can do." He drew out the glass-and-copper contraption and handed it to her.

Rose almost pulled her hand away.

Hink caught her slight hesitation and paused with the battery balanced over his palm. "Problem?"

"No. None." She held her hand out again.

"Rose. Tell me true."

"I don't like touching it."

"Because?"

"It . . . I can hear it in my head."

The silence that stretched out made her wish she'd told him that some other way. It sounded like something a crazy woman would say. And she'd been accused of being odd, strange, mad, for much of her life. She could handle people judging her, but she wasn't sure she could handle Hink thinking she was . . . frail in that way.

"Like a thought? A voice?" he asked. Not judging. Not yet. But not exactly believing her either.

"Never mind." She forced a short laugh. "I'm just being silly. Let me take that and see if it fits. . . ."

"Rose." A gentle reproach. "I told you you're the only woman who brings the truth out in me. I'd be pleased if you'd answer me truthfully. How can you hear this in your head?"

She swallowed hard to get the dry out of her throat. Then she told him something she'd never admitted to anyone. "When I was little, when I was first learning to talk, I used to tell my mother that I could hear the plants. That they said they were happy with sunlight, or water, or bugs. I told her I could hear the trees and flowers, and if I listened carefully, moss."

"Moss?"

"It's the quietest."

He didn't say anything else. Waiting. Waiting for her to continue proving she was tetched in the head.

"By the time I was seven, people in town were talking. I was adopted, which made me strange, and I was talking to trees. You can imagine how well that went over.

"I stopped telling my mother what the plants were saying. Stopped . . . just stopped talking about all of it. I found my way to Mr. Gregor's shop. The metal there in his blacksmith shop didn't talk to me. But my hands seemed to know what to do with it. How to make it change from a lump, or a cog, or a spring, into something wonderful. Something just as vital as the plants and other living things. It was still strange for a girl to spend her time in the blacksmith shop, but my mother allowed it for a while. Then she didn't even allow that."

Rose had hoped she could end her story there, but he was still waiting, as if he knew she wasn't done yet.

Good glim. Why did she have to hook up with a man who paid so damn much attention to a person? Wicks would have likely been bored by her story by now, and suggesting a book on botany or some such thing.

"I never stopped hearing green things talking about dirt, bugs, the weather. It's just a pleasant chatter in the background, like always being in a slightly crowded room.

"Only ever since I got hurt, since the tin bit of the Holder hit me, I don't think I've heard growing things. But when I put my hands on that . . . on that cold copper, it speaks to me in an overwhelming sort of way. Saying what it can do, saying what it might have been made for, like too many pictures rolling through my head all at once."

"Does it hurt you?" he asked.

"It's not painful, no. Just . . . just strange. I don't like it as much as I like hearing from plants. They're so simple in their needs and functions. This . . . that thing is very complicated."

"So what did it tell you it can do?"

"Power something, store something, trap something. It's copper and glass, obviously, but it's more. I think . . . I think there might be glim worked into that metal."

Hink nodded slowly. Odd thing was, that didn't seem to surprise him. "We've heard, well, I've heard that could be true. That someone may be working metal with glim. And glim-worked metal doesn't behave like other metal."

"Who have you heard that from?" she asked.

"The doves."

This time he waited for her reaction. She realized she wasn't as angry about it anymore. A spy network among those women made a lot of sense when she thought about it. Even with the . . . temptation present. "What have they heard it can do, glim metal?"

"That's the thing. No one's talking about what it can do. There are rumors, but nothing's been confirmed. And the rumors say it's best used as a weapon. A weapon that can be used to bring this country to its knees."

"That's a big weapon," Rose said.

"Or many small ones. Maybe say roughly the size of a man that can be shipped in parts in a railcar, then pieced together at every destination the rail, boats, or airships can reach."

Rose glanced at the puppet man she had constructed on the floor. Headless, it looked like some kind of gruesome toy.

"Do you think that's what that is?" she asked. "A weapon?"

"One way to find out." He lifted the copper device again. "Have you figured out exactly how it powers with this thing?"

"No. I have ideas, but . . ." She made up her mind. "Let me do it. If I see pictures of what it's made for, or what it can do, maybe that will help us figure it out."

"Are you sure, Rose?"

She nodded. "Won't be the first time I've heard funny things in my head. I can handle that."

Hink reluctantly rested the copper and glass in her hand. The cold and weight of it still surprised her. And then, just like before, a rush of knowing about the thing thrashed across her thoughts. Power, holding, storing, feeding, and other things: how it was made, pounded flat of cold copper and bound to glim by . . . something slippery there. She got the image of herbs and hands and . . .

"Witches!" she exhaled.

"Rose?" Hink put his hand on top of the copper piece, ready to pull it away. The noise from the device dampened down, like a plucked string with a palm over it.

"Witches. I think the glim was bound to the metal by witches. Oh, God. Do you think that was why Margaret was delivering the crates? Do you think they made this?"

"Hold on now, hold on. Are you sure it's a spell?"

"No. Yes. I mean, when I pick this up, I sense hands and voices and herbs. A sort of mixing up of the things I consider unique to the coven. I'm not sure it's a spell put on glim and metal to make them bind, but I'm sure the witches are involved."

"Can you tell who?" he asked.

Rose shook her head. "But the night before I left the coven I heard some of the sisters talking. Saying witches shouldn't choose sides in a war. Saying they shouldn't be involved in curses. Maybe it's not the same thing. Maybe it's not this." She held up the device. "But it might be. You haven't heard of the witches being involved in the homunculus thing have you?"

"There has been some whispering of deals made between different covens across the country and people who are involved in movements for and against the government. Covens choosing sides."

"Sides for what?"

"You know how Alabaster Saint was raising a force to see that the glim trade funneled through him to someone above him so they could start up a new war? I'm beginning to believe Alabaster Saint was just the tip of that sword. There are people who want this government overthrown. People who know just how vulnerable the United States is right now, since the war."

"Is it that serious?"

"Much more. Anything else you can tell me about that?" He nodded at the copper device.

She considered the device in her hand. "I don't get the impression this is all that needs to be together for that"—she pointed at the puppet on the floor—"to work yet. It seems to be missing something; some part of what it does isn't here yet."

"Think we can get some power into that thing on the floor now that it's all together?" he asked.

"Without repairing the glass, I don't think so. Maybe if we patch it, though. Is there any oilskin around here? Glue?"

"I'll look." Hink checked the labels on crates, broke open half a dozen, and finally found waxed parchment and glue.

Rose cut a piece of parchment to the correct size to patch the glass, then glued it in place.

Hink walked over to the puppet and groaned a little as he knelt next to it. "So what a ways do you think we should fit it this time?"

Rose knelt on the other side of the construction and handed him the battery. "This way, I think. Those wires should thread into the holes there, which isn't what we did last time. I don't understand what they're used for. One string at each compass point."

"Got it." He lowered the device, and made sure to thread each wire before dropping it down carefully in the metal band. It fit perfectly.

"How do you think it starts up?" he asked.

"Maybe . . ." Rose searched her memories, searched the pictures that had flashed through her mind. "I'd turn it counterclockwise."

"Might want to stand back," he said. Rose got on her feet and stepped back a bit. Hink twisted the device by the patched globe, one firm turn to the left.

And then the parchment and remaining glass lit up with the uncanny green-white glow of glim.

"Well," Hink said. "I think you were right. Well done, Rose Small."

She smiled and was going to walk closer so she could see what it might be capable of. But she didn't have to get any closer.

Because the puppet man twitched. All the limbs flexing one at a time like pistons pulling and pushing. Then it whirred somewhere inside, as if fans and cogs and springs got under power.

And then it stood up.

CHAPTER SEVENTEEN

Cedar walked up the wide polished stairs to the city hall library. Marble pillars supported an arched entryway to a tall double door wide enough for a wagon to pass through.

He was suddenly aware he hadn't had a decent hot bath in a couple weeks, and that his clothing was the sturdy sort made for the trail, not tailored wear appropriate for fine institutions such as this.

He removed his hat, smoothed his hair, and entered the building.

And a fine, grand building it was. The whole of it opened up to walls filled with books, only interrupted by six arched windows marching down both sides. Half a dozen tables took the center of the place, each with a padded chair, inkwell, and sheaves of paper at hand, and green-shaded lamps waiting for the user.

The wooden floor glowed softly in the evening light, a wide, rich red carpet taking up the centermost of the room. There were doors at the far end and, as he walked through the room, more to each side beyond the collection of books. The doors likely led to the trial room and smaller chambers, respectively.

He passed a small study area and noted Miss Dupuis inside.

She had removed her coat and rolled up her sleeves, not a state he usually found her in. She sat at the head of the table, head bent as she read over broadsheets and newsprint, several smaller record books opened and stacked on the table within her reach.

He knocked softly on the half-open door, old manners and habits from his days in universities falling upon him as easily as stepping into worn slippers.

She looked up, the frown fading as she recognized him. "Mr. Hunt. Please come in."

"How is the case going?" he asked as he entered the room, which was also filled with walls of books. He dragged his finger along the tabletop to the end chair, where he finally settled.

By glim, he was tired. And just the short walk through the building had left him winded. He needed sleep. A lot of it. Soon.

"There are some inconsistencies in the reports of what happened to Roy Atkinson all those years ago. Still . . ." She sighed and sat back. "It does not look good, Mr. Hunt. Not just that there was a man murdered, but that Mayor Vosbrough is the witness who can best testify to what he saw that day."

"Did he see the murder?" Cedar asked. "Was he there when the man was shot?"

"No. But he saw the Madders riding off to the mayor's manor with guns at the ready. And he overheard them saying they were going to end a man's life. The circumstantial evidence is a mile high. And since the judge was appointed by the mayor, who has a personal grudge against the Madders, I do not see how I can do much more than delay the hanging."

"Then that's what you'll do. Delay it. How many days do you think you can hold it off?"

"Two, perhaps. No more than that. Maybe not even that." She leaned forward and laced her fingers together, elbows resting on the table. "We should plan to break them out before then," she whispered.

"We'll have a plan in place by morning." He looked around the room and for a long moment savored being surrounded by knowledge.

Savored the silence of the place with the hustle of city life just beyond the walls, savored the connection to the life he'd given up years ago. He had been a different man then, but not in a bad way. He wondered if he'd still be happy with this sort of life, had he the chance for it.

"Do you miss it?" she asked. "The days you spent in places like this?"

"Very much so," he said quietly. He stood and held back a grunt at the ache in his bones. "Have you seen Mae or Father Kyne since you came to town?"

"Yes. They found the herbs they needed and went back to the church. They asked me to tell you to meet them there, if I saw you."

"Then I'll be on my way. Good luck to you, Miss Dupuis. In case the Madders haven't seen to thank you lately for taking on this task, let me extend my gratitude on their account."

She smiled. "Such fine manners, Mr. Hunt. A brief encounter with civilization suits you."

"Perhaps it does," he said as he walked out the door.

But that was not the full truth. The beast lingered just beneath his skin, growing strong as the moon grew fat. Just like a veneer of moonlight over shadow, his civilized manners were fleeting at best, and misleading at worst.

Back outside, he untied his horse from the watering trough, and swung up into the saddle. The wind shifted, bringing the first scents of the night—a razor cold sharpened by ice.

The clouds had thinned enough he could see the angle of the sun near the horizon. An hour perhaps until dark. No more.

He should turn back to the church. Give Mae and Father Kyne time to break the curse.

Instead, he guided his mount toward the jail. He needed some answers, and the Madders seemed to be the only people who could provide them for him.

The townspeople sensed the failing light too. The few, very few, children he saw on the street with parents were held firmly by the hand

and taken into homes where doors were shut, bolted, and shutters latched tight.

All before the sunset. There was a hurriedness to it, an apprehension in the air, a tangible fear. Fear of the night. Or of what happened in the night.

By the time he made it to the jail, the streets had half emptied out, leaving only the saloons and parlors full with laughter.

He rode around to the side of the jail, hitching his horse out of the way a bit, out of the wind that was hard rising.

He walked through the front door without knocking.

There was only one lawman there, Deputy Greeley, who stood behind a desk drinking coffee.

"Evening," Cedar said.

"Evening. Mr. Hunt, wasn't it? Something I can help you with?"

"I understand you have three men behind bars here, Alun, Bryn, and Cadoc Madder."

"That's so."

"I'd like to speak to them."

The wide-built deputy considered him, then sucked his teeth a moment, making the scar on the side of his face pucker. He placed his cup down and walked out from behind the desk. "I'll need your weapons. All you got on you, blades included."

Cedar complied, placing his guns and knives on the desk.

"They're back in the far holding cell at the end of the row. Put them together so it'd be easier to shoot the lot of them if needed."

Cedar nodded and strolled down the line of cells, passing by hard-eyed or desperate-looking men until he came to the cell at the end.

The Madder brothers had made themselves at home, somehow between the three of them managing to sling up three hammocks and turn the bunks into a table and chairs, at which they currently sat, playing poker.

"Nice of you to visit, Mr. Hunt," Alun called out cheerily. "Any news on how construction on the gallows is going?"

"Haven't looked in on it myself," Cedar said. "Could stop by tomorrow morning to let you know, if you want."

"I would indeed. There's been a startling rise in the preference toward the new drop systems. I myself would prefer a bucket I could jump off of, don't you agree, brothers?"

"I don't know," Bryn mused. "Snapped neck is quicker than slow strangulation."

"Bah," Alun said. "You want to go that easy? Crack and it's done? Rather kick and spit and make a scene as I choke to death. Last chance to be on stage. Shouldn't want to waste it."

"I didn't come here about the gallows," Cedar said before Cadoc could enter the argument.

"What then, Mr. Hunt?" Alun asked with a twinkle in his eye. "Something on your mind tonight?"

"Roy Atkinson."

The brothers stopped smiling. All of them, simultaneously, seemed more interested in their card hands.

"Don't know that I know a man by that name," Alun said.

"I wouldn't suppose you would." Cedar placed one hand around the thick cell bar. "Seeing as how he's dead."

"That so?" Alun said. "I'll take two."

Bryn thumbed two cards off the top of the deck.

"Did you kill him?" Cedar asked quietly enough; even the deputy out front shouldn't be able to hear him.

The brothers played their hands a bit longer, Bryn giving Cadoc four new cards, though Cedar was sure he hadn't asked for them, and Bryn taking only one.

"Aces high. Cadoc loses," Bryn said.

Cadoc heaved a sigh and pushed up to his feet. He walked over to the bars and stood in front of Cedar. "That man is dead. It is true. Not by our hands, though we helped with his crossing. He wasn't meant for this world, Mr. Hunt. He'd done his good. And we gave him his reward for it. The reward he asked for."

"Death?"

"Only to some eyes. To others, we gave him eternal life."

"Careful there, brother," Alun said quietly. "All the world is made of ears."

"Eternal life. Is that a fancy way of saying murder?" Cedar asked.

"We . . ." Cadoc looked up to the ceiling and frowned, as if working his way through his thoughts. Finally, he returned his gaze to Cedar and regarded him, for just a moment, as if he were gauging a stranger's trust-worthiness.

"You've seen things, Mr. Hunt. Been affected by a world most people can only imagine. One might think there are other curious things set near our world. Perhaps even other places that are wholly dif-ficult to discern. Like darkness hides in shadow, some things and places hide in plain sight."

Cedar tried hard not to sigh. He usually didn't much mind Cadoc's roundabout riddle answers. But tonight the moon was calling. Calling for blood.

"Just so." Cadoc nodded toward Cedar as if he had listened in on his thoughts. "Things beyond the naked eye that are nonetheless very real. Things that can speak and even . . . change us."

"What does this have to do with murder?"

"Why, everything," he said, clearly surprised. "Haven't you been listening to me?"

"You are difficult to parse on the best of days, Mr. Madder," Cedar said. "And tonight is not my best day."

"Tell it to a child, brother," Alun suggested while Bryn reshuffled the deck.

Cadoc raised his eyebrows in surprise. "Oh. Well, then." He patted

Cedar's hand like an uncle to a fond nephew. "Mr. Hunt. Cedar. We just made him appear dead so that he could live a different life. His time of being a mayor was over and only the illusion of death would release him from his promises."

"To whom?"

"To us. Or as much as."

"As much as," the other two brothers repeated.

"So you faked his death?" Cedar said. "But the mayor found him dead. Robbed. He put a price on your heads for it."

"That devil found what he wanted to find," Cadoc said. "No more."

"Did you break into the safe? Did you rob Atkinson?"

"No," Cadoc said. "Those valuables always belonged to Roy Atkinson. No one took them from him."

"So where is he?" Cedar asked. "If you tell me, I can bring him here. He can stand as witness, as proof that you didn't kill him. You'd go free."

"Free?" Alun said. "Why . . . I can't . . ." He exhaled one hard grunt. "Mr. Hunt," he began in the tone of an orator as he stood and strolled slowly over to the bars of the cell. "We do not wish to be free. If we wanted to be free, we wouldn't be in a jail cell, now, would we?"

"Can't say as I've ever seen the logic in what you do and don't do," Cedar said.

That made Alun grin. "Even so, this should make sense to you. We are here to buy you time. Time to fulfill your promise to us. A promise that if gone unfulfilled will mean disaster and death for many innocent people. A promise that you are apparently not doing since you are instead standing here talking about something long finished in days gone by."

"Buying me time? You don't think I can do my work if you're free?"

"I know you can't. It would quickly become . . . complicated between the mayor and all our companions. He's the kind of man who enjoys tying off loose ends, and that's what you would become to him. Right now, well, when you aren't under the jail roof, you are out of his notice. He doesn't give a damn about you, Mr. Hunt. But if you draw attention to yourself by fraternizing with us, he will notice. And when he notices, he will get in your way."

"You think I should fear him?" Cedar asked.

Alun nodded, but he did not smile. "You should, Mr. Hunt. You should. Now," he went on, as if they were discussing the weather, "the night is near to us. I'd say you'd best be on your way to do your important things for our country. On your way." He waved his hands as if shooing a child off on errands.

Cedar clamped his back teeth to keep from saying anything more. The beast was pushing for his body. The blood hunger was growing stronger and would soon be too close to the surface of his thoughts for him to control it.

"Is there anything more you can tell me about the mayor, or about the copper mine and devices he's built?"

"Copper mine?" Alun said.

"Devices?" Bryn asked.

"Have you seen these things?" Cadoc asked.

"Yes. In a mine outside of town. Vosbrough found me there, searching for the lost children."

"Mr. Hunt," Alun said gravely. "That is our promise to fulfill. You must find the Holder. You must. All else will fall into place once that is found. You do still think it's nearby, don't you?"

Cedar inhaled, caught his breath, and then was set upon by a coughing spell. He pulled his handkerchief out of his pocket and wiped his mouth.

The brothers were exchanging concerned looks. "Are you falling ill?" Bryn finally asked.

"It's the cold," Cedar said. "It doesn't agree with me."

"All the more reason to be done with this quickly," Alun said as he stumped back over to the table and picked up the new cards Bryn had dealt. "Go on now, Mr. Hunt. Go."

Cedar tucked his handkerchief back in his pocket and left the Madders to their cards.

"They're an odd bunch, aren't they?" Deputy Greeley said.

Cedar reclaimed his weapons and shook his head. "You don't know the half of it. Good night, officer."

Cedar left the jail and glanced at the sky. The sun dipped low, nearly on the horizon. He might have cut this too close.

He pointed the horse toward the church and somehow found his way down the right streets and alleys and finally to the lane that led to the church.

By the time he had taken the rudimentary care to put his horse away, that luxurious promise of losing his body to the beast was lapping at the back of his mind.

He still had hold of his thoughts, of his reasoning. But it was a tenuous thing.

He didn't remember walking to the church. Didn't remember going through the kitchen. His next clear thought was when his knees hit the floor—a cushion on the floor—in a room that was unfamiliar to him.

"Calm and clear," Mae was saying. "Trust in my voice, Cedar, and I will lead you to rest.

"Rest," she said again from behind him. He tested his wrists. Tied together at his back. It was a thin string, maybe even a thread, but for some reason, he could not muster the strength to break it.

He waited for Mae to walk around in front of him.

And she did. To his eyes, Mae was brighter than moonlight, and infinitely more beautiful. She smiled, searching his eyes for what was left of his reason—which was a lot more than he expected at this point—and he smiled at her.

"Hello, Mae," he said softly. The beast wanted him to say more. To claim her as mate. To take her in his arms as a man does a woman. But that thin thread at his wrists crossed over the blood moving beneath his skin, and cooled it. Giving him reason. Giving him thought.

"Hello, Cedar," she said. "Do you trust me this night?"

"Yes. And more," he replied.

"Do you give yourself to me?"

That took longer to answer, the push of blood and heat and want stealing away his words. He knew she saw his desire for her, his need. But she waited. Needing his words to use her spells.

"Always."

"Then my hands will hold you and guide you. Rest, Cedar Hunt, and give the night to me."

Cedar wanted to answer, but her words, and the spell they carried, wrapped around him. There was darkness. And then there was nothing else.

CHAPTER EIGHTEEN

"Um," Rose said, since she couldn't think of anything else to say now that the puppet creation was on its two legs and standing there like a soldier awaiting orders.

"Don't move," Hink said quietly behind it. "We don't know what it can do."

"But it doesn't even have a head."

"Lots of things don't have heads and still do a lot of harm," he said. "Back away from it slowly."

"You just told me not to move."

"Well, now I'm saying back away." He pulled his gun.

"You're not going to shoot it, are you?"

"Not unless it shoots first. Or maybe before that."

"Oh, no you won't, Captain. I just made the poor thing. I won't watch you blow it to bits."

"It ain't a baby, Rose."

"I know what it is and isn't. More than you do. And I also happen to think it isn't a threat to us."

"On what grounds?"

"It has no mind."

"Neither does a gun."

"Neither do you, Lee Hink. Listen to me," she said. "There's nothing to tell it what to do. No steering device. No telegraph wire, no levers or pulleys sending it to do anything. I don't even think it could take a single step if it tried." To prove her point, she walked toward it.

"Woman, you want me to shoot you too, so you and I can still be alive to argue this issue? I said stop moving."

"Just wait. For once, think first, shoot second." She put her hand on the puppet's shoulder, careful to be beside it and not in front of it just in case she was mistaken about what it could do.

The puppet soldier did nothing.

"It has no head," she said again to Hink, who had walked up behind it, gun still drawn. "No trigger, no driver. A power source, yes. But that's all it has. Put your gun down."

Hink scowled at her, and she gave him a wide-eyed look. "You aren't afraid of a puppet, are you?" she asked.

"I'm not afraid of anything," he snarled. He slammed the gun into the holster and hissed, likely at the pain from jostling his wounded side so hard.

"But you," he said, "are too trusting."

"I just know what goes into the things I make. And this thing—soldier maybe?—this soldier isn't complete enough to do harm. Like I said, something's missing."

Hink walked around to stand in front of it, and Rose backed up too. They stood there a while, tipping their heads and staring at it, like two patrons in an art gallery trying to see the craftsmanship in a painting.

"Gimbals well with the shift of the car," Hink noted.

"Has a sort of ball and rocker system set up in the ankles and torso. Keeps it standing."

"So you think it's made for ships? Sea or air?" he asked.

"I think watching it keep balance proves it can at least stand a deck," Rose said.

"What else do you think it can do?"

Rose shook her head. "If I had to make a guess? It walks like a man, or does the kind of work a man does, but doesn't tire until the . . . the battery there runs down. It could be a worker. For a factory or a mine of some sort?"

"I'd think it would cost too much to make a thing like that, metal and rubber and wires. Men are cheap. Maybe it's something for the rich. A toy?" he said. "A servant?"

She shrugged.

"How long do you think the power in it lasts?" he asked.

"I don't have the foggiest idea."

Silence as they stared at it some more.

Finally, Hink said, "Well, I'm done being baffled by it. Let's turn it off."

"I agree. No need for it to just stand there doing nothing. Also, it's giving me the goose chills."

Hink grinned. "I thought you said you weren't afraid of it."

"I'm not afraid. Just unnerved, I think. It has no head."

"There is that," he agreed. "Do you suppose I just turn that orb the other way to unscrew it?"

"I think so, yes."

Hink walked up to it and did so. The entire thing stiffened, then slumped, falling forward. Hink caught it, grunted a bit. "Heavier than it looks," he said as he lowered it to the ground. That he did gently, as if it contained nitroglycerine.

He stood back up, the copper and glass device balancing on his palm. That had come loose a lot easier than Rose expected.

"Did you break the wires?" she asked.

"Which wires?"

"The copper ones."

He gave her a look. "Rose, all the wires are copper."

"Oh, for heaven's sake. The copper wires attached to the battery."

He lifted the thing, held it so the lamplight caught it and studied the edges. "Nope. Doesn't appear I did. Four wires, just like before. Do you have any complaints if I keep it in my pocket?"

"Other than it's not yours? No complaint from me."

"Come on now, Rose. Tell me you don't like a man who isn't afraid to just reach out and grab what he wants out of life."

"Oh, sure. Confidence in a man is one thing. Thievery—"

The train car tilted so hard she was thrown off her feet and landed on her back end and elbows, then slid down the sloping floor and slammed into the door.

Hink was upended right behind her but somehow managed to land by locking his arms on either side of her, so he didn't completely crush her when they collided.

The puppet came sliding toward them next, and Rose had a moment to be grateful the door she had fallen against was locked tight on the outside.

Then the dead body started speeding their way.

"Move!" Rose yelled. "Dead body, dead body!"

Hink pushed to one side, rolling, and grabbed ahold of her coat lapels as he did so, yanking her aside with him.

The puppet soldier thunked into the door where they had been only moments before. Then the dead body smacked into it with a meaty thump.

Rose suddenly realized she was sitting, well, mostly lying, across Hink's body, their legs tangled in a most improper manner.

"Hey," she breathed.

"Ma'am," he said with a suggestive grin. "I do believe we have gotten ourselves into a bit of a jumble."

"You're going to kiss me, aren't you?" she asked.

"I'm confident I am." He did just that, and Rose was not shy about kissing him back. This was it, the last straw. She could feel it in every inch of her bones. Her heart was well and truly set on this man. He might infuriate her, test her patience, but she loved him. Not just because he was the first wild-minded fellow she'd met outside her little town.

She loved him for challenging her, for caring for her, for the wild, adventurous troubles he seemed to constantly land himself in.

Plus, he had a sweet airship. She couldn't deny that added just a bit to her feelings for him. The *Tin Swift* was a place she could belong. A job she would love, running the boilers across every sky in the world. And Captain Hink was a man she could happily spend her life with.

All these thoughts flickered through her mind in a rush, then were replaced with this: his mouth pressing gently against her lips, catching at the curves of her with delightful attention to detail.

Just to see what he'd do, she opened her mouth a bit and gently bit his bottom lip.

What he did was groan, but not in painful sort of way. Then his mouth was over hers with a bit more intention and he did something with his tongue that made her lose all breath and all thought, and go wobbly at the knees.

She liked the feel of him, the taste and scent of him. She savored his body, strong beneath her, arms possessive around her.

And then the entire world crashed around them.

They were untangled and unkissed in a most startling way. One second the freight car and everything inside it went weightless and stirred up; the next second everything was thrown to the ground with a bang.

"Rose," Hink called out. "Are you okay?"

She took in several hard breaths before she could push words out of her lungs. "I am. I am fine."

She had landed against a wooden crate and scratched up her back a bit, and lost the belt on her coat, which might have been Hink's doing, but other than straw in her hair and stuck to her dress, she seemed to have all her limbs in the right places.

Hink pushed himself up off the dead body, and straightened his coat, checking for the copper device in his pocket.

"You have a gun on you?" he asked quietly.

Rose checked to see if her gun was still tucked in her pocket. "Yes," she said. "I have it."

"Good girl. Now come stand here with me, back to mine, facing that door." He pointed.

She walked toward him, the tone of his voice telling her this was not the time to ask questions. She did it anyway. "Why?"

"Because we just landed. Any minute now someone's going to open one of these doors to see if their freight is intact. And they aren't going to like finding us inside."

She said no more, but stood, back-to-back with her airship captain, U.S. Marshal, and love. Rose Small raised her gun, cocked back the hammer, and waited for the door to bust open.

CHAPTER NINETEEN

O ut of the blackness came moonlight. And from that moonlight, came Mae. Cedar felt very, very relaxed, more rested than he had felt in at least a decade. There was no pain. It was a wonderful sensation, and he knew it would end soon.

All good dreams must bow to the morning light.

"It is done," Mae said. She frowned slightly and pressed a cool cloth against his forehead. "The spell is complete. Are you awake? Cedar, can you hear me?"

"Yes," he said, from both far away and near. Something, something wasn't right with his body. He felt, strangely, as if he were in two separate places at once. It was . . . disconcerting.

"Good," Mae said. "Very good. Let me help you sit."

She did more than help, as Cedar lost track of where up and down were located while the room seemed to swing into place around him.

There was something at his back—a pillow. And he was sitting on a blanket spread out on the floor. Next to him lay Wil. Only Wil was not in wolf form as he should be. He was once again his brother, needing a shave and a haircut, asleep and covered by a heavy blanket. Around his neck was a thin thread, and on that thread was a cross.

"What?" Cedar cleared his throat and then looked back at Mae. The room didn't spin this time. Even though it had only been moments, he felt less split in two. "Did you break it? Mae," he said, unable to hide the relief in his tone, "did you break the curse for both of us?"

"Temporarily," she said offering him a cup of water, which he drained. "The spell will last a few hours. Perhaps six or seven. That means you'll need to return to the church before dawn."

"What happens when the spell wears off?" he asked.

"We don't know."

"We?"

She nodded at Father Kyne. He lay on a simple cot, breathing heavy enough Cedar could clearly hear each inhalation and exhalation. His lips were moving. Praying, Cedar realized. He was saying prayers.

He felt something cool at the hollow of his neck and touched it with his finger. He too wore a cross.

"How? What . . . part in this has Kyne taken? Is he holding the curse at bay?"

"He is carrying your burden," Mae said. "As is his faith to carry the burden of his fellow man. The binding of the curse hasn't been broken; it has been . . . diverted to Father Kyne. I didn't think it would work. But he insisted to have faith. Faith in God. Faith that a Pawnee curse would rest a while with him, if invited. Faith that God would help him remain strong. So you can hunt for the children. And for the Holder tonight."

"Wil? Why isn't he under the curse?"

"The curse was cast on you both. It was meant for you both to carry, each brother light and darkness. We could not lift it and bind it to Father Kyne for one without needing to do so for the other."

"Is the preacher carrying both curses? The . . . the weight of both?"

Mae nodded. "I have eased it some, and could only bind it to him in the most shallow of manners. Nothing bone deep. Nothing blood deep. Nothing that will twist his mind. Just . . ." Here she cast about for words to describe what exactly she did with magic that no other witch could do as well. "It is bound to his faith, for lack of a better way of saying it. To his will. As long as he does not waver in this task, the curse and binding will hold. But it will tire him. And when he tires, the spell will unravel."

"Is Wil awake?"

"Yes," a hoarse voice said from the blankets next to him. "Wil is awake. And naked. And hungry. Again."

Cedar couldn't help but smile. He had seen his brother too briefly over the last few months, only for the three days over the new moon each month. So this, nearly two weeks before he should have a chance to talk with him, was a welcome happenstance indeed.

"I offered to put pants on you in wolf form. You didn't seem interested," Cedar said.

Wil chuckled, then coughed. Mae walked over to him and handed him a cup of water.

He drank, then handed her back the cup. "Mrs. Lindson, you're looking lovely this evening. I am sorry to catch you in my unavailables."

"Thank you, Wiliam, but don't worry about that. I thought we agreed you would call me Mae."

He rubbed his hand over his eyes, scrubbing at them for a good bit. "That's right. We did, didn't we? My apologies, Mae?"

"None needed," she said. "How are you feeling?"

"Human. As I prefer. Thank you. For that." He smiled, and that charm he'd possessed since birth shone through. "Though I have a strong hankering for cinnamon. I don't suppose there's a stick of it anywhere around these parts? Or a dash of it in tea?"

"Might have something in my coat pocket," Cedar said.

"Did you hear what it is we intend to do this night?" she asked as she found Cedar's coat hanging on the chair, and rummaged in his pocket.

"I think so. The Madders are set on us hunting the Holder, because that is what the Madders are always set upon, near as I can tell." He pushed up and sat, resting his back against the wall without a pillow to ease him. "Father Kyne is hoping we will search for the children. We'll be looking for the children, won't we, brother?"

He rolled his head to the side and gave Cedar a knowing look.

Cedar nodded. "Children first." He didn't have to add *of course*. After he'd suffered his own daughter's death, he'd lost his strength to brush the pain of any child aside. If he could help, he would. "We hunt the Holder at the end of the night, if we have we have time."

"You never disappoint," Wil said, not unkindly.

"Put on your pants," Cedar said. "I'll find your boots."

Cedar stood, and was glad there was no pain. He had expected to suffer for this respite of the curse he had carried for so many years. But this was Mae's spell. She had yet to cause him pain.

"Your things are here, Wil. I brought them from the wagon." Mae placed a folded stack of clothes on the blanket. "Boots are by the door. Also, this." She handed him the small cinnamon hard candy Cedar had kept in his pocket.

"Oh . . . you are an angel," Wil said as he reverently pulled on the candy's wax wrapping and held up the disk of sugar like a man studying fine wine.

"Thank your brother. He's the one who remembered it last town we stopped through. I'll leave you to dressing."

Wil popped the candy in his mouth. "God. Oh, God. This . . ." He closed his eyes, rolling the candy around in his mouth. "How did you know?" he sighed.

"You always want cinnamon when you're back in your own skin."

"True. I tried it in wolf once." He frowned. "It was like licking a rusty pipe. Hideous. But this, this is so . . . so . . ." He just closed his eyes again, a smile across his face.

Mae walked out of the room and shut the door behind her.

Cedar stared at the door for a moment, wondering if casting the spell had fatigued or harmed her. She didn't appear to be overly tired, but then, she often kept such things behind a calm exterior.

"Have you asked her yet?" Wil asked.

COLD COPPER • 209

"Hmm?" Cedar said, coming out of his thoughts. "Asked her what?" He reached over for his gun belt hanging on the wall peg.

"You know what."

Cedar did indeed. He had confessed last month in those scant hours when he and Wil could converse that he wanted to marry Mae. He had also said he didn't know when to ask her.

"It hasn't even been a year since her husband passed," Cedar said, plucking up his ammunition belt. "I don't want her to feel I'm expecting anything of her."

"You do see the way she looks at you, don't you?"

"Wil. There isn't time for that now."

"There is tonight. And I'll have plenty of time to convince you that there is an honest woman who I'd love to share our family name with, in a brotherly way."

"I am aware. Very aware."

"So then, brother. Do I need to also remind you that most women won't wait forever? Not in this quickly changing world. What if some handsome man comes along and persuades her away with his wiles?"

"Wil. I have never taken your advice when it comes to matters of the female persuasion. I see no need to be doing so now."

"Life changes quickly, brother. As I reckon it, you and I change rather quickly ourselves." He chuckled under his breath and stood up, stretching up onto his toes and reaching fingers toward the ceiling. "Love being tall. Love it. Don't love being unfurred in this weather, though." He shivered, then quickly dug about for his undergarments, and pulled those on, followed by breeches, shirt, and an overshirt.

"Socks. I've been looking forward to these." He sat down and bunched up a pair of thick wool socks, then dragged them over his bare toes. "So . . . snuggly. Ah, my loves, how I've missed you. Seriously and completely. I'd wear six pairs, if I had them."

"Your feet wouldn't fit in your boots," Cedar said. Wil was like this when he took man form. No, Wil had always been like this. Enthusiastic about life, with a delight for all sorts of things. His attitude was infectious.

"Almost wouldn't care," Wil said. "But this. This is a boot." He held one up and kissed the top of it, then shoved his foot into it. "Plenty of room in the toe, soft on the arch, royal of bearing. Built for a king."

"Hurry up, your majesty," Cedar said. "There's work to be done."

"Tell me you don't love a good boot after tromping around barepads for days on end." Wil stood and buckled his belt.

"True. Although I'd go without, as long as I could have a cup of coffee."

"Right, of course. So would I. Speaking of which, are we in luck?"

"We are. Kitchen's this way."

"So is Mae, I believe. How are your knees?"

"Why?" Cedar asked.

"Just wondering if you're capable of a bended one."

"Won't be asking her tonight, Wil."

"If we don't keep hold on the life we want, it's likely to just wander away."

"It's been a while since I've heard you in a philosophical mood," Cedar said. "Must be the full moonlight's set you romanticizing."

Wil laughed. "My words are falling on deaf ears, I'm afraid."

"For now," Cedar said, settling his coat over his shoulders and buttoning it up. "We have hunting to do."

Wil strapped on his gun and gun belt before shrugging into his coat, tugging it straight, and then latching it closed.

Making a point not to meet Cedar's gaze, Wil said, "Last I knew there were no laws against a man hunting more than one thing at once."

"I suppose," Cedar said.

Wil hooked laces up his boots and pulled them tight. "So you're still not going to talk to her tonight?"

"There are children to save, Wil. Everything else can wait." Cedar gave his brother a smile. "But the night's young. I'm of a positive considerance you're not going to stop talking about it until dawn."

Wil grinned as he adjusted his hat. "Reckon you know me pretty well."

They left the room and found Mae waiting in the kitchen. She had on her long coat, a pair of breeches tucked into her boots, and a hat pulled tight to her chin. She was also carrying a shotgun.

"Are you ready then, gentlemen?"

"I'd be wasting my time asking you to stay, wouldn't I?" Cedar said.

"Yes." She opened the door. "I've hitched the mules to the wagon and filled it with blankets. If we find the children, we'll need some way to bring them back. I promise I won't get in your way."

"I've never once worried about that," Cedar said. Then, "Are you sure you shouldn't stay with Father Kyne? To see that he's tended?"

Wil tugged on a thick pair of gloves and worked on settling a length of wool around his throat to cover the grin he was giving Cedar. *Ask her,* he mouthed.

Mae had, thankfully, turned her attention to the weather through the door's window.

"Thank you, Mr. Hunt," she said as she drew her scarf around the bottom half of her face, "for thinking of him. But he will be fine. Now. Let's hunt for the children so you can hunt for the Holder."

"Have I mentioned how I always enjoy your company, Mae?" Wil asked. "And my brother, he just can't stop talking about how much he likes having you around." Wil stepped outside and gave Cedar a big wink before offering his arm to help steady Mae across the icy ground to the wagon.

Cedar sighed and followed them, closing the door behind him.

For a moment, the world slipped and his vision split in two. He was outside the door to the church and he was inside, lying in a bed, staring at the ceiling, the beast calling his name.

He shook his head and the double vision faded. But for that second, he had seen through his own eyes and through Father Kyne's. He glanced at Wil, who hadn't missed a step. He must not be experiencing the same thing.

He considered saying something, but decided this was too rare an opportunity to turn away from. They'd hunt for as long as they were able.

Mae had seen to it there were two horses saddled along with the wagon.

After making sure Mae was settled in the driver's seat of the wagon, Wil swung up on one of the horses. "I've missed this," he said as Cedar, already in his saddle, sent his mount across the snow. "Would you like me to take the lead?"

"No," Cedar said. "We can't strike out into the night on a gut feeling. Not in this weather. Mae?" He took his horse to the side of the wagon. "Is there any kind of spell that might locate the children? I've done some hunting and found no real signs of them today other than frozen footprints by the river."

"I don't think so," she said. "I tried scrying for them when you were in town." She shook her head. "Father Kyne gave me this."

She handed him a pink ribbon. "He said it belonged to Florence, the Peters' daughter. He didn't know if it would be useful. Perhaps for a scent?"

Cedar took the ribbon fluttering in her fingers and held it in his palm. The song of the Strange rose soft from that thin strip of silk. The Strange had touched this ribbon. Maybe they had touched the girl who it once belonged to.

He offered the ribbon to Wil. As soon as Wil grasped it, his eyebrows hitched up. "Strange," he said. "Think you can follow that?"

Cedar nodded. "You can't?"

"Usually I'd say yes, but this"—he pointed at his chest—"change makes me a little uncertain about the whole thing."

"Just tell me if you see something I don't." Cedar took the ribbon back and placed it in his pocket next to the small piece of copper.

He turned his horse down the lane following the hint of Strange song caught and muffled in the cold wind.

Wil's senses might feel unreliable, but Cedar's were very foggy. He could hear the Strange, he could smell them, but he didn't see a single creature.

When they reached the end of the lane, Wil spoke. "Do you see that?"

Cedar scanned the darkness. "No."

"There are ribbons of light, like trails tracing along the street."

"I don't see anything."

Wil dismounted.

"What are you doing?" Cedar asked.

"I'm going to find out what they are." Wil stepped into the center of the street, spreading his bare hands as if trying to catch the nature of the wind upon his fingertips.

"What do you see?" Cedar asked.

"A thin pink string of light runs down the street. There's other lights, like ribbons in all sorts of colors, coming from all the roads to this one. And none of them are higher than my waist."

"Do you think it's the Strange passing through?"

Wil shook his head. "I hear singing, Cedar. Children singing. Laughing. Some are crying. When I stand in these ribbons, I hear their voices. They walked this way, drawn away in the night. Lost."

"Are you sure?" Cedar asked. "Finding them shouldn't be this simple."

"I know." Wil walked back over to his horse, shaking his hands out as if shedding water. "You really can't see that?"

"No."

"So?" Wil asked. "What do you reckon?"

"It's a trail. A trail the children walked. One ribbon for each child, pouring out of the heart of this city."

"That's . . . convenient," Wil said. "So you think the Strange made these trails? To lure us?"

"Possibly," Cedar said.

"We're going to follow them, aren't we?"

"We shouldn't."

Wil's eyes crinkled up to make room for his grin. "It is the only trail. If it's a trap, let's spring it and move on to the next." Wil clicked his tongue and urged his horse down the road following the lines of light.

Mae brought the wagon up beside Cedar. "He's always so full of fire," she said, not unkindly.

"That he is," Cedar agreed. "And it has often burned him. He says there's a clear trail that the children, many, many children followed this way. We're going to follow it."

"You sound concerned."

"I can't see it, and he can. I know Wil and I perceive the Strange differently, but"—he peered at the road, and at the city ahead of them—"I see nothing of the Strange. At all. Even though it is the full moon."

"Maybe it's the spell we cast?" Mae offered.

Cedar shrugged. "And to find a trail lit up bright as a torch and nearly on our doorstep? It's too easy."

"You think it's a trap?"

"It seems likely to be."

"And Wil?"

"Like you said, he's filled with fire."

"So are you," Mae said. "You just keep a closer mind on the draft."

Cedar smiled, then set his horse after his brother.

They followed the road in relative silence, the only sounds coming from the city itself and the occasional high drone of airships landing in the field north of town. They passed no more than a handful of souls, a worker coming in on foot from the coal mines, a cart leaving town to farms and fields more distant.

Other than that, it was as if the town were intent on making itself deserted, hidden from what it knew roamed the night.

Wil kept a running report on the trail. It took a sharp turn, looped into a muddled knot, and strung in ragged tatters down a single street into town.

"I'm beginning to think there might be a wild goose at the end of this chase," Wil said with a grin.

"You're the one who wanted to spring the trap," Cedar reminded him. "You know the Strange. They'll lead a man down a twisted road, then right off the edge of a mountain, if they can catch his eye with a shining light."

"This doesn't look like no will-o'-the-wisp," Wil noted.

"I know," Cedar said. "That's why we're still following it."

The street widened and grew toothy with cobblestones. One thing the city did well was keep the roads mostly free of ice and snow. But it was full dark now; there would be no need to have workers clearing the roads if there wasn't going to be anyone using them.

They reached an intersection and Cedar pulled his horse to a stop.

A sound was rising, far off and high, but not in the sky and not carried by the wind. It was growing louder and louder from the earth beneath his feet. Loud enough his and Wil's horses both whickered and fidgeted, unsettled.

Cedar dismounted, pressed his hand against his horse's neck to calm him, then knelt, spreading his fingers out across the street.

The sound wasn't anything he'd heard before. It rumbled, but also hissed and crackled like lightning snapping the sky. And behind it all was a single chord of notes, the trumpet of some great beast.

Something—something big—was beneath the city.

And it was moving, growling, waking up.

"Tell me you hear that," Cedar said.

"I do," Wil said.

"Mae, do you hear anything unusual?" Cedar asked.

"No." She paused, then said, "Yes, like a horn of some kind?"

"Yes," Cedar said. "If you can hear it, then it's not a Strange song."

"Which I couldn't be happier about," Wil said. "Their songs lead to dances that last for the rest of your days. Hate to wear out these boots. I've barely worn them in."

"I wouldn't worry," Cedar said. "They wouldn't dance you to death. The Strange only like pretty men."

Wil let out a loud laugh and Cedar couldn't help but join him. He'd missed his brother. Missed his laugh. Even though this was not the best of their times, it was still time together. Valuable. And the longer they spent hunting Strange or, hell, the Holder across these states, the more of a chance they'd have to pay on their promises, break the curse for good, and make their days their own again.

He was looking forward to many long years together with his brother. And with Mae.

"It sounds like gears to me," Cedar said. "It might be the generator we saw in the copper mine."

"But why would it make this sound? What could it be powering?" Wil asked.

"I don't know," Cedar said.

"Huh," Wil said. "Maybe they know."

Cedar glanced up at his brother. He was looking west, down the road that jagged between brick and wooden buildings, and beyond that, the fields, forests, and river.

"Who?"

Wil glanced at him, worried. "The Strange. You don't see them? There's"—Wil paused—"dozens. Ghostly, but real. Well, real as they get without bodies to possess. Tall as chimney stacks and thin as thread, short and squat like toads."

"I hear them howling, screaming," Cedar said. "But I can't see them."

"That's . . ." Wil lost his voice for a moment, swallowed the words back into place and tried again. "Not right. Something's wrong with them. Something's very wrong with the Strange."

"Talk to me, Wil."

"They're coming this way fast. Real fast."

"Mae, keep tight hold of the mules," Cedar said. His own horse was dancing and snorting, trying to bolt. Cedar tightened his grip on the reins, but didn't even try to swing up into the saddle.

The curse that Father Kyne was holding fell around him like an icy cloak. His vision split again. He saw the room where Father Kyne was standing. And watched as he strode through the church and into the night air. He felt the push of the beast, urging Father Kyne out into the night. Needing to kill the Strange. Needing to hunt and run.

"Get out of the way, you damn fool!" a man's voice yelled.

Cedar blinked and it seemed that the entire world came burning back around him with singular heat and color and light. The vision of Father Kyne was gone.

"Something wrong with your ears?" the man yelled again.

Cedar peered down the other end of the street behind him. Seven men stood in the street, wearing dark-lensed goggles, heavy leather coats and boots, and overlarge gloves more suited to smelting metal. They held wide-muzzled shotguns equipped with copper tubes that connected to a box, which was slung over their shoulders like bulky canteens.

A soft green fire licked around the edges of those copper tubes. Glim. Those guns were powered by glim.

"Mr. Hunt?" a familiar voice asked. "Is that you?"

Cedar recognized the figure driving the steam carriage at the back of the line of men. It was Sheriff Burchell. He also wore goggles, a heavy coat, and a thick scarf around his neck. He carried a slightly different version of the copper-box gun, this one slender with a bayonet fixed at the end.

"I'd move aside, Mr. Hunt. There's trouble in the air tonight, and you don't want to be on the wrong end of our guns."

He said it affably enough, but he was dead serious.

Cedar managed to lead his horse over to Mae's wagon, which she had tucked up tight against a feedstore.

Wil followed, silent in the darkness. He somehow kept his horse in hand, and stopped next to Cedar.

"Who's that?" Wil said quietly.

"The sheriff," Cedar replied.

"Don't like him."

"Neither do I," Cedar said. Then, "Is there something I can help you with, Sheriff?"

"Have an entire posse of men to help me, Mr. Hunt," Burchell called out over the huffing boiler of his cart. "And you're about to see just what my forces can do."

The rumbling beneath their feet grew louder, and brought with it the eerie trumpet call that stroked higher and higher until it was a piercing whine.

The Strange screamed and sobbed. They were crying. Whether from pain or fear or loss, Cedar did not know. But the lawmen spread their feet as if bracing for a wave, and toggled the triggers on their guns.

"Steady," the sheriff said, his voice loud and strong. "And . . . fire!"

Seven guns shot out lace-fine netting that crackled with pure bolts of glim.

Seven nets caught seven Strange. And since the Strange were little more than spirits, once the copper and glim struck them, they lit up with an eerie green glow and even Cedar could see them.

Mae gasped, seeing, Cedar knew, for just that moment, the Strange as he and Wil always saw them. He supposed the men with guns saw them too.

"Draw!" the sheriff shouted. "Ready for the rush."

The men reeled in the nets, fast as starving fishermen, dragging the Strange down the street toward them. Once the nets were in reach, they triggered another lever on the gun and the bellows on the side pumped, sucking the Strange into the copper box.

With a flick of levers, the nets were ratcheted back into the firing chambers and the copper wires snapped with glim again.

"They'll never be fast enough for the rest," Wil said.

"The rest?" Cedar asked.

Wil pointed. "The Strange. That mob of them. You don't see them?"

Cedar shook his head slowly. "No."

Wil gave him a sideways glance. "That's not like you."

"Maybe it's the magic," Cedar said. "How many Strange do you see?"

"Dozens. They aren't crying anymore. They're attacking."

Cedar did not move. Neither did Wil. It was disconcerting, almost surreal, to just stand aside while other men fought the Strange, Strange who only became visible to Cedar when the nets struck true.

Those goggles the men wore gave them some kind of sight that picked Strange off the bones of shadows. And those guns fired again, nets snapping, glim crackling, and men reeling in their eerie catch.

But there were twice as many Strange as there were men.

The sheriff stood behind the wheel of the buggy. He'd put his gun down and was tapping on a telegraph key mounted near the buggy's steering wheel. His fingers flew through code, slinging messages.

Just before the wave of Strange should be upon him, just when Wil told Cedar they had surged past the men he hid behind, suddenly the Strange were gone.

"Blown out like a light," Wil said.

At that same instant, the moment when the sheriff's fingers stiffened to a halt, the underground call went silent.

Only the ticking metal of the net guns' gears rolling the remaining nets into position broke the quiet. Then, from some far off corner in the city, a piano picked out a rambling tune.

The sheriff laughed. "Well done, gentlemen! Well done, indeed. I'd say the citizens of Des Moines are safe for the night. We'll patrol the streets until dawn, but I'd wager we won't see more of those nightmares."

"Is that what those things were?" Cedar asked. "Nightmares?"

Sheriff Burchell tugged at his goggles, and let them fall down into the scarf he wore around his neck. Across the darkened intersection of roads, Cedar could see his smile, friendly as a coyote.

"What you just saw was some of the troubles a civilized town falls upon in this modern age. That was the Strange, Mr. Hunt. I'd think you'd have run across them in your travels."

"That was more than I've ever seen in once place," Cedar said. "What brings them on like that? Coal? Or is it want for those fancy copper-and-glim guns you have there?"

The sheriff paused, still smiling, but there was something different about how he held himself, as if steel had staked his spine in place.

"Maybe it's nothing but the moon, Mr. Hunt," he said, his voice barely glossing over the anger he held in check there. "You know what an odd master it can be. Brings out all sorts of unnatural things at night. Unnatural things in men too."

"And children?" Cedar asked. "Do you suppose the full moon sends children wandering out of town into the cold arms of winter?"

"I wouldn't know, Mr. Hunt," he said with what almost sounded like real concern. "I've seen to it that we have patrols of men on the streets every night. Folk have taken to tying their children to the bedpost and locking every door and window. And still there are empty cradles in the morning. I don't think that's the moon's fault. I blame the very creatures we just burned off of the street."

"Burned?"

"Those guns carry boxes packed with hot coals. Once the Strange are sucked in there, they never come back out. Like straw up a chimney flue."

"You've thought this through," Cedar noted.

"You can thank the mayor for that. He knows what's best for this town, and sets to seeing that it's done. But now we have roads to cover. Good night to you and yours, Mr. Hunt."

He pressed the throttle down, and the carriage rumbled to life, the back stacks puffing a thick cloud of smoke that rolled upward like the edge of an ocean wave, silvered by the moonlight. The other men turned and followed him.

"Well, he was unpleasant, wasn't he?" Wil said.

"He knows something," Mae said. "Something about the children, I think. But he is right: there is no power the full moon can give to take children away."

"What about a spell?" Cedar asked.

"Witches?" Mae didn't sound very surprised. Cedar wondered if she'd been thinking that could be a possible cause for the children's disappearance for some time now. "It's . . . I think there are some spells that can send someone wandering. And the full moon brings most magic strength. But magic doesn't lend to wicked ends. The very practice of magic is peaceful, gentle. Tried and true."

"What did you just say?" Cedar asked, as a memory slipped through his mind.

"Magic is gentle?"

"The last thing."

"Tried and true."

He had heard those words before. Heard them from a man. "Is that a saying among witches? That magic is tried and true?"

Mae nodded. "I suppose it is. When I lived in the coven we said it often enough. The old spells are the best for they are tried and true. Why?"

"I've heard it recently. From a man. But I can't remember where or who."

"Father Kyne?" Wil suggested.

Cedar shook his head. "I don't think so. It's something more. It feels important."

"Well, the trail's gone cold. No more ribbons of light," Wil said.

The side of Cedar's neck stung, and he cupped his palm over it to ease that pain.

"So how about we follow that trail instead?" Wil pointed to the mouth of an alley, at the figure standing there. Not a man—well, not a man made of flesh and bones. It was a Strange, the Strange Cedar had seen three times now.

Instead of bits of wood and dirt, it was made of things found in the city. Scraps of cloth, torn newspaper, and wrappers off bottles and crates that formed the arms, legs, and body, along with bits of wire, rusty nails, a broken watch fob, and a sparkle of glass. All those pieces seemed to be constantly moving, as if a small wind tangled them together to make the humanish shape of the creature.

Even with all those castaway bits of life giving it shape, the eyes were not human. And they were very much not alive.

They were nothing but the ghostly light of the Strange. It raised one hand. And in that hand was the pink ribbon—Florence's ribbon.

Then it opened its mouth and whispered softly, "Help her."

CHAPTER TWENTY

Rose's arm was getting a little tired, raised as it was, holding her gun trained on the opposite door of the railcar.

"Hink," she said quietly.

"Mmm?"

"It's been near half an hour. I don't think anyone's opening these doors."

He shifted behind her, taking a step forward. "I'll have a look."

While he did that, she walked to the stack of crates and stepped over the puppet man lying on his back and staring at the ceiling as if he had a head with which to stare.

"Dark out. I can't see anything in particular. Ship fans have gone quiet," he noted.

"We should go now, before we're noticed," Rose said.

"Do you still have that torch?"

"I think so. But do you think we could just go out through the roof instead? Quieter that way."

Hink struck flint to steel and Rose winced, expecting another one of the many flares he'd been throwing around lately. But this time it was just a single flicker of light, a wick caught to flame. He held it up, walked to the highest stack of crates, and studied the ceiling.

He kept the light low, but it was night out and the freight car had the two holes Rose had burned into the doors. Also, the walls themselves weren't exactly air tight. If there was someone watching out in that dark, they'd see slants of light slipping out of the freight car, and that would surely send them searching.

"You up to climbing?" Hink asked.

"If it means getting out of this box, I am." Rose plucked a signal light off the wall and held up the glass chimney while he lit it.

The lantern light seemed like a whole sun compared with the little flame he'd been using. It was easy enough to find a rope, and Hink was a dead aim throwing it out the hatch in the roof they'd come down through.

"I'll go up first," he said. "If it takes my weight, it will take yours. Once I've reached the top, tie this end of the rope around your ribs, and I'll help pull you up."

"I know how to climb," Rose said.

He nodded. "Good. But tie it anyway. I don't know how much time we'll have once I top that roof."

He tugged on the rope one more time, then held on to it while he climbed the height of the boxes stacked along the wall. He hoisted himself up the rope, hand over hand, with impressive speed. Rose was once again reminded that Hink was an airship captain, and likely spent more than half his time crawling over ropes and riggings. Of course he was quick at the climb.

His boots disappeared over the top. After a pause, he leaned over the hatch. "Come on up. Quick now."

Rose blew out the lantern, set it at her feet, and tied the rope in a loop under her arms. She made sure her skirts were tied up and out of the way and thought, not for the first time, that Molly Gregor, Hink's recently departed boilerman, had it right by wearing men's trousers. As soon as Rose had a chance to do so, she was changing back into her practical overalls. The modern adventurer didn't need fluff and ruffles.

She needed good boots, a reliable pair of suspenders, and a level head on her shoulders.

Rose was good to her word and climbed the rope while Hink hauled back on it, bringing her over the top of the train car with more speed than she'd expected.

She sat and Hink let go of the rope and crouched down next to her. "Are you okay?"

"Good as glim," she whispered back. Rose worked the knot on the rope. "Any idea where we are?"

"Too dark to see much, but I heard the airship fans fade off east of us, and that"—he pointed—"looks to be a work shed or factory of some sort."

"So people might be that way," Rose said, pulling the rope off and tossing it back down into the freight car. Hink did one better and tugged the other end of the rope free and kicked it down the hatch.

"I reckon," Hink agreed. "Town should be that way. My guess is Des Moines."

"So we go to town?"

"We find a telegraph office."

"Why?"

Hink stood and offered her his hand, which she took. They crossed to the side of the freight car, to the rungs set down the side, which they could use as a ladder.

"I have information that needs passing along. That thing in there? It's something my superiors want to know about. Telegraph will be quickest." Hink lowered himself down the side, feet sure on the rungs. He was on the ground in an instant.

Rose followed, cussing a bit under her breath as her boots got tangled in her skirts.

"Problem?" he asked when she reached the ground.

"I'm just thinking Molly Gregor was smart to wear men's trousers, with all the climbing and cavorting that goes into this sort of life."

Hink tightened just a bit. The death of his crew member still hurt, even though it had been months ago, and not his fault.

"She was one of a kind," Hink said kindly. "And smart."

"Yes," Rose said, "she was. I might even buy myself some tailored trousers that I could wear about town. Something more sleek and fitted than all this fluff."

Hink had taken a step and stopped. He looked back over his shoulder with a grin. "Woman, why did you go and have to put that vision in my head?" He started off again. "I do not have time for such distractions."

Rose smiled and followed on his heels. The freight car had been placed surprisingly accurately on a rail spur, which connected to a line that ran parallel to the warehouse they had seen from the top of the car. At this late hour, no trains appeared to be coming or going, and the airship that had transported the car here was not visible in the sky.

Hink moved from shadow to shadow with clear purpose. He wasn't going toward town. He was headed straight to the warehouse.

"Wait," Rose whispered when they paused by an empty wagon. "Why aren't we following the rail or road into town?"

He pointed at the telegraph pole standing at one corner of the warehouse. "Telegraph line. Shouldn't be manned this time of night. I'll send the message here, then we'll bolt to town."

"Is the homunculus that important?"

"Yes."

Hink strode away from the wagon, straight toward the warehouse. Rose supposed if someone came along to stop him, he'd tell them he was a U.S. Marshal here to inspect the place. Or, just as likely, he'd hit them in the face and consider that explanation enough.

They rounded the corner of the warehouse. Four doors were spaced up the length of the building, the one at the farthest end looking the most likely to lead to an office.

That's where Hink was walking.

Rose followed. The only windows were up higher than her head, and all of them were dark and still. If this was a working warehouse and not just a place of storage, then it was silent and waiting for dawn to bring its workers back. She had heard of many big businesses in big cities keeping at least one person on the grounds to watch for robbers and other undesirables, but since this building was so far from town, she doubted anyone would leave portable valuables behind.

And though some factories chugged away through the night, this place was silent.

Just before they reached the door, a man stepped out of it. He tugged his bowler hat down tight, then looked ahead and behind.

And saw Hink, who had closed the distance between them.

"Hey!" the man said, startled.

Hink grabbed hold of his arm, twisted it behind his back, and shoved him up against the warehouse. "What are you doing out here at this time of night, friend?" he asked.

"I'm . . . I'm." The man paused. Just as Rose recognized his voice.

"Mr. Wicks?" she said.

"Ms. Small?" He twisted to try to see her, but Hink pressed a little harder, keeping him in place.

"It's Thomas," Rose said. "Let him go."

Hink didn't seem to be listening. "What are you doing here? I thought you were up in first class sipping tea in your stocking feet."

"Well, there was a robbery. . . ."

"Yes, I recall," Hink said. "Shot a man for trying to nick my valuables. What I'm wondering is just how much you are involved in the whole thing. Seeing as how you obviously took a smoother ride to this warehouse than we did."

"I'm not—" He grunted as Hink pressed a little harder. "For the love of decency, Mr. Hink. Will you please let go of me so I can explain?"

From the look on Hink's face, the answer was no. Rose reached over and placed her hand on Hink's arm. "We don't want to draw attention."

Hink considered her for a moment, then loosened his grip on the man. "Hope I didn't wrinkle your accouterments, Mr. Wicks," he noted conversationally. "You do understand I'll shoot you if you run."

Wicks turned and took a moment to straighten his jacket, cuffs, and collar.

"Well," he started. "This is unpleasant. May I inquire as to why you are following me?"

"We're not following you," Rose said before Hink started yelling at him. "We were following the train car being lifted by an airship."

"I am extending to you my patience, Mr. Wicks," Hink said. "But that's about ran out now. Why are you here? What interest do you have in this enterprise?"

The two men regarded each other for a moment as if Rose weren't even standing there. Fine, let them argue. She wanted to know what was in the warehouse.

She stepped up and opened the door.

"Rose," Wicks started, "you shouldn't."

"Oh, I think we all should," Hink said.

But Rose ignored them both. The building was very clearly a warehouse. Stacked within it were crates, just like on the train, and just like the freight in the train, these were stamped with the initials VB. She could guess what was in them. Copper-and-glass battery bits and pieces. Maybe even a few parts of those puppet men.

It was too dark to see much of the warehouse, but the boxes appeared to line the entire place, with at least one or two clear aisles for walking.

And to her left was a small office space, a rolltop desk, and beside that, a table with a closed ledger book, a lamp, and a telegraph key.

"What were you doing in here, Wicks?" Hink asked. "Stealing goods?"

"If you must know, I sent a telegraph. Now, I really do think we should be leaving in all haste. Miss Small?"

"Who?" Hink asked. "Who did you send a message to? What part in all this are you playing, Wicks?"

Wicks smiled, and it was a hard, bright slash in the darkness of the room. "I see no need to tell you, Marshal Cage. My business is my own. And yours, which I believe includes pirating glim, smuggling goods, and trading in secrets, strikes me as against my best interests. Perhaps even against the best interests of this United States. I've been sent to look in on you."

"You're a spy?" Rose asked startled. "For who?"

"I never said I was a spy, though I do operate under the direction of those few people in higher places than I."

"So what I'm hearing," Hink said, "is I should just shoot you now, since you're just going to talk riddles all night."

"What you're hearing, Marshal Cage, is I am your boss."

Hink opened his mouth, but no sound came out of it. He shut it, scowled, and tried again. "Unless you are the president of this here States United, like hell you're my boss."

"Chief Territorial Director of the United States Marshals, Thomas Wicks." He nodded once. "Recently appointed to oversee all lawmen on the ground and in the air."

"Horse crap."

"Appointed by the president himself, as a matter of fact, and sent out to investigate the . . . goings on out west. I assure you I am your superior." His smile seemed to add: "in every way."

"And I'm just supposed to take your word for that? Do you think I fell out the hatch last week?"

"You tell me. Have the doves mentioned a change in the overview of lawmen?"

"Information is cheap," Hink said. "And can be planted with a penny and a pretty word."

"So you're telling me you don't trust your own spy network?"

"I'm telling you that, as of now, you haven't done a lick to convince me that I'd be wasting a bullet just to shut you up."

"Interesting." And that appeared to be all Mr. Wicks was going to say, for he just stood there, waiting.

"I don't want to interrupt this, um . . . discussion, but about these crates?" Rose asked. "Do you know what those devices are being used for, Thomas?"

His eyes shifted to Rose. "Why in the world would you want to know? I find it odd that a woman who claims to have only stayed with the coven in Kansas out of convenience is suddenly mixed up with this glim pirate, stowing away on freight trains and meddling with contents that may be used to destroy this country."

"Pirate?" Hink asked with a dangerous grin.

"Meddling?" Rose said. "You were the one who broke the lid off the crate. You can't really think I'm part of some kind of plot?" It both frustrated and saddened her. She had been honest with him when they'd been together. But it appeared Mr. Wicks had been lying about who he was, and what he was made of.

"I really can't rule it out, can I?" he asked. "You are traveling with *this* man."

"Aw, don't be tender on me, Wicks." Hink's voice held a casual sort of threat. "Tell me just what it is you think I am."

Rose let out a hard sigh. This wasn't getting them any closer to figuring what the copper batteries and puppets were used for. "Excuse me," she said, a little louder than necessary. "I am tired of being defined by the men I travel with. I make my own choices. I'm here for my own reasons. And one of those reasons is to find out what those devices in the crates are used for. And guns"—here she gave Hink a hard look—"aren't going to help with that none. Neither is standing around pissing on each other's boots."

Both men looked a little shocked at her language, but Hink smiled.

"Mr. Wicks," she continued, "I am not involved in any plot. What I am is tired, cold, and in need of a good hot meal. Gentlemen, I'll leave you to your threats and wrasslin'. I'm going to find a way into town and, if I'm lucky, a warm hotel and steam bath."

"Don't go far," Hink said. "Steam bath sounds nice, and it won't take me long to send a wire."

Rose walked out of the warehouse, angrier than she'd expected. She had liked Wicks. But he was yet another man dealing in secrets, like Hink.

No, not just like Hink. She knew for a fact Hink really did work for the president of the United States, and she'd seen him do some heroic things to save lives.

She couldn't say the same about Wicks. While he had seemed nice, she hadn't actually seen the measure of his character.

She pulled her coat closer around her shoulders, suddenly all out of fire for adventure. It was bitter cold here, most of the ground covered in snow and ice. She was hungry, dirty, and at the same time, restless to be moving on.

Far off, the sound of music, maybe piano keys, tumbled down in the dark. She didn't hear gunfire, which meant maybe the men had managed to settle their differences with fists, although it had barely been a minute since she stepped out into the cold. They might just be warming up on threatening each other.

Then she heard footsteps in the snow. More than one person, a lot of people—men. Coming this way.

CHAPTER TWENTY-ONE

The Strange in the shadow of the alley drew the pink ribbon closer to its chest. Then it started down the road, not so much clinging to shadows as becoming a part of them, then reforming as a man-shape with the bits of trash from the city whenever moonlight touched it.

"You heard it speak, right?" Wil asked.

"Yes," Cedar said.

"And you saw it?"

"Yes," Cedar said again.

"We're following it, aren't we?"

Cedar hesitated only a second. "Yes."

They did just that. The Strange avoided full moonlight, avoided open spaces, preferring to cling to structures. When those became fewer and fewer, it lingered against trees, brambles, and even drifts of snow.

But as soon as they reached the forest, the Strange changed. It dropped all the scraps of trash from the city, and instead drew together a body made of twigs and dirt and snow that glittered darkly in the shadows.

The only thing it kept with it was the pink ribbon, Florence's ribbon, clutched with one hand against its chest where a heart should be.

The trail through the woods narrowed until there was no room for the wagon Mae drove.

When they stopped because of the wagon, the Strange did too, just ahead of them, waiting, its hand held out imploringly.

"Following that thing is a trap," Wil said. "Makes my teeth hurt for the want to do . . . something." He gave Cedar a fast grin, and there was more wolf in that look than man.

Cedar felt it too. The curse was returning, growing stronger. Soon Father Kyne wouldn't be able to hold it at bay.

At that thought, his vision split again. He was running, no, Father Kyne was running, down the roads of the town, following the Strange, following the blood need to kill the Strange.

The rumbling sound of something moving underground caught Father Kyne's ears. The high-whirring chorus grew and grew, like a great engine building steam.

Through Father Kyne's eyes, sharpened as they were by the curse, Cedar could clearly see the Strange. And he suddenly knew it was that underground sound that pulled the Strange into the city and pushed them, unwillingly, through the streets toward the men with guns.

Father Kyne ran for the Strange, jaws snapping. He was no longer in the form of a man. The curse had taken him whole, his body and his mind. He ran the streets as a beast. But it was not just the Strange that he wanted to kill.

Cedar opened his mouth to tell him to stop, but could not manage it.

Father Kyne ran after the Strange, followed them as they followed the call. Kyne might not recognize where the call took him, but Cedar did. The entrance of the copper mine. Where the Strange hovered outside the metal door that still stood ajar, caught like flies in a web made of sound. Sound coming from Vosbrough's generator.

"Cedar?" Mae's voice shattered his vision and brought him again to his own surroundings.

"Kyne," he said. "I think the curse has him. I think it has changed him."

"What?" Wil asked. "How?"

"Can you see through his eyes?" Cedar asked.

Wil frowned. "No."

"I can. Just flashes. He hunts the Strange. And the Strange have taken him to the copper mine."

Mae set the brake on the wagon and made sure the mules were secure. "What copper mine?"

"Just north of town," Cedar said. "It looks deserted, but there is a chamber there, with tanks and other devices built to create or store energy. There are copper wires connected to it, cables that run underground."

"And you think the Strange want that device?" she asked.

"No," Cedar said. "I think they fear it, but cannot resist it."

"But the preacher," Wil asked, "he's not . . . not in his right body?"

Cedar tried to see through Father Kyne's eyes, but couldn't. "I don't know," he said. "It seemed that way. Felt that way."

Wil exhaled one hard breath. "So do we go find the preacher and take back our curse? Or do we look into whatever it is that is leading us to first?" He pointed through the trees to the Strange that stood there, still clutching the pink ribbon.

It moved aside, revealing a small opening in a moss-covered tumble of stones. It took a step toward the opening, paused to see if they were following, waited.

"It wants us to go in there," Wil said. "Trap, of course. So, brother? A plan?"

"Mae," Cedar said, "I want you to stay here."

"No." Mae caught his sleeve. "I don't think that is just a tumble of stones."

"Neither do I," Cedar said. "There are pockets where the Strange gather. Where they dwell. Pockets like that."

He dismounted. "Stay here, I'm going to see what I can."

Wil dropped off his horse right behind him. They approached the edge of the clearing, the sound of their boots breaking the snow and filling the night air.

Cedar and Wil stopped twenty feet away from the tumble of rocks.

The Strange remained beside the cave, its body a swirl of tiny snow-flakes that rose and fell. Thin catches of moonlight slipped out of the clouds to pour patches of white on the ground through the gaps of its skin.

"We followed when you asked," Cedar said, his voice pitched low. "We followed because you have a child's ribbon. Do you know where the missing children are? Do you know who has taken them?"

The Strange nodded, an odd bowing motion for a creature with very little neck. And then it tipped toward the opening in the stones, and slipped inside it like smoke in a draft.

"Me." Wil clamped his hand briefly on Cedar's shoulder and ducked into the narrow opening that Cedar would have had a hard time squeezing through.

"Wil, don't," Cedar said, but Wil was already off, swallowed by the darkness.

Cedar pulled his gun, knowing bullets would do no good against the Strange.

After a moment, Wil called out. "Children. Dozens. Maybe a hundred. They're . . . sleeping, I think. I can't quite reach them; it's too narrow in here."

"Can you wake them?" Mae asked. "Can you bring them out of there?"

"I . . . I'll try."

And then a force, as strong as an explosion, pounded through Cedar's head. He stumbled back as his surroundings faded and the vision took him.

Mayor Vosbrough stood in front of that huge copper contraption in the mine beneath the city. In his hand was a gun, smoke curling out of the barrel. In his other hand was a heavy metal bar, which he swung with vicious accuracy.

Pain cut across Cedar's ribs, buckling him to his knees. Pain that exploded through him again and again as Vosbrough beat Father Kyne bloody.

"Cedar!" Mae called. She was beside him, her hands on his arm to try to steady him.

The vision went black.

"What is it?" she asked.

"Vosbrough. It's . . . Vosbrough."

Cedar pushed up onto his feet. "Wil."

Wil was thrown out of the rocks and slammed into the ground in an unconscious heap. The Strange burst out of the cavern right behind him.

Moonlight, full and hard, finally broke the clouds and shot white fire against the earth, bathing them all in its light.

The Strange screamed and launched itself at Cedar.

Just as the curse dug teeth into his bones and blood, demanded its due, and racked his body with pain.

CHAPTER TWENTY-TWO

Rose ran back into the warehouse and quickly closed the door behind her. "There are men coming."

Captain Hink still had his gun drawn. Pointed straight at Mr. Wicks's head. Mr. Wicks held his gun at Hink's belly. Apparently, they hadn't pulled the trigger to decide who was boss yet.

"I suggest you settle real quick if you're going to work together, or just kill each other," Rose said. "There are men coming. Men who won't want us to be nosing around their warehouse. Do we hide? Fight?"

"Hide," both Hink and Wicks said simultaneously.

"Dammit," Hink added.

Then they both offered their hands to her. Rose just rolled her eyes and jogged down the row of boxes on her own, looking for decent cover in case the men came into the warehouse and decided to put on a light.

Hink and Wicks did the same, all of them settling near one another between a stack of boxes and a boarded-up window.

"How many?" Captain Hink asked.

"I heard maybe six voices."

"How far?" Wicks asked.

"Close. Very."

The door opened and Rose curled down lower.

". . . isn't any better, I'm telling you," one of the men said. "Hob, get the light."

"How can you know?" another voice, this one accented with a southern sort of drawl, asked. "They aren't like buffalo. Can't just stand on a hill and count out the herd. Ain't no bones left behind either. Might be we've done our part to kill them off. Might be this is the last night we'll see them on the street."

"You can't be that dumb," the first man said. "Until we go a full moon without someone losing their youngest, they aren't gone. Maybe not even then. It ain't just children they snatch. There's crops going bad, and that bout of fever that set in last spring? Brought on by the Strange, plain and clear."

A switch snapped, metal against metal, and gaslights caught one to the other in a line across the top of the building. Rose blinked hard to get her eyes adjusted to the bright, and hunkered down a little tighter. They'd chosen a good enough hiding place, and the men, five she could see still near the door with Hob walking back from a little farther off, didn't seem to suspect they were anything but alone in the big building.

The men were of a height to one another, most of them wearing beards and mustaches cut trim to their faces. She'd guess them all of an age too, maybe even as old as thirty or so. They wore a mix of styles: pants in dark, heavy wool plaid, plain leather, or sturdy denim blue; boots in black polish or oiled hide. The only thing their coats and hats had in common was they all looked warm and useful in the hard weather.

But there was one other thing that they each sported—a wide-muzzled gun of some sort with a copper box attached to it, hanging at the side.

One look at that gun sent her mind spinning with possibilities. She'd never seen anything like it, and her fingers itched to figure what it was made of and why, exactly, it was modified in such a manner.

A hand reached out and pressed gently downward on her arm. She glanced up. It was Hink. He wasn't looking at her, but crouched as he was at her side, he must have sensed her coiling up with curiosity. He must have known she was pulled by the knowing of something worse than a cat by yarn, and given too much a chance, might just walk up there and ask those men what the guns were for and how, exactly, they worked.

"Mayor says there's an end to them," the second man said. "Won't need a second warehouse, and this one's nearly full. I say there'll be no ghosts in the night come spring."

The men each hung their guns on wall pegs, then freed the copper boxes from the contraptions by thumbing off a couple latches and giving them a good tug.

"Want to put money on that, Sal?" one of the other men asked.

"Didn't say I'd bet for it."

"Here now. A man who ain't willing to back up his opinion with money shows you exactly what his opinion's worth."

The men chuckled and walked off with the copper boxes, heading deeper into the warehouse, out of Rose's sight. In a moment, a clattering of cogs and wheels and chains filled the quiet of the place as some large device was activated. After a bit, there was silence.

"Should we follow them?" Rose whispered once the racket had died down.

"No," Hink whispered back. "We stay here."

"We do not stay here," Mr. Wicks said. "We investigate."

Hink just shook his head slowly. "I don't know how you can't seem to understand a two-letter word, but let me try again: No."

"As your director, I order you to follow my orders, Mr. Hink."

Hink snorted.

Mr. Wicks scowled at him. He stood and very quietly and quickly made his way down the aisle, pausing at the end of the stack of crates and peering around the corner to where the men had wandered.

"Blasted yatterhead," Hink whispered. He turned and gave Rose a look that said she would share the blame if Wicks got them all killed.

There was no use calling out—the other men would likely hear them. So Rose did the only thing she could think of. She pulled her gun and got ready to shoot if Wicks was discovered.

Thomas didn't dash out from behind the crates. But it wasn't long before the men were back, talking over more mundane market prices of buckwheat and potatoes. They crossed over to the door.

Wicks ducked down out of their line of sight as the men reconnected the copper boxes back to the guns, shouldered them, shut down the lights, then left through the same door they'd come in.

Rose's heart thumped for a minute, maybe two, as her eyes, once again, got the hang of darkness. Then Captain Hink was on his feet, just as quiet as Wicks, but twice as large and twice as temperamental as he strode in a killing sort of way down to where Wicks sat.

"What in the hell do you think you're doing?" Hink growled.

"Gathering information." Wicks stood, dusted his coat, and adjusted his hat, though neither looked out of place to Rose.

"They could have found us."

"Yes. Then we would have killed them, I suppose," he said nonplussed.

"Idiot," Hink grumbled.

"'Sir,'" Wicks added. "You will address me as 'sir.'"

"When hell burns holes in my boots," Hink said. "And not even then."

"What exactly will convince you of my station above you, Marshal Cage?"

"Paperwork signed and sealed by the president. Don't have that, do you?"

"Let's find out, shall we?" Wicks dug in the satchel he carried, thumbed through a small stack of paper, and pulled out one clean sheet.

In the dark of the place, Rose could just make out a seal of an eagle worked up in red and blue ink.

"Will this do?" He handed the paper to Hink.

Hink took it and tipped it to the meager light slipping in through the cracks in the ceiling.

"Anyone could forge a document. There's practically a printing press on every corner nowadays." He shoved it back at him.

Thomas paused, looking for a moment like he might have just noticed the depths of Hink's stubbornness.

"Yes. Well," he said. "I want to know where they went with those copper boxes. Go and see where they put them and report back to me."

Hink inhaled. His hand clenched into a fist.

She didn't know if he was fighting the urge to yell at the man or just fighting the urge to fight.

"Lady said she wants to go to town," Hink said. "Find a nice hotel and a bath. I say that's the way I'm walking."

"I'm sure Miss Small won't mind one little jaunt to see what's behind that door." He pointed.

Rose walked over to the both of them. Then walked past them so she could see what he was going on about.

There at the far end of the warehouse was, indeed, a door. "Armory?" she suggested.

"Won't know if we don't look." Wicks took the distance at a quick clip, placed his hand on the door handle, and leaned in a bit as if listening for something moving behind the door. Then he tried the latch.

The door opened. Wicks turned, grinned, and stepped over the threshold.

"Idiot," Hink said. "And a fool. We should leave, Rose. Now."

"You want to know what's in there," she said. "You know you do. Doesn't matter if he's your superior or a horsefly. You'll always wonder what was really back there. Got a case of the curious in a bad way."

Hink glanced at the boarded-up windows, then shook his head, a smile easing the edge of his anger. "Woman, the trouble you find." He turned and stormed off after Wicks.

"I like to keep my eyes out on the world," she said.

"Thought you wanted a bath."

"I do. After we find where they went with the copper boxes."

Hink pulled his gun again, and stepped away from the stacks of crates and into the darkened room. "Wicks?" he called out softly.

Thomas seemed to melt out of shadows, a small flame tucked tight in his hand so as not to give more than an ember of light to his face. "Some kind of device here. I think it's a hoist for the goods. The men used it."

Captain Hink never seemed to fail when a light was needed and this time was no different. He pulled a flint and steel from his pocket and lit up a small torch.

"You hear that?" he asked.

Rose nodded. "Like trumpets, but higher? And . . . water? Maybe there's a waterwheel that runs the equipment under here?"

"No," Hink and Wicks said at the same time.

"You first, Marshal Cage," Thomas said.

"Call me Captain Hink. I don't go by Marshal unless I'm about to bring someone to law."

"Really? Seems a hassle to change your names around like that. Why not just Cage for Captain and Marshal?"

"Because no glim pirate should be known as Marshal Cage. They'd shoot the ship right out from under my feet." Then he said, "Down." He nodded at the platform in the middle of the floor between a rise of gears and pulleys surrounding it.

From the look on his face, Wicks didn't like to be ordered around either. Still, he strolled over and stood on the boards of the hoist. "I assume you understand how to set this device to working?"

"Haven't run across a matic I can't figure. Rose?"

"What?"

"Get on the platform with him."

"You want me to go down there with him? I thought you didn't want me anywhere near the man."

"He didn't?"

"No," Hink said.

"Yes," Rose said.

"No," Hink said a little louder. "You aren't going down there with him alone. We all go. Don't plan to turn my back on you now, Mr. Wicks. Fancy papers or no."

Hink set the matic in gear and then mounted the platform next to them. He pulled a lever and the entire contraption lowered, far more smoothly and silently than Rose expected. They dropped only one floor down, into a basement.

But that basement was massive, carved out of solid stone and at least three times as large as the upper floor. A series of connected tunnels with arched ceilings braced by metal connected to this huge center room and splayed out in every direction like the petals of a half-bloomed flower. All the tunnels and ceilings were lit with what must be electric light, strung with copper lines and shining like dewdrops catching sun.

The floor was water-smooth with rails down each tunnel and crossing at each junction.

A train station? No, Rose knew it wasn't just that. Perhaps it was built for transporting something: coal or some other valuable.

Against the wall stood massive tanks and coils that looked like huge snail shells lit up from within and wrapped in copper wire. That copper wire ran through tubes across the ceiling, down the metal bracers against the walls, and looped across hundreds of other wires that suspended huge glass balls in a dozen colors, each glass ball wrapped in even more copper.

It was a fairyland of wires, cogs, glass, and power. Ideas she'd never been brave enough to imagine sat right here, already a reality. She knew what this was, though not what it was being used for.

"Power," she said. "Acres and acres of power. Generating it. Storing it. And pushing it down those cables, I think. It's . . . magnificent."

"What in the world is this for?" Wicks asked. He glanced over at Captain Hink. "What do you know about it?"

"Rose." Hink stepped off the platform behind Rose, who was already wandering out into the chamber.

The wonder of the place set her head to buzzing. She couldn't seem to take it all in, to know what it all might mean. And she so very much wanted to.

"It's connected," she muttered as she started toward the towering tank on the nearest wall. "All of them. They're made of . . . what is this? Copper? It's the wrong color, too green and white, almost turquoise." She stopped directly in front of one of the huge contraptions and stretched her fingers to touch it.

"Rose." Hink pulled her hand away, then stood in front of her. He wasn't big enough to block her view of the entire thing, but just the sight of him made her realize she had been foolishly wandering the place like a moth drawn to fire.

"There's glim involved," he said, not letting go of her hand. "And there's Strange. Look."

He turned her about so that her back was toward him. Across the room, stacked from floor all the way up to the ceiling, were dark metal shelves filled with copper and glass devices. Just like the copper and glass battery they had found in the train and put in the puppet man.

But instead of the glass globe in the middle of all that copper being empty, each globe was filled with something alive and skittering.

"God in heaven," Rose breathed. "Something's trapped in there."

Hink, for just a moment, wrapped his arm around her waist. For just a moment, she was held against him, protected in the strength of his arms, his body.

"It's the Strange," he said very quietly. "Can you see them?"

Rose nodded.

"So can I, though I don't usually. Do not touch them," he said.

Then he gently let go of her and walked across that room toward them like he was approaching a wall full of rattlesnakes.

It took all the will Rose had in her not to turn and run from this place. The Strange were evil, mindless, brutal creatures that enjoyed nothing more than torturing people. She'd seen what they could do. She'd seen them make the dead walk. She'd seen them do worse.

Suddenly, she was too hot and too cold at the same time. She wanted to be anywhere else but here, yet she could not make her feet lift to run.

Hink was almost at the globes. He was going to touch them. He was going to reach out and then there would be nothing but a thin curve of glass between him and the creatures that were destroying the world.

They'd kill him. Draw him in. Devour him.

"Lee." She said the word all in an exhale. "Please, Lee. Don't touch them. Don't leave me."

Hink didn't stop. Didn't pause. He stepped up to the towering stack of caged Strange and stared at them, making a decision. Then he reached out and pressed his palm against the glass.

CHAPTER TWENTY-THREE

Cedar landed hard on his shoulder and hip. He gritted his teeth against the pain spearing through his side and leg. He'd broken a rib for sure, maybe done worse to his leg. He pushed up and out from under his brother, his head pounding. Even though it was cold enough to see his breath coming out in steamy gasps, his skin was on fire.

He struggled to get on his feet, but couldn't do any more than rise up upon his knees. Every inch of his body hurt more, much more, than it should. His mind slipped between conscious thought and raw hunger to kill.

The curse wrapped around him, broken free from Father Kyne's hold, stretching his body, twisting him into the shape of the beast. Changing from the body of a man to that of the wolf had never been a painful experience.

Until now.

Cedar yelled as the curse broke the spell and claimed him again, turning him into a creature that hungered for the blood of the Strange.

But even with the curse in full force beneath the power of the moon burning bright, the thin chain he wore that the Madders had given him months ago managed to separate just enough of his thoughts that he retained the barest vestiges of logic. Still, he had very little control over the beast.

Control that slipped.

The world broke apart into color and fragments of trails and scents: shattered bits of all the things, living and dead, that had passed this way.

Above it all, the scent of the Strange was strongest, tangled though it was in the smells of Wil next to him and of the wildflower scents of Mae from where she stood with the horses.

Mate.

The beast demanded he run, hunt, and rend the Strange until they broke and bled.

Wil was on his feet next to him, and like him, wore the skin of the beast. They would hunt, together. They would kill, together. It was what they were made for. It was all they breathed for.

To kill the Strange.

Cedar howled and Wil lent his voice to his brother's song, to his rage. There was a Strange nearby. A familiar Strange. Cedar growled. That Strange stood, just on the other side of a fallen tree. It held a ribbon in one hand.

Cedar could smell its fear, could hear the sour song that bled from it into everything it touched. He knew the Strange understood what he was. Knew the Strange understood he was death to its kind.

But still it stood there, not attacking, not running. It lifted its hand with the ribbon, as if making sure Cedar knew it carried a human token, a child's ornament.

And then it ran.

Instinct curled and exploded in his chest. He would hunt it, track it, run it down, kill it.

Wil was right beside him as they pounded across the snowy terrain. Through the forest and over hills, across a field spread wide beneath the moonlight. The Strange ran faster, always just ahead of them, leaving a trail so strong Cedar could have found it with his eyes closed.

And then he heard water, a river flowing hard beneath a layer of ice. He knew that river. He had been here before, here where the road split in two, branching toward the city of people and away through a stand of trees to the frozen river.

Danger. The beast knew it was a trap, and so did his logical mind. He stopped, hidden in the shadows, Wil at his side. They waited, watching as the moon slipped in and out of the clouds at the horizon.

The moon would soon set. Dawn was only a few hours off. Though the curse was still strong, Cedar could already feel the power of it fading.

There was no reason to wait. They should kill the Strange.

But something held him back.

Danger.

The Strange was waiting for them. Waiting on the bank by the frozen river. Waiting to kill.

Cedar moved out of the shadow, drawn by the unbreakable need to kill the creatures that tread the earth. He held near the curve of the path, slipping silently through brush. This was a trap. He knew it must be.

And as he neared the river, he heard more than the song of the Strange. He heard children crying in the night, calling out for mothers and fathers. Calling out to be saved.

Wil heard it too, and whined softly, his ears flicking forward and back.

Because even though they heard a hundred children calling, crying out, there was only one child they could see.

A little girl, maybe three years old, barefoot and shivering in her nightshirt, her hair braided at each ear. She clutched a tattered blanket close to her chest and walked across the snow-covered stones as if she were blind or sleepwalking, following the sound of children's voices straight to the icy river.

The Strange stood upon the ice, the pink ribbon pinched between its fingers and trailing in the predawn breeze. It stared at Cedar, watching his every move with those odd eyes.

He growled, but the Strange did not move.

It waited.

When Cedar had the clarity of a man's mind, he would say it was not afraid; certainly he no longer smelled fear on it. Nor did it seem set to attack the child. When he had the clarity of a man's mind, he would say the Strange was waiting for him to understand. It was desperate. And sad.

But the beast warred with his thoughts: *Save the child or kill the Strange.*

"Help," the Strange whispered. Not asking. Showing.

The wind rose with the early light, bringing with it more than the sound of the children calling, crying, begging. That wind brought with it the scent of the Holder.

Cedar jerked his head up and took a backward step.

The Holder was here, and as the Strange pointed at the ice, he knew the Holder was there, in the river, hidden beneath the ice.

Calling the children.

The little girl was almost at the river's edge.

Save the child, his logical mind demanded.

Cedar ran for the girl.

Just as the Strange ran for her.

She collapsed before either reached her. But it was the Strange that somehow whisked her up and, faster than the wind, pulled her away from the river and ice and ran away with her into the forest.

Cedar dug claws into the frozen ground, twisting to catch at the Strange, launching after it.

But the sun broke the horizon, lifting the curse. He writhed in agony as his flesh and bone once again snapped, shifted, and compacted, forcing him too soon into the shape of a man.

CHAPTER TWENTY-FOUR

ink didn't blow apart or fall down dead from his hand on the globe. So that was a good thing. The bad thing was the six men who came striding over from a door across the way. Men who were armed with ordinary, but no less deadly, sorts of guns and rifles. Men who looked an awful lot like a sheriff and his posse.

"Step away from the glass, mister, or I will blow your hand off."

Hink, wisely, stepped back. "Evening, gentlemen," he said smoothly. "Or is it about morning now? We got ourselves turned around, trying to find a hotel. We've just come to town. Found an open door and took shelter from the wind."

The men didn't move. Worse, they didn't put their guns away. A man with a long, drawn-out sort of face and cold black eyes said, "What's your name?"

Thomas took a small step forward and every gun shifted to him. He looked a little startled at that, and Rose thought he also looked a lot like a bumbling greenhorn who had stumbled into a situation he couldn't quite get the hang of.

That was an act. The same act he'd used on her to make her believe he was just a nice young man showing her through the library, and offering to walk her home, when really he was probably trying to gather information about Captain Hink.

"I'm sorry if we've wandered into your, uh"—he craned his head and squinted at the ceiling, then down at the wall across the way—"building. Would you be so kind as to point us toward a hostel?"

"Name," the man repeated.

"Oh, yes," Wicks said. "My name is Thomas Wicks. Pleased to make your meet." He tapped the brim of his hat and hitched a short bow.

"And this is Mr. Hink, and Miss Small, my traveling companions. We're recently out of Nebraska, and on our way to Minnesota. The snow seems to have set us off course a bit. Is the nearest town Des Moines or Council Bluff? You see, Mr. Hink and I have a gentleman's bet riding on it."

"What you and your friend have here is a problem." The men split their attention so that their weapons were aimed at the three of them equally. "This is Mayor Vosbrough's town, and this"—he pointed to the floor—"is Mayor Vosbrough's private property. We are under orders to shoot any man who trespasses on this land."

"We mean to cause no trouble—," Captain Hink said.

"Shut up, and get walking." The man gestured toward a short tunnel that must have a door at the end of it.

At least Rose hoped it had a door. Here, underground, it would be easy to kill them and leave their bodies to rot. No one would know.

She tucked her hands in her coat pockets, and fingered through the bits there, trying to come up with something that might help them out of this mess.

Twine, bolts, a smooth lump of lead, but nothing that could take down six armed men.

Hink threw Rose a look, and she decided the plan was to cooperate with these men. He started down the tunnel, and Rose finally unfroze her feet and started after him.

As she passed near the globes filled with the Strange, the creatures slammed against the glass, slapping it with their hands, shoulders, causing the whole wall to take up a sour chiming, like someone was hitting milk jugs with wooden spoons.

A few of the Strange called out, their voices too faint and hollow to carry words.

Chills stuttered down her arms and spine, and her stomach turned. There was something very wrong about this. Something very wrong about trapping the Strange in those copper batteries.

And there must be something about those devices that allowed her, and the others, to see the Strange.

"I really don't think there's a need for guns," Wicks was saying. "I assure you we mean no harm. This was just an unfortunate misunderstanding. Perhaps if we could speak with Mayor Vosbrough, we could explain our case and apologize properly."

"You'll see him," a man with a scar on his face said. "Walk."

The tunnel did indeed end in a door, which one of the men had opened, letting the rising dawn breeze in. Rose paced up the sloped floor behind Hink, and then through the door and up a ramp that must be for wagons.

The men turned to face them again in a half circle, guns pointed. Off to the right was the airship landing field. Now that dawn was purpling up the horizon, the buzz of airship fans broke the stillness, and in the distance, she heard a train whistle blow. Steam and smoke and the sharp stink of hot metal drifted through the still-dark morning.

Behind the men were three more warehouses, and off a ways, a building was being erected, a strange bric-a-brac structure made of wood and brass that tipped upward at over a hundred fifty feet high. It wasn't an airship tether: too wide, with no looks of a landing platform. Maybe a water tower?

The entryway to the lower section of the warehouse was cleverly hidden by a gear and track system that silently closed a wooden floor over the ramp, so it looked for all the world like a place to park a wagon, not a place to hide captured Strange and rail tunnels.

She had no idea how they even captured the Strange to begin with, nor how they trapped them in the glass. Most people couldn't see the

Strange. And that wall had been filled floor to ceiling with globes. There were easily several thousand Strange in those copper batteries. She didn't even think there were that many Strange in the entire world, much less in a warehouse in Des Moines, Iowa.

Did they ship them in on the train? They shipped the copper batteries. Maybe there had been Strange on the train with them.

Before she could grapple with that nightmare idea, a steam wagon rolled over from one of the warehouses. It was built closer to the ground than most horse-drawn wagons, and the back of it was boxed in by wood sides and roof, leaving room for a driver and passenger up front to work the boiler and steering devices.

"You're all going to get in this wagon. Now," the man with the scar said.

Hink gauged the men. Rose knew what he was deciding: to fight or go along with them. And she knew what decision he'd come to. There wasn't a fight Captain Hink would walk away from. Didn't matter if he came out the winner or the loser.

"Of course," Wicks put in cheerily. "We are happy to do as we're told. Aren't we, Mr. Hink?" he added.

"We?" Hink drawled.

"Yes," Rose said quickly. "We are." She walked off to the back of the wagon, a smile set on her face in hopes it hid the fear clogging up her throat.

Please don't start a fight, she thought desperately. They were outnumbered, outgunned, and so far outside of any civilized part of town, they could be shot and kicked down that shaft, which would put a short end to all their adventuring days.

She had a lot of the world left to see, and watching Hink get killed over whether or not he should get in a wagon was one sight she intended to avoid.

He finally turned and walked after her, his boots crunching through the layer of tamped snow. Wicks was ahead, between the two men who stood at the back of the wagon. He nodded to the men and stepped up into it.

Rose climbed into the wagon next. It was dark, windowless, stank of old beer, sweat, and leather. The floor was wood, and there were benches along two walls. Wicks sat on one side and Rose settled across from him.

The wagon springs dipped as Hink climbed up the step. His wide bulk blocked out what little light there was coming in from the open doors. He ducked low and swung onto Rose's bench, nearest the door.

The doors slammed shut behind them, punctuated by the slide and clank of a bar being thrown across to keep them locked.

"We could have taken them," Hink said quietly. But there was no chance anyone would hear him. The steam boiler kicked up, starting the wagon to squeaking and rocking over the uneven ground. He could probably yell and not be heard by anyone outside the vehicle.

"No," Mr. Wicks said. "We couldn't. You may be a fast draw, Marshal, but we were outgunned in close quarters. And besides, this suits our needs all the better."

"What needs?" Rose asked.

"There has been information coming out of these parts that the Vosbrough family is gearing up to make a move against the United States government. We don't know how, and we don't know when . . ."

". . . or where, or who, exactly," Captain Hink added, "or even why. So basically, we know squat. And squat ain't nearly enough to die for."

"What we know," Wicks said with cool disapproval, "is that the Vosbroughs are involved, and are likely the figureheads and money behind the unrest. They are gathering glim, through legitimate and illegal suppliers."

"I shut down Alabaster Saint's operation," Hink said.

"I read the report. Nasty business. Torture." Here he went silent, and Hink just returned his look with his single, remaining eye.

"Yes," Hink said, "it was."

"Don't you see?" Wicks said, leaning forward a bit and using his hands as he spoke. "This is a perfect chance for a face-to-face meeting with the mayor, Vosbrough."

"Because he'll think favorably of us trespassing in his warehouse. A warehouse that contained more than a thousand trapped Strange?"

"What?" Wicks asked.

"Did you look at those glass-and-copper globes?" Hink asked.

"Well, it was dark."

"They were filled with Strange. Each and every one of them."

Wicks didn't say anything for a moment. Outside the wagon, the sounds of the working city grew louder and quieter as they made their way through streets. The yells of a news hawker and of a fishmonger, the hammering of a smithy, the clanging chains of horses and wagons, and the puff and bells of steam matics all navigated in such a tight space made Rose wish there was a window in the wagon. Des Moines would have been the largest city she'd ever seen. If she could have seen it.

"Why?" Wicks finally said. "Why capture the Strange? And how, for that matter?"

"Maybe you can ask the mayor," Hink said. "I'm sure he'd be happy to just spill it all out for you."

"Batteries," Rose said. "That's what the man on the train told us it was. Somehow the Strange and the glim in those globes make batteries."

"Power storage for glim?" Wicks shook his head. "I don't understand that at all."

"Think of it as a watch that doesn't need winding because glim sees to the powering of it," Rose said.

"Watches?"

"No. I don't know what the batteries are powering, exactly." Here she glanced at Hink.

They had an idea: the battery fit in the puppet man they had pieced together. If the Strange could be somehow used to power that creature. To work as a heart or drive a spring . . .

Rose wrapped her arms around herself, suddenly cold. She'd seen what Strange did when they took over dead bodies. They killed, devoured, tortured. And if they had puppet bodies, would they do the same?

Why would anyone want to use the Strange as a power? Or maybe the use of the Strange drained them and killed them.

"What have you heard about the Vosbroughs raising forces?" Captain Hink asked.

It looked like he'd given up on believing Wicks was lying about being on the same side of the law. Either that or he was doing what he always did: gathering information on the glim trade, the Strange, and other unlawful things.

"Not much," Wicks admitted. "We know Alabaster was raising men and dealing in glim trade he transported by air. One of the main drop points was Cedar Falls, just west of here and easy rail to Des Moines. If those copper globes were filled with glim, it likely came from the western mountains to Alabaster, then by airship to train, and train to here."

"Are all the Vosbroughs set up in this town?" Hink asked.

"No. Killian is here. His brother is in Chicago and sister is in New York."

Hink nodded. That was something he seemed to already know. Rose wondered why he didn't tell Wicks about the puppet, the possible homunculus, but maybe he was smart not to do so. Wicks had fooled her before; she wasn't feeling favorable to trusting him again so quickly.

"Any news on what the Vosbrough siblings are doing, specifically?" Hink pressed.

Wicks shook his head. "Nothing the papers wouldn't print."

The wagon jerked and came to a full stop. Moments later, the bar was lifted from the doors, and when the door was opened, the full light of dawn freshened up the darkness. Rose held her hand over her eyes to block the worst of the glare.

And saw the row of men outside the wagon, all armed, all wearing green and gold with armbands embroidered with the initials VB. A personal guard? Or maybe just the town police? She didn't know.

"This way." It was the same dark-eyed man from the warehouse.

Hink sighed, as if tired of the whole thing, slapped his thighs, and then stepped out of the wagon, being sure to stretch up to his full six-and-a-half feet.

The men in the line below gripped their guns a little tighter. Hink could be an intimidating presence when he wanted to be.

"Fine city you got here," Hink said. "Real nice welcome a fellow gets, plus a free ride to town." He stepped down to the ground and held his hand out. Rose took his hand and walked down the steps. She tried to smile, but couldn't hide her worry.

That was a lot of firepower pointing at them. She heard Wicks climbing out of the wagon, but her eyes were suddenly too full of the sights to pay him much attention.

They were standing on a lovely street with brick buildings that reached high enough to scratch the underbelly of heaven. Windows lined the buildings in neat rows, trimmed with scrolling edges and woodwork. And all the way down the street, she could see people in winter coats and bright scarves hurrying here and there. Some stopped to stare at them curiously. Women in fine wool and furs, men in sharp hats, and lots of working folk too, in heavy boots and practical headwear to ward off the cold.

At the farthest end of the street, hovering over the building like a child's kite, was a plump little airship. It was tied by cable to the street, and its open-deck gondola showed cargo being lowered by rope and pulley—bags of grain and barrels of oil or maybe wine—to the building below it.

It was a loud, busy, exciting place, and even though she should fear for her very life, she couldn't tamp the thrill out in her heart. This was such a grand sight; something she'd never seen before, never known before. The giddy rush of it warmed her like a fire against the winter.

A city. She, Rose Small, was standing in a city.

"Rose," Hink said softly.

She looked away from the wonders and to him. He spared her a slight raise of eyebrow and smile. He knew how much this meant to her. He knew how much she loved seeing the world. And would willingly spend her whole life seeking out and unwrapping new bits of it to savor.

"This way," he said.

That's when she noticed Wicks and four or so men were already walking into the building they had stopped in front of. Hink started off toward it, and she went with him.

"What did I miss?" she whispered as the men closed in behind them.

"Just that we're to meet the mayor."

"Oh," she said. And the wonder and excitement went cold under that notion.

She stepped through the door and into a carpeted room with walls painted cream and blue, broken up a bit by oil portraits framed in gold. The ceiling was made entirely of copper, and buffed to an ember shine.

It appeared to be a large meeting room or a place where official business might be conducted. A slab of wood the color of rubies filled the center of the room, with ornate chairs set around it. A small desk rested in the corner of the room, and from that desk, a twist of copper cables the size of her arm attached to the wall near a window. A telegraph station was set up on the desktop and a box with other levers and curious switches stood nearby.

But for all the grand nature of the room, it was the man who sat at a kingly desk at the far center who caught her eye.

"Well, well. What do we have here, Sheriff?" he asked in a friendly tone.

The man was of medium height, blond hair caught in a curl beneath his ears, and nose broken and healed at least once. He smiled from behind his desk, and leaned forward a bit in his chair, propping his elbows across a spread of paperwork. One of his hands was bandaged and it appeared his other was rather badly bruised.

Looked like he'd recently been in a fistfight, even though he was dressed in a fine brown pinstripe suit with fur trim at the lapels that probably cost more than all the belongings Rose could call her own.

"Mayor Vosbrough, we found these people in the warehouse by the ship fields."

"Really? Where exactly?"

"Underground."

The mayor's friendly smile tightened along with his eyes.

"Who are you, friends, and why were you on my private property?" he asked.

"Sir, Mayor, sir," Wicks said, walking forward and offering his hand to shake. One of the sheriff's men stood in front of him, blocking his approach.

"I am Thomas Wicks," he said, dropping his hand and giving a nervous smile. "Very pleased—no, honored—to be in your presence." He bowed.

"I like your manners, Mr. Wicks," the mayor said. "Thomas, was it? But I don't stand on such formalities here. Come on up closer. We're all friends."

The gunman moved aside and Wicks pulled off his hat and held it in front of him. "I do hope we haven't offended you in any way," he said. "We just came into town, and got turned around by the weather while looking for lodgings."

"It has been cold out, terribly so," Vosbrough agreed. "And I suspect you only dashed into the warehouse to duck the wind. Is that the story you're going to tell me, Mr. Wicks?"

Vosbrough was still talking like they were the best of friends, but there was a hard glitter to his eyes.

"Well, it's . . . it's the truth," Wicks said, doing a damn fine impression of a man who was flustered and confused and nervous.

Rose might hate that he had fooled her with his acting, but right now she sincerely hoped he could do the same to Vosbrough.

"And you, sir? What's your name?"

"Captain Hink, of the airship *Tin Swift*."

The mayor paused. "I've heard of the *Swift*. Rumor is she's fast."

"There isn't a ship faster that burns the sky."

"What are you doing in my fine city, Captain?"

"We ran into some trouble back out Oregon way," Hink said. "Looking for some parts to repair my ship."

"You've come a long distance for a bolt or cog," Vosbrough noted.

"Don't need a bolt or cog. I need a deal."

Wicks frowned, looking genuinely confused this time. Rose tried not to bite her bottom lip or otherwise look concerned. She had no idea where Hink was going with this.

"A deal? With whom?"

"You, Mayor. I've got the fastest ship in the western sky, can harvest more glim in one haul than any of the bigger blowers, and am in need of money for repairs."

Vosbrough sat back and a grin spread wide on his face. "You came here to ask me for money?"

"I came to make a glim deal. Heard it's the sort of business a smart man like you might be interested in."

Vosbrough's grin remained, but he pressed all his fingertips together while considering Hink over the top of them. "Am I to assume you intend to trade via legal channels?"

"Not all the men who fly the skies are pirates," Hink said.

"Rather high percentage, I'm given to understand," Vosbrough said.

"Takes all sorts to make the money go round," Hink said. "So are we doing business?"

"True. So very true," Vosbrough said. "You know what? I like you too, Mr. Hink. But I'm afraid I can't do business with glim pirates. Sheriff, lock them up."

"What?" Wicks said. "In jail? Hold on, Mayor. You must understand I am in no way associated with that man."

"I do not care, Mr. Wicks. You were trespassing on my property with intent to do harm, I can only assume. Be happy it's only jail time you're serving. We have a brand-new gallows built in the central square. And people do enjoy a good hanging."

The sheriff's men moved in and Rose glanced up at Hink, then over at Wicks, to see if they had some kind of plan she didn't. Neither of them said anything. So she did.

"Who is the gallows for?"

The mayor turned and looked at her. Maybe for the first time. She had to admit that her coat was loose, having lost her belt, and her skirts were dirty and tattered at the hem. She wore a practical hat a cowboy might find himself comfortable doffing.

She was no vision; that was certain.

Still, his eyebrows went up, as if he'd just noticed two things: that she was in the room and that she was, indeed, a woman.

"My apologies, miss. But I doubt you know them. Set of murderous brothers. Real rough lot. Go by the name of Madder."

Rose was very careful not to let her shock show. "Well, God be with them," she said quietly.

Vosbrough looked between her and Hink, who stood closest to her. Hink's arms were crossed over his chest. It didn't take a genius to read what he was thinking while he glared at the mayor.

"God gave up on them years ago," Vosbrough said with a sigh. "Pity to see three lives wasted. Still, it's my place to see that justice is done and they are sent down to the fires they crawled out of. Take them," he ordered.

Hink and Wicks exchanged one brief look, and then neither of them put up a fight as they were pushed back outside. The lawmen didn't touch Rose. They simply pointed to the door, as if she were a child who needed instructions on how to get out of the place.

Once outside, they were shoved back into the steam wagon.

"Do you have a plan?" Rose asked.

"Escape sounds good to me," Hink said. "When they open the door, I'll take the first one and get his gun."

"You'll die." Wicks sighed. "Sometimes the best plan isn't to attack directly."

"Was your plan working any better?"

"Got a look at him at least," Wicks said. "Got a look at his forces, the setup of communication. He's wired the entire town with cables. Also noticed he's a bit roughed up—that's interesting. So I wouldn't say it was a complete loss. But as for our escape, we'll watch for a chance and we'll take it. But our chance does not involve rushing a half-dozen armed men. Do you understand me, Cage?"

"You are not my boss," Hink said.

"What about the Madders?" Rose asked.

"What about them?" Wicks asked.

"They're friends of ours."

"Friends?" Wicks sat up straighter.

"Acquaintances," Rose corrected. "We have to save them."

"That'll be a mite hard if we're behind bars," Hink said.

"Maybe not," Rose said. "Do you still have the copper battery?"

"Think so."

"Battery, what battery?" Wicks asked.

Hink pulled the glass-and-copper device out of his pocket.

"You have a battery?" Wicks said again. "Why didn't you tell me you had a battery?"

"Because it is none of your business."

"That's stolen property. And it's proof. What part of that isn't my business?"

"The part where I said it ain't."

"Let me carry it," Rose said. "They might search you, but there's less of a chance they'll make me strip to my underdress."

Hink tipped his head down just a bit. "So. You're going to strip now?"

"No." Rose was busy unbuttoning her coat, and then the back of her collar so she could stuff the thing down her blouse.

When Hink didn't say anything, she glanced up at him. "Well?"

"I was just waiting to see where you were going with this," he said, giving her a knowing smile.

"I'm going to drop it down my blouse. It should . . . fit." Rose was blushing madly now, her cheeks so hot they stung. She just hoped the dark interior of the wagon didn't show it.

"Maybe I can be of some assistance? I'm a deft hand with buttons."

"No."

Wicks snorted.

Hink handed Rose the copper device and she was once again caught by the song of it, by the cold of it, by the possibilities of what it could be. Glim and cold copper and Strange, bound by witch's spells. Her hand was shaking, though she'd only been holding it for a moment.

Then Hink's hand was under hers, supporting it. "Are you sure, Rose?"

She pressed her lips together and was surprised to feel a tear at the corner of her eye. Maybe she'd been sitting there, unbuttoned with the odd device in her hand for more than a moment.

She didn't know why she heard this metal so loudly in her mind. She only hoped that when she placed it between the cloth of her blouse and her underdress it would be dampened enough—and not touching her skin—so she didn't hear it at all.

It wasn't easy, but then, she'd done plenty of other difficult things. Finally, she got the copper tucked into her blouse and the back of her collar buttoned up again. The wagon had already stopped moving and she wasn't done buttoning her coat.

Her fingers flew through the closures, hoping she lined the holes and buttons up straight.

"How do I look?" she asked Hink.

He visibly swallowed. "Beautiful." And then he bent down, and right there, in front of Mr. Wicks, he made to kiss her.

Just then, the door was thrown open and Hink pulled away.

It took Rose more than a bit to get her breathing under control, and all the heat in her cheeks had migrated down her chest and stomach, even though he hadn't even kissed her.

"Get out," the man outside ordered.

"You sure your mind's made up?" Hink asked Wicks. "There's only five of them."

"Quite sure," Wicks said a little stiffly.

And then Wicks ducked out of the wagon, and Rose was right behind him. Hink was last out and, true to his word, went with the men peacefully.

The jail wasn't as large as Rose had expected. She'd never been to a big-city jail before, but had hoped it might be several stories tall, and trimmed up with all the bric-a-brac the rest of the city seemed to be dripping with.

No, this was a short, square brick building, with narrow windows and a door made out of metal.

They were brought inside and quickly marched past several cells occupied by rough-looking men who hooted and whistled as she passed by.

Hink and Wicks were shoved into one cell, and when Rose went to step in, the sheriff pulled on her arm.

"You'll be in a separate cell," he said.

"Plenty of room for her in my cell, Sheriff," one of the prisoners yelled. "You know you want me, pretty thing. Come on in and let me get a good look at you."

"Touch the lady and I'll be shoveling you into your grave before sunset," Hink said calmly.

The bars slammed shut behind Hink, and Rose was pushed down the hall farther.

To her left was another cell with a big brute of a man who paced and mumbled what sounded like the Lord's Prayer to himself; then the next cell held a man lying on a crude cot.

He seemed to be of native blood, though he wore the styles of a white man. He appeared shirtless beneath a blanket tossed across the middle of his body. He also looked pale and sick, and there was a pool of blood at the side of the cot.

He was dying.

But before she could even see the all of him, she was shoved into the next cell and the bars were snapped shut behind her.

"Wait," Rose said. "Please."

The guard had taken several strides down the hall, but turned and looked at her. "What is it?"

"The man in that cell we passed. I think he's badly hurt."

"He is," he said. "But if I were you, I'd worry about your own business."

"You'll just leave him here to die?" For some reason Rose was shocked about that. She shouldn't be, not after everything she'd seen. Cruelty was all too common in this world. "What did he do?"

"He broke the law, miss. Just like everyone else on your side of the bars." The man walked away.

"I haven't broken a law," Rose said quietly, knowing he wouldn't hear her. "Not yet, in any case." She put her hands on her hips and turned to assess just what she had to work with in the tiny cell. Not much: bars, a cot, a blanket, two buckets—one filled with water, the other empty. That was all. Certainly not much to plan an escape with.

And then a voice drifted down from the end of the line of cells. A very familiar voice.

"Rose Small?" Alun Madder asked. "Is that you, girl?"

CHAPTER TWENTY-FIVE

Cedar took a deep breath, savoring the warmth and ease of the soft bed. Nothing hurt. He could sleep all day and not be the worse for it.

But the soft bed was rocking enough he began to wonder if he were still aboard Captain Hink's airship, or maybe in the back of the wagon forcing its way through the blizzard toward Iowa.

That—a moment of sheer fear that he was still trapped in the blizzard, drowsy from the cold, and possibly on the edge of death—sent him rushing up through the warmth and comfort to wakefulness.

He was indeed in a wagon, the back of their traveling wagon, bundled beneath several layers of blankets. Wil lay next to him, sleeping in wolf form.

Cedar shook his head, trying to shell reality from dream. Wil had been a man, and so had Cedar. The curse was temporarily lifted by Father Kyne.

And then the curse had fallen upon them again, leaving Cedar a beast until the sun rose and Wil a beast until the next three nights of no moon.

Dawn must be upon them. And with dawn, Cedar had once again regained his man's body.

Which explained why he was naked.

Other memories tumbled through his mind, a chaotic mix of double images he could hardly put reason to. A few stood out clearly. He had followed the Strange with the pink ribbon. He had heard the children trapped in the icy river, and sensed the Holder down in that black watery grave. He had watched the Strange steal away that sleepwalking child, and had felt the pain of Father Kyne being beaten by someone.

Vosbrough. Father Kyne had been beaten by Vosbrough.

He rubbed his face. There was more: the children in the rock-tumble cave. Wil thought they might be alive, but how could they be after all this time, stashed away behind rocks?

The Holder, though—that he knew was beneath the river. He knew it like he knew his own heartbeat. He had to find a way to pull the deadly device free. He had no idea how to do that.

The wagon hit a bump, and he realized they were driving some-where. Mae. He hoped she was holding the reins. He searched the wagon for clothing, found a pair of breeches and a spare shirt, not as heavy as his other shirt. He'd probably lost his clothes when he'd shifted shapes.

These would have to do. He had an extra pair of boots with a hole in the heel, but a wad of cloth would keep them mostly watertight.

Wil was going to be so disappointed his favorite boots had been left behind. Cedar combed his hair back with stiff fingers and paused at the pain tightening his chest. He inhaled too quickly, which set him to coughing. His lungs hurt, his back hurt. Usually when he took the form of the beast, all his injuries were healed. But the spell Mae and Father Kyne had laid upon him must have changed that.

When his cough was settled, he scrubbed the sweat off his face and blinked to clear his eyes. He took several short, careful breaths to test that his lungs were still whole. Breathing hurt, but his cough was the least of their worries.

He gathered himself and swung out the back of the wagon, leaning wide so he could see their surroundings.

He was surprised to see the tall buildings and crowded street of the city. A quick look at the shadows told him it was just an hour or two past dawn. With his heightened senses from the change, he knew the two voices at the head of the wagon were Mae and Miss Dupuis.

Mae was there. Mae was safe. His heart seemed to unclench as relief flooded through him.

The wagon turned down a side street. Cedar recognized it as the alley that ran beside the courthouse. Mae called the mules to a halt, and then he heard her and Miss Dupuis jump down from the driving seat to the snowy ground.

They walked around the wagon and Cedar called out softly to Mae, "Good morning."

She glanced up at him, the worry slipping away for a moment as dawn brushed her soft features with the watery tones of spring roses.

"You're awake," she said.

"I am. Why are we in town?" He jumped down to the ground beside her.

"Because," Miss Dupuis said, coming up from the other side. "I have very bad news. The Madders are scheduled to be hung this afternoon."

"What? Have I lost days? There was to be a court hearing. You were to defend them. To stay the hanging."

"You've only been asleep a few hours," Miss Dupuis said. "The mayor has changed his mind. He has decided the charges against them are too egregious and numerous against the nation for a jury of peers to decide their fate. He has declared them guilty and the judge agrees. The jury hadn't even been assembled. But the court clerk was there and made note in the record."

"Is there no way to stop this?" Cedar asked. "Legally?"

"I sent a wire to the attorney general of the United States, but I don't believe I will receive a response before noon."

"And the mayor?"

Mae spoke. "He's set to kill them, Cedar. No matter what the law says. The Madders said it was an old rivalry between them, an old hatred. And for Vosbrough there was only ever one way to end this: with the Madders' death."

"They're still in jail?" he asked.

"Yes," Mae said.

"So we break them out."

"I agree," Miss Dupuis said. "But there is more you must know. Father Kyne is injured. And he too is in jail."

Cedar nodded. He remembered the injuries from his visions last night. "Can he walk?"

"I don't think so."

"Mae, could you help him with that? Heal him enough for us to free him?"

"I could try, but healing is gentle and difficult to speed along. And if we're running from the law, it will be even more difficult."

"What weapons do we have at our disposal?" he asked.

"The things you see here," Mae said. She pulled open the back of the wagon, and drew away an extra blanket that he didn't recognize. Beneath that blanket were rifles, pistols, and a couple sticks of dynamite.

"Where did you get these?"

"Some from the church, some from the Madders' supplies," Mae said. "I took you and Wil to the church first. Miss Dupuis met me there and told me the news. I assumed we'd need guns to work our way out of this."

"You are a practical woman," Cedar said with a smile.

"I can hold my own in a pinch."

"They're set to hang at noon?" Cedar asked.

"Yes," Miss Dupuis said. "We have a few hours."

"And no plan." Cedar rubbed his face again. Hunger and a lingering ache were stealing his thoughts away. He needed food. "Do we have water?"

"Yes," Mae said. "I'm sorry, Cedar. I should have told you that first. I brought you some food." She walked around the front of the wagon and returned with a saddlebag. He could smell the hardtack and jerked meat even through the leather.

"I didn't have time to make anything," she said, opening the bag.

"It's fine," Cedar said. "More than fine."

Mae handed him the bag. His hands were shaking from the hunger, but he managed to chew before he swallowed. Mae also gave him a canteen of cold water in which she had steeped some dried tea leaves. It was a humble meal, but more than a feast for his needs.

He saved half the meat and water for Wil, but finished all the hardtack, which he knew Wil wouldn't eat in wolf form.

His hunger temporarily abated, he went through the things at their disposal: guns, dynamite, the wagon, horses.

"Maybe in the middle of the night," Cedar said, "we'd have a chance. But to break them out in broad daylight, just the three of us, and somehow make it to the wagon with an injured man, and then get out of a town this size without being stopped . . . I don't know."

"Perhaps Wil could be a distraction?" Miss Dupuis suggested. "A wild wolf in the middle of town is sure to draw attention. And the law."

Wil must have heard his name. He lifted his head, then stood and stretched. He walked to the end of the wagon. He didn't step outside of the shadowed interior, but he was listening now.

Cedar quickly repeated the situation with the Madders and Father Kyne, and told him Miss Dupuis's suggestion.

"You could get into the jail," Cedar said, "lure out the lawmen. We could go in behind you, take out anyone else who was left, then get Kyne and the Madders out. We'll need to have the wagon close by for Father Kyne, and once we're out of that jail, we will need to leave town as fast as we can."

"It seems our best chance," Miss Dupuis said.

"There is one other thing," he said. "I know where the Holder is."

"What?" Miss Dupuis said. "Where?"

"In the river not too far from here. At the bottom of the river under ice," he clarified.

They were silent a moment, and Miss Dupuis closed her eyes and whispered something in her native French.

"You must retrieve it," she said.

"It's under ice."

"But you must. If it falls into the wrong hands, the world will suffer."

"Maybe the world's going to have to suffer a bit until spring. The lives of our traveling companions and Father Kyne are more important than a piece of a weapon no man can reach."

"Men will reach it," she said. "Men always do. The Holder must be contained."

"Not before we save the Madders."

She took a breath, held it, then said, "I believe they would think otherwise."

"Well, then, they can tell me I'm wrong while I'm dragging their hides out of this town and away from the gallows strung up for three."

"They will come with us if we break them out, won't they?" Mae asked Miss Dupuis.

Miss Dupuis shrugged. "I have known the brothers Madder for many years. But I still do not understand their ways. There is one thing I am certain about, however. They will risk anything, and anyone, to see that the Holder is gathered up and securely, permanently locked away."

Cedar started around to the driver's side of the wagon. "Well, we're about to tell them they're going to risk leaving it behind. Let's get this done."

CHAPTER TWENTY-SIX

"Mr. Madder?" Rose said. She walked to the farthest side of the cell bars so she could look down the hall toward where she'd heard his voice.

At the end of a hall was another cell. And standing with one elbow resting on a crossbar, holding several playing cards, was Alun Madder.

Rose had never been so happy to see him in her life.

"What trouble have you gotten yourself into now, Rose Small?" he said with a smile and a wink. "Always knew you were a spirited woman."

"Trespassing, apparently," she said. "Do you know they mean to hang you? You and your brothers?"

He nodded. "Building a gallows in our honor, I'm given to understand. Did you come in alone?"

"No, Captain Hink is with me, and a Mr. Thomas Wicks."

"Wicks?" Alun said. "Thin fellow, curly hair, tends toward bowler hats and books?"

"Yes. Do you know him?"

"We've made acquaintance."

She couldn't tell by his tone of voice whether they had met on good or bad circumstances, but made a note to herself to ask him, if they ever got out of this place.

"How long have you been here?" she asked.

"Came into town two nights ago. And were thrown in jail yesterday morning or so."

Bryn Madder and Cadoc Madder both walked up to the bars and gave her a wave.

"Good to see you, Miss Small," Bryn said.

"Hello," Cadoc added.

"Hello," Rose replied. "Why did they throw you in jail?"

"That's a long story," Alun said. Then, to Bryn, "It has been a full day and night now. I suppose that's long enough for Hunt to find what we're looking for, don't you think, brothers?"

"Should be," Bryn agreed. "Cadoc?"

Cadoc stared at the ceiling. "Lots of cracks in that mortar."

"There is, isn't there?" Alun said. "Rose, you'll want to stand back a bit."

"Rose!" one of the other prisoners called. "Is that your name, sweetheart? When I make bail, I'll come and get you and show you what a man can do for a woman."

"Or at least as much a man can do with a broken neck," Hink said placidly.

That got all the men in the cells riled up, and threats, the like she'd never heard before, sprinkled with more than a little blue language, filled the air.

Rose ignored the taunts and whistles, and moved away from the bars of her cell as the Madders had told her.

But the noise brought the lawman back to the hall. No, not just the lawman, the sheriff himself.

"What's all the racket back here?" He ran a nightstick against the other prisoners' bars, then headed down the rest of the hall. "You." He pointed at the Madders. "Stand away from the bars and shut your yaps."

Rose could hear the scuff of the Madders' boots as they each took one step backward.

"I said get away from the bars."

"You know, Sheriff," Alun said conversationally. "These bars are pretty strong. Solid steel. Good quality too; the mayor does not disappoint. I don't think even three men could break them down."

"However," Bryn added. "Stone is another matter."

"A Madder matter," Cadoc echoed.

"Don't make me shoot you, gentlemen," the sheriff said. "Mayor would hate for you to bloody up the new gallows before your necks snap."

"There's no need for guns," Alun said.

Rose snuck up to the front of her cell again. The sheriff had walked past her cell and was standing just out of arm's reach in front of the Madders' cell.

Just as she'd thought, each brother had stepped away from the bars. As a matter of fact, Bryn and Cadoc were even farther back in the cell, each of them leaning one hand against the stone wall there, as if loitering in front of a saloon.

Only Alun stood in front of the sheriff. And he was smiling.

One thing Rose had learned in the time she had known the Madders was a smile like that meant they were intending to make trouble.

"These metal bars are more than strong enough to hold us right where we stand. Only thing is, I can't say the same thing about the stone in which they're anchored. Do you see that?" Alun pointed to the ground.

The sheriff looked down. "The floor?"

"The floor," Alun agreed. "Brick and mortar. Stone held together by more stone."

"Your point, Mr. Madder?"

"Well, stone isn't at all the same thing as metal. Stone is known to crack, break, to move about if it so chooses. Metal? It stays in one place unless a man goes through some hard sweat to shift the stone aside and break the metal free. If a man really wants to set metal free, all he has to do is convince the stone to step aside a bit."

Bryn and Cadoc both had something small and shiny in their hands that looked like a brass piston. They placed the bottom of the piston against the wall where they were leaning and then depressed a button at the top of the device.

The building filled with the sound of ice cracking. Rose glanced at the ceiling and floor. The sound wasn't coming from outside the building; it was coming from inside. Every wall around her, the floor, the ceiling, was breaking apart. Cracks in the stone nearly a finger width snaked out from the base and top of each bar of her cell and ran lines up the walls.

The entire jail was cracking apart, all the stone crumbling.

"Rose!" Hink yelled. "Are you all right?"

"Fine!" she yelled back.

But the noise had brought all the rest of the lawmen crowding into the hallway.

"What in the hell is going on?" the deputy demanded.

The sound faded like the last rumble of a distant drum, and it was eerily quiet inside the jail again.

Until Alun spoke. "The rocks moved aside a bit," he said. "So the metal could come free."

And then Alun pressed one finger against one bar of his cell. The bar creaked and fell out into the hall.

Like a cascade of dominoes that just needed a push, all the other bars of his cell fell out too. And so did all the bars of the other cells.

There wasn't even time to take a deep breath before the entire jail-house erupted into a brawl. Prisoners rushed for freedom, prisoners rushed the lawmen, prisoners rushed prisoners, raising bare-knuckled fists or brandishing the bars of their cells.

The Madders were right in the thick of it, throwing punches at every man who wore Vosbrough green and laughing their fool heads off.

Rose ducked through the space of two fallen bars and kept her back against the side of the hall as she made her way toward the main room. The fight was an undulating sea of men and sweat and swearing. There were twice as many prisoners in the place as she'd seen on her short walk down the hall. Maybe the jailhouse was a lot bigger than it looked from the outside.

Right behind her was the cell with the dying man. She glanced in. He turned his head and opened his eyes, just slits of pain.

He didn't say anything. Didn't ask her to save him or give him mercy. Still, there was something that caught at her, caught at the deep parts of her, and made her want to help him.

"Time to be moving." Hink came up behind her and grabbed hold of her arm.

"We have to take this man with us."

"No, we have to get out of here," Hink said.

"I'm not going if he's not going," Rose said.

Hink scowled down at her, and she held his gaze.

"Oh, for the love of glim, woman." He gave her a small push out of the way so he could enter the man's cell. "Death of me. Always thought it'd be my ship, or some pirate come to stab me while I sleep, but now I'm pretty sure it's going to be you. You're death in petticoats."

He bent and without much fuss, picked up the man and slung him over his shoulder.

The man groaned, and promptly passed out.

Hink turned. "You." He pointed at Rose. "Get walking. Now."

Rose turned to do so and nearly ran into Bryn Madder.

"Rose? Thought you'd be long gone. Hey, there, Captain. What are your plans with that man?"

"Rose wants him carried out of here. I'm carrying."

"Aren't women curious contraptions?" Bryn asked.

"They are at that."

"Curious contraptions?" Rose said. "It's not as if men are exactly a deciphered wonder."

"Rose, darlin'," Hink said, "let's finish this argument after we escape from prison."

Bryn Madder stepped aside, and held his arm out for her like he was escorting her to a dance.

She took his arm, and they made a dash for the door, avoiding fists, broken bits of chairs, and swinging metal bars.

They were separated only once, and Rose made use of a lost boot to hit a man over the head, and then Bryn pulled her forward and out the door, Mr. Wicks on their heels.

Alun Madder stood outside the jail, smoking his pipe. "I do love a good morning brawl," he said as he exhaled smoke. "Helps to get the blood moving. What exactly are you thinking of doing with that man, Captain Hink?"

"Ask Rose," he said.

"What connection to him do you have, Rose?"

The fight seemed to be dying down inside, or at least there were fewer sounds of fists. There was, however, a gunshot.

"I think we can talk that over on the run, don't you, Mr. Madder?"

"I surely do," he said.

They took off at a run down the street and Rose couldn't help but think of what a motley crew they made: Hink, with a man bleeding over his shoulder; the well-suited Mr. Wicks; the three rugged Madders; and herself—still dusty and unbelted—dashing away from the jail and down streets and darkened alleys at break-leg speed.

A few people stopped and stared, but no one took after them, nor stood in their way. That was nearly unimaginable to Rose, though she was grateful for their indifference. In the small town she'd grown up in, there would have been half the population of Main Street out to chase down people running away from a jail.

Here in the city, it appeared to be nothing more than a passing curiosity.

And then a great whistle went off, piercing the air and rolling over the rooftops like a banshee screaming. It must be a siren telling the city they had escaped. It must be calling in more men, more guns, more matics to stop them.

"Where are we going?" Rose asked as Mr. Wicks paused at the end of the alley and turned left.

"Did you bring your ship, Captain Hink?" Alun asked.

"No. Came in by other means," Hink panted. He looked a little flushed and Rose suddenly remembered that he'd been shot before pounding his way through a brawl. Some of that blood on his coat might not be from the man he was carrying. It might be his own.

"Train," Hink added. "And air cable."

"Both?" Bryn asked, suddenly seeming interested in the conversation. "How so?"

"I'd be happy to tell you, Bryn Madder," Hink said. "So long as we survive this. You gents have any notions up your sleeves? Like, say, a bomb or two?"

"Not as much as," Alun said. He pulled up short at the next opening to the street and reached out and grabbed hold of Wicks's coat to drag him back into the shadows. "You hear that?" he asked.

Mr. Wicks shook his head. "Hear what?"

"Wagon wheels."

"It's a city, Mr. Madder. It's filled with wagon wheels."

"But these wheels are special."

"How so?"

"They're mine." He stepped out and put his fingers to his lips, letting off a piercing whistle Rose had heard many times when traveling with them.

"Your wheels?" she asked. "Someone has your wagon?"

"I'm hoping it's Mr. Hunt or Mae Lindson."

"Hoping?" Mr. Wicks said. "You're betting our lives on a vague hope?"

"I've bet more on less," Alun said. "Haven't regretted it. Often."

"This . . . this is ridiculous. Risky."

"Says the man who just broke out of jail."

Wicks shut up and gave Madder a slight smile. "You and I have had too little time to come to a full understanding of where we each stand for the good of this great country," he said.

"Let's not lose the mystery." Alun patted Wicks on the shoulder, then stood out in the middle of the street and waved the wagon down.

CHAPTER TWENTY-SEVEN

Cedar knew that whistle. He guided the horses down a side street and up another.

There, in the middle of the road, stood Alun Madder. He had his pipe in one hand, blood drying on his knuckles. One eye looked like it was swelling shut. He also had a huge grin on his face.

"Ho there, Mr. Hunt. Have you found the Holder yet?"

Cedar set the brake on the wagon. "We came to break you out of jail."

"Kind of you, but as you can see, unneccessary. As we told you, we Madders come and go as we please. The Holder?"

"I know where it is."

"Is it at hand?"

"Not exactly."

"Then by all means, be exact, Mr. Hunt."

"There's no time. We need to get you . . ." He glanced up, saw Captain Hink, Rose Small, a man who he didn't know, and the other Madders.

"Rose," he said. "What are you doing here?"

"Currently, I'm running for my life. Mind if we put this man in the back of the wagon? He's hurt terribly."

And that's when Cedar realized it was Father Kyne over Hink's shoulder.

"Yes, of course," Mae said, hopping down from the wagon and rushing to the back, where she helped Hink and Rose get Father Kyne settled.

"Did you bring your ship?" Cedar asked as Hink strode by.

"Nope. Flew a train."

Cedar wasn't sure he'd heard that correctly.

"We won't be needing a ship, Mr. Hunt," Alun said. "We need an answer." He rested his hand on the side of the wagon. "Where is the Holder?"

"Nearby, but beyond my reach."

Alun grinned. "You're beginning to sound like my youngest brother, Mr. Hunt. Can't have that, he'll get jealous. Tell me."

"I'll tell you when we're out of town."

"Perhaps you haven't been listening to me," Alun said. "We can't leave this town. *Can't.* Not won't, not might. Can't. That man?" He tipped his head toward the back of the wagon where Father Kyne was being laid out. "We're bound by our promise to his words and his exact words were . . ." He looked over at Cadoc.

" 'You will find every child lost by this city and return them to their family and homes, and will not leave this city until you have done so,' " Cadoc intoned.

Alun nodded. "Those words, Mr. Hunt, those exact words bind us. We must find every last child and bring each home. Our feet won't cross the boundaries of the city until we do just that."

"Maybe it's time you consider breaking a promise."

"Thought about it," Alun admitted. "If we let Father Kyne die, then we'd be released from the promise. Should we let the man die, Mr. Hunt?"

"Some might."

"Maybe we should. But then, that's the problem with promises. Each side offers up a little something of their soul for them and has a vested stake in the outcome. I don't see any reason to leave, or to break our promise to the father back there, if you're not doing your part to fulfill your promise to bring us the Holder. You say it's here; I see no reason to leave."

"I said it's beyond my reach."

"Where?"

"Beneath the ice, beneath the river," Cedar said. "Out of my reach and any other man's. Now, are you going to get in the wagon or wait for the lawmen to find you standing in the middle of the street?"

"Depends on where this wagon is going."

"Father Kyne needs medicines," Mae said. "We go back to the church and tend him."

"Mae," Cedar said, "We don't have time."

"He's dying," she said with a blank sort of matter-of-factness that did little to hide the anger in her eyes. "He'd want to do that in the heart of his church. That much we can give to him for what he's given us."

"Doesn't much matter where a man exhales his last breath," Alun said.

"I disagree with you, Mr. Madder," Mae said, and her words were made of iron. "He'll have the house of God around him."

Then she climbed up into the seat next to Cedar. "As quickly as you can, Mr. Hunt."

Alun caught the running board as the wagon started rolling. "Don't suppose you know what injured him so?" Alun asked.

"He carried the curse while I hunted," Cedar said. "While Wil and I hunted."

Alun was silent, then finally shook his head. "The Kyne men are some of the toughest I've even known." It was the first time Cedar had heard respect in Alun's tone for the father.

"I'll clamber back," Alun said. "The church is as good as any place to hole up while you go get us the Holder, Mr. Hunt."

"I'm not doing that for you, Mr. Madder."

"If you want this man's death to be worth anything, if you want the world to be safe from plague and famine and destruction, you will change your mind, Mr. Hunt. You and I can have a difference of opinion, but in the end, all that matters is the Holder. If we don't bring it to rest, then the living won't be living for long. And there will be no hope to save a single soul from the devastation that will befall us all."

Alun worked his way back along the wagon, nimble and quick, then swung in beneath the cover.

"Do you think he's telling the truth?" Mae asked.

Cedar nodded. He knew the danger of the Holder being loose, knew the poison it could spread in the land, and in the people. And he knew that if it fell into a man's hands, a man like Mayor Vosbrough, that the warning Alun Madder had just given them wouldn't be nearly dire enough.

"First we tend Father Kyne," Cedar said. "Then we decide what to do about the Holder."

Mae reached over and slipped her hand up beneath his arm and tucked herself more tightly against his side. He could sense her worry. He could sense her fear. And more than that, he could sense the magic that leaped to her hands, eager to be used.

"Were you able to heal him?" Cedar asked.

"I . . . I bound his soul to his bones with magic, and that is all I could do with my supplies here. But I will need to release his soul before . . . before he passes. Otherwise he'll be trapped there. Dead, but knowing."

Cedar didn't say anything. He could feel the shiver of revulsion that ran through her body. Once again he cursed the sisters of the coven who had gone to great lengths to convince Mae the power of binding and vows turned to nothing but evil in her hands. Many times her skill with spells had done just the opposite and seen that a merciful outcome was assured.

"You made a good choice," Cedar said. "A kind choice. It will give him time—give us time to get him home."

They rode the rest of the distance at as leisurely a pace as they could afford so as not to attract attention. Though Cedar saw lawmen on foot and on horseback obviously looking for the escaped prisoners, he did what he could to look all the while as if he were just going about his business and nothing more.

It helped that the Madders' wagon wasn't much to look at. It blended in well with all the other street traffic.

"Can you feel him?" Mae asked once they had made the far end of town and were turning down the lane that led to the church.

"Who?"

"Father Kyne. I can sense a bind still between you. It's thin, faint, but there is still something of him that clings to you. To your curse."

Cedar hadn't wanted to admit it, but he could feel him. "Some," he said. "An occasional drifting pain, or warmth or cold. No thoughts, no images."

She nodded. "His body won't hold against those wounds for long." She took a breath, then shook her head slightly and let it out.

"What?" he asked. "What were you going to say?"

"I could—I *think* I could bind health to him, strength to him."

"Would he heal from it?"

"Yes. I believe he might, if it's done soon enough."

"Why do you hesitate?"

"The strength would need to come from somewhere. The health I bind to him would have to come from somewhere. His body is too injured and lacking in resources to heal on its own. He would need another living person to offer their strength to him. And the wounds and pain he bears would slowly drain that person, giving the healing time to take."

"And if the healing didn't take?" Cedar asked.

"I think I could break the binding." Then, she said, stronger: "Yes, I could break it."

"I'll do it."

She thought on that a moment. "We already know you can be bound to him. That he can carry your burden."

"And I'll carry his. For a short time. Long enough to know if he can survive."

Mae squeezed his arm a little. "You are a good soul, Cedar Hunt. A very good soul in this world."

Though Mae's words made his heart swell, he wasn't sure he could agree with her. He had done bad things, many bad things. And one kind gesture didn't erase his past. Still, he was glad she, at least, found comfort in his decision.

He pulled the wagon up to the back door of the church. No use hiding it. If the sheriff and his men were looking for Father Kyne, they'd come out this way. If they were looking for the Madders, they might be on their way now to see if Cedar and Mae and Miss Dupuis were involved.

They might have only an hour or two or even just minutes before they were found.

Everyone, including the new man, Wicks, got busy taking the supplies—guns, dynamite, blankets—into the church. They moved the wounded Father Kyne as gently as they could on a makeshift sling and took him off to his bedroom, where he was to be laid out upon his bed.

As soon as everything and everyone was inside and the kitchen door had been closed behind them, Rose flew into Mae's arms and gave her a fierce hug.

"I was so worried about you," Rose said.

Mae hugged her back, gently rubbing her back. "I thought you were going to stay with the sisters," she said. "And help Captain Hink repair the *Tin Swift*."

Mr. Wicks moved around to stand at the opposite side of the table, keeping it between him and Wil, who paced the kitchen hungrily. Cedar knew his brother hadn't had enough to eat, so he walked off to the kitchen's larder to see if Kyne had any meats hanging.

A pork hock was wrapped and set on a shelf, and Cedar took it, un-wrapped the cloth, and brought it out for Wil.

Wil sniffed it, then took the bone in his jaws and walked—purposely—past Mr. Wicks, eyeing him the whole time, then settled in a corner where he could watch the door and all the people in the room.

"And then I thought I'd be better off on my own," Rose was saying to Mae. The two women were busy at the stove now, stoking the fire and heating water.

"Can I help?" Cedar asked.

"Not yet," Mae said. "You should eat, if you have the stomach for it."

Cedar glanced over at the man standing, not exactly nervously, more like with heightened awareness, behind the table.

"Mr. Wicks, is it?" Cedar asked.

"Thomas," he said. "Thomas Wicks."

"Hungry?"

"Starving."

Cedar gestured toward the larder and Wicks accompanied him there.

"What part of this brings your involvement, Mr. Wicks?" Cedar asked.

"I found myself aboard a train with Miss Small and Captain Hink. I'm afraid I'm just a bit caught up in their wake."

Cedar found a round of cheese and a loaf of flat bread. He pulled both out, and a handful of dried apples.

"Let's not lean on falsehoods," Cedar said. "You have a stake in this, or you'd have run down your own road and let us go our way."

"You're a perceptive man, Mr. Hunt," he said. "Perceptive enough to know a man doesn't reveal his secrets indiscriminately."

"Then I'll set my stake in this straight for you, Mr. Wicks. I am bound to the Madder brothers by a promise given. I will lay my life down for most the people in this church." He turned so he could glare down at the slight stranger. "And if you cross me, or otherwise cause harm to these people, I will break you in two and feed you to my wolf."

Mr. Wicks swallowed, his color going a shade paler than just a moment before. "Do I look like a man you need to threaten, Mr. Hunt?"

"You said I was a perceptive man. Has your opinion changed?"

Mr. Wicks smiled, and there was cunning, maybe even delight, in his eyes. He was impressed Cedar had seen through his bumbling greenhorn act.

"No, Mr. Hunt. It hasn't changed a bit. Where did you school?"

Here it was Cedar's turn to be impressed. "East."

Wicks nodded. "Strange how our roads lead us onward, isn't it?"

"I've no complaints."

"Other than fraternizing with escaped criminals?"

"Is that what you are?"

The corner of his mouth twitched again. "No. Not exactly."

"Then this isn't fraternizing. Exactly." Cedar handed him the dried apples and pushed past him out of the larder.

Cedar drew his pocketknife and shaved off a thick wedge of cheese while he walked back to the kitchen, then placed the cheese and bread on the table. The cheese was a bit sharp but surprisingly rich. To better fill his stomach, he tore off a chunk of the bread and ate that too. Then Mae was pressing a small cup of tea into his hands.

"You won't need to drink much of this, just a swallow or two. It's very bitter."

Cedar sniffed it and pulled his eyebrows up. "What's it for?"

"The binding."

"Binding?" Mr. Wicks said. "What do you mean by that?"

Mae glanced over at the man. "I mean that I'm a witch, Mr. Wicks. And I intend to cast a spell to bind health to Father Kyne. Mr. Hunt has offered to be a part of that spell."

Wicks's gaze darted to Rose. Rose just shrugged. "She is telling you the truth, Thomas. It won't change one whit whether you believe her or not."

"I . . ." he began, then recovered his wits. "I've just never met a, uh, a woman who so willingly claims to follow such . . . preoccupations."

"Have you drank it yet?" Mae asked Cedar.

He took a breath, held it, then sucked down two mouthfuls of the vile tea. He didn't know what she'd put in it, but wouldn't rule out boiled leather and rusted nails.

"Good. I think this will be best done near Father Kyne."

Cedar stood. He hadn't noticed Wil, who padded up silently next to him. If he had, he might have been fast enough to stop him from standing and placing his paws on the table. Might have even been fast enough to stop him from lapping up the remaining tea in the cup.

"No," Cedar said.

Wil was near Cedar's height when he was up on his back legs like this. And his eyes were those of a man, not beast. He knew very well what he was offering by drinking that tea. He was offering to help carry the burden of Father Kyne's life.

"Wil," Cedar said. "You should not do this."

Wil dropped down onto all fours, looked up at Cedar, then at Mae, and walked out the door toward Father Kyne's bedroom.

"Mae, I don't want you binding Wil's life to this."

Mae pressed her lips together, her hand on the tatting shuttle she wore around her neck. She only held that shuttle when she was very uncertain or frightened. But right now she looked like she was working a complex formula in her mind, or going through an unfamiliar dance to set each step in her memory.

"It might be better," she finally said. "No, it will be better. Two lives, two men's strength and health will lighten the burden. And he is also bound to Wil. Yes." Her soft brown gaze rested on him. "This is right. This is the best choice we can make."

"Then let's get it done." Cedar didn't hear anyone approaching the church yet, but it was only a matter of time. The faster they dealt with Father Kyne, the faster they could come up with a plan that included getting Mae, Miss Dupuis, and Rose out of this city.

Cedar strode off to Father Kyne's bedroom, and found the Madders gathered there, staring down at him. Captain Hink had found a chair and was sitting in it, his head resting against the wall. He didn't look in top shape.

The beast gave Cedar sharp senses, and in this room he could smell the deep, old blood weeping from Father Kyne's wounds, and also the fresh blood dripping out of Captain Hink. From the sweat on Hink's face and stink of pain, he knew the airship captain hadn't come out of that jailbreak unscathed.

"So, Mr. Hunt," Alun said. "We've returned the man to his own bed to die. A decent gesture. And now it's time for you to fulfill your promise to us."

"You'll have your promise," Cedar said. "But you'll wait."

"I grow tired of waiting, Mr. Hunt." Alun turned, and so did the other two Madder brothers, as if they were all soldiers in a line.

"We are all tired of waiting," they said with one voice.

There were times, like this right here, when Cedar questioned just what, exactly, the Madders were. They'd once told him they could talk to stone. They'd parlayed promises with him that cut deep as any metal shackle, and they seemed bent on a mission to retrieve the Holder, no matter the man, creature, or law that stood in their way.

But they did not go about their business as ordinary men might.

Cedar turned away from them. "What do you need from me?" he asked Mae.

"Just a drop of your blood," she said. "Please, brothers Madder, if you'll move aside, I'll do this quickly."

The brothers didn't move, didn't exchange a single word, but then, all at the same moment, they seemed to exhale, losing that intensity they had just possessed.

"You are a man made of steel will, Mr. Hunt," Alun said. Then, "What have you cooked up now, Mrs. Lindson? Some spell to get us our Holder, I hope."

"No, a spell to bind strength and health to Father Kyne, Mr. Madder."

"You think it a kindness to prolong a man's death?"

"I think it a kindness to save his life."

The Madders moved out of the way and Cedar stepped up by the bedside along with Wil. Cedar used his pocketknife to nick his finger, drawing a red bead there.

"And Wil," Mae said.

Wil put his left paw on the edge of the bed and Cedar drew blood near his claw.

Mae had a white handkerchief with pretty blue and yellow flowers embroidered in the corners. She dabbed the cloth in Wil's blood, then pressed it against Cedar's finger.

"This won't hurt," she whispered to him. She stood so close all thoughts were washed from his mind, replaced with only the need to hold her, to have her.

"I know," he whispered back.

And then Mae turned to Father Kyne.

She began humming, then singing a soft song with words Cedar did not understand. They caught at him and carried him along, and the room, the danger, the worry of the world was, for one blessed moment, lifted from his shoulders and mind.

The song was Mae, her voice, her soul, her love, and he wanted to lose himself in her forever.

Then she pressed the folded handkerchief with their blood into the wound over Father Kyne's heart.

And all the world came back to Cedar, bringing with it pain.

CHAPTER TWENTY-EIGHT

Rose stood just inside the bedroom door. There wasn't a lot of room in there with all the people gathered around the bed. Miss Dupuis and Mr. Wicks waited in the hall, talking softly. She even heard Miss Dupuis laugh once, a rare sound from a woman who had lost her longtime companion and lover only a few months ago.

Thomas was charming. She'd certainly fallen for his smooth manners. Rose glanced down the hall. Thomas and Miss Dupuis leaned on opposite sides of the hall, drinking tea. Miss Dupuis was a beautiful woman. Refined, poised, elegant. Somehow, even with all the wind and dirt, and running from the law, she had remained composed, not even a ruffle out of place or smudged.

Rose sighed. She'd just have to face that she'd never have that kind of grace. She was dirty, tattered, and her hair had come undone from its pins. She had other skills, though: metal and steam and cog. She didn't worry about her abilities in that area. She had a hands-on knack for the tinkering and devising things of the world.

Those skills were just as worthy as being able to stroll comfortably though social situations or remember which fork you were supposed to stab your vegetables with. Weren't they?

She looked back in the bedroom, and found Hink staring at her. He was sitting in the only chair, his arms crossed over his belly, his hat on his thigh, leaning back with both legs out, taking up the walking space. He looked a little pale, his hair slicked with sweat from the run he'd just taken.

He must be in pain from the bullet wound he'd gotten on the train, but he just raised one eyebrow and gave her a smile. "How do you like the horizon so far, Miss Small?" he asked. "Adventurous enough for you?"

She nodded. "Plenty, thanks. Maybe I should see to your wound."

"Don't worry. I'm just catching my breath."

She took a step into the room. "You are an incorrigible liar, Captain Hink."

"Call me Lee."

"All right, then. You are an incorrigible liar, Lee."

That made him smile a little more. "Aren't I just?"

He stood and closed the distance between them. She was caught once again by the sheer mass of the man, tall enough he had to duck doorways and with shoulders wide enough to send him at a tilt through hallways, corridors, and other tight spaces.

No wonder he loved the sky. There was all the space a man of his construction could want for.

"You're thinking about the *Swift*, aren't you?" he asked as he stopped in front of her.

"I . . . why?"

"I can always tell." His hand slipped down to rest on her hip, casually, as if it belonged there. She could feel the heat of his palm, even through the heavy coat and her layers beneath.

"You can? Tell what?" she asked.

"When you're thinking about my ship. You get this dreamy look in your eyes." He leaned in close over her. "Always makes me want to kiss you."

"Oh?"

He placed his other hand on the wall above her head. "What about that, Miss Small?"

"Kissing?" she said a little out of breath. "I . . . you do remember we just broke out of jail? Men are probably headed out here to kill us right now."

"I remember jail. All those long minutes without you beside me. Stirs up a fire in a man."

Rose grinned. "Minutes? It only takes you minutes away from a woman for your fire to get stirred up?"

"Well, not just any woman," he said. "You." And then the talking was over because his lips were against hers, in a most inappropriate and public display.

By glim, she didn't care. She had almost died today. She'd been thrown in jail. And Hink could act as relaxed as he liked; she knew there were men on the way with guns to make sure one or the other previous events were carried through. She kissed him back with abandon. If this was their adventure, their horizon, she didn't want to live it without him. Without his passion.

She was so busy with that kiss she figured she was missing most of the spell Mae was casting.

She finally pressed her palm against Hink's chest, telling him without words that the kiss was as far as this moment was going to go.

He pulled back, and for a quick moment she saw something more than humor and fire in his eyes. She saw pain.

"Come with me to the kitchen. I want you to take off your shirt," she ordered.

His eyebrows hitched up. "Go on. I like where this conversation is headed."

"I'm going to look at that hole in your side."

"I stand corrected. There's no time for that, Rose."

"I don't care. Paisley Cage, don't make me pull rank on you."

"You don't outrank me."

"I'm your boilerman, aren't I?"

He paused for a moment. "If you still want the job," he said hesitantly.

"Then I have the right to tell you when your ship is flying and when it's not. Right now, we're not going anywhere until the captain is taken care of."

"And just like that, I'm back to liking where this conversation is headed."

"Out," Rose said with one last glance at Mae, Cedar, Wil, and the Madders. Mae had stopped singing and Cedar swayed a bit on his feet, groaning like a mule had just kicked him in the chest. Bryn Madder was there to steady him, and Alun nodded, as if approving of the work Mae had done, work Rose could not see with her bare eyes.

They were nothing but in the way here, and Mr. Hunt would likely be needing the chair Hink had been occupying.

She started down the hall, and Miss Dupuis looked up. "Is it done?" she asked.

"I'm not sure. It might be. I'm going to tend Captain Hink's wounds. Are there clean cloths in the kitchen?"

"Yes, there's a cupboard with everything you'll need. We'll be right in."

We. She was already talking for Thomas now too?

Rose tried not to let it bother her. She had made up her mind about Thomas long before now. It was just that his falling in with Miss Dupuis was so sudden it stung a bit.

Although it shouldn't. She had just spent the last few minutes kissing another man.

"Sit," she said as she crossed the kitchen and began searching cupboards.

Hink made some noise getting settled in a chair.

Miss Dupuis entered the kitchen next. "Can I help, Rose?"

"No," she said a little too quickly, then, "I think I've got it. Do you know what we're going to do next?"

"The Madders will have only one desire," she said.

"The Holder?" Rose walked over to Hink. Instead of taking off his coat, he'd just unbuttoned it and tugged up the shirt beneath it to mostly reveal his side.

The makeshift bandage she'd put there from the train was soaked through with blood, not a stitch of white remaining.

This was worse than she'd thought.

She knelt and slid the kitchen blade up beneath the cloth, cutting the wrapping free as carefully as she could.

"Cold," he noted.

"It'd be easier if you took your clothes off. Just coat and shirts, down to skin," she clarified.

"All right, then." He shrugged out of his coat and then shirt. Rose was close enough to see that he held his breath through it all, his jaw clenched tight. It hurt. A lot. But he refused to show his pain.

Swinging from a chain at the center of his chest was the finder compass she had given him.

"You kept it?" she asked, surprised.

"What?"

Rose touched the necklace.

"Of course I did. It's the first gift you've ever given me."

"Oh," Miss Dupuis said, coming over to look at the wound more closely. "That does need some tending."

"It's a scratch," Hink said.

Rose looked away from the tenderness in his face, and assessed the wound. No, the wounds. Somewhere in that struggle he'd gotten the worst end of a blunt instrument across his ribs. From the black bruise and tears in his skin, it was probably one of the cell-door bars. From the lumpy look of his side, he had several broken ribs.

"Miss Dupuis," Rose said, "I think I could use your help."

"Of course. More hot water?" she suggested.

"Yes," Rose said. "Do you know how to make a compress? I saw comfrey on the shelf."

"Yes." She got busy putting that together and Rose looked up at Hink.

"You've got a bullet wound open and bleeding, and broken ribs. Someone also appears to have decided to tenderize all the meat on your bones. It's a mess, Lee. And you'll do as I say so that I can see it all doesn't go to rot and kill you."

"Pleased to see you so concerned for my welfare," he said.

"Of course I'm concerned. Not much use for a boilerman if there isn't a captain to fly the ship."

He grunted and then slouched back a bit and stared at the door. He was breathing with a hitch, and his skin was hot to the touch, though he shivered. Fever, for certain. Not a good sign.

Rose lost herself to cleaning his wounds and trying not to make him flinch. Miss Dupuis proved to be invaluable, and handed her fresh water, wraps, and compresses just as she needed them. Even Thomas was helpful in finding a shirt from Father Kyne's things that fit Hink well enough.

Once she was sure she had done everything she could think of, she helped him put his coat back on.

He was shivering still. "Rose," he said.

"Mmm?"

"You still have that copper bit on you?"

"Yes." She'd wanted to take it out of her shirt ever since they'd fled the jail, but there hadn't been time.

"Good. Give it to Mr. Wicks. He'll get it in the hands of someone who might know what to do with it."

"We can do that. You and I can do that."

"I'd rather cover our bets."

"You're not going to die, Lee Hink."

"I know that," he said.

She wasn't sure if he was going to say something else, but right then, the Madders strolled into the kitchen.

"You up for this dance, Captain?" Alun asked Hink.

"Still got my boots on, don't I?" he answered calmly.

"Do we have a plan?" Rose asked.

"We?" Alun helped himself to a hunk of cheese from the round Cedar had brought out, then poured himself a cup of the plain tea brewing on the stove. "I think we might have several plans."

"And what would those be?" Miss Dupuis asked.

Alun had a mouthful, so Bryn picked up the conversation. "Cedar Hunt, of course, will retrieve the Holder. We Madders will search for the lost children, and the rest of you." He narrowed his eyes, as if working hard to see just who he had fallen in league with.

"Mr. Thomas Wicks!" Bryn declared. "It's been a year or two, hasn't it?"

"Or five."

"Just so. Did you decide which side of the law suited your needs?"

"The right side, Mr. Madder. I am the Chief Territorial United States Marshal now, appointed by the president himself."

"Why, that puts you"—he turned and made a show of looking at Captain Hink—"in a position directly above our good captain here, doesn't it?"

"Yes," Wicks said, giving Hink a look. "It does."

Alun slurped his tea. "Would love to know what the chief territorial marshal is doing in this town. Some kind of trouble you're following, Mr. Wicks?"

"Something like that."

"Then we'll leave you to it." Alun handed his tea to Cadoc, who had finished off a chunk of bread, and swigged the tea to chase it.

"Mr. Hunt," Alun said as Cedar walked into the room. "It's time you bring us the Holder. We are done waiting."

"Under ice," Cedar said.

Rose glanced up at the hoarseness of his voice. He looked like he'd gained a year in just the few moments since she'd last seen him. She'd seen pain age a man like that, but not so quickly.

Dark circles shadowed his eyes, and he held his shoulders back and to the side as if any other position just set off more pain.

Wil, beside him, walked carefully. He too looked to be in pain, but not nearly as bad as Cedar.

"Aye, Mr. Hunt. So you've said," Alun agreed. "You'll find a way to draw it up from that river and quickly, before the life you're giving to Father Kyne gets in the way of your promise to us."

"Unless you have a device that can do that for me, Mr. Madder," Cedar said, his voice little more than a low rumble in the room, "then the Holder stays right where it is until spring melt."

"I'll do it," Mae said.

Alun's eyes went wide, and he leaned so he could see around Cedar to Mae standing in the doorway.

"I can . . . there are spells that might bind it. Cedar, I'll go with you and Wil. We will find a way to retrieve the Holder."

"Good," Alun said. "It's all settled then."

"Settled? How?" Cedar moved across the room—slowly, Rose noted—and poured himself a cup of hot water.

"You, Wil, and Mae will retrieve the Holder," Alun said. "Brothers Bryn and Cadoc and I will search for the children, which is what we've promised, and the others will do"—he waved his hand dismissively—"whatever it is they choose to do."

"We know where the children are," Cedar said after he took a long drink.

"What's that you say?" Bryn Madder asked.

"The children," Cadoc echoed. "Where have you found them?"

"There's a stand of woods just east a ways. The road past the tinker's shop leads to it after a fact. About a half mile in, there's a tumble of stones with a small opening. A Strange pocket. Wil went into that tumble and saw the children sleeping—he thought they were sleeping—in a chamber beneath those stones."

"Outside of town?" Alun asked.

"That's what I said."

Alun and the other two Madders all nodded once at the same time.

"Done," they said. Then they buckled coats and pressed hats tighter over bushy hair.

"Farewell to you, one and all," Cadoc Madder said.

He stepped out the door and Bryn simply gave a half salute, half wave and was out on the heels of his brother.

Alun was last to leave. He paused at the door. "Rose," he said. "Hurry up now; there isn't time to waste."

"Excuse me?" she asked.

"We'll need a spare pair of hands. And you're just the person for it. Grab your coat. We'll be waiting in the wagon."

Rose looked over at Cedar, who gave her a shrug, then at Hink, who was still slouching in the chair.

"I should stay with you. Mae told me children were missing," she said, "and it's part of a promise between the Madders and Father Kyne, but I don't know how I'm going to be any good in finding them."

"If the Madders find the children," Hink said, "and they're alive, do you think they're going to follow those old coots back to town? I'd say the children might take comfort in a woman being there."

"But if I leave, leave you . . ."

He raised his eyebrow. "Rose Small. Go find that horizon and stop worrying about me. I'm in the middle of a church with plenty of people and plenty of guns. What could possibly go wrong?"

"Father Kyne and fellow fugitives," a voice bellowed from the front of the church. "This is Sheriff Burchell. I've got all my lawmen and half the town out here. We know you're in there. We have the church surrounded. Come out with your hands up, or we will burn this place down."

"Well," Wicks said, putting on his bowler hat and pulling a gun out of the satchel he carried, "that could possibly go wrong."

CHAPTER TWENTY-NINE

Cedar knew the sheriff wasn't intending to negotiate with them. Half the people in the room, including the Madder brothers, had fought their way out from behind his city's bars. He was most likely hoping they'd walk out, hands up, so he could shoot them in cold blood and not have to worry about stringing the gallows.

Alun held the back door open for Rose. "Now's the time to decide. Wagon's rolling."

Rose grabbed her coat and rushed across the room. She must want to say good-bye to Mae and Mr. Hunt. She must want to say good-bye to Hink. But the entire kitchen was in a jumble of people hurrying up to either run for the back door or take a stand.

"What about Father Kyne?" Mae asked as she snatched up a cloth tied around a bundle of herbs for her spell casting.

"We'll stay with him." Miss Dupuis walked into the kitchen with her rifle and sidearm. "We'll protect him."

"I'll stay with you, Miss Dupuis," Mr. Wicks said. "See if I can talk some sense into the men out there. Either with words or bullets. Whichever seems to get more results."

"Go," Hink said as he stood. He wavered a bit and planted his palm on the table to keep himself steady. "Get the children. Get the Holder.

Get whatever it is we need so we can get the hell out of here. We'll be fine." Then he added a little more gently, "I'll be fine, Rose. Go."

Cedar wondered if she heard the good-bye in his tone.

Cedar strode to the door and put his hand on Rose's shoulder. She pressed her lips together, then let out a breath. And with that look of determination she often wore, she turned and ran after Alun Madder, who was already on the slowly rolling wagon, his hand held down for her to catch. As soon as Rose was safely up in the wagon, Bryn Madder snapped the reins and set the horses to galloping. Straight at three mounted lawmen who stepped out from behind the barn to stop them.

Cedar knew what the Madders were doing. They were causing a distraction so he, Mae, and Wil could reach the barn, the horses, and hurry out to the river.

Mae had her gun drawn and so did Cedar as they made a run for the barn. The sheriff had been stretching the truth a bit. The church wasn't completely surrounded, and there were no other men around the barn.

The horses inside the barn were saddled. He didn't know who had taken the time to see to it, other than maybe Miss Dupuis and Mr. Wicks. Whoever it was, he silently thanked them. There was an ax hanging on the wall, and he took that before swinging up into the saddle. Mae was already astride her horse.

Then they rode as quickly and quietly as they could out of the barn and across the field through spindly trees and shadows, Wil leading a winding path to the river.

Cedar was breathing hard. Everything was more difficult with the tie between him and Father Kyne. He felt Father Kyne's pain, felt the draining weariness of his wounds as if they were his own. And the aches and pains he'd been enduring since he came to town felt even worse. Wil felt Kyne's pain too, but seemed to tolerate it much better than he did.

Cedar could bear this pain for a few hours, maybe for a day or two if he could spend them in a sickbed, but if Kyne didn't begin to mend or heal in that time, Mae would have to break the spell. Cedar felt a need to repay the debt of Kyne carrying their curse, but both of them, or all three of them, dying wouldn't do the world a bit of good.

They urged the horses into a slow lope, following Wil as he carved a path through trees and brush toward the river.

The crack of gunfire broke across the cloud-heavy sky. Then return fire rolled out.

"The church," Mae said.

Cedar nodded. Leaving Hink, Miss Dupuis, and Wicks back to guard Father Kyne was really no more than a gunfight waiting to happen. They'd be wise to surrender. As far as he knew, the three of them weren't on the mayor's hanging list.

Even though he wasn't a praying man, he found himself wishing there was more he could do, more any of them could do, to turn that fight in their favor.

The gunshots were constant, then became more sporadic, but did not cease.

Wil, panting, stopped short of the river, which lay on the other side of a thin line of trees. He lifted his head and looked up at Cedar.

"Is this the place?" Mae asked.

Cedar dismounted, throwing the horse's reins over a low branch and drawing the shotgun out of the saddle holster.

"River's just that way," he said. "It rushes between two rocks, but is iced full over."

"And you are sure the Holder is beneath it?"

"I am sure. And there's more. When we came out this way last night, following that Strange, it stood on top of the ice, pointed at the river, and said one word: 'help.'"

Mae frowned. "So you think it wants the Holder too?"

"I don't know what it wants. I don't know what help a Strange thinks

I'd be willing to offer. But it wasn't the call of the Holder that brought me to the river. We followed the Strange, and as soon as we were near the river, we could hear the voices of children."

Mae had dismounted and was in the middle of tying her horse to a bush. She looked up at Cedar, startled.

"Children? But Wil said he saw them sleeping in the old mine shaft."

"Strange like to play with a man's mind. Show him roads off the edges of cliffs, show him lights down the bottom of ravines, or promise him his heart's desire and deliver nothing but smoke."

"So you don't think the children are really here? You think the Strange somehow made you imagine their voices?"

"I don't know. It makes the most sense."

"Do you hear them now?"

Cedar pushed the pain away and listened with ears sharper than any man's. Wind scrubbed through sticks, birds and beasts in the forest searched for food, the city clattered and clamored behind them, while far-off trains whistled and airship fans rose and fell. Plenty of noise in the silence of the day.

But no children crying. No voices calling out. No sorrow.

"I don't hear them," he said. "I don't even hear the Holder. But I know it's here."

"Then let's go get it." Mae settled her satchel across her shoulders. It was filled with herbs and other small tokens to help focus her spell craft.

She had also made sure to holster a gun at her hips, and when she looked up at Cedar, he reached out and brushed the hair away from her cheek.

"Be careful," he said.

"I will be. Is the binding too much?"

"It's bearable." It wasn't a lie. Yet. "Do you think it's helping him?"

"More than I expected," she said. "I'm not practiced enough with what bindings and vows can do. I've spent too many years without using spells, and now that I am free of the coven . . ." Her words drifted off. Cedar knew that in some ways she regretted leaving the sisters. The coven had been her home, her sanctuary for most of her younger life. If Jeb Lindson hadn't wandered through their fields and led her heart all the way to the wedding aisle, Mae would likely still be living her life with the women in Kansas.

". . . now that I am free of the coven's restrictions and rules," she continued, "I am finding magic useful for so many things."

"I would have never survived the blizzard before we came into town without your warmth," he said. When she tipped a smile at him for how exactly that sounded, he smiled back. "Also," he clarified, "without your spells that bound warmth to my bones."

"I'm just happy we . . ." She shook her head. "I'm just happy. And it's been a while since I could say that."

Cedar nodded. He felt the same.

But time was slipping away. He walked down the rough path to the river, Wil sliding, like a shadow, beside him.

The wind went dead, though there was nothing to block it. Wil growled softly and stopped well before they left the edge of the trees.

Cedar felt it too.

"Witchcraft," Mae said. She stood at Cedar's left.

"A spell?" he asked. "Can you tell what kind?"

He shouldn't be surprised to find spell work in the area, though he was certain this spell had not been in place just last night.

"I'm not sure. It's powerful. Whoever cast it is very practiced in the arts."

She pressed her fingers on his sleeve as he took a step forward. "Why? Why would someone cast a spell over this section of this river?"

"Is it made for repelling people from this road? From this river?"

"Yes, and more than that. Can you feel the . . . well, it's sort of a deeper rooting that runs beneath the road too. That line of stones?" She pointed at the row of small stones carefully set front to back in a straight line blocking the way to the river. "If we walk over those stones, or disturb them in any way, we'll let whoever cast this know that their spell has been disturbed."

"We need to reach the river." Cedar rolled possibilities through his mind. "Unless you can draw the Holder up from the bottom?"

"With a spell?" Mae shook her head. "I could call it to itself, bind it to its own if it were broken, but to just call it free—I do not have that power."

"You could bind it to me," Cedar said. "And we could break it."

"No."

He had been studying the icy water, but at her tone, looked down at her.

"I bound one piece of the Holder to Rose, and she is forever changed because of it. If I bound a weapon of such Strangework to you . . ." She pressed her lips together and shook her head again.

"Then we'll have to go in after it."

"Diving in that river will kill you."

"Not if you cast a spell of warmth around me."

Wil walked up and gently put his mouth around Cedar's wrist.

"Warmth around us. Wil and I will dive for it."

"Wil doesn't even have thumbs," Mae said.

"But he senses the Holder differently than I do. If I can't find it in that dark, he'll be able to lead me to it."

Another round of gunfire echoed in the distance.

"Mae," he said. "We are all running out of time."

She closed her eyes. "Yes. I'll do it. Give me a moment." She dug in her satchel and tucked several small items into her palm. He knew that whenever she could she'd been gathering tokens that represented the elements of earth, air, water, and fire—things like unstruck matches, stones, and an odd assortment of cotton threads, buckles, bones, and buttons.

"I'll need you both to hold very still. I am going to ask the warmth to wrap you as one."

Wil leaned a little closer to Cedar and Cedar knelt down so he was of the same general size as the wolf.

Mae cast the spell, and just as it had when they were forging through the blizzard, it settled around him like a heavy, hot blanket. It wasn't exactly comfortable, but since he was about to dive into an ice-covered river, he was happy for the weight of the spell and its protective heat.

They just might survive this dive.

"You'll need to do it quickly," Mae said. "One dive and right back up. The spell won't last long for both of you."

Cedar stood, and took half a step, leaning over Mae. He wrapped his arm around her, pulling her full against his body.

The spell surrounding him felt of her, smelled of her perfume. It even tasted of her.

It made him want her.

She reached up and kissed him. He had intended it to be a gentle kiss, but she was fierce, clinging to him, knowing, as he knew, what a very slim chance it was that he and Wil would survive this.

Wil growled.

Children's voices rose around them, sighing, crying, sobbing. And behind that sound was the eerie ring of the Holder. Calling. Calling Cedar and Wil down to their deaths, just as it had called the children.

Mae pulled back, and so did he.

"I need to . . ." Cedar started.

"Yes," Mae licked her lips to catch the last of the taste of him on her tongue. "You should."

"I'm coming back," he said.

"I know." And then she gave him a look of faith that he'd never known before. She believed he'd find the Holder. With her spell, with Wil.

He wasn't about to disappoint her.

Cedar shrugged out of his coat and hat, and carried them, along with his shotgun and the ax, over to the river. He left all his clothes and his boots on, but even in just his shirtsleeves, winter could not touch him through Mae's spell. He glanced up and down river, then crossed over the line of stones.

There was no sound, no shadow movement in the forest, no gunmen. It appeared as if there was no warning attached to the stones, as Mae had worried there would be.

It could be another trick. Stones stacked in a line by the Strange to make a man think there was magic there.

To keep him and Wil from the Holder.

Cedar bent, loosened the laces on his boots, then left them beside the river, his coat and hat and gun all stacked with them. He held the ax loosely in his hand.

Wil's ears were up as he searched the ice covering the river. They'd need to go in directly above the Holder, dive straight down, catch it up, and pull back onto the bank fast.

A man couldn't live long in that water. Not more than a handful of minutes. But there would be enough time to dive to the bottom if the river wasn't too deep. There would be enough time to find the Holder.

Cedar walked upriver just a bit, toward the rush of water pushing between the huge stones on either bank. The heat of Mae's spell was beginning to make him sweat, as was the tie of pain with Father Kyne.

Wil paused, then took a step onto the ice. Cedar tipped his head, listening for the children's cries, but more than that, listening for the music from the Holder.

He stepped out on the river in his stockinged feet, following Wil.

His brother took just a few steps downriver and then stopped closer to the far side of the river than the side Mae waited upon.

Cedar agreed. The Holder was here, beneath his feet, calling. Calling for their death.

And when he looked down, between the bare ice spread out under a dusting of snow, he could see the children, trapped beneath the ice like shadowy ghosts, pounding and clawing at the ice above them.

Screaming to live. Begging to be free.

CHAPTER THIRTY

Rose held on tight as the wagon rumbled down the road at top speed. Bryn was driving and let out a whoop when anyone got in their way on the street. He was not slowing down, no matter who or what was in his way, a fact that was quickly proved out by all the cussing and swearing going on around them.

"You want to put this on, Miss Small." Bryn handed her a leather harness.

"What for?"

"For our escape," he shouted.

She hesitated, then wrapped the harness around her ribs and latched it in place with several snaps. It fit tight as a corset, with just enough room for breathing.

While Bryn was busy trying to keep at least two of the wheels on solid ground, Alun and Cadoc crawled down the side of the wagon, facing the back of it, each carrying a gun.

"What are you doing?" Rose yelled from the bench beside Bryn.

"Taking care of this like we should have when we first rolled into town," Alun yelled. "Ready, brother Cadoc?"

"Days ago," he yelled back.

They already had their guns drawn, but instead of shooting, they both tucked a finger into their pockets and threw something at the riders closing in behind them.

"One!" Alun yelled.

It wasn't dynamite, but whatever they lobbed on the street kicked up enough light that Rose went half blind, even in the full light of day.

She'd seen the Madders use those light tricks before. They'd told her it was glim mixed with a few other things, in small, corked bottles. When the bottles were shook up good and hard, say like when they hit cobblestone and shattered, the mixture of glim turned into a light that would blind the sun.

As if that weren't enough, they started shooting at their pursuers.

"Two!" Cadoc yelled back.

"And . . . three!" they both said.

Bryn let go of the reins. "Hold on to your hat!" he said.

Rose grabbed hold of the brim of her hat just as Alun, Cadoc, and Bryn all fired their guns straight up in the air.

"What are you doing?" she yelled. Before Bryn could explain, she'd figured it out.

He wasn't shooting bullets into the empty sky; he was shooting a grappling hook, straight up at the cabled airship above them. A cabled airship that was zipping faster than a gallop over the tops of the buildings, the cable buzzing down the street rail line, and hooking hard down a side street.

This was madness.

She took a breath and held it.

Bryn slipped one arm around her through the harness loops across her back. His other arm was buckled at wrist, arm, and shoulder and attached to the leather strap around his ribs and to the grappling-hook rope.

Three hooks hit their targets with the distant sound of knuckles rapping hollow logs.

She was yanked up out of the wagon so fast and hard she lost her breath completely.

The Madders did not whoop and holler as they usually did during death-defying stunts such as these. Bryn was, however, grinning like a cat in a bird's nest, and so were Alun and Cadoc, who dangled from their own grappling ropes not far from them.

Rose was pressed against Bryn's side, locked there. She squinted her eyes against the icy wind to see where the airship was dragging them.

They were dashed away from the wagon and the chase below at an alarming speed. And since they had exited so quickly, the horses kept running a good block or so farther into town before slowing down.

Blinded, and expecting gunfire, the lawmen had followed a little more cautiously, but had not seen them fly free from the wagon. And she knew the weight of four people wouldn't do much to make the airship fly any differently. Not with the load of cargo roped below its envelope, and the cable doing part of the work to push the airship to its intended drop point.

The airship sped nicely above even the tallest of the city's buildings, ensuring it wouldn't get buffeted by a stray wind into a chimney or spire.

But the Madders' ropes were so long, they dangled between buildings, about five stories up from the ground. No one looked up, except a dog or two that barked. Everyone in the city was too busy rushing, and too used to simply stepping aside for the cable as it passed to notice anything amiss.

"How do we get down?" Rose asked.

"You might not want to know, Miss Small."

"I most certainly—"

"Now!" Alun yelled.

Bryn glanced up and shifted his grip on the gun.

Shifting his grip actually caused a cutting device to snap the rope.

Rose grabbed Bryn's arm tighter as they fell.

A flat rooftop was coming up fast. Too fast. She didn't know if they'd hit it, or if the force of breaking the rope while they were being towed by the airship cable would mean they had overshot the roof completely and would fall to their deaths in the street.

"Out!" Bryn yelled as he pushed her away just a bit.

Rose readied herself for the landing. *Just like falling out of a tree. Just like falling off a fence. Just like falling off a cut rope from the bottom of a cable airship.*

She hit the roof on feet, then knees, lost all contact and rolled, caught by Bryn's larger mass and momentum until she lost track of which side of her was up and which was down.

Pain shot through her arm, and she screamed.

Then the world stopped.

And she was still on it.

The airship fans faded away off to her left. She opened her eyes.

She was lying flat on her back, scuffed, bleeding, and sore, her stupid skirts untucked from her belt again.

A shadow moved next to her: Bryn, pushing up on hands and knees and shaking his head to try and clear it. Somehow he had unhooked his arm from the harness that bound them together in enough time that they fell separately and landed, mostly, whole.

"Miss Small?" Bryn asked in a dusty voice. He coughed, tried again, "Rose, dear?"

Dear? In all the time she'd known the Madders, she'd never heard one of them address her with such familiarity.

"Is she all right?" Alun asked from farther off. "Is she breathing?" He was concerned. Truly concerned.

On the one hand, it warmed her heart to hear the Madders' worry for her. On the other hand she had knocked her noggin pretty hard. She could just be imagining their concern.

"I'm fit as a fine," she slurred. That wasn't right, was it? Fine as wine? Fiddle fine? "Whatever is fine, I'm that," she said.

She blinked several times to get the focus back into her eyes. Sky up there, heavy with unspilled snow. Then a round, bearded face with a round nose and round eyes that were clearly narrowed in pain.

Alun Madder bent down over her.

"Rose, are you all in one piece?" he asked.

"I am. I think." She moved to sit and yelped again.

"What is it?" Alun asked.

"Her arm," Cadoc said from far enough away she didn't know how he had guessed at her injury.

"Can you bind it, brother Cadoc?" Alun asked.

"No," Rose said. "It's . . ."

But then Cadoc was there, helping her sit. And then Cadoc gently took her arm in his big, wide calloused hands, as if lifting a bird's broken wing.

She whimpered, but he was as careful as could be, assessing the break. He withdrew two smooth wooden dowels from inside his coat, steadied her arm with both sticks, wrapped a length of cloth around it all, then used a wider, soft cloth that smelled of lemon balm to sling her arm against her chest.

"Now, you will not want to move your arm, Rose Small," he said kindly. "Well, you may want to move it but you should not. There is healing that must be done, bones that must latch and clasp and mend. It has been a fine arm for you. It will be a fine arm again. If you let it rest. If you let it heal."

"Thank you," she said, still feeling a little woozy.

"Always happy to help one of our own."

He was standing and walking away before she could really get her thoughts in order about that statement. She was one of their own? How?

"How much farther?" Alun asked.

Rose glanced over at Alun and Bryn, who were standing at the edge of the rooftop.

"Just there." Bryn adjusted the monocle over his eye, then pointed. "Far as we'll go."

"It will have to be good enough, then," Alun said. "Do you have your breath, Miss Small?"

"I can walk." She proved it by strolling over to them.

"I hope you'll consider a jog or two," he said as he pointed to the iron ladder that clung to the edge of the building, "once we hit the ground."

"I'll be fine," Rose said.

Bryn nodded, and started down the ladder.

"You next, Miss Small," Alun said.

Rose walked to the edge, tucked her skirt back into her belt so the ruffles wouldn't be in her way, then crouched and eased her foot down to the first rung.

It took more effort with one bad arm, but Rose knew how to climb a ladder and did so swiftly.

Once her boots were on solid ground, she took several deep breaths to steady her heartbeat. She had never minded flying. Falling, she didn't enjoy.

"Come, now, Miss Small," Alun called as he started down a dark alleyway at a slow lope. "We're almost there."

"Where?" she asked as she tried a few faster steps and mercifully found that her arm could bear the jostling.

"Edge of town. Beyond that if you're willing."

"Willing? To find the children?" she asked.

"Yes, that. Which we can do if you make us a promise."

The alleyway opened up onto the unpaved road that cut across the north end of town.

"Brother Bryn?" Alun asked.

Bryn flipped the spread of lenses up and away from the monocle, then snicked them into place, one by one.

"Promise?" Rose asked. "Why do you need a promise from me? You've already promised Father Kyne you'll find the children, haven't you?"

"Oh, yes, that promise remains exactly as he stated it. We are not to leave the city until we find the lost children. It's a problem."

"A puzzle," Cadoc said distractedly.

"A predicament," Bryn added.

"And we Madders have discovered, over time, that even the most devious problems are quickly solved by a simple promise," Alun said.

"Right," Rose said. "Just as this Small knows that no promise is simple when it's made with a Madder."

Bryn laughed and Cadoc chuckled.

Alun gave her a wide smile and a wink. "You are a clever girl, Rose Small."

"It's there," Bryn said. "A hollow, the Strange pocket, on the other side of those trees."

"Can you tell if there are children within it?"

"No."

"It will be our risk then. Do you see that stand of trees, Rose Small?" Alun asked.

"Of course."

"On the other side is our best guess of where the lost children of this city might be held."

"All right," she said. "Why aren't we going there right now?"

"Because this," he pointed at the side of the road beneath his feet, "is where the city ends."

Rose stared at the road, then looked back to Alun. "I don't understand."

"We are bound to not leave the city until we find the lost children."

"You are locked here? By a promise?"

"It is an old promise," Alun said.

"Made of blood," Bryn added.

"Sealed in faith," Cadoc said.

"Unbreakable," Alun finished. "So we'll need another promise, from you, Rose Small."

"Will it help us find the children so we can all leave this place?"

"Yes."

"Will it do any harm to the people I care for?"

"No."

"Then what do you want from me?"

"Your word," Cadoc began.

"Your blood," Bryn added.

"Your body," Alun finished.

CHAPTER THIRTY-ONE

Cedar shifted his grip on the ax, set his feet, and swung at the icy river.

The ghost children cried and screamed, reaching for the ice, reaching for the ax blade as if it alone could pull them free.

He swung the ax again.

Again.

The river cracked. The children slapped and pounded at the ice.

And then the ice broke free.

Wil dove into the water, narrowly missing the blade of the ax as he did so.

Cedar swore, then swung the ax one last time to bury it in the ice. Diving into the river was easy. Getting out was going to be much more difficult. The ax would serve as something solid to grip so they could pull themselves up.

Cedar bent and reached down for the child who floated just beneath the surface, eyes wide and blank, staring at the sky. But as soon as Cedar's hand closed around the boy's arm, the boy was gone, as if he were made of nothing but water and light.

They weren't real. They might sound like the children, and they might look like the children, but they were ghosts, spirits. Perhaps nothing more than disembodied souls.

Cedar took no time to ponder the situation further. He held his breath and dove into the river after Wil.

Blackness, complete except for the ghostly light of the sobbing children.

Silence, unbroken except for the sound of grief.

Even with Mae's spell around him, he could feel the pressure of cold around him, as if he pressed bare skin against a window while winter raged on the other side.

He kicked toward the river's bottom, working against the current, knowing he'd have to find the hole he'd chipped in the ice if he wanted to breathe again.

The Holder was here; he knew it was. He could hear the unsprung sour melody of it coiling through the water from all directions. Calling him on.

There was no light to show him where the Holder lay. There was only the sound of it, the feel of it. He shifted left and kicked harder, downward.

He didn't know where Wil was in the water, but Wil's instincts were as good as or better than Cedar's here in the dark and cold. Cedar stretched his fingers forward, feeling grassy dirt and stones, odd and slick, their rough, cutting surfaces dragging at his palms as he scoured the river.

The Holder was here. It had to be here.

But he didn't know the shape of it, didn't know exactly the size of it. It could be as small as a pea.

He was blindly grasping for something he'd never had a clear look at, underwater, in the darkness, in the dead of winter.

He searched for the Holder, and he searched for more. The drowned bodies of children should be here. They might have been killed. Thrown in this river or lured into it by the Holder. That might be the reason their ghosts lingered around this place.

His lungs clenched in pain. There were no dead bodies. Not that he could see or feel.

He needed air. Now. Cedar kicked upward, searching for a spear of light through the hole. Spotted it, upriver farther.

He pushed through the water, kicking hard, the glim green ghostly children swimming alongside him, tugging on his arms and legs with insubstantial hands, begging him not to leave them to this watery death.

The light was there, just ahead of him. Wil was swimming too, moving toward that hole, moving toward the promise of air.

And then the warmth spell broke.

The cold of the river hit him as hard as a train at full throttle. The pain of it, the overwhelming ice of it, slammed into his chest, driving all the air out of him. He struggled not to inhale. Not to fill his lungs with the water.

Wil struggled too, thrashing, mouth open, wolf eyes wild with panic.

Cedar's muscles screwed tight, arms and legs unwilling to move.

He pushed to lift his arms. It took all his strength to force his feet to kick.

Wil was not doing as well. His movements became weaker and weaker, and he began to sink.

Cedar pushed up to him, grabbed him by a front leg, and swam to the oval of light.

He grappled at the edge of ice with a hand and arm he could not feel, pulling his head and Wil's above water.

He inhaled. The air sliced through his lungs, and his heart stuttered.

Too cold. They had been in that water too long. Much too long.

And they had failed. Had failed to find the Holder. Failed to bring this nightmare to an end.

The world drained down to darkness, but he kept moving, until finally his hand hit the buried ax. He wrapped numb fingers around the haft, then pulled, heaving himself and Wil out of the river in bits and lengths until they were both lying half-frozen and shivering on the windswept ice.

He blinked, the blackness took him, blinked again, and was coughing, every muscle in his body knotted in pain.

Slowly, too slowly, thoughts formed again. He needed heat. Needed to get out of the wind. Was Wil alive? Where was Mae?

And through those thoughts came the knowledge that someone was speaking. Someone had been speaking for some time. A man's voice.

Mayor Vosbrough.

"I thought I'd made it clear that this city belongs to me. I locked your friends, the Madders, away. I warned you quite clearly at breakfast.

"I thought you, Mae Lindson, a witch of your . . . reputation—now don't look so surprised; the sisters have told me about you and I am impressed with your work. Still, I thought you would understand just how strongly I feel about keeping my city safe, and in my control. Didn't Sister Adaline explain how this new world operates? The rich own the witches. Well, certain rich. And I am that certain rich. I own you, Mrs. Lindson. And it's high time you behave accordingly."

"Do not come any closer," Mae said.

"Or what will you do, Mrs. Lindson? Cast a spell against me? Do you even know who I am? Do you even know the things I have done right beneath your notice?"

"I don't have to use a spell, Mayor Vosbrough. I have a gun."

Cedar knew he had to help her. Had to turn his head, see where the mayor was, see how many men he had with him. Had to fight. But it was all he could do to draw in each breath.

"You think you can shoot me?" The mayor chuckled. "That is *very* confident of you."

"I said step away, Mayor Vosbrough." Mae did not sound frightened. But then, she had faced down nightmares and Strange in equal portion. She was made of steel in the face of fire.

"Maybe," the mayor said in a hard, cold tone, "*you* should step away. Witch."

Cedar pushed up, moving on instinct alone, unable to feel his body. He somehow got to his knees, and looked around him.

Wil lay still on the ice, a short distance away. How had they gotten so far from each other? He was too still, though Cedar saw his chest rise once and fall. Breathing, but barely.

Mae stood on the riverbank, just downstream from him and Wil. She'd pushed her hat off her head, and stood with her rifle aimed at Mayor Vosbrough.

The mayor was dressed in rich green velvet, a black fur coat, a top hat, and fine black leather gloves.

Cedar recognized those gloves. Vosbrough had done something to him, hurt him, wearing those gloves. He shook his head, trying to clear his thoughts. Was it just his memory of Father Kyne being beaten filling his mind?

Beside Vosbrough stood some kind of strange matic. It looked like a headless man, taller at the shoulder than Vosbrough's head, and wider to match. On its back was a tank wrapped in tubes and hoses that draped over its shoulder and strapped to its arm. Those hoses and wires were wound tightly between small glass tubes filled with colored liquids.

And in the center of its leathery chest was a copper contraption with a glass orb marking the direct heart of it.

Cedar blinked, unable to believe what he was seeing. For he knew, without a doubt, that inside that glass orb wrapped in copper and glowing with green glim light was a Strange. Was the Strange trapped in that monstrosity, or there willingly?

"Put your gun down, witch," Vosbrough said. "This is only a small portion of the weapons at my disposal. Weapons my family has devised and tested. This is only a small portion of the great advances we will use to bend the world to our favor. You have a choice. Be a part of this new age, the Vosbrough Age, or be crushed under the wheels of our domination. Choose your side."

322 • DEVON MONK

Cedar tried to call out to her, to tell her to put the gun down so Vosbrough wouldn't shoot, but nothing more than a groan escaped his lips.

But Mae was already bending to set her gun on the ground at her feet.

"Is that your pet, witch? I didn't expect him to be breathing after that fall into the river. Although I do wonder why you are out here so intent on killing yourselves."

"We are looking for the children who have gone missing," Mae said. "Something you and your men should be doing."

"Why? They are just casualties in our struggle with the Strange. We need the Strange for our devices, so we draw them here."

"That was the sound of horns in the night?" Mae asked.

"Yes. A device, a generator, calls the Strange, and a netgun in the hands of my men traps them. When transferred into these batteries and mixed with glim, the Strange have remarkable, and powerful, properties." He tapped the glass globe in the center of the headless matic. The Strange there jerked away from his touch.

"It is the perfect use for the Strange. We harvest and harness them. With the Strange under our control, the witches at our service, and a nearly unlimited supply of glim and gold, the war is won before it even begins. We will own and rule this land and any other that suits our fancy. You, Mrs. Lindson, are looking at your new king."

"I am looking at a dead man," she said quietly. "And a fool."

She lifted her hands, whispering the words to a spell.

Cedar struggled up onto his feet—and fell. The cold, the pain, dragged at him as surely as a weight around his neck.

Mae didn't turn toward him. He didn't know if she could even hear him trying to call her name.

Vosbrough pressed something that looked like a telegraph key at his belt, tapping out a message, and the headless, bloodless creature fueled by Strange and glim raised its weapon at Mae and fired.

CHAPTER THIRTY-TWO

Captain Hink's head felt like a swarm of bees had taken up hiving there. He'd gotten hit in the head, along with more than a few good thumps in the side, during that jail brawl. He'd lost blood and the lump on the back of his noggin was making him see double between blinks.

In any normal circumstance after a brawl like that, he'd hit the sky, hole up a while, and drink away the pain until the world straightened out again.

But he was without his ship, without booze, and stuck in a dying man's church. He was also the last chance Rose Small, the Madders, the Hunt brothers, and Mae had to grab up the Holder and finish off finding the young folk.

He'd told Rose to go. He told her he'd be fine. And he supposed that was true. For as long as their ammunition held out.

"So what weapons do we have left?" he asked.

Miss Dupuis and Mr. Wicks, who apparently had been in the middle of a conversation, both looked over at him.

"We're surrounded, correct?" he asked as he walked to the back windows and looked out.

"What supplies do we have to fight with?"

"Who said we have decided to fight?" Miss Dupuis said.

"And who said you are the one to make the decisions around here?" Wicks asked.

"I was a captain in the war," Hink said.

"I am your superior," Wicks said. "Is there another language in which you'd rather I say that, and in which you might understand? Pirate, perhaps? Or fists?"

"Guns," Hink said, ignoring his yatter and talking to Miss Dupuis instead. "How many do we have, how many do they have?"

"Father Kyne doesn't appear to own anything but a hunting rifle. I have my gun, Wicks has his, and you have yours."

"Bullets?"

She shook her head. "We have two sticks of dynamite, though. We can make a stand, but we won't win a firefight."

"This is Sheriff Burchell," the man yelled. "We've given you time to put your guns down, walk out, and turn yourselves in so that justice can be done. If we don't see every man and woman out here on the ground in front of us in one minute, we will be forced to take care of this in a much less civilized manner."

"How many men out there?"

Wicks pulled off his glasses and wiped a clean white cloth over the lenses. "Sheriff and his deputy, and the posse they rounded up. Perhaps thirty men, wouldn't you agree, Miss Dupuis?"

"At least that, yes."

"Sounds good to me," Hink said.

"Do you have a plan?" Miss Dupuis asked.

"Of course I have a plan," Hink said as he pulled his gun and strode out of the kitchen toward the front of the building. "Keep shooting until I run out of bullets."

CHAPTER THIRTY-THREE

"Mr. Alun Madder," Rose said, her good hand sliding down to her gun, "you must know that I respect you and your brothers for those fine deviser minds of yours. And I certainly can understand when a brain slips a cog and goes off to wander down a whimsical path. But you will never have my body as a bargain for your gain. Never."

Alun regarded her through sharp eyes. "Rose Small, I find myself becoming more and more fond of you as time goes by. I agree. Your body is your own. Perhaps I misspoke."

She kept her hand on her gun. She knew that the Madders used words like a watchmaker used tools: precisely and with intention.

"Then respeak yourself, Mr. Madder. Clearly."

"We come from . . . old blood, we Madders. Blood that stretches back for more days and years than people have numbers for. We are uncommon men, and we walk the earth by choice, for reasons of our own. Old blood brings with it certain advantages. You've seen only the barest hint of the things we know, the things we can do."

He paused, and Rose was glad for it. She found it hard to breathe when he was speaking. Alun Madder and both of his brothers were miners, devisers, and brawlers. But sometimes, in the rare moments when the flame of their humanity was uncovered and let burn free, they were more than just three men: they were a force, a unit, brothers like none she had known. And when one of them intended to use words to capture your attention, even breathing seemed an unnecessary distraction.

"The reason I tell you these things, things I do not willingly explain to most men," he continued, "is because you too are of uncommon blood, Rose Small."

He waited, they all waited, as if they were listening for the first call of a bird to signal the dawn.

"You think I'm like you?" she asked.

"Not think. Know."

"You think we're . . . kin?"

Alun hitched one shoulder in a shrug, but his eyes were steady, unreadable. "There are stranger things that have happened in this world."

Brothers Bryn and Cadoc both chuckled.

"We can't know," Rose said. "You can't know. Unless there are records?"

"None that we have. None that we've seen. But we have blood. And so do you. That's all we need today."

"For what?"

"To find the children." He frowned just a little. "You have been listening to me, haven't you?"

She ignored that. "How will blood do any good in finding them?"

"Just blood alone wouldn't, but when the word is added, a promise"— he nodded once—"that is the thing that can change the winds."

"Mr. Madder," Rose said. "I am not a slow thinker, but your words don't mean a thing to me."

"It's the promise *and* blood," Cadoc said, "that will give us reach. Our feet are tied, bound to this side of the road. Our lives are tied to the promise of finding the children. We alone, Madder blood, must find the children to be released from the promise. If anyone else finds them, we will remain, locked to this city."

"Unless Father Kyne kicks off," Bryn noted.

Cadoc nodded at that. "His death will release the promise. But that is not what we want. We want to fulfill our promise, bring closure to our word given to his father's father. To do that, we need you, Rose. Blood of our blood, in some curious manner. You will be our hands and our feet. You will reach the children since we cannot."

"The practicalities of it," Bryn picked up, "are simple. You vow to us to join in our promise to rescue the children and fulfill our debt to the Kyne family. A drop of your blood mingled with ours on a rope or wire"—he pulled a thin length of copper wire on a spool out of the pack at his side—"this wire, will be enough to stretch our reach, carry our blood and our promise."

"Wire?" she asked, wondering where and when he'd had the chance to steal it.

"Each of us will keep hold of it," Alun said. "And linked by it, we'll stand as far on the other side of this road as we can, the wire carrying our promise to span the distance, just like a cable carries the dash and dot of words down the line. You'll have the wire around your wrist or waist. If there's any luck left for us, the wire will hold long enough, far enough, that you'll be able to find the children in that tumble of rocks through those trees, and bring them back right along this string between us, to the city proper."

"What if . . . if they aren't alive?" Rose asked.

"Then we'll carry them home, one by one, and give them their rest," Alun said.

Rose knew the promise was keeping the Madders here in town. And she knew Father Kyne might not even make it another day or two without Mae's witchcraft to help him heal. But missing children struck at her heart like a heavy stone. She had no children of her own, but she was an orphan. She knew what it was like to be lost. Knew what it was like to lose home and family.

She could only imagine how frightened the children must be. And how their parents must worry.

"How many?" Rose asked. "Children? How many are lost?"

"Father Kyne says a hundred or more," Alun said.

"A hundred?" Rose brushed the hair from her face with the back of her good hand. "How can we carry a hundred children home?"

"Let's find them first," Alun said. "Then we'll devise a way to help them. Are we agreed, Rose Small? Is there to be a promise between us?"

"Yes," Rose said. "I'll give you my word and blood. For the children."

"Well, then, let us seal our words to it," Alun said. "Brothers?"

Bryn and Cadoc stepped up close until they were all standing in a circle at compass points: Rose east, Cadoc west, and Alun and Bryn at north and south, respectively.

"This we enter as four and exit as one," Alun said soberly. "This bond of our word, this bond of our blood."

The three brothers simultaneously drew knives from their pockets and in the same motion, nicked the thick of their left thumbs. Blood welled there.

"Rose," Alun said.

She offered her hand in the center of the circle. Bryn, straight across from her, placed his hand flat behind hers, then nicked her pinky. "Thumbs are useful, and you have only the one to spare right now," he said, pointing the knife at her arm in a sling.

"Thank you," she said quietly.

"Our blood seals our word, and our word is this," Alun said. "From this day onward, we are bound together. Until our promise is fulfilled, until the lost children of Des Moines are found and returned to the city. I, Alun, so swear."

The brothers intoned, "So I swear."

Rose said, "I, Rose Small, so swear."

Bryn held the coil of wire in the center, and each brother grasped it, thumbs smearing a drop of blood on the rough twist. Rose added her hand, and her blood.

"Good," Alun said. "Now that's out of the way, let's forward."

Rose hadn't felt anything change. When Mae cast spells, she could at least sense the magic in the air, or sometimes something more subtle, like a change of temperature or a honey scent. But for all the world, it seemed like the speech and blood and wire business hadn't done anything to change her or make her feel owing to the Madders in any way.

"Is that it?"

"Is that what?" Alun asked.

"The, uh, promise?"

"We all agreed, didn't we?"

"Yes, but I just thought. Well, when Mae uses magic it's different."

"Ah, there's your mistake, Rose Small. It isn't witchcraft that holds a promise to bones. It's a much older magic than that."

"Magic?"

"Superstition, soul, the will of the mind, magic." He waved his hand. "Men have plenty of names for the things they can't explain. None of them quite right, and none of them matter. All that matters is what we know is promised between us. Because that is our truth now, and that truth will have to do. Here. Let me tie this about your wrist."

He quickly twisted the end of the copper wire into a bracelet of sorts, his thick fingers cleverly bending the latch into the shape of a rosebud, and all the rest of the bracelet into a leafed stem.

"That's beautiful," Rose said.

Alun grunted and made sure the bracelet was latched securely. "Just because we're in a hurry doesn't mean we shouldn't do things right."

"Now what?" Rose asked.

"Do you have a gun on you?"

"Yes."

"Good. Keep it. There are still men out looking for us, though I think we gave them a good slip. Airships." He shook his head. "Lovely invention. Now, we'll each walk as far as we can."

Cadoc took the spool from Bryn's hands and stood with the toes of his boots touching the side of the road where the city ended.

Bryn and Alun each put a hand on the line between Rose and Cadoc.

"Rose," Alun said. "Please walk across the road."

Rose did so, and Alun and Bryn walked with her.

Bryn chuckled. "This will do, brother. Nicely."

"Then let's do it faster," Alun said. "Miss Small, straight to that stand of trees. Quickly now."

Rose picked up the pace and Alun and Bryn jogged right behind her, holding the unspooling wire. They were just at the line of trees when Bryn grunted as if he'd hit a brick wall.

Rose looked back.

"That's as far," Bryn said, already in a sweat, "that the bond will stretch between Cadoc and me. Go on."

"But—"

"We go on," Alun said.

Rose could tell by how he was walking that he too was in pain. But if the Madders were willing to spread the distance and the pain between them, then she was inclined to do her part too.

The forest opened into a clearing. Mr. Hunt had said the stones that held the children were just beyond.

She realized Alun was no longer following her and glanced back at him. He stood, copper wire clenched in his hands, feet spread as if bearing a heavy weight or pain.

"Go on. Should be beyond the trees," he said.

Rose nodded. She continued through the trees.

The farther she walked away from Alun, the more her legs, her back, and arms began to hurt. It was a slow-growing pain, but it was a real pain. And each step she took away from the town where the Madders were bound—where she was bound too now that their blood and oaths had mingled—caused that pain to sharpen.

Just on the other side of the trees was a stone hill. A small opening in the hill was clearly visible, but it was only large enough for someone her size or smaller to slip through. She didn't know how Wil had crawled in there. Certainly, the burly Madders would not be able to clamber through that crack.

"I see the rocks," Rose called. "I see the opening."

"That must be it. Do you see children?"

"Not yet." Rose walked closer to the cave, every step like needles beneath her feet.

"Can you see them?"

"Wait." Rose ducked and turned sideways and slipped into the small opening. She didn't go any farther, catching her breath against the pain that was crawling down arms and legs, and clenching at her chest, and waiting for her eyes and the darkness to make amends.

"Rose?" Alun's voice was muffled by the layers of stone, but plenty clear enough for her to hear him. "Do you see the children?"

She did. But she could not find her voice to answer him.

The small entryway opened into a wide, high-ceilinged cavern just below. And the floor of that cavern was covered by children, all of them old enough to be walking, but none of them over ten or eleven years of age. They lay one to the next, like carefully placed tiles in a great mosaic. At least a hundred children. All of them unmoving. All of them made of stone.

CHAPTER THIRTY-FOUR

Cedar pushed onto his feet. "Mae!" This time his voice carried. This time she heard him.

But it was too late.

Vosbrough's matic soldier fired its weapon. Liquid flame roared out of its gun, melting snow and cracking rocks.

Mae threw herself to the side, yelled one final word of her spell, and grabbed up her gun.

Before Cedar could take so much as a step, snow began to fall.

Thick as a blizzard, the world was erased, swallowed whole. It was snowing so hard that even if there were a wind to break it, there would be no end to the white. It was as if the entire sky of clouds had fallen whole cloth to smother everything on the ground.

A gunshot cracked and echoed. Mae's gun.

Mayor Vosbrough laughed. "Good, Mrs. Lindson. You are as strong as they say. Calling winter and binding it. A difficult spell. Very difficult. I could use a witch like you on my side. Don't think of it as a service. I will pay you handsomely, beginning with sparing your life."

Mae didn't answer. Smart. Her voice would only give Vosbrough a target to fire at.

Another arc of fire blasted through the snow, setting the air glowing deep red and orange, as if Cedar stood in the stirred ashes and flame of a frozen bonfire.

He knew Mae wasn't far away. Took another step toward her.

A figure appeared out of the snow in front of him.

But it was not Mae.

It was not Wil.

It was the Strange he had seen so many times before. The Strange he had followed. It did not have Florence's pink ribbon. But it pointed at where Wil was lying on the ice. The snow moved aside for that gesture, like a curtain pulled by cord.

"I can save," the Strange said with the reedy song of water through grass, "him. I can save"—the Strange pointed the other direction, and Cedar knew it meant Mae—"your own."

"Then save them," Cedar said.

"You must." The Strange was made of windblown snow, though there was no wind. It swirled, losing eyes and mouth and shape, and then re-forming again. "Agree. Free my kind as I free yours."

"I don't save Strange." Even numb, freezing, hurting, Cedar felt the heat of the beast in his blood. Wanting to kill this Strange. Wanting to destroy.

"Your . . . bro-ther," it said, as if the word were awkward for it to speak, "is dying."

Cedar knew it was right. Wil's side had barely lifted with breath, and the binding between them and Father Kyne was sapping his strength. As it was, Cedar could barely think straight, and shook uncontrollably from the cold.

"I can save your bro-ther," the Strange whispered. "I can save your own. If you free my kind. From the light."

It lifted a hand and grasped at the falling snow, impossibly dragging it aside again so that the air was clear of it. Farther downriver stood Mayor Vosbrough, hands raised, chanting.

A spell. He was spell casting. But only witches could cast spells.

That's when the truth of it hit him. Vosbrough was a witch. He knew it was true. And Vosbrough was using glim, cold copper, and the Strange to power that monstrous matic. The light pouring from the orb in the center of its chest burned bright even through the snow. In that light he could see a Strange. It was in pain. Trapped. Tortured.

The Strange waved its hand, and all the air around Cedar was solid white again. "Free. Free my own."

"Yes," Cedar said. "I will free your own. Save my brother."

The Strange bowed gracefully. "Oath."

"Oath."

Snow parted like water around stone. The Strange walked on weightless tiptoe over to where Wil lay. It bent, placed its hand over Wil's eyes, and then the Strange was gone, dissolved into a chalky mist that Wil inhaled.

"No!" Horror crawled through Cedar's mind. What had he just done to his brother? What was the price of this bargain?

Cedar staggered to Wil.

Wil opened his eyes, and exhaled.

Then his wolf form stretched, molded, changed. Fur was replaced by skin, muzzle by lips, paws by hands.

And it was Wil, lying naked on the ice. He turned his head, looked up at Cedar, confused. "Did we find the Holder?" he asked.

Cedar shook his head. "Wil, the Strange. You breathed it in. It's in you."

Wil's eyes went wide, then he sat up smoothly, as if the ice and snow and wind had no effect on him. As if he were not in pain. "In me? I don't feel any different."

And then everything about Wil changed. His face went blank, and a light burned copper behind his eyes. "This. Oath," a voice that was not Wil's said through his mouth.

"No," Cedar said. "I take back my oath. I break it. Get the hell out of my brother."

"Oath," the Strange said with Wil's lips.

Wil stood in a graceful, liquid motion, then he took two steps and dove into the water.

"Wil!" Cedar grabbed for him. Wil was gone, disappeared beneath the inky black water.

The entire exchange had taken no more than a few seconds. He could dive in after him.

It would be his death.

The snow thinned. Cedar glanced at where he'd last seen Mae. She was standing just inside the line of trees by the road, her hands out to both sides, curled in fists, as she called on the elements to fuel her spell.

He didn't know what she was casting. Whether it was a curse, a binding, or a vow. But Vosbrough stood at the riverbank, unmoving, arms clamped to his side at an awkward angle, as if a rope were tied around him and cinching tighter.

"Whore!" he yelled. "Demon spawn. You are an abomination on this earth. And not even a very good one at that." He pushed his arms out to the side and flexed his fingers. "Strong, though. Which I like. I'll give you that."

He crooked his finger and Mae gasped. She grabbed at her neck with one hand as if a wire had just wrapped around her throat, her other hand still tight in a fist.

"Goddamn it," Cedar swore. If ever there was a time for the beast to lend him its strength it was now.

He ran for his rifle. Stumbling at first, his feet fell faster and faster as anger gave him strength over his pain. And like kindling starving for oxygen, that anger caught a spark of rage and woke the beast within him.

His senses heightened and heat and power rolled through his bones. One step and he bent, scooping up his rifle. A second step and he had the headless matic in his sights. It was still, bound by a spell, by a spell that Mae still held and Vosbrough had not yet broken.

Cedar shot at the matic, aiming for the glass globe, but the bullet ricocheted, and sent out a spray of glim and copper sparks like flint rubbing steel.

"So now the hero wants to join the fight," Vosbrough said as Mae struggled to breathe. "Haven't I said this to you enough, hunter? I am your death. And the death of your woman. You do realize I could snap her neck with a twitch of my wrist, don't you, Mr. Hunt?"

Cedar held his place and did not lower the gun. "Let. Her. Go." It was all he could force out through his teeth, all his rage would allow.

"I was willing to give you the hospitality of this fine city if you played by my rules. But now . . ." He shook his head. "Well, you're consorting with witches, Mr. Hunt. And damned men. A decent civilized world has no room for such things."

"And you," Cedar snarled as he shifted his aim to Vosbrough's head, "talk too much." He squeezed the trigger.

CHAPTER THIRTY-FIVE

Hink was surprised they were still alive. After the sheriff had let every damn man in town unload a round or two into the walls of the church, they'd settled down to a more random aim and fire, mostly only when he, Wicks, or Miss Dupuis stuck their head out a window long enough to take a shot of their own.

The sheriff knew it was only a matter of time before those inside the church ran out of bullets. He seemed willing to wait them out.

But being low on bullets only meant each shot had to count. And they'd made sure to do just that. There were more wounded men on the street, or being transported by wagon to doctors, than there had been just a few minutes ago. Hink knew Miss Dupuis was a steady aim, but he had to grudgingly admit Mr. Wicks was no slouch with a gun.

The sheriff had tried to burn the place down too, but the recent snows made for difficult burning.

Miss Dupuis and Mr. Wicks had taken the time to bring Father Kyne, mattress, blankets, and all, into the main room with them, and put him on the floor, bundled for warmth. Less likely he'd be shot up here than back in his bedroom near a wall getting peppered with lead.

"I don't like how quiet it is out there," Wicks said.

"Shoot at them," Hink suggested. "Seems to wake them right up."

"They're planning something," Miss Dupuis said.

"My thoughts exactly, Miss Dupuis," Wicks agreed. "Someone should scout to see what they're doing. Captain Hink, I elect you."

"Go to hell," Hink said.

The puffing of a steam wagon pulling a heavy weight drifted into the room. Whatever matic was out there, it was coming closer, coming to the church, while men shouted directions.

That didn't sound good.

"Train?" Miss Dupuis said.

"No," Wicks said. "Wagon, I think. But it sounds like it's on rails."

"It's hauling," Hink said. "Under a heavy load."

"What is it hauling?" Wicks asked. "What would the sheriff haul all the way out here to the outskirts of town?"

"Something to kill us with?" Miss Dupuis suggested.

"A gun," Hink said. "Don't know what kind, but it will be a gun. A big gun."

"Cannon?" Wicks asked.

"Maybe. When that puffing stops, I'll stick my nose out and look."

None of them argued, so Hink took a swig out of the canteen of water Miss Dupuis handed him and leaned his head back against the pew behind him. They'd stacked the wooden pews up against the doors, then used the rest as a barricade to take some of the sting out of the bullets that found their way through the thin walls.

He closed his eyes for a minute or so, tired of seeing the room in double. That knock on the back of his head wasn't doing him any favors. His body was begging for sleep, but he knew sleeping right now would just be a shortcut to the grave.

"It's stopped," Mr. Wicks said. "Marshal? You'd better look."

Hink opened his eyes and held his breath a minute until the room stopped yawing side to side.

"Are you all right?" Miss Dupuis asked.

"Low on bullets and bleeding? Oh, yeah, I'm just aces." Hink pushed up to his feet. He supposed he should crouch low and scuttle to the window, but he was damn tired of scuttling.

He walked up to the side of the window, then glanced outside.

A bullet winged through the wood above the window and Hink pressed against the wall for the scant protection it provided, then glanced out the window again.

The wagon scraped the brush on both sides of the road as it lumbered toward the church. It was pulled by a steam muler with tracks for wheels that belched thick, black smoke into the snow-heavy sky. Behind that muler was a massive cannon, black as the devil's heart and long as the wagon. The thing had three barrels, the center one big enough to stuff an ox into, the two barrels flanking it only slightly shorter and smaller.

Six men stood atop the flat wagon, working the cranks and wheels to lift and drop the cannonballs into all three snouts, while angling the beast down so it was aimed directly at the church.

"Dammit all," Hink growled.

"What?" Miss Dupuis asked. "What kind of a gun is it?"

"The kind that can blow this church into splinters. We run. Now!"

"I don't take orders from you," Wicks said. "And there isn't a gun on land that can take down an entire building."

"Well, then you can stay here and let me know if you still hold that belief when the roof is falling on your head. Miss Dupuis, help me with the father."

Miss Dupuis levered Father Kyne into a sitting position. It was enough to rouse the preacher. He opened his eyes.

"What . . . where are we?"

"Take a last look at God's house," Hink said, bending to haul the man up onto his feet and then bracing him there with an arm around his waist. "It's about to be decommissioned."

Kyne did Hink a favor by not passing out and not arguing as Hink mostly dragged him toward the back of the church. Miss Dupuis followed, and Wicks must have decided to go look out the window himself, because he suddenly got his cussing on.

Man had an impressive list of words to chew.

"Why would they have built such a thing?" he said as he came up on Father Kyne's other side and thankfully helped to carry the man toward the kitchen.

"Don't know," Hink grunted. "Indian wars?"

"No. That thing is built to tear down walls. Or buildings."

"Just what we need," Miss Dupuis said as they ran for the back door of the place. "A gun big enough to destroy cities."

"Ain't progress just dandy?" Hink asked.

And then there was no time to talk. No air left to talk with anyway. An explosion blasted out and the world shook like a wet dog.

CHAPTER THIRTY-SIX

Rose made her way down the slope into the cavern. The closest child lying on the floor was a little girl, maybe three, hair braided at each ear, a tattered blanket clutched in her stone hand.

Statues? Who would go through the trouble and time to carve statues of a hundred sleeping children? It was an eerie thing, and gave her the same feeling had she been walking a graveyard.

She knelt and placed her hand on the little girl's blanket. It was wool and ragged at the edges where it must have been dragged behind her. Then she touched the girl's cheek.

She was warm and at Rose's touch she exhaled ever so slightly.

Rose pulled her hand back and rocked up onto her feet, startled. That was no statue. These children, all of them, weren't statues. They were enclosed in stone, but they were still alive.

She wanted to run. Thought maybe a good scream was in order too. But Alun's voice cut through her panic.

"Rose Small, what do you see?"

She backed all the way to the opening of the cave, unable to look away from the children. Afraid to do so.

"There are children here," she called. "A lot. Maybe a hundred. They're all sleeping, I think. But they are covered in stone like moths in cocoons. Like statues."

There was a moment of silence while Alun worked that through.

"Strange work, most likely," he finally said. "Old trick. Hard to do for one, much less a hundred. Can you carry them out of there?"

"Not with only one arm." Just the knowledge that this was something Alun Madder had heard of helped make Rose feel a little less horrified at the scene before her. If they knew what was causing the children to be stone, they might know how to fix it.

If it was some kind of spell, they'd need a witch.

"Should we get Mae?" Rose called.

"No," Alun said. "We can't last this pain, and her blood wouldn't fulfill our promise. We Madders, or you, bound by this bloodline, must find the children *and* return them to the city. No other can help in this deed."

"What do you want me to do?" Rose asked.

"Can you reach the children?"

"Yes."

"Then touch one. Skin would be best. And wait; don't let go."

Rose moved back to the little girl with the blanket and sat down beside her. "Wait, he says," she said to the girl. "What in the world can they do? They can't come any closer. I don't think they have a witch in their back pocket. And even being this far from the city is giving me a headache. Not that I'm complaining," Rose said, just in case the girl might have heard her words.

"I'm sure sleeping under a stone blanket isn't all that much fun either." She reached down and put her hand on the little girl's hand this time. Soft. Warm. She thought she heard the girl sigh and wondered what sort of dreams she might be having.

"We'll get you out of here, honey," she said. "You'll be home soon."

The copper wire around her wrist grew warm. Not so hot as to be uncomfortable, but warm enough she looked down at it, almost expecting it to be glowing. But it was just as it was before, dark copper spun into the tight petals of a rosebud, with a stem and latch.

The Madders were doing something, like sending a message down the wire. She could feel a low rumble at the base of her spine, a subtle hum that seemed to grow and roll out from the wire, out through her body, like the deepest thrum of a train in the far distance.

The hum spread until the cave picked it up, vibrating softly.

No, not the cave, the stones.

The Madders had bragged about talking to mountains. They'd said rocks and stones were an amiable sort that didn't mind giving up their secrets if a man knew how to talk to them. They'd said their people, their blood, were from the old country, where men and stones had often sat down to converse.

And now, here, in this winter country, in the cold heart of a cavern used for a Strange spell to trap living children, the stones sat up and listened to old Madder blood.

Rose held tight to the little girl's hand. Held tight while the stones rumbled and grumbled. Tiny cracks spread out from where Rose touched the girl, cracks stretching across the girl's hand, just like the cracks in the jail cell. Stone fell in dusty rivulets away from the little girl, building soft piles of sand around her.

The child coughed, opened her eyes, and whimpered. Then she leaned up into Rose's arms, clutching her blanket tightly.

"Hush, now, hush," Rose said, rubbing her back gently. "You're just fine now. Just fine."

And then she heard another child cough. Another child wake. In one big rush, the stones released all of the lost children of Des Moines out of their grasp and returned them back to the living world.

The rumbling faded to a chuckle, faded to a soft garbling grumble that gave way to silence. The cave was just a cave again. The mountain had had its say. And the copper wire around Rose's wrist was no longer warm.

The message from the Madders was sent, received, and answered.

"You're all going to be all right now," Rose said to the children, who were waking, rubbing eyes, and looking about. "We're just a little way from your homes and we're going to take you back to your parents. Can you all try standing up?"

The children were too dazed to panic, and she hoped they listened to her and trusted her long enough to get them back to town. Whatever it was the Madders had done to talk the stones into freeing the children had cost more than just heating the copper wire. All the pain she'd been feeling was doubled now. And if she were feeling this much pain, the Madders must be in agony.

"I want you all to hold hands," Rose continued. "Can you do that for me?"

She stood and set the little girl on her feet, then held her hand out for her. The little girl took it. Seeing that, the other children each took the hand of the child next to them.

"Very good," Rose said. "You're doing very good. Now, we're all going to walk out into the daylight. Ready?"

The children just stood there, blank-eyed. She didn't know what was normal and expected for a child who had just been turned to stone and back, but these children acted as if they were still in a dream.

Or that they were mindless, empty—and as stonelike inside as they had been outside.

A shiver ran down her spine as Rose glanced at all those blank eyes staring at her. They weren't behaving much like children at all.

She swallowed hard and pushed her unease aside. The children were alive. They were breathing, standing, and they could understand what she was telling them. That would be enough. Maybe if they got out of this cave, farther away from this spell, they would begin to act like children again.

"Here we go," she said. "This way. Don't let go of hands."

Rose walked back up the slope to the cave opening, then ducked and pushed her way out into the daylight, still holding the little girl's hand.

In the short time she had been in the cave, it had begun snowing rather heavily. She couldn't see more than a step or two in front of her, but there was no wind behind the snow. There was just snow, a constant, blinding, wet curtain of white closing down on everything.

But with the wire around her wrist, she could find her way back through total darkness.

"I have them," Rose called. "I have the children."

The copper wire tugged gently, and she followed the draw of it as the Madders spooled it in.

Alun's hand appeared out of the snow and caught her wrist. "Are you all right, Rose?"

She nodded. "Fine. I don't know what you did, how you talked the rocks into letting them go, but it worked. Look." She pointed back at the line of children who each steadfastly held the next child's hand and followed behind her like a string of beads.

Alun Madder touched her cheek gently, in a very fatherly sort of gesture. "You are a delight. This couldn't have happened without you, Rose. Now let's take these children home."

They followed the tug of copper as Cadoc Madder gently reeled it in, each step growing a little easier, the pain lifting and fading the closer to town they traveled.

Bryn held up one hand in welcome when they reached his side, and fell into step with them until they reached the road, where brother Cadoc stood on the other side, winding the spool of wire in his hands, solid as a mountain in a storm.

Alun, Bryn, Rose, and all the children crossed the road. As soon as Rose's boots were firmly on the other side, the pain in her legs, arms, and chest were finally gone.

The snow lightened and then stopped altogether.

"Odd weather," Cadoc noted.

"Odd town," Bryn said.

"We'll let the weather and town be," Alun said. "We've got our hands full with children who need returning."

"Something's wrong," Rose said.

"Plenty's wrong." Alun unlatched the copper rose from her wrist. "Strange stealing children and stacking them like cordwood in a cavern under a dust of stone doesn't make a lick of sense. Mr. Hunt seems incapable of fulfilling a promise we've given him days to do, and Vosbrough, well, Vosbrough has been a very naughty man."

"I mean something's wrong with the children," Rose said.

Alun paused, and took a hard look at the children, who had gathered silent and uncomplaining as ghosts around Rose.

None of them were crying. None of them were speaking. None of them were running off toward their homes. They just stood there, staring blankly up at Rose.

"They're quiet?" Alun asked.

"They're more than quiet," she said. "They're dazed. Almost as if they can't think for themselves. Like a part of them is still dreaming."

He knelt and looked at a boy of about six years straight in the face. The boy did not move. Did not even blink.

"Do the stones still have something of them?" Rose asked. "Is the waking part of the children back in that cave somewhere?"

"Bryn?" Alun asked, standing away from the child.

Bryn walked up and dug a jar out of the pouch at his side. He also withdrew a fine horsehair paintbrush. He opened the jar and dipped the brush into it. Red dust clung to the brush tips. "Turn your hands up, son," Bryn said. "I'm not going to hurt you."

The child did not appear to hear him.

"It's okay," Rose said. "You can turn your hands up now."

The boy turned his hands so they faced skyward.

Bryn drew the brush across each of his tiny palms.

The dust in the boy's hands turned black.

COLD COPPER • 347

"Strange touched," Bryn said, as he replaced the brush and jar into his pack, then used a cloth to wipe the boy's hands clean.

"We knew that, didn't we?" Rose asked. "That a Strange somehow put them in that cave?"

"Yes," Alun said. "But the child is still Strange touched, under Strange influence. This isn't a spell, this isn't a daze. A Strange is doing something, at this moment, to keep these children dreaming."

"Can we find it?" she asked. "Use that dust to track the Strange?"

"The dust won't work on anything but skin," Bryn said. "We'd need Mr. Hunt."

"No," Cadoc said. "His brother. I believe his brother may have answers we need."

"We can't take all these children rambling around looking for Mr. Hunt," Rose said. "They're in their nightclothes and most of them don't have shoes. We need a safe and warm place for them to rest while we sort out how to undream them."

"The church?" Bryn suggested.

"Too far," Alun said. "And likely under gunfire or burning down."

Those casual words hit Rose like a hammer at her chest. "Lee," she breathed. "Lee is in there."

"We passed a warehouse a while back," Bryn said, mostly ignoring her. "Room enough for the young folk."

"Quickly," Cadoc suggested. "Winds are changing. Men are coming."

Alun's head snapped up, as if he too had suddenly sensed a change riding the breeze. "Let's get them out of the weather," he said. "Rose, are you coming?"

She took a step or two away, but the little girl clung tightly to her hand. "You can take the children," Rose said. "That's what you promised. And now we're in town." She shook her hand, trying to dislodge the little girl, but the girl would not let go.

"Please," Rose said. "I have to go to him. I have to know if Lee is all right." She took a few more steps and all the children walked with her, surrounding her like hands trying to warm to a fire.

"They're following you, Rose," Alun said. "They see you, they hear you. They don't hear us. It was your hand that freed them, and they must know it. Wherever you go, they will follow."

A hundred children. No shoes, thin shirts and pants, some in only nightdresses. No hats. They were shivering, though they didn't seem to notice and did nothing to warm themselves.

Hink, at least, had a gun and a quick wit to defend himself with. The children were completely defenseless.

"Where is the warehouse?" Rose asked.

Bryn pointed toward the buildings a ways off behind them. "Just about a block that way. Saw it from the rooftop."

"Far enough into town the law will find us?" Rose asked.

"Probably," Alun agreed.

"Good," Rose said, setting her shoulders. "Let's go. Now."

CHAPTER THIRTY-SEVEN

Cedar was cold, bootless, hurting, and angry. None of that got in the way of his aim. The hard crack of his rifle fire slapped against the snow-covered stones.

Vosbrough threw himself to the side. Too late to dodge it completely, he fouled the shot and took the bullet in the shoulder instead of the head. He grunted and stumbled over stone, then fell to the ground.

Which was fine with Cedar. He didn't want to kill him. Yet.

Cedar strode over to the mayor. "Don't make me unload this into your head," he said. "Keep your hand away from your gun and release Mae. Now."

The matic stood still. The Strange inside the globe of glim in its chest was a ghoulish tatter of white smoke with two mouths and no eyes. It was also frozen.

The matic and Strange were bound by the spell Mae had cast. It was all that was keeping the matic from firing its weapons.

Vosbrough leaned on his knees and one hand, the other still fisted, clenched around the spell that was choking Mae. Killing Mae.

"It would be no disappointment for me to see your guts spread across this snowy ground," Cedar said. "Drop the spell."

Vosbrough stared up at Cedar and the hatred that creased his face spread out into a smile even more vicious. "You do not know whom you threaten," he said, "nor what you have walked into, Mr. Hunt. I have seen to your death. You just don't know it yet. Step away from this fight. Now."

"This gun," Cedar raised the barrel even with Vosbrough's head, "is all the wisdom I need. Release her."

Vosbrough looked between Cedar's eyes and the muzzle of the gun. He uncurled his fingers.

Mae gasped and took several long, grating breaths. Cedar didn't turn to look at her.

Vosbrough was wounded, and only more dangerous because of it. Cedar knew better than to turn his back on him. Instinct told him there was more about the man he didn't know. And he was not inclined to ignore his gut feelings about the man.

"You know what they say about you, Mr. Hunt?" Vosbrough asked, his voice strong, even though blood soaked the dark wool of his coat over his shoulder.

"They say you killed your wife. They say you killed your child. They say you ran from the law and then, when your brother tried to turn you in, you killed him too."

Cedar's heart beat harder. None of that was true. Not a word of it. But Vosbrough was telling him the rumor he would spread. Telling him how he would ruin his life.

"They're wrong," Cedar said.

"Are they?" Vosbrough shook his head. "Well, I suppose they are wrong about one thing. You haven't killed your brother. Until today. And I will make sure everyone knows. Every lawman, every court, every desperado with a gun will know. As of this moment, as long as you live, you will have a price on your head, Mr. Cedar Hunt."

Cedar chuckled, a low rumble. "If that is the worst you can do, Mr. Vosbrough, you have vastly underestimated the hardships I have endured."

"It is only the beginning," Vosbrough said. "I will tear your world apart like a crow picking flesh from bone. Not slowly—no, there's no need for that. I will destroy you before you have time to realize what you've lost."

"Cedar!" Mae yelled hoarsely. "No!"

The matic turned, so quickly, it was a blur at the edge of his vision. He heard the blast from its gun even before he had thrown himself to the ground, bruising his back and hip in the fall. The heat of blood and pain rolled down his left arm.

He twisted, back flat, and brought his rifle around.

The matic towered over him, Strange heart pulsing with light and flashes of teeth and claws, as the Strange battered the cage that held it. Then the inhuman, unthinking, but horrifyingly graceful hands of the matic manipulated the settings on the gun.

"This is just the beginning of my power," Vosbrough said as he stood. "There is no force on this earth—man, Strange, matic, or weapon—that can stop me."

"There is now." It was Wil's voice; yet it was not quite Wil's voice. It was also the voice of the Strange, and the voices of a hundred children crying out.

With no time to think, Cedar trained his gun on Vosbrough.

Too many things happened in too little time. Cedar's bullet struck Vosbrough in the thigh. The matic's bullets rained down around him, buffered by a spell of warm wind scented with spring flowers.

A copper bolt of light shattered the day, burning all sight from Cedar's eyes. The scent of flowers was gone, replaced by the searing copper stink of hot blood.

Cedar pushed himself up, away, scrambling to get out of the line of fire, out of the reach of the matic.

"Wil!" he yelled, then, "Mae!" But only the sound of children wailing, and a booming roll of thunder exploding on the heels of the copper lightning, filled his ears.

Cedar swore and wiped his palm over his eyes.

His vision cleared. The matic lay a yard or two away from him, arms and legs akimbo, like a puppet cut from its strings. The glass globe in its chest was shattered, glim and a thick ichor leaking out between glass and copper.

Vosbrough lay there, dead.

Silence filled the air. No thunder. No sound of crying children.

Cedar spun. Mae was making her way across the rocks toward him, like an angel walking. It was snowing again, dusting the world in white.

"Are you all right?" Cedar took a step, his bare foot hitting the sharp edge of a rock. Where were his damn boots?

"I'm fine." But her voice was hoarse and a bruise smeared red and black across her throat.

Vosbrough had nearly killed her. Cedar turned and put another bullet into the man just to be sure he wasn't breathing. Then he looked out over the river.

"Wil?"

Wil stood naked on the riverbank, water dripping off of his pale skin in slick rivulets, his dark hair smoothed back away from his face. He stared at the copper Holder in his hand with a mix of curiosity and caution.

The piece of the Holder was shaped like a crescent moon, with intricate scrollwork etched down the flat of it. Wires and springs hugged the concave length and glittered like fine jewelry in the late-afternoon light.

"Wil?" Cedar said again.

Mae was at Cedar's side now. "Let me," she said. "I'll get your boots."

She took the dozen or so steps over snow-covered stones to the edge of the river. "Wiliam," she said. "Are you cold?"

Wil tipped his face toward her. "Mae? Is this?" He glanced back at the Holder in his hand. "Um, I think I found the Holder."

"You did. You've been touched by the Strange, Wil. Do you remember that?"

His smile was wry. "I can hear . . . it. Hard to forget a thing when it's all up in you and itching."

"Let me take that so you can get dressed." Mae held out her hand.

"No." Wil straightened. That, suddenly, was not his voice. Even the way he stood didn't resemble Wil. "Flesh will burn. Your flesh."

"Cedar?" Mae said, her hand still extended, but otherwise not moving.

"Listen to it," Cedar said. "And throw me my boots."

Mae tossed his boots back to him, and Cedar put them on quick enough, even though his hands and feet were numb.

"Wil," he said. "How much control do you have over that creature?"

Wil grinned. "None at all. Haven't tried to control it yet. Look. Fingers." Wil wriggled his fingers. "And daylight. I do love daylight. Cold, though."

"Give me the Holder." Cedar closed the distance and held his hand out for him.

Wil plunked the Holder into his palm without a pause. The curse made it so that the Holder did not burn their flesh. He didn't know if it would burn Mae, but after seeing what it did to Rose, he didn't want to chance her touching it.

"Thank you," Wil said. "So." He bent and shoved feet into Cedar's socks, sighed at the pure pleasure, though Cedar doubted he could even feel his feet, then pulled Cedar's coat around his body. "We found the Holder at the bottom of the river? Does that mean we can leave this town? I'm a little hazy on the details."

He held his hand back out for the Holder and Cedar gave it to him and shrugged into his own shirt. "You found the Holder at the bottom of the river. And you did so with help from a Strange."

"That part I remember," Wil said. "Everything was quiet and calm and all of a sudden there's another voice thinking in my head. Darndest thing."

"Wil." Cedar took hold of his brother's arm. "It's my fault. You were dying. I panicked. I gave it permission, an oath, if it would save you. But I didn't know it would get into you. I'll find a way to make it leave. Mae could help with unbinding spells."

Wil put his hand on Cedar's. "Ease down, brother. You aren't the only one it made a deal with. It spoke with me too. For as long as we're freeing its kind, whatever that means, it can hold off the beast. Enough, at least, that I can walk as a man most my days. Drink coffee. Oh, God, I could eat sticky buns. Cedar, I could, you know"—he leaned in toward Cedar a little closer, turning his back so as to hide his words from Mae—"give a woman my intimate attentions."

Mae just coughed politely to cover a laugh.

"You're not angry about having that thing use you?" Cedar asked. "You don't feel trapped?"

"Ever since our lives went to hell, it seems one thing or another's been trying to use me. The Pawnee God. Shard LeFel. That monster Mr. Shunt. This time, for once, it's mutual."

"And if it isn't," Cedar said.

Wil nodded and gave Cedar a slow smile. "Then you and I will do something about it, won't we?"

"Cedar, Wil," Mae said. "Riders."

Cedar heard it, had heard it for some time. Horses coming this way. Mayor Vosbrough never traveled alone. Cedar had been surprised to see him by the river with nothing but the Strange matic. It appeared his lawmen had been called to the river to finish what Vosbrough had started.

"Go," Cedar said. "Now."

"Should we do something with that?" Wil pointed at the matic and dead man lying near the river bank, as they quickly gathered guns and ran across the rocks.

"No time," Cedar said.

"It must not remain," Wil said in a stilted tone. Wil stopped and raised the Holder. The Strange said words that Cedar had never heard, not from men, not from Strange.

The Holder glowed in Wil's hands. With one last word, a blast of lightning arced wildly around the Holder, snapping there in a globe of electricity.

Wil wavered on his feet, then directed the arc of electricity toward the matic.

The lightning struck the matic so hard it was thrown across the riverbank and onto the icy river. The ice cracked from the impact, and the headless puppet sank quickly out of sight.

Wil nearly collapsed, but Cedar wrapped an arm around his waist, and helped him walk as quickly as he could away from the river as thunder rolled.

Cedar took the Holder out of Wil's hands before he dropped it. He didn't know how the Strange knew to use this piece of the great weapon, but whatever it was that went into doing so had left Wil nearly unconscious.

Mae was already at the horses, and Cedar shoved Wil up onto his mount, then swung up behind him.

Time to run. More than time to run.

Cedar jerked the reins, sending his horse into the sparse woods.

"Mae," Cedar said. "Can you slow them? Can you hide us?"

A gunshot broke through the air, striking a tree just behind them.

"I can try."

They pounded across snow, pushed through brush and brambles and fallen logs in a headlong race to reach the city.

They were losing ground, the men behind them closing in. And the men knew the city far better than Cedar and Mae. Where could they run to? The church had been surrounded when they left. Unless Miss Dupuis, Mr. Wicks, or Captain Hink had a smooth way to talk the lawmen out of believing they'd just escaped and destroyed the jail, they were either already in custody and back behind new bars, or they were dead.

A far-off humming grew louder and louder above the treetops. There was an airship coming in fast. Fast enough she sounded like she was screaming through the air.

He didn't know how she had found them, but he knew the sound of those engines. Knew them very well.

Cedar Hunt laughed.

The *Swift*. Gunfire from behind took chunks out of trees, just inches from Cedar's head. He ducked, turned his horse to match the airship's path, and made for the break in the woods.

CHAPTER THIRTY-EIGHT

Rose was glad the children did as they were told and were silent about it, to boot. She had managed to round them all up and lead them into the warehouse, which stored leather. It stank of old hides, the strong solutions it took to soften them, and the odd hickory smoke of meat and burnt hair curing.

But at least it was warmer in the shed. Rose gathered the children in a huddle close together on the sawdust floor. She wished they'd found a wool or cotton warehouse, or even a hay barn. Any of those would be warmer by far. Still, this was better than standing in the snow.

She brought over some of the supple pieces of leather, which were carefully folded and tied with twine, and draped them around the children to keep some of their warmth near their skin.

"Still mighty quiet," Alun said as he helped drape some of the softer and warmer folds of leather over the children.

"So," she said, putting her good hand on her hip. "How do we wake them up?"

"We'll need to find the Strange that's put them sleeping," Alun said. "Could take days."

"Months," Bryn added.

"Minutes," Cadoc said.

Rose turned to the youngest of the Madder men. "Minutes? Do you know a way to find the Strange?"

"No," he said. "You do."

"I can assure you, Mr. Madder," Rose began, "if I knew how to fix all this, I'd be right about doing it—"

Cadoc tipped his head to one side, as if waiting to see if she caught on to the sense in his words.

She still didn't understand what he was saying, but she suddenly didn't care.

"The ship!" she said, tipping her face to the ceiling as if she could see through the boards and bracers there. "It's the *Tin Swift*!"

She turned and ran toward the door.

"Thought the *Swift* was in pieces in a barn in Kansas," Alun Madder said.

"She was," Rose called back, already breathless with hope. "But you can't keep her out of the sky for long. I'd know her fans anywhere!"

Rose ran out into the street and scanned the section of sky slotted above the buildings. That was the problem with a city grown so tall: it put its teeth into most of the sky.

She couldn't see the ship, but she heard her.

And her heart soared with hope. Hink had said he sent a wire when they were on the train. He must have told Seldom to bring the ship.

If they had the *Swift*, they'd have a way out of this town. They'd have all the wide sky trails to ride, and the men and Strange in this snowed-down city wouldn't be able to touch them.

The *Swift* could save Hink.

Rose ran. Ran toward the sound of that beautiful ship. She didn't know, and didn't care, that the Madders were shouting at her. She didn't know, and didn't care, that the children followed behind her, running as she ran, heedless and determined to save the man she loved.

CHAPTER THIRTY-NINE

H earing the *Tin Swift* screaming through the sky was enough to make Cedar Hunt laugh, but the trouble with airships was trying to get their attention from the ground.

He didn't have any of the bright orange flares Captain Hink always carried, and he was certain the sparse tree cover they were galloping through wasn't helping their visibility any.

"Can you signal them?" Cedar asked Mae.

"Yes." Mae urged her horse to the left, out of the cover of trees. Out where she'd be an easy target for their pursuers. An easy target for the crew of the *Swift* too, if they thought she was trying to shoot at them.

She tugged on the reins, pulling her horse up into a hard stop. Then she turned and lifted her hands toward the ship.

A small but bright yellow light flickered in her hands, growing larger until her entire hand shone like a small sun.

The *Swift* cut fans, swiveling in the sky until the port door, filled by the ship's cannon, was bobbing just above Mae.

"Mae!" Cedar yelled.

A voice called down from the ship—the operatic baritone of one of Captain Hink's crewmen, Mr. Ansell: "Howdy, Mrs. Lindson! Care for a ride?"

"Yes," Mae yelled back. "The men behind us—"

"Don't worry about them."

The *Swift* wobbled in the air again and gunfire from the ship hailed down on the trail behind them. The rope basket dropped from the port door and Mae helped Cedar get Wil into it.

Then the ladder was lowered while the basket was being cranked back into the ship.

"Go," Cedar said.

Mae started up the ladder and Cedar was right behind her.

Before they reached the wooden floor of the ship, before the sound of return fire from the men on horseback had finished its echo, the *Tin Swift's* fans roared to life and the ship climbed sky, out of the bullets' reach.

"Good to see you, Mrs. Lindson." Mr. Ansell was short, rounded, and dusky-skinned. He was also the most nimble and sure-footed man in the air Cedar had ever seen. He offered his hand to help Mae safely into the ship. The basket with Wil in it was already stowed and latched tight. Wil rubbed his face, as if coming up out of a hangover.

"Even more pleasant for me to see you and the crew, Mr. Ansell," Mae said. "How did you know to come here?"

"Got a wire from the captain a while back. Mr. Seldom put the last rivets in the *Swift* and we came right away. Didn't expect to find you on the run. Welcome aboard, Mr. Hunt," he said, offering Cedar a hand for the final step into the ship.

"Thank you, Mr. Ansell. Wil, are you all right?"

Wil nodded. "That was a hell of a thing."

"Don't suppose you'd mind manning the port guns?" Ansell asked. "We're running a thin crew."

Cedar glanced at the crewmen. The *Swift* was a small ship and usually ran on a skeletal five people, including the boilerman and captain. Aboard the ship there was only Mr. Seldom, Hink's second at the helm; Mr. Guffin, a thin, pale, sad-eyed man with a mop of unruly yellow hair, who was locking the starboard door and stowing the guns; and Mr. Ansell.

"Happy to help," Cedar said. "We know where Captain Hink is," he added.

"So do we," Mr. Seldom called back from the front of the ship. "Have a tracker locked on him."

"Tracker?" Mae asked. "I don't understand."

"Some thing Miss Small cobbled together." Ansell made his way to the navigation gear at the helm.

Mr. Guffin nodded his tousled mess of hair and stomped his way up toward the front too. "That finder compass has held straight as an arrow for fifty miles. Hell of a way to keep track of a person. Not surprised Miss Small thought it up. She's got a head full of clever."

"Doesn't she just?" Cedar said with a smile as the ship shot through the air, over the town and dead set toward the church.

CHAPTER FORTY

When Hink could hear again, the first sound that reached his ears was a double-barreled shotgun racking a round about two feet from his head.

"You are under arrest," the sheriff said. "All of you. Drop your weapons and get on your feet."

The cannon blast had done just what Hink thought it might do. It had torn half the building off and left the other half of the church sagging dangerously. The stink of gunpowder, smoke, blood, and burning wood filled his nose and lungs.

They had been thrown out of the church and had landed in a heap about twelve feet behind it, wood piled on top of the four of them.

That made it easy for the sheriff and his men to surround them, and to point a rather impressive array of guns their way.

"I said, get on your feet."

Hink looked for his companions. Wicks was already helping Miss Dupuis stand, but Father Kyne was unconscious again.

"The priest is hurt," Miss Dupuis said. "He cannot stand."

"Wasn't talking to the priest, ma'am. You," the sheriff said, "move. Now."

Hink spit some of the dust and grit out of his mouth, poked at a loose tooth with his tongue, then pulled himself up to standing. Blackness closed down around him as the world decided to set up shop out there at the end of a tunnel. He took a deep breath and the darkness pulsed back with the beat of his heart. He was pretty sure he wasn't going to be conscious for long.

"Problem, Sheriff?" Hink asked.

"You broke out of my jail, tore it down, and released every criminal in custody. Then you beat up my men and spent the last hour shooting holes in the good people of this town. So, yes, I have a problem. But it ain't no kind of problem I can't solve with a trip to the gallows."

"We are allowed due process of the law," Miss Dupuis said.

"Law says I'm the due process," the sheriff said. "And I say there's plenty of room on the gallows for all of you."

"Fine," Wicks said. "We'll walk. But if you plan to hang the priest, you'll need to provide him safe transport there."

Hink knew what he was trying to do. He was buying time. Maybe time for one of them to come up with a plan. Only Hink didn't have a plan, and from the look on Miss Dupuis's face, she didn't either. While a long walk might jog some idea out of his head, more likely he'd just pass out halfway there.

Father Kyne groaned and lifted one hand, then somehow managed to get himself sat up. He glanced at the sheriff and guns, then up at Hink, Wicks, and Miss Dupuis. He seemed to put two and two together, and found a way to stand.

"Look at that," the sheriff said. "Now we have all our ducks in a row. Walk."

Hink took a step, saw Father Kyne nearly stumble, and reached out to steady him, but Wicks was already there.

"We'll fight when the chance presents itself," Wicks said quietly as Hink and he got Father Kyne walking again.

Hink grunted in agreement.

By the time they'd picked their way through the wreckage to stand in front of the sheriff, there was a buzzing in Hink's ears he could not shake.

Not a buzzing, more like a high-pitched scream coming from somewhere far off.

They were shoved toward the road into town and got to walking. Hink was surprised the sheriff hadn't just shot them yet. He must really want to give those new gallows a try.

Then he figured it out. Alongside the road stood long lines of people. It looked like half the city had turned out to gawk and stare at the escaped criminals. Women and men, reporters and workers, poor and old all drawn up tight together to see how the great jail escape ended, to watch the shootout, and probably clap and cheer the sheriff on while that beast of a cannon shot the old church to sawdust.

As a matter of fact, they started clapping now.

Beyond the clapping, that far-off buzz was getting louder. Annoying.

Hink lifted a hand to his ear, cupping it and frowning at the noise.

And then he knew exactly what that noise was.

"Oh," he said quietly. "This is going to be nice. Real nice." He grinned and lowered his hand, then stopped walking.

"Told you to walk," the sheriff said. "Not stand there grinning."

"Now why would I want to walk," Hink asked. "When I have wings?"

And just like that, the *Tin Swift* swung down out of the sky, a quick silver bullet skimming the tops of buildings and threading the city like a needle through a patchwork quilt.

The ship came to a stop overhead, and Cedar Hunt's voice boomed out over the growl of her fans. "Put your guns down and release them. Or we will open fire."

Hink glanced up at the ship. Looked like Mr. Seldom had done the girl some good, and put in the flamethrowers they'd been talking about.

Flamethrowers that Cedar Hunt currently manned at the starboard door, aiming downward.

"Problem with a ship like that," Hink said to the sheriff, "is she can be out of your range before you pull a trigger, but that flamethrower doesn't have to be close in to do serious damage to all these nice folks gathered here. And neither do the cannons, dynamite, and guns her crew keeps on board."

"How do you know what's on board that ship?" the sheriff asked.

"Because I am that ship's captain."

"That so?" The sheriff spit to one side. "Then I know your crew isn't about to kill their captain on the way to killing me."

"You overestimate the morals of my crew," Hink said. "They do what I pay them to do. And if I tell them to shoot, that's what's going to happen. Even if I'm in the way."

Hink was ready to reach for the gun he had stashed in his coat. But before he could pull it, he heard his name shouted out.

"Lee!"

That was Rose's voice. Rose's voice calling over the roar of the *Swift*. But not from above.

Rose stood on the snow-covered road that wended away from the church, back the other way. She was staring at the demolished remains of the building. Her hat had gone missing and her hair was tousled free of its pins in a glorious tangle of brown and red.

One of her arms was slung tight and tied to her chest, and there was a bruise across her forehead. She looked away from the church and caught sight of Hink standing down the road a ways. Her free hand flew up over her mouth, as if it could hold back the half sob, half laugh that escaped her lips.

Then her hand slipped down, revealing her smile. And she ran. Straight toward him, as fast as she could, ignoring the men, the guns, the ship, ignoring everything. Running as if there were no time left for walking in this world.

Hink started toward her too, as fast as his injuries would let him.

The clack of guns racking rounds filled the air, but he didn't care and he didn't stop. Rose was running for him and he was running for her. Bullets wouldn't keep him from that woman.

"Hold your shot!" the sheriff yelled. "Do not shoot! You'll hit the children."

Children?

Hink looked away from Rose. Sure enough, she was surrounded by dozens of children, none of them taller than her waist, most of them in nightclothes, and all of them running, just as she was running, right toward him.

And all the people on the street, men and women, rich and poor, crowded up to see just what was happening.

They cried out in surprise, in confusion and joy, calling their children's names.

"Henry! Victoria! Donald!" Dozens of voices calling dozens of names.

Strolling along behind the bundle of blank-eyed children were the three Madder brothers, looking as if they were going on a walk round the park, not that they were returning to a town full of people who wanted to see them swing by the neck.

Hink wrapped his arms around Rose and she clung tightly to him with one arm, looking up at him.

"You shouldn't have come back, Rose," he said, near out of breath, his head pounding darkness into the corners of his vision again.

"I'm right where I intend to be, Lee Cage."

"Well, isn't this a pleasant sight?" Sheriff Burchell said.

"So good to see all the criminals come into the town, all the law-breakers and justice dodgers, right here in one handy place. Looks like justice will be done this day. Men," he said. "Fire."

CHAPTER FORTY-ONE

"Hold your fire!" Alun Madder called out loud enough Rose thought his voice could be heard in the next county. "We have found the children gone lost in this town. There will be no shooting."

The gunmen hesitated.

"My baby!" a woman cried out. "You found my baby." The woman was short and thin, with dark hair caught back under a blue silk-flounced bonnet. She broke out of the crowd and ran toward the children surrounding Rose.

The woman plucked up a little boy and pulled him into her arms, standing there rocking and murmuring comforting words.

Then a flood of people came forward, pulling their children toward them, crying, hugging, holding. More than one man clapped Hink on the shoulder in thanks as they walked by; more than one man shook hands with the Madders.

Rose found herself overwhelmed by the surge of happy people, and did her best to see that the children fell into the hands of family and loved ones. The sheriff was surrounded by townspeople and was receiving congratulations too, and several of his men had youngsters in their arms.

The gunmen were fathers, brothers, and uncles. They put their guns away.

The Madders stood near Rose, staring at the sheriff across all the happy people.

The sheriff glared at them. But he couldn't just shoot the men who had solved his city's greatest mystery, couldn't kill the men who had brought happiness back to families who had been wrapped in grief.

The Madders looked like three pleased foxes who had dined on prized hens.

The sheriff holstered his gun.

Rose was relieved that the children had been found and returned. But there was still more that wasn't settled. The children weren't talking. None of them seemed to even recognize their families.

Something was missing. And she wasn't the only one who noticed. It began as a small murmur. One or two people asked their child what was wrong. And then it grew. They knew. They knew their children might be there in body, but that some part of them was still lost.

"What the hell now?" Hink muttered.

"It's the kids," Rose said. "Some Strange has a piece of them. We haven't found it yet. Haven't found the Strange. Well, haven't had a chance to look for it. I thought . . . I thought you were dying, so I just ran."

"Sheriff," Cedar said. "May I speak with you?"

Rose looked over and was shocked to see both Cedar and Wil Hunt striding down the road. Wil had on borrowed pants and boots, one hand rested in his coat pocket as if he carried something there. His grin was wicked and his eyes glittered.

Seeing the two of them together, as men, was such a rare thing, she had to admit to being a little caught by the sight of them.

They were of a height and build, though Wil was leaner and narrower than his older brother. And whereas Cedar Hunt looked like he could bear the weight of the world's troubles across his wide shoulders, Wil looked more the type who might enjoy stirring up that trouble.

The brothers passed Miss Dupuis and Wicks, and Cedar told them both to get aboard the ship that hovered to one side of the ruined church. Neither of them argued, though Wicks opened his mouth, but closed it quickly when Miss Dupuis tugged him by the arm to the *Swift*'s ladder.

The sheriff met Cedar in the center of the road. Close enough Rose could hear them over the townsfolk and airship fans.

"We came to this town with no animosity toward the town or these people. And though my companions have been jailed, and escaped, it was to do this great good. To find the children of this town. And if you want the children to laugh and grow and thrive, to have their reasoning minds, you will let us go."

"What game are you playing, Mr. Hunt? Are you holding our children's minds hostage for your release?"

"It seems I am."

Rose glanced around. She couldn't believe Cedar was standing there blackmailing the sheriff. She slipped her hand in her pocket and wrapped her fingers around her gun.

"Is there some kind of guarantee you're going to give me?" the sheriff asked. "I'm not about to let you fly off on the strength of a promise."

"Keep us here and those children will never recover."

The sheriff frowned, glanced over at the children, many of whom just stared straight ahead.

"We'll stay behind as collateral," Alun Madder said. "My brothers and I."

"No," Cedar said.

"Now, now, Mr. Hunt," Alun said. "You should know better than to turn down the best offer you're going to get. According to the law, there's still some reason Sheriff Burchell here might want to keep us. We'll stay while you see to the children's needs. And when it's clear those children are once again their normal selves—something I encourage you to do quickly—then Sheriff Burchell will uphold his side of the bargain and let us all go."

The sheriff nodded slowly. "You belong behind bars."

"As you may have noticed, bars can't hold us," Alun said. "We will leave your town and give our promise to never return."

"Agreed," Burchell said. "Let some other lawman see you swing."

"Just so," Alun said happily. "Off with you, Mr. Hunt. If you do your job correctly, we'll see you on the outside of town."

Rose tugged on Hink's hand and hurried with him to the *Swift*. The Madders always had a plan. She knew that if they had to, they'd find a way to get away, even if the sheriff wasn't true to his word. And it appeared Cedar knew that too.

Rose climbed the ladder to the *Swift* as quickly as she could with a bum arm, Hink right behind her. He hollered for his crew to lower the basket.

Cedar and Wil helped Father Kyne into the basket.

Then Rose was up in the hustle and hurry of the ship, that beautiful, sweet ship, hugging Mae and helping to work the wenches to get Father Kyne aboard. She glanced up to see her airship captain walk up the narrow interior, already more steady on his feet as his hands grasped and released the ship's metal framework, like a blind man gently stroking the face of a long-missed loved one.

Last into the safety of the ship came Wil, who was smiling, and Cedar Hunt, who looked exhausted and in pain. He took hold of one of the metal bracings and leaned against the wall a moment, breathing heavily from his climb.

She had never seen him so ill before.

"Tell us where to fly, Mr. Hunt," Captain Hink said. "So we can put this town behind us."

"A warehouse," Wil said. Only it wasn't Wil's voice coming out of his mouth. Rose shot a glance at Cedar.

"Listen to him," he said. "The Strange saved the children from following the Holder's call and drowning in the river. But they put their bodies in that cave. Their minds are trapped with the Strange."

"Strange are keeping the children's minds?" Mr. Wicks asked.

"Oath given," Not-Wil said. "To free your own. To free my own."

"I don't understand," Miss Dupuis said. "What is . . . is that even Wil speaking?"

Cedar pulled himself together with what looked like extreme effort. He walked over to stand by his brother. "It's not just Wil. I have a promise to fulfill. To free the Strange. They're somewhere in this town, trapped."

"And all he can tell us is they're in a warehouse?" Miss Dupuis said. "There must be hundreds of warehouses in this town."

"I know where they are," Rose said. She pulled the broken battery out from under her blouse and held it out so Wil could see it. "Are they trapped in something like this?"

Wil's eyes went wide and his lips pulled back in a snarl. He took a step toward Rose, reaching for the battery. Cedar clamped his hand around Wil's wrist and Wil stopped.

"That looks like a yes to me," Captain Hink said. "Take us northeast, Mr. Seldom," he said. "Toward the airship field. Look for boxcars on a side spur with a warehouse to the west."

Captain Hink's crew scrambled to see to his orders and Rose took hold of a metal bracing, setting herself for the welcome speed of the ship beneath her feet.

CHAPTER FORTY-TWO

Captain Hink spotted the warehouse from above. There weren't any airships in the immediate sky, nor did there seem to be men moving about down there.

Not that either thing would matter. He was tired, hungry, and in pain. He wanted the hell out of this town. If that meant turning the *Swift's* cannons on the buildings below, or burning it to cinders, he wouldn't shed a tear.

"Is this the place?" Cedar asked.

Hink glanced over his shoulder. Cedar wasn't asking him. He was asking his brother, Wil. Or whatever it was that was looking out from Wil's eyes. Hink had seen a lot of afflictions in his life, but whatever it was that made it so that Wil Hunt was standing among them in man form set his hackles rising.

Wil was looking out the window. He nodded. "Yes. Dying. Trapped."

"I'll set them free," Cedar said. "As I promised."

"You won't do it alone, Mr. Hunt," Hink said. "Seldom, bring her around to the south."

"There's no need for you to accompany me, Captain," Cedar said.

Cedar looked like he had aged a hard year since they'd been in town. He didn't know what illness the man had picked up, or if it had more to do with whatever business he and his brother had gotten into with the Strange, but the man was clearly not at his best. All the more reason to hit the air trail. Soon.

Hink reached up into the overhead storage bin and pulled out several half sticks of dynamite, which he shoved in his pocket.

"The front door's on the east side," Rose said, coming up beside Hink.

"Ain't planning to go in the front." Hink strode past her to the door. "Mr. Guffin, lower the winch line." Hink pushed the door open and stepped out on the running board, holding the deadman's bar as he leaned out, looking for the covered loading entrance they'd been escorted out of earlier this day.

Spotted it. He ducked back in. "That's it. Hold here," he said to his second. Then to Cedar, who stood no more than three feet away from him, "You aren't going down there alone. I trust my crew with the ship, the witch with the father's injuries, and Miss Dupuis to dealing with the problem of Wicks."

"Problem?" Wicks called out from halfway across the ship. "May I remind you—"

"No," Hink said, "you may not."

"You don't trust me, Captain?" Cedar asked in that low dangerous way that made Hink wonder just which of them would come out breathing if they ever happened upon a serious sort of disagreement.

"I trust you," Hink said. "Not so sure I trust what's looking out from your brother's eyes. You aren't going down there alone, and I'm not staying behind to argue."

Hink kicked the ladder out the door and climbed down it at speed.

The Hunt brothers were right behind him. Moving a good bit slower, which provided Hink with time to grab hold of the winch line—a sturdy chain with a locking hook at the end—and walk it with him over to the closed-over entrance in the ground just outside the warehouse.

"Right down there." Hink adjusted his hold on the line, making sure there was plenty of slack between it and the *Swift*.

"Have you been here before?" Cedar asked.

"Unfortunately, yes."

"What's down there?"

"I'll show you." He didn't set the hook. Instead, Hink lit a stick of dynamite, tossed it at the boards that covered the ground, and then he and the other two men stepped back.

The explosion was enough to shake the *Swift*, but not so much as to send anything high enough to hit her.

"Down there is where the Strange are trapped," Hink said. "Let's set them free."

He strode through the rubble, down the sloping road that led to a door, which he shot the locks off, then into the huge underground chamber filled with copper wires, tanks, rail lines, and dark tunnels.

"There," he pointed at the wall of glass-and-copper globes, stacked up nearly two stories high, with Strange skittering behind curved glass.

"Son of a bitch," Cedar breathed.

But Wil walked over to the wall, silent.

"Wil," Cedar warned.

"Don't worry," Wil said, and it was him, just the man, not the thing inside him. "I'm not going to touch them. What in hellfire is this for?"

"Trapping the Strange," Cedar said. "Using them."

"There must be hundreds," Wil said.

Hink strode over with the winch line. "More like thousands. Stand aside, gents. I'm going to shut down this horror show."

Cedar and Wil both moved back while Hink latched the hook to the center bar holding the shelf to the wall. He then proceeded to wedge two sticks of long-fused dynamite at each end of the shelf.

"You're just going to blow it up?" Cedar asked. "What makes you think the devices will break?"

"Rose threw one just like these at a man and the glass shattered. I'm thinking that's exactly what will happen here. Especially when I have the *Swift* rip the shelf off the wall." He lit the fuses. "And now it's too late to argue. Out the road and up the ship," he ordered. "Unless you want to wake up in hell."

Hink jogged for the door counting off the seconds left on the fuse. Wil was already running that way, and Cedar was not far behind them.

Five . . . four . . .

Hink whistled, one piercing blast, and then he motioned the brothers onto the ladder, jumping on the bottom of it just as the *Swift* lifted for the sky.

Three . . . two . . .

Her fans strained as she angled down and south, the winch-line chain pulling tight.

"Up!" Hink yelled. "Faster!"

Cedar and Wil flew up the ladder. Hink crested the top and was pulled aboard by Rose and Wicks.

One . . .

"Full throttle!" he yelled.

The explosion pounded at their backs just as Mr. Guffin released the winch line and the *Swift* tilted into the sky.

Wil stood in the door of the ship, staring back at the billows of smoke coming out of the warehouse.

"They are free," Not-Wil said.

"And so are the children," Cedar said.

"Good," Hink panted as he shoved back up onto his feet and made toward the front of the ship. "Mr. Seldom, take us up high and head back toward the church. We have one last problem to deal with."

"But what about the Madders?" Rose asked.

"They're the problem I'm talking about."

CHAPTER FORTY-THREE

The Madders were right where they'd left them, standing among the church ruins, smoking pipes. The sheriff stood to one side of the road, but the townspeople and children were gone, having all recovered from their dreaming state.

It took no time for the Madders to come aboard.

The sheriff did not look sorry to see them leave.

While Captain Hink ordered his crew around and the Madders got settled, Cedar stepped up close to Wil.

"I want to talk to it, Wil."

"Can't we just, can't I just rest a bit?" Wil asked. "Besides, it seems . . . sad."

"Wil."

"Fine, fine. I'll try to make it hear you." He nodded. "Go ahead."

"Our bargain is done," Cedar said. "I freed your kind. Now you leave my brother alone."

Wil's face changed minutely, eyes relaxing wider, but jaw tightening. He didn't look quite Wil-like. Because it was the Strange looking out through Wil's eyes.

"Not all. My kind. Still. Many dying. Many trapped."

"But I freed those—we freed those in that warehouse."

"Our promise holds." Then Wil's face was just Wil again, and it was

Wil who spoke. "I get the impression there are more of those copper-and-glass things. More Strange trapped inside of them. Maybe shipped off by rail or river?"

"We can't track them all down," Cedar growled.

Wil put his hand on Cedar's shoulder. "Not today we can't. Maybe tomorrow. Cedar, I'm fine. I feel fine. It's not difficult to live with. Not yet. So let's enjoy what we have today. While we have it."

"Wil," Mae said, "I'll need you here a moment."

Wil worked his way down the length of the airship and paused next to the hammock where Father Kyne had been bedded down. Cedar followed along.

"It's time to break the healing bond," she said.

Wil glanced at Cedar.

"I'd forgotten," Cedar said. "Suppose we should be sitting?"

"No, I don't think it will be painful."

Mae said a simple prayer and gently broke the healing bond.

Cedar and Wil both took in a deep breath. Cedar felt as if a rock had been lifted from his chest, allowing his lungs to fill. The absence of that pain was intoxicating, but breathing in too deeply set him into a long coughing spell. He pulled his handkerchief up to his mouth and noticed the speckling of blood there.

"Cedar," Mae said. "Are you all right?"

He folded the bloody cloth and tucked it away in his pocket. "I'm fine. Just fine."

Father Kyne lifted his hand. "Thank you," he said to Cedar and Wil. "For all you have done. For me. And for this town."

Wil smiled. "It was fun. Hell of a way to spend a day or two." He gave Cedar a pointed look. "And I wouldn't have it any other way." Then he turned and wandered back down the airship, as if restless to walk in a man's body again.

"Let me get you some tea," Mae said to Father Kyne. She made her way to the very back and tended the small stove there.

"You were the one who stood your ground for those children," Cedar said to the father. "We were just part of the people who helped make things right."

"You have done so much more." He lifted a hand toward the others on the ship. "Gathered together these people. Created a . . . family."

Cedar looked over at the Madders who were making themselves comfortable on the floor midship, leaning against the wall and tamping tobacco in pipes, feet stretched out in front of them, to Miss Dupuis and Mr. Wicks who stood with their heads bent toward each other near one of the windows, talking quietly.

Captain Hink was at the helm and Rose stood next to him, her arm around his waist. His crewmen were on either side of them, Mr. Ansell humming the strains of a song Cedar realized was one of Bach's concertos. Lastly, there was Wil, slowly walking through the ship, not yet content to settle down.

Wil had given Alun the Holder as soon as the ship had been under way. Cedar had never seen a man stash a bit of metal away in his bags so quickly. He hadn't asked Alun what he was going to do with it, but he had a fair idea. The Madders said they could lock the Holder away and ensure that all pieces of it were safely out of the hands of every man in this country.

"I don't know that it's a family," Cedar said. "Friends, yes." Rose leaned her head against Hink's arm and Miss Dupuis chuckled softly at something Wicks had said. "Maybe more than friends. Comrades in the fight. Whatever the fight might be."

"The fight's the same as it ever was, Mr. Hunt," Alun said around a mouth full of pipe smoke. "We find the Holder before it falls into the wrong hands. We save the world from destruction. Not a bad note to leave in the margins of history, is it?"

The Madders chuckled and Bryn pulled out a small bag of dice. "Of course, there are other ways to pass the time."

The rattle of dice caught Wil's ear and he ambled over to join the game.

"Family," Father Kyne repeated. "Not of blood. But of choice."

Cedar nodded. "Maybe you're right."

"What heading have you taken, Captain Hink?" Alun asked.

"East," Hink said. "There's a place we can tuck in out Chicago way, if that suits most."

"Suits us fine," Alun said.

"Chicago will do for me as well," Mr. Wicks said.

Wil leaned back a bit to look at Cedar. Cedar shrugged. Chicago was as good a place as any to wait out the storms and look for the trail to lead them to the next piece of the Holder. There would be work there, lodging. And it did not slip his notice that Chicago was also where Killian Vosbrough's brother lived.

"Good," Captain Hink said. "It's settled. Take the helm, Mr. Seldom. My boilerman and I are going to see that this ship's fires are properly stoked."

Mr. Seldom slipped over to take the wheel and Hink and Rose strode down the ship toward the boiler room in the rear.

Rose's complexion was rather pink at the cheek, but she was smiling like the sun rose and set on the airship captain.

It was good to see more than infatuation in her gaze. There was love. If Cedar was any judge of a man, Hink returned her feelings more than she realized.

He looked over at Mae, who was pouring hot water into two cups by the stove. His heart caught at her beauty, her strength.

"Cedar," Mae said. He realized he'd been staring, and looked away to try to sort his wants.

Mate, the beast whispered in his mind.

"Would you like some tea?" she asked.

He strolled over to her. "Tea would be fine," he said. "Just fine."

He took a drink and closed his eyes a moment, savoring the sheer warmth and sweet green of it. A man could get so mixed up in unworldly things, in dangerous things, but a simple cup of strong tea brought times more wholesome rushing back to him like memories lost.

"Where will we go once we reach Chicago?" she asked. "What will we do . . . with everyone?"

"We'll search for the Holder," he said. "There are five pieces still missing."

"Four, Mr. Hunt," Alun said. "You gathered up the tin bit a few months ago, but we pocketed the iron piece of it back in Hallelujah before we started off east."

"Don't recall you telling me that," he said.

"Consider yourself told," Alun said cheerfully.

Cedar sighed and Mae touched his hand gently.

"But Wil," she said. "The Strange. You made a promise to it too."

"To free the Strange?" He took another drink of tea and studied his brother over the rim of the mug. Wil threw the dice and laughed. The Strange might be in him, but it didn't appear to be hurting him.

"I'll uphold my promise to the Strange. Somehow. Just as I'll find the Holder, and then find a way to break the curse Wil and I carry. For good. After that?" He took another drink. "We'll settle down. Find a piece of land. Build a home."

Mae brushed her hand back over her hair, pulling the wayward strands out of the way. She took a sip of tea then smiled softly. "I believe you will do all of those things," she said. "But it does sound wonderful right now, doesn't it? A house. A fire. A quiet sort of life."

"Is that what you want, Mae?" he asked.

"It's what I've always wanted," she said.

Cedar placed his tea carefully on the edge of the stove. Then he turned to her, close enough he could feel the warmth of her exhale.

"Mae," he said, uncertain of how to voice the thoughts that were making his heart race. "I'd like to give you that. All of that. A quiet life. A house."

She searched his face, a small line of confusion knitted between her brows.

Cedar didn't know if this was the right time, but Wil had been right. If he didn't enjoy what they had today, while they had it, it could be gone forever.

"Mae Rowen-Lindson," he said, taking her hand and bending down on one knee. "I don't have a ring. All I have to offer you is my heart. Will you do me the honor of being my wife? Will you marry me?"

Mae's eyes went very wide. She held still, not breathing, not blinking. And for those slim, crushing moments, his world faded away, replaced only by her. Mae. His heart. His love.

Mate.

"Yes," she said in a rush. "Yes, of course. Yes, I will."

Cedar grinned and surged up onto his feet. He wrapped his arms around her and kissed her long and full while Wil and the others clapped and cheered.

This, he thought, this woman, was his family. No matter where their path took them, no matter what stood in their way, no matter how long they had, they would face it together.

Mate, the beast whispered again.

Yes, Cedar thought. She was his mate—and his love.

EPILOGUE

The airship *Tin Swift* took to the sky, but it was not the only wings upon the air. A tiny clockwork dragonfly made of gold with crystal wings fluttered down along the icy river and landed, gently, on Mayor Vosbrough's chest.

The mayor was dead. Unbreathing.

It was a perfect state for the Strange who waited just inside the forest's edge. He had been looking for the dragonfly, the rarest device of all, worth an emperor's ransom.

And now the dragonfly was here, resting on that dead man, wings pumping like the softest heartbeat.

An invitation?

Yes.

The Strange slipped through the trees, nothing but a shadow of a man. But if he wore a shape of his choosing, he would be tall, with a top hat to hide his eyes, scarves to cover his jagged teeth, and needles at the tips of each finger.

This dead man was not the shape of his choosing. But it would do. It would do nicely.

The Strange hovered above the dead man. Then, in the manner only his kind could accomplish, he slipped into that flesh and bone like a man donning a winter coat. He sat the body up, and swiveled his head while he dug through the knowledge left inside it.

This body was an important man. A powerful man. Yes, yes. That was pleasing.

He picked at the cuff of the man's coat, freeing a thread from the seam. Then he used that thread to lash the dragonfly down into the hole in the man's chest, trapping it tight so that the heart would beat and the lungs would fill. He would do a finer job of caging the rare clockwork device when he found a proper needle, a proper thread, and perhaps a drop of glim.

For now, he needed to know the name of the powerful man he had become, for names carried their own power.

Ah . . . Vosbrough. Killian Vosbrough. A familiar name. Not as fine as his own—Mr. Shunt—but it was fine enough.

He rose to his feet, far too graceful for a dead man. But then, he hadn't been dead.

The Holder had been here, or a piece of it at least. It had been stolen by the hunter. He had watched that happen, seen it all from the shadows. He had watched the hunter win. Again.

Rage filled him. Rage and revenge.

But then Mr. Shunt smiled. The hunter's small victory was no matter. Mr. Shunt was a new man now. And he had all the time he desired and all the power he needed to kill Cedar Hunt, and destroy the world.

Devon Monk has one husband, two sons, and a dog named Mojo. She writes the Allie Beckstrom urban fantasy series and the Age of Steam steampunk series, knits silly things, and lives in Oregon.

CONNECT ONLINE

www.devonmonk.com